THE GINGERBREAD HOUSE IN MISTLETOE GARDENS

JAIMIE ADMANS

Boldwood

First published in Great Britain in 2023 by Boldwood Books Ltd.

Copyright © Jaimie Admans, 2023

Cover Design by Alice Moore Design

Cover photography: Shutterstock and iStock

A CIP catalogue record for this book is available from the British Library.

Paperback ISBN 978-1-80483-861-7

Large Print ISBN 978-1-80483-860-0

Hardback ISBN 978-1-80483-862-4

Ebook ISBN 978-1-80483-859-4

Kindle ISBN 978-1-80483-858-7

Audio CD ISBN 978-1-80483-867-9

MP3 CD ISBN 978-1-80483-866-2

Digital audio download ISBN 978-1-80483-865-5

Boldwood Books Ltd
23 Bowerdean Street
London SW6 3TN
www.boldwoodbooks.com

For everyone who believes you're never too old to enjoy the magic of Christmas.

1

'Dim uchelwydd, dim lwc.'

— AN OLD WELSH PROVERB – NO MISTLETOE,
NO LUCK

'Now, the most important topic on tonight's agenda – a date for my daughter to the Mistletoe Dance.'

I shrink in my seat at the side of the stage. There are some benefits to your mum being leader of the town's resident committee, but this is *not* one of them.

'Mum,' I hiss. '*That* is not the most important thing, tonight or any night.'

Before I've finished, Mr Arkins, a pensioner who runs a dinosaur shop and remains permanently in character by wearing a dinosaur costume at all times, has raised his hand.

'Thank you, Mr Arkins,' my mum says smoothly. 'I was hoping for someone a tad younger, but we'll keep you in mind, seeing as Essie is determined to go alone this year. It's nice of you to volunteer. Again.'

I cover my face with my hands. Just when I think things can't get any worse, an old gent dressed as a dinosaur takes pity on me. I begged my mum not to do anything embarrassing tonight, but no parent ever listens when they can embarrass their offspring in public, do they?

'Well, you know where to find us if you're at a loose end on the twenty-third of December and want to take Essie to the Mistletoe Dance. I promise she scrubs up nicely and doesn't *always* have flour on her face.'

'Mum!' I wonder if anyone ever has, actually, died of embarrassment? If not, I feel it's a distinct possibility tonight, and I rub a hand over my cheek self-consciously. I'm *almost* positive I checked myself in the mirror before leaving the bakery, but flour on faces is a regular occurrence. See also: sprinkles in hair, chocolate on clothes, icing on forehead.

'Right then, the next topic of tonight's meeting – there is no mistletoe in Mistletoe Gardens.'

'Mum,' I hiss again. 'There's plenty of mistletoe. There's just nothing *else*.'

'Oh, yes, I know, but it sounded delightfully theatrical, didn't it? Got to engage the crowd.' She titters and turns back to said crowd. 'Usually the local council would've begun the makeover of Mistletoe Gardens by now, but it's already late November and they haven't started yet. Tonight we're joined by Mervyn Prichard, leader of Folkhornton council, who has come to offer an explanation for their tardiness this year.'

Mervyn Prichard is sitting next to me at the stage edge, and he audibly gulps as Mum invites him to her podium at the front of the town hall. He's wearing a hard hat and a neon safety vest and looking like he wishes they were both bulletproof armour. I have a bad feeling about what he's going to say. Surely the only reason to wear a hard hat indoors is if he's expecting people to throw things at him.

Mistletoe Gardens is the best thing about Folkhornton. Throughout the year, it's just a park, a Victorian-era green space at the edge of town, but every December, it's transformed into a winter wonderland. Once the leaves have fallen from the trees, the only thing that remains in the bare boughs are the masses of mistletoe that give the park its name. The council workers string fairy lights around tree branches, and there's a circular walkway that passes underneath every tree, illuminated with glittering Christmas lights. The gates open after dark and blissfully happy couples come to walk beneath the mistletoe, sharing kisses at the base of every tree. There's an old legend that says anyone who kisses under the mistletoe on a December night is guaranteed another year of love and happiness in their relationship.

And that's certainly true in my family. It was my great-great-grandmother who sowed the first mistletoe back in 1848, and every generation since has a romantic story of sharing kisses with a significant other in Mistletoe Gardens every Christmas. Except for me. I'm thirty-six and *still* the only member of my family who's never had anyone to kiss under it. A fact that my mum *never* lets me forget.

Mervyn Prichard's knees look like they're shaking as he approaches the podium and looks out at the gathered Folkhornton residents. As a council leader, he must be used to addressing large crowds, although maybe there's not always a bloke dressed as a dinosaur sitting in the front row. That's enough to make anyone nervous.

'Now the thing is...' He swallows and if I didn't think he was about to tell us something horrible, I'd take pity on him and offer a glass of water. 'Unfortunately, due to financial constraints, Mistletoe Gardens is no more.'

A gasp of shock floods through the crowd.

'There will be no winter wonderland this year. The council have taken the decision to flatten Mistletoe Gardens completely in January, and then construction will begin on a new apartment complex, which will provide many jobs, bring new people to the area, and reinvigorate our town. I'm sure you'll all agree this is a much more sensible use of the space.'

Even though I had a feeling something bad was coming, I didn't think it would be *this* bad. This is awful. I can't imagine our little town without Mistletoe Gardens. On those magical December nights, it becomes a Christmas market too. Local shop-keepers set up stalls to sell a selection of handmade goods, crafts, and food and drink. Mum and I have a stall for the bakery, and I *love* spending December evenings there, serving loved-up couples with heart-shaped spiced shortbread, gingerbread iced with a mistletoe pattern, and mince pies topped with fondant holly leaves, sipping hot chocolate, and vicariously experiencing the romance of Mistletoe Gardens.

The anger in the room is palpable. I was joking when I thought people might start throwing things, but some residents are definitely looking around for projectiles.

Mervyn Prichard is obviously getting worried too. 'Mistletoe Gardens no longer earns its keep. It's costing an increasing amount to maintain, and the winter wonderland isn't as popular as it was in years gone by. Tourists simply aren't interested these days. And the silly myth about a kiss under the mistletoe granting couples another year of health and happiness... No one *really* believes that. People don't believe in magic any more. No one will miss Mistletoe Gardens.'

'I'll miss it,' someone says near the back of the hall and it starts a chorus through the residents.

'Well, I'm sorry, Mr Prichard, but that simply won't do.' My mum approaches the other side of the microphone. 'The resident committee will not allow you to destroy the only green space this town has. Where will we go to eat our lunch on summer days? The only place we can walk our dogs, or have picnics, or that children can kick a ball around. Where will we have outdoor yoga classes with our friends?'

'Where will I hold my Wild Crochet Club?' Beryl, who owns a knitting shop, asks. 'Wild' suggests an outdoor crochet group, and while that's exactly what it is, 'wild' can also be applied to some of their more *interesting* creations. She's sitting at the front, merrily crocheting a zombie version of Santa.

'The only things who have any lingering attachment to it are the pigeons who attack anyone daring to walk through with a cone of chips,' Mervyn continues. 'It's dead space sitting at the edge of our town – space that can be well used in other ways.'

'There has to be something we can do,' Mr Arkins pipes up, his words muffled behind the dino suit.

'You can't wipe out such a huge part of our town's history without letting us have a say!' Lynette from the chemist shouts. 'That park has stood there since Victorian times. Queen Victoria once kissed Prince Albert underneath *our* mistletoe! That must give it heritage status! Who of us here *hasn't* kissed someone we love under that magical mistletoe on a cold December night?'

Well, *I* haven't, but now isn't the time to mention it, or my mum will be asking for volunteers to kiss me, not just to be my date for the Mistletoe Dance.

'Folkhornton council makes decisions for the good of the town, and I am confident you'll all come round in the next few months, even if you can't see the benefits now.' Mervyn Prichard sounds anything *but* confident.

'Condescending wazzock!' Mum gives him a look capable of turning a cow into a hamburger at ten paces.

Similar shouts erupt from the others, although few of them stick to descriptions as polite as 'wazzock'.

'Let's talk about this like civilised people, from one leader to another.' Mum gestures for Mervyn Prichard to step behind the stage curtain with her and then flaps a hand at me. 'Essie, take over!'

Take over? Me? There's angry murmuring throughout the residents and I have no idea how to calm them down. I approach the podium on shaking legs, listening out for a yelp in case she wallops him. It wouldn't be the first time.

What am I doing here? I was supposed to be leading a round of brainstorming for Santa's replacement grotto, not getting to grips with a room that's been left reeling, and trying to referee a fight between my mum and a man who's been her rival since secondary school. From friendly competition to a love-hate relationship to full-on loathing.

'Um, so...' My mum is a natural public speaker who thrives under the adoration of expectant gazes. I am *not*. 'As you know, Santa's been evicted from his usual spot in the supermarket, so we need to find a new home for his grotto this year...' I nod to the man on the right side of stage, in full Santa regalia despite the fact there isn't a child in sight.

There's yelling coming from backstage and it's absolutely plain that *everyone* wants to listen to that and not to me. My face has gone so red that it'll camouflage completely with my hair, which I've just dyed a bright Christmas red in honour of the festive season.

Eventually, my mum emerges, smoothing her skirt down with a satisfaction only usually felt after despatching a particularly large spider found lurking in the bath, and Mervyn scuttles out after her, rubbing his arm like it really did descend into violence.

'While we appreciate resident feedback, Folkhornton council

is committed to doing what's best for the town, and this new apartment complex will bring in a level of investment unseen for decades. The decision is final – the contracts are signed.' He looks around uneasily.

My heart sinks. 'What about the winter wonderland this year? If the build isn't starting until January, there's still time to get everything set up this Christmas – one last time. You could at least give Mistletoe Gardens the send-off it deserves.'

'I'm sorry, Miss Browne, it isn't worth the time, manpower, and cost of sending out a team of workmen. Tourists won't come – just like they didn't last year, or the year before, or the year bef—'

'We could do it!' Mr Arkins calls.

'Yeah, we're not giving up on it! We could decorate it ourselves,' someone else says.

Mum looks to the gathered residents. 'We need to show them that Mistletoe Gardens means something to this town. Folkhornton wouldn't be Folkhornton without our magical mistletoe and our December nights spent underneath it. Essie's right – it deserves a decent send-off at least.'

Everyone's looking at me expectantly, and I'm not quite sure how I got in the middle of this. The mistletoe is our family's legacy. There are two framed photographs on the wall in the bakery – one of the gingerbread house display my great-great-grandmother made for Queen Victoria's arrival, and one of Queen Victoria herself eating my great-great-grandmother's gingerbread in Mistletoe Gardens on the day she came to Folkhornton to officially open it in 1848.

Murmurs of potential tourist-attracting events rustle through the crowd, and they're all good suggestions, but none of it is *enough*. We don't need a series of events to get people talking – we need to do something spectacular. Something *bigger* than the council's new apartment complex. Something that's going to make people sit up and take notice of Mistletoe Gardens. Something that's going to go viral on social media, that's going to put our story of magical mistletoe onto a world stage.

Mistletoe Gardens started with gingerbread... Maybe it should end with gingerbread too. A karmic full circle thing. A send-off to mark its departure in the same way it began.

'How about gingerbread?' I suggest so quietly that only a few people in the front row hear. 'A display like my great-great-grand-mother made to celebrate the opening. We could recreate that. Use the old Victorian recipe she once used...'

'It's a little small, Ess. I can't see tourists travelling for miles to visit a few modestly decorated gingerbread houses...'

'Small!' An idea flashes into my head in full living colour. 'That's it! *Not* small! The opposite of a small gingerbread house display! A giant gingerbread house! A life-size one!'

The murmurs that crackle through the room this time suggest I'm a few fries short of a Happy Meal, but the idea gathers speed so fast that I forget I'm in front of a microphone and barrel onwards. 'Think about it – we've got a Santa without a grotto and we need to do something *big* for Mistletoe Gardens, even if it's only a final goodbye. No one's going to talk about a few events, but people *are* going to talk about a real-life full-size gingerbread house. People are going to visit Santa if his grotto is *inside* a ginger-bread house. It'll be a nod to what my great-great-grandmother did for the opening day – gingerbread, but modernised. And hopefully it will attract the kind of crowds that Mistletoe Gardens attracted back in the day because we could do with even a fraction of the people shown in those old photographs!'

'Is a life-size gingerbread house even possible?' Mum side-eyes me.

Maybe I should be worried that my mum who – when she's not busy terrorising council leaders and trying to set me up on dates – is head baker at Dancing Cinnamon bakery doesn't think it's possible.

It *must* be possible... right? 'We make gingerbread houses all the time. Why can't we work on a slightly bigger scale? A really, *really* big scale?'

The thought makes me feel like a child again. I can imagine the wonder of staring up at a life-size fully edible house towering above me, peaks of bright-white royal icing and twinkling gumdrops of giant proportions.

But when standing on a stage in front of a crowd and getting overexcited about something, deathly silence is not generally the desired response.

'Oh, come on. Where's your imagination? We need something that's going to get people talking about Mistletoe Gardens – something that people are going to come *to* see. If there's nothing we can do to save Mistletoe Gardens, then we can at least send it out with a bang.'

'That bang might be our ovens exploding, Ess,' Mum whispers. 'Do you have any idea how much gingerbread that's going to take? How much time it will take to put it together – *if* it's even possible to get a structure of that size to stand up?'

Well, no, because I haven't thought about the logistics yet, but I'm a firm believer in ideas coming at exactly the right moment and things working out when you need them to. I'm fizzing inside at the idea of building a gingerbread house to such a large scale. 'Can you imagine how magical it would be for a child to go to visit Santa in a *real* gingerbread house? The smell, the look, the taste. It would be like something from a fairytale. A part of a winter wonderland that no one will ever forget.'

'Wouldn't it get wet in the rain?' Edna, the retired librarian, calls. 'This is South Wales, we're not known for our dry and sunny winters.'

Oh, *snowdrops*, I hadn't thought of that. You *can't* leave ginger-bread outside, it would melt in the first shower, and she's right, we're not short of rain in this valley. There has to be a way around it... 'The old bandstand! It's more than big enough to fit a house in, and it's got a roof, so the gingerbread would be protected.'

'And what about that sleety, driving rain that comes down sideways with howling wind?'

'We could put something around the edges... a circus tent or something. I don't know. It's a spur of the moment idea, obviously it needs some planning first, but it's the best plan we've got so far...' As usual, I do not excel at having confidence in myself and my ideas. I was hoping for a slightly better response than the indifferent mutterings that sweep through the audience.

'Ess, who's going to do this?' Mum sidles closer and whispers from the side of her mouth while projecting a bright smile outwards. 'You?'

'Of course. I'd love to. What an amazing way to spend December and honour our family and the tradition *our* grand-mother started. She sowed the first mistletoe – it's brought a lot of joy to Folkhornton over the years. If it's going to be the last time, people should remember her.'

'I can help,' my best friend and co-worker, Saffie, says from her seat in the front row.

'You can't both do it! What am I supposed to do for staff at the bakery? There's only the three of us and you know how often I have to dash out for my resident committee duties.' Mum's face contorts in distress. 'Do you have any idea how long this is going to take? Do you even know *how* to build a life-size house out of biscuits?'

'No, I haven't got a clue, I'm going to need help on that front, a builder or someth—'

'Right, attention, folks!' Mum claps her hands in front of the microphone, so loud that it attracts the attention of not just this room, but probably a fair half of the rest of Wales too. 'Essie's volunteering to build the gingerbread house, but there's the small issue that she doesn't know how. Anyone out there have experience of building houses?'

In slow motion, every eye in the room swivels to a corner at the back. Slouched in a chair at the furthest edge of the room is Joseph Hallissey Junior, owner of Hallissey Construction, a building company well known around this area. Joseph, who always attends these town meetings but never speaks or offers any input whatsoever, has a black baseball cap pulled so far down that I doubt he can see out, a black scarf pulled so far up that it covers most of his face, and he seems to be shrinking in his chair under the weight of so many gazes.

No one speaks. The entire town hall is waiting for him to volunteer his services, but his arms fold and his cap sinks lower.

The silence stretches out, and my mum isn't one for patience. 'Mr Hallissey! You are a builder, are you not? In fact, you're the *only* builder in Folkhornton. Would you be so kind as to offer some advice?'

No response.

'Maybe he's asleep,' someone murmurs.

My mum does the deafening crack of a clap again, loud enough to wake ancient mummies in the Egyptian pyramids, never mind any napping builders in the vicinity. And he's definitely not asleep. His arms have pulled his black coat even further around his body and he's sunken so low in his chair that he might be trying to slide off it and crawl away unseen.

Nothing.

'Mr Hallissey!' Mum barks again.

'No.' The cloud of blackness in the corner finally speaks,

muffled from under the baseball cap and scarf. Just the one word, which to be fair, is more than he's ever spoken before.

Mum gasps into the microphone. 'No?'

He doesn't respond, but he looks like he's hoping to make himself so small that he'll simply disappear.

'But Mr Hallissey,' Mum booms into the microphone, but she's making things worse. This is obviously not a man who wants to be the centre of attention. I can sense the discomfort pouring off him in waves. 'Your father would've loved a project like this. Won't you at least consider it?'

He gets to his feet, pulls his cap up and his scarf down, and looks around the room. 'It's impossible. *You're* insane.' His gaze falls on me and lingers for a moment. 'No. No, no, and no. And in case it wasn't clear the first time – *no*.' He sits back down with a clunk, refolds his arms, pulls his scarf up and his cap back down.

A man of few words. Joseph Hallissey has always been an odd one. His father, Joseph Senior, was the life and soul of town meetings, always throwing around ideas and meeting challenges with spark and enthusiasm, but he died a couple of years ago, and Joseph Junior moved into town and took over Hallissey Construction. He comes to every meeting, like his father used to, but he sits silently in the back corner and offers no input or opinion. He never even bothers with the free tea and biscuits.

The room is silent, like everyone's unsure what to make of having heard him speak for the first time, and I realise my mouth has gone dry from having *his* attention on *me*.

'Okay, well, we can't win 'em all,' I stutter, trying to get everyone's focus back to the task at hand. 'I'm sure there are plenty of builders who'll be willin—'

'Your father would be ashamed of you!' Mum bellows into the microphone.

The whole room turns to look at Joseph again.

'Mum! You can't say tha—'

'No, I *will* say it. We all knew Joseph Senior, much-loved friend and neighbour that he was. He'd be mortified to see such rudeness from his son. You are an embarrassment to your father's good name!'

'Mum!' I try to cover the mic with my hand. My cheeks have gone red on Joseph's behalf.

She's still wrestling the mic away from me when Lynette pipes up. 'Hear, hear!'

'Joseph Senior was the kindest man,' Mr Chalke from the shoe shop says. 'Would've done anything for anyone. He loved this town and he *loved* Mistletoe Gardens.'

Joseph's father was the kind of loud and overbearing Welshman who made himself a friend of everyone. There was no one who didn't know him. A nice man, of course, and quite clearly the opposite of the one currently looking like he wishes the ground would swallow him whole.

'Look, no one has to help us,' I say loudly into the mic, sending whistling feedback reverberating through the room. 'People are busy at this time of year. I can find someone else, it's no bother.'

'You shouldn't have to! Not when there's a builder right here who doesn't even have the decency to offer advice.'

'Oh, I'll offer some advice all right.' Joseph Hallissey gets to his feet again. 'You can't build a house out of gingerbread and you *definitely* can't do it in three weeks. Don't be so stupid.' His eyes fall on me again, and then he turns around, jams his cap so far down that it looks painful and stalks out. The room is stunned into a silence punctuated only by the loud swinging of the door behind him.

'Well, I never...' Mum says. 'No wonder he doesn't speak to anyone if that's how rude he's going to be.'

'You were rude to him! You can't use someone's dead father to shame them into doing something they don't want to do. He isn't obligated to help with this – no one is. That was unfair.' I'm half-tempted to run after him and apologise, but what would I say?

'We can find someone else,' I say instead, but it falls on deaf ears as they all start muttering about Joseph. My mum has never had much of a filter with words, but even she must've been able to see that someone crossed a line there, and it wasn't him.

'If I may?' Mervyn Prichard rises from his seat next to Santa. 'You're all missing a fairly important point here. You *can't* build a life-size gingerbread house.'

I turn to him, glad of someone getting the conversation away from the unpleasantness with Joseph. 'Do you mean that from a legal standpoint or because you believe it's impossible?'

'I don't *believe* it's impossible, Miss Browne – it *is* impossible.'

'Nothing's impossible at Christmas.' I give him a grin. 'Do we have your permission to use the bandstand in the park?'

He ums and ahs, twisting his fingers together, but he eventually answers. 'If you want to waste your time, effort, and presumably a great deal of money on ingredients, then the council will have no legal objections to your project. Mistletoe Gardens will be razed to the ground in January. What you do with it in the meantime is up to you.'

'Hurrah!' Santa cheers and stands up too. 'The only thing we need is a little belief in Christmas magic!'

'We can do this,' I tell everyone. 'I just need a couple of days to work out a plan and find a builder. Hallissey Construction are not the only builders in the universe. As soon as I get home, I'm going straight online to find a whole slew of builders who will jump at the chance to do something so fun. There will be millions of them. We'll be holding builder auditions by the end of tomorrow. It'll be like a *Bob the Builder* set around here!' Let's hope none of them know *Bob the Builder* is an animated programme most favoured by those under three years of age.

I smile broadly at the sea of faces looking back at me, hoping the doubts don't show on my face, because internally, I'm wondering what I've got into here. It seemed like such a good idea at the time, but Joseph Hallissey's reaction and Mervyn's 'impossible' comments have left me feeling overwhelmed and like I'm grasping at straws.

I can bake gingerbread until the cows come home, but I don't know where to begin when it comes to building a house with it. There's a good possibility I've bitten off more than I can chew, in more ways than one, and this cannot be another 'big idea' that turns out to be a big mistake.

2

Queen Elizabeth I is credited with creating the first gingerbread man. At a banquet in the sixteenth century, she had gingerbread figures made in the likeness of her guests.

Okay, there are no builders. Most of them were polite enough to say they were booked solid for December, and *some* of them were kind enough to wait until *after* they thought I'd hung up the phone to start laughing out loud. Most of them thought it was a practical joke.

'Thanks for your time.' I sigh as I hang up on the twenty-third construction company I've tried this morning and cross out the final name on my list.

Mum's baking the day's stock and Saffie's covering the shop floor, and they're both expecting me to go and tell them we've got a choice between several builders when the reality is that we have none.

I traipse down the stairs from the flat above the bakery where I live, wondering what on earth to do now.

'From the look on your face, I'd say not many builders are

interested in using gingerbread as a construction material,' Saff says gently while Mum's out of earshot.

'None of them took me seriously. Not even *one* would discuss it.' And the mountains of screwed up paper littering my living room floor are proof that I have no idea what I'm doing. Badly sketched house ideas with pencil lines drawn through them where I'd tried to work out how to divide them into small enough pieces to fit into the bakery ovens. I've made a *lot* of gingerbread houses over the years – customer commissions, display pieces for the shop, but the biggest I've ever made would fit on a small cakeboard.

Failed gingerbread house designs weren't the only thing haunting my dreams last night. I can't get Joseph Hallissey's face out of my head. When he stood up that last time, he sounded angry, but he looked... something else. He looked miserable. Crestfallen. Hurt. The eyes that lingered on me. The urge to apologise hasn't lessened since last night, but I suspect that if I'm not quite the *last* person he wants to see, I'm definitely near the bottom of the list.

'You're not seriously considering asking Hallissey again, are you?' Saffie asks.

This is what comes from working with someone who's been my best friend since we were six years old and my co-worker since she started a Saturday job at the family bakery when we were fourteen. 'Do I have a window in my forehead or something? How do you know that?'

'I know that look, Ess. I just don't know why you'd bother. He votes against every suggestion that's put forward.'

'To be fair, Mr Arkins's giant neon dinosaur slide into the duck pond was a terrible idea and we all voted against it.' I sigh. 'I felt so bad for him last night. It was like the whole town turned on him for not being like his father. It wasn't right.'

'Doesn't hurt that he's absolutely gorgeous too, does it? I'd never noticed before, but *wow*. If I was single, *I'd* be asking him again too.'

'It's nothing to do with that. Maybe he could give me some pointers or something because I don't know where to start. And I want to apologise. I know better than anyone that comparisons to our parents do none of us any good.'

'Who's comparing you to me?' Mum appears from the bakery kitchen. 'Ah, good, you're back from the builder hunt. Did you find one?'

'I'm still working on some... possibilities.'

'You need to get a move on, because I don't believe the contracts *are* signed. Mervyn's eye was twitching when he said that – it's a dead giveaway.'

'It's interesting that you've studied your worst enemy *that* well.' I waggle my eyebrows and Saff giggles.

'Oh, hush, you two!' Even as she says it, she's gone red. Saff and I have often said that Mum and Mervyn's love-hate relationship springs firmly from a place of love-love many moons ago. 'What I mean is I think the council could be persuaded out of the idea of an apartment complex if someone comes up with something better. So it's down to you now, Essie. Don't mess up the "something better".'

I feel wholly inadequate in the face of my mum's superior confidence and skills. There is *nothing* she can't do, but I've failed at every 'great idea' I've ever had – I can't fail at this too.

* * *

'Does anyone know where Hallissey Construction is working today?' I ask Mum and Saff when I get down to the shop floor after lunch, with a basket of baked goods over my arm.

'You're not seriously...' Mum gasps in such horror that she can't finish the sentence.

'No,' I say. Let's manage our expectations here. 'I'm going to apologise for *your* behaviour last night. And I *might* be hoping that this basket of baked goods will make Joseph Hallissey willing to at least talk to me. If he could suggest how to make sure a gingerbread house of that size can stay stable, I'd be landed.'

'Essie, I don't think you should give that man another moment of your time.' She nods to the basket. 'And don't tell me you've been up there baking for him all that time.'

'No. I wanted to make a few things anyway,' I lie. 'Anyone seen their van around today?'

They both shake their heads, so I head out onto the paved street and ask a few of our neighbours.

'Oh, don't go looking for him,' Lynette says from beside the chemist's till. 'He growled at me once. I was only offering my condolences after his father passed, and he *actually* growled. He might be a werewolf, you know. We never see him around on the night of a full moon.'

'We never see him around on *any* night, Lynette. I don't think he comes into town very often, regardless of the moon phase.'

Mrs Allen in the clothing boutique and Mr Selman from the antiques shop don't know either, but finally Mr Arkins, still dressed as a dino in The Dinosaur Shop, tells me they're repairing the roof of Folkhornton's swimming baths this week.

The swimming baths are on the outskirts of town and at the top of an unnecessarily large hill – by the time you've climbed it, you've had your exercise for the day and don't even need a swim any more. It's been closed for the past few months after a storm caved in the roof, and as I approach, embarrassingly breathless and sweatier than you would've thought possible for a chilly November day, I'm glad to see the white van with the black 'Hallissey Construction' lettering emblazoned across the side. There are two men on the roof, and one in the car park shovelling sand into a cement mixer.

'Hello,' I pant. 'Is Joseph here?'

'Died a couple of years back,' the man replies without looking up.

'No, I meant his son. The one who runs Hallissey Construction now? Joseph?'

'Oh, right.' He stands up and leans on his shovel, laughing to himself like it's an inside joke. 'I wouldn't call him that if you want to stay on his good side.'

'What should I call him then?'

'If he's even vaguely interested in what you've got to say, he'll tell you. And if he isn't, he won't.' He shrugs and points me towards the main doors, covered in yellow and black warning tape, and then goes back to the shovelling, clearly not going to provide any further insight into his boss.

I pull aside a broken piece of 'do not enter' tape, hoping it's not a bad omen, and push my way through the double doors into what was once a lobby, but now looks like a weather-damaged builder's yard. There's a workbench set up in the centre, huge sheets of plywood stacked against one wall, and Joseph Hallissey is carrying one across the room.

He looks up at the sound of the door clattering shut behind me. 'Oh, it's *you*.'

I give him a bright smile. 'Well, if that isn't the warm welcome every girl dreams of, I don't know what is.'

He grunts in response as he manoeuvres the huge sheet of wood onto the bench.

'You're a very difficult man to find,' I say when he doesn't make any move to continue the conversation.

'I think you'll *find* I'm a very difficult man, full stop. And I didn't want to be found.' He'd look more approachable if he was wearing barbed wire and carrying an 'I hate people' sign.

I try not to be discouraged. 'I came to apologise.'

He picks up a set square and starts marking out measurements on the sheet of wood. 'And there was me thinking you'd come to try bribing me with whatever's in that basket.'

'It's an apology basket. I'm sorry for what happened last night. My mum was out of line to call on you so publicly like that. I didn't mean for it to make you so uncomfortable.' My cheeks have gone red just thinking about it.

'It's fine. They spoke nothing but the truth. My father was bright and lively and easy to get along with. I am none of those things. No offence taken – no apology needed. Don't let the door hit you on the way out.'

I glance backwards at the door and it takes me a few seconds to realise he's telling me to leave. 'Oh, no, wait, if I could have a moment of your time...'

'I'm busy.' He continues marking out measurements on the board using a pencil and the square. 'There's the door, take your bribe basket with you.'

'It's not a bribe basket.'

'No? So you *haven't* come here to try again? See if you could talk me into helping you? Butter me up with whatever's in the basket?'

I go to answer, but I can't.

He finally turns to look at me. 'Let me guess, you phoned every builder within a five-hundred-mile radius and they laughed in your face or put the phone down *or* laughed in your face and *then* put the phone down on you?'

I stutter for a moment. 'It wasn't a *five*-hundred-mile radius.'

'Well, those within the UK's land borders then.'

'Only those that could reasonably get here.' I sigh. 'Please, Joseph, you're my only hope.'

'Firstly, I am no one's hope. Secondly, the number one rule of trying to get around me – my name is Joss. Joseph was my father and I am *not* him. It's Joss, always.'

A little spark of hope flashes through me. *If he's even vaguely interested in what you've got to say, he'll tell you.* I take a step further into the room. 'Sorry, I didn't know that. No one knows that. Maybe if you spoke to people once in a while and told them things like that...'

'Why would I speak to people? I have nothing to offer anyone in this town.'

'Your dazzling personality and incessant wit?'

He gives me a scathing look and continues his work.

'I'm sorry,' I say, annoyed at myself. I was determined to be as nice as possible, but his grouchiness is getting to me. 'I'm not asking for your help. I just need a few pointers. I can bake gingerbread blindfolded, but I don't know how to build a house. If you could give me some tips, like how to get it to stand up, how to make it in small enough pieces to fit in an oven... It'll take five minutes of your time and I'll be eternally grateful.'

As if on cue, the men on the roof start hammering something, the noise making me wince as it reverberates through the building.

'Please, Joss.' I like that name. It suits him. He doesn't look like a Joseph.

He looks up at me, his blue eyes meeting mine and for just a moment, I think he's wavering, and then he looks away again. 'You can't teach someone how to build a house in five minutes, especially if that someone is stupid enough to try to build it out of gingerbread.'

'Ten minutes, then. Please. I don't know who else to turn to.'

Bang, bang, bang, bang. The incessant hammering from above makes me feel as unwelcome as his frosty attitude.

'I hate this town. I couldn't care less if they *bury* Mistletoe Gardens. Why should I do anything to help?'

'Because it's neighbourly?'

'Well, we're in luck then because I won't be a neighbour for much longer.' He glances upwards as the hammering continues. 'Go on, go. You shouldn't be in here without a hard hat on.'

My eyes shift to his thick, dark brown hair that looks like he's tried to spike it with product but it's a bit too long so has flopped forwards instead. 'You're not wearing a hard hat.'

'I'm not wearing one because, quite frankly, it would be a blessed relief if a ceiling fell on *my* head.' He lifts a hand to gesture towards the door again and for just one second, I catch his eyes, and that sentence doesn't seem like the sarcastic joke I thought it was.

I take another step nearer. 'I brought gingerbread.'

'I don't like gingerbread.'

'I foresaw that and I also made you flapjacks.'

'I don't like flapjacks.'

I grin. 'I also foresaw that and made some clementine brownies too.'

'I don't like brownies.'

I walk across the room and hold the basket out to him. 'Well, maybe you've got a wife, girlfriend, boyfriend, friends, or children who might enjoy them.'

'There's just me.' He makes no move to take it.

'There must be *something* you like?'

'Yep.' He looks me directly in the eyes. 'Silence, and being left alone.'

'Well, you aren't going to get much silence around here with all that banging, so you may as well talk to me for five minutes.' I put the basket down on the plywood, deliberately in the exact spot he was about to mark up.

He gives me an annoyed look, but uses his pencil to lift one corner of the tissue paper covering it and peers in. 'Gingerbread in the shape of a house. Your persuasion tactics are impressive.'

I thought it was quite ingenious when I was using my house-shaped cookie cutter on my lunchbreak. 'Is it working?'

'Nope.'

I wish Saff hadn't mentioned how gorgeous he is because now I can't see anything else. His hair is so dark that it could almost be black, and it makes his blue eyes look even sharper. A layer of dark stubble covers pale skin, and he's wearing paint-stained jeans with holes in them and a black T-shirt that's smeared with the dust of the wood he's been cutting.

He nudges the basket aside and carries on putting pencil lines on the plywood. 'Isn't a gingerbread house a bit... Hansel and Gretel-ish? You know, are you trying to be Christmassy or are you trying to lure unsuspecting children into the forest so you can eat them?'

I roll my eyes. 'Because it's festive and it'll be magical when it's done. Can you imagine being a child and finding out Santa lives in a *real* gingerbread house?'

'No. I like to think I never was a child. I've always been as cynical and grumpy as I am now. Santa is a commercial figure invented to sell soft drinks.'

'No, he's not. Santa's been around since ancient Turkey. Nicholas of Myra?'

'And I think this conversation has been going on for a similar amount of time. Is there a reason you haven't left yet?'

'I need your help. I have no one else to turn to, and I'm good at failing at things. Now I've suggested this, I can't fail at it too.'

There. He seems direct and like the kind of person who'll appreciate honesty.

'Not my fault, nor my problem.'

'I know that.'

'But you were assuming I'm the kind of person who has a "better nature" that would be swayed by biscuits?'

'No, I...' I try to explain about the short notice and how this is something that should've been planned out months in advance and how I can't even start making the gingerbread because I don't know what formation it'll need to be baked in, and he carries on marking up the board like I'm not there, even when my voice rises to be heard above the banging.

'What if I pay you?' I say eventually. 'You say you don't want to help the town but you're fixing the swimming baths roof, presumably because the council are paying you. What if it was like any other job? I'll pay you to help me. I mean, I can't afford much and a fair chunk of the ingredients are going to come out of my wages, but if you'd let me pay in instalments into next year...'

He stops and thinks it over for a moment, and then he looks up and shakes his head. 'No, I couldn't take money for it. That would feel hideously awful and goes against everything I stand for.'

I draw in a breath of excitement because it sounds like he might be considering it, but he cuts me off. 'Of course it would be morally wrong to accept money for something I'm *not* doing.'

I sigh.

He puts the pencil down and leans on his elbows on the plywood. 'Look, I'm about to lose my business. I can't waste time working on some whim of a project. I need to spend the next few weeks getting everything in order, not building a gingerbread house.'

'Hallissey Construction is in trouble?' I say in surprise.

'Yeah, and if you could *not* repeat that to *every* busybody in Folkhornton, I'd be extremely grateful.'

'How come? Hallissey Construction has been going for decades. Everyone uses you guys for everything.'

'Everyone *did*. But that was my dad – it's not me. I took over after he died, and since then... Word gets around that I'm not him. People don't like me. I'm not as good as him. Construction is not my strong suit. He ran this company for twenty years, and I've run it into the ground in just two.'

'I'm sorry, I didn't know that.' I chew my lip. 'Again, no one knows that. If anyone knew you were in trouble, they'd help.'

'I don't want anyone's help.'

He really is impossible. 'I won't tell anyone.'

His gaze locks onto mine again. 'Thanks, I appreciate that.'

I'm captivated by his eyes. Not because they're captivating but because I've never seen anyone with such sad eyes before. He hasn't smiled once since I've been here. Come to think of it, I'm not sure I've ever seen Joss Hallissey smile. 'People in this town aren't so bad, you know. You might be surprised if you engaged once in a while.'

'I engage the perfect amount, thank you.'

'You growled when Lynette offered you her condolences at a town meeting once!'

'I didn't growl.'

I raise an eyebrow, and he sighs. 'That was the first town meeting after my dad died. The first one I went to in his place. I was struggling, okay? You know when you're holding onto your emotions by a thread and someone being nice to you makes it worse? I didn't mean to growl at her, but having a full-on emotional breakdown in the middle of the town meeting would've made even more local headlines than the growling did.'

'I'm sorry, I didn't know that,' I repeat. It seems there are a lot of things people don't know about Joss Hallissey.

He sighs again, but this time it's the heavy sigh of someone who's fed up with not just this conversation, but *everything*. 'I didn't know she was still upset by that. I'll apologise next time I see her.'

'That means you'll have to speak to another human being.'

'Well, the delights of talking to you will certainly tide me over for another few years, so maybe you could be a gem and tell her I didn't mean to growl at her?'

'Shall I also tell her you're *not* a werewolf or shall we let her go on believing that one?'

He laughs, but it's a quiet, curtailed laugh. 'Yeah, no one's *ever* correcting her on that.'

And then he shakes his head, his thick hair flopping with the movement, and the pseudo-laugh is gone and he's serious again. 'If you're so short on time, you shouldn't be wasting it here. I can't help you. I'm sorry.'

God, his eyes. They're such a beautiful dark blue, but they show something his voice doesn't. When he says the word 'sorry', his voice sounds sharp and sarcastic, but his eyes look genuinely sorry. He pushes himself up off his elbows, and he looks like he can barely move under an invisible weight pressing his shoulders down.

And I feel like I'm making it worse. I hate giving up, but I don't know what else I can say, and he's already been more open than I expected. 'Okay. It might not seem like it, but I *can* take a hint. I'll leave you in peace.'

Bang, bang, bang, bang.

I glance upwards. 'Well, maybe not that much peace, but still. Thanks for your time. Have a good day.' I give him what I hope is a genuine smile. He seems like he needs it.

My hand is millimetres away from the door handle when he calls after me. 'How would you do it?'

I turn back. 'That's kind of where you'd come in. I don't know anything about construction. I don't know how to get a structure of that size to stand upright and be safe. Usually when I make gingerbread houses, four sides and two roof pieces all fit in the same oven, but there's not an oven in the world big enough for a life-size gingerbread wall...'

'Maybe like a greenhouse...' He doesn't sound convinced by the idea. 'You ever put together a greenhouse?'

I shake my head.

'It's a metal frame and the glass is in panels which are held in place by clips... but then the pressure on the lowest panels would be too much...' He sounds like he's mentally constructing it as he speaks. 'And if one cracked or got ruined, you'd lose the whole side. And standard greenhouse panels are sixty-one centimetres, so you'd have to work smaller than that...'

'That sounds feasible. And I can look up instructions for putting a greenhouse together... and that's glass. It doesn't get much more fragile than glass and it works for greenhouses.'

'Firstly, it's horticultural glass, and secondly, it's not a biscuit.'

'The whole point is building with biscuit. Doing something unfeasible. Something that people keep telling me is impossible. I want children to look up at it and be unable to believe it's real. Adults, too. I want miserable adults to believe in the impossible.' I give him a pointed look. 'I want it to be like something from a fairytale. Something that makes people believe in magic.'

That sarcastic smile flashes across his face again. 'Use a greenhouse frame. Work out the maximum size gingerbread panel you can get in your oven, and do the maths to divide it into enough pieces to fill the frame. Bake it as thin and solid as you can...' He trails off.

'You don't think it's going to work, do you?'

'I think...' He glances upwards as the banging above us continues, and rubs a hand across his forehead. 'I think there's probably a better way but I can't hear myself think. But maybe a greenhouse will give you a blueprint to work from. I wish I could help more than that, but I can't.'

He flinches like he's got a headache.

'Okay. Thanks, Joss. I really appreciate it.' I give him a nod of thanks. I hadn't even thought of using something like a greenhouse as a template. A gingerbread greenhouse doesn't exactly bring to mind the cosy, homely cottage I was imagining, and God knows how to get gingerbread panels as thin as glass... But it's certainly the best idea so far, and my mind is buzzing as I walk away. I'm excited again, instead of overwhelmed and stressed like I've been feeling since last night. It feels achievable again with his input.

'Essie?' Joss calls after me again. When I turn back this time, he gives me a wink. 'Thanks for the basket.'

I grin to myself. The way to a man's heart is *always* with baked goods in the end.

3

In Sweden, it's believed that gingerbread can grant wishes. You hold the gingerbread in your palm and make a wish, and then break it with your other hand. If it breaks into three pieces, the wish will come true.

'How'd it go with Joseph Hallissey yesterday?' Saff asks as we open the bakery on Wednesday morning.

Mum's gone to referee a parking dispute between neighbours, so it's just the two of us, and I've been making loaves of bread since 5 a.m. as they're always snapped up first thing.

'I don't know. I mean, it was a total bust, he said no, obviously. But he was... nice, I guess. He explained things I didn't understand before, and he was... unexpectedly open. Kind of helpful without actually helping.'

She raises both eyebrows.

'Joss suggested using a greenhouse as a template. I've been online looking up greenhouses, but I don't know how it's going to work. Gingerbread so thin would turn to charcoal in the oven.'

'Joss?' Saff's already-raised eyebrows turn extremely waggly. 'You got on so well that you've already given him a nickname?'

I'm convinced she's missed every word since his name. 'It's what he goes by. Believe me, he couldn't have been more stand-offish if he'd tried.' I play it down because the last thing I need is my mum getting wind of a nickname. She's traumatised Joss enough for one week, she doesn't need to start trying to set me up with him as well, and he fits her criteria in as much as he's got a pulse. Only the recently deceased are off limits to my mum when it comes to finding me a potential date. I wouldn't be surprised if she soon turned to necromancy.

'What are we going to do now?'

'Give it a go myself, I guess?' It comes out sounding like a question even though there aren't any other options. 'People put together greenhouses all the time. And Mr Arkins has offered to help. Maybe that's the answer – make it into a community project where everyone comes along and has a go. Maybe we'll be in luck and stumble across someone who's really good at building life-size gingerbread houses.'

'Ess, Mr Arkins wears a dino costume twenty-four-seven. I have severe doubts he even takes it off to sleep. He'll build a wall and then send it crashing down with his dino tail. No one's seen what he looks like since 1985.'

Admittedly, the dino suit may be a little cumbersome in a fragile gingerbread greenhouse. 'All right, well, maybe we could get a garden shed and glue gingerbread to it...'

'That's not what you wanted.'

'Well, no, but I don't think the greenhouse idea is viable, and I've got to face the fact I can't build a whole house by myself. We'll be able to find someone capable of nailing a shed together, and then... a hot glue gun and flat pieces of gingerbread stuck to every part of it. We could decorate it with real icing and real sweets.' I try to sound upbeat, but I wish I'd never opened my mouth about this idea. I should have done some research first and spoken later. I get another crate of fresh bread from the kitchen and start arranging loaves into the display baskets on the shop shelves.

My back is to the door as I carry on talking. 'We could make it *look* like a gingerbread house. And it would still do for Santa's grotto. If we slap enough icing on, children might still have the same sense of wonder when they look at it, it's just me who feels disingenuous about—' I'm still trying to talk sense into myself when Saff interrupts me.

'Ess,' she hisses urgently as a chilly draught rushes in from the door opening. She jerks her head to the side, and I turn around to see an unexpected figure in the doorway.

'Joss,' I say in surprise, not entirely sure I haven't imagined him into existence.

'Morning.' He's carrying a tray of four coffees with a fifth one balanced on top and he walks across to the counter and looks at the cakes inside the glass display unit that runs from the front of the shop to the back.

'Hello, stranger.' I approach him cautiously, like you might go up to a wild animal and you weren't sure if it was going to rub your hand or tear out your carotid artery. 'Never seen you in here before.'

'I don't shop locally. I hate these people. I don't want to support their businesses.'

'Apart from the coffee shop.' I nod to the cardboard tray in his hands.

His dark hair flops forwards as he looks down like he's forgotten he's carrying it. 'My need for caffeine is stronger than my morals, and my workers would go on strike if they didn't get coffee.'

Saff has stayed safely behind the counter, looking like a safari park ranger who might need to grab a stun gun at any moment, and eventually Joss uses his elbow to indicate towards the ring doughnuts, iced green like a festive wreath with a red fondant bow at the bottom. 'I'll take four of those, please. And can you put one of them in a separate bag?'

As Saff grabs the tongs and starts popping them into bags, Joss slides the coffees onto the counter so he can pull his wallet out, and then turns to me. 'I'll also take 1,500 gingerbread bricks.'

'Gingerbread bric...' I start in confusion before I realise what he's saying and gasp in delight. 'You'll do it?'

I let out such a squeal that he looks alarmed and takes a step backwards. 'Not if you continue looking like you might be about to hug me. Physical contact turns it instantaneously into a no.'

'I wasn't going to hug you,' I huff. 'Some ego you've got there to consider yourself a huggable person. I'd rather hug a wasp.'

'Good. Their sting is less painful than mine.'

'Bricks?' I say to cover the embarrassment of momentarily forgetting he isn't a normal person and I can't hug him like I would a friend.

'That's how we do it – gingerbread bricks. A wooden frame, and we build the walls with gingerbread bricks, and then it's going to have a wooden roof that you can tile with gingerbread. Can you make gingerbread bricks?'

'Yes! Er, not that I've tried, but I hadn't even thought of bricks. I was trying to convert a normal gingerbread house into being life-size, not build a real house using gingerbread... This is exactly why I needed you.'

'I couldn't stop thinking about it last night. If I make mistakes today, I'm holding you personally responsible because I got barely any sleep. To calculate the exact number of bricks, I need measurements of the bandstand to size it properly. What time do you finish work tonight?'

'Five.'

'I'll meet you in Mistletoe Gardens at five past five?'

I nod enthusiastically. 'It closes at six. I'll contact Mervyn Prichard today to find out when we can get the keys.'

He slides a fiver onto the counter and I hold up a hand to stop him. 'They're on the house. It's the least I can do.'

He pushes the money closer to Saff. 'Not a chance, thanks all the same.'

Saff looks between me and him, and I shrug, so she picks up the note and rings it into the till, and Joss takes his two paper bags and picks up the tray of coffees again. When she holds out his change, he lifts his chin towards the charity donation box on the counter. 'Put it in there.' He gives me a nod as he goes to leave. 'See you later.'

'Joss,' I call after him. 'What made you change your mind?'

'You.' He gives me a wink, and then he's gone.

'Oooooh!' Saff whistles and reaches across the counter to punch my shoulder. 'I thought you "just talked". Did you *talk* about persuasive sexual favours or what?'

I laugh, even though I've gone red. 'I think I talked him into losing the will to live.'

'Or our baked goods really are *that* good.'

'Yeah, maybe.' I'm staring distractedly at the empty doorway, trying to do a calculation of my own.

'*Duw, duw,* he's a laugh-a-minute, isn't he? It was like a cloud descended as soon as he walked in. I don't envy you having to work with *that*. He's living proof of why girls always go for guys with personality over looks. And what kind of person doesn't shop locally? He's so weird.'

'I think he's quite sweet under the gruff exterior. He was nice yesterday. He didn't have to be as open as he was. And I definitely didn't expect him to change his mind about the gingerbread house or to have spent half the night thinking about it. And that was nice with the change, right? Not many people do that these days. And... that was the wrong amount of coffees and doughnuts. Five coffees, four doughnuts. That doesn't add up.'

Saff makes a noise of confusion, but I stick my head out of the door and look in both directions.

The tall, dark-clothed figure of Joss is walking away from Santa, and Santa's now rustling his doughnut out of the bag. 'He gave them to Santa,' I say more to myself than to Saffie. 'Santa's up by the fountain collecting for charity, and Joss gave him the extra coffee and the doughnut in the separate bag.'

'Trying to get himself on the nice list?' She glances at me. 'Why do you look like you're trying to do the Pythagorean theorem?'

'He didn't buy one for himself. He works with three other guys. He gave a doughnut to Santa, so there were only three left. He didn't get one for himself.'

'I feel like I'm about to re-sit a school maths exam. If I have fifteen apples and I'm driving at thirty miles per hour, how many sandwiches will there be in Swansea at four o'clock?' She giggles. 'Maybe he had enough with that basket you took him yesterday. Maybe one of his employees is off today. Maybe one is diabetic and wouldn't want a doughnut. Maybe he dislikes doughnuts as much as he seems to dislike everything else.'

'Yeah, maybe.'

'Essie Browne, I know that face. What are you thinking?'

I'm staring out the door again, watching Santa sipping his coffee. 'I'm thinking Joss Hallissey is nothing like we think he is.'

* * *

'I should take him something.' I peer into the mostly empty display case. Closing time is not ideal for having much choice, but there are two Christmas tree cupcakes left, vanilla cake iced with green swirls and an edible tree on top.

'Good luck.' Saff hands over the box she's put them in. 'You're going to need it.'

While I have no doubt that Joss's reaction to the cupcake will be one of disdain, I don't want to turn up empty-handed. I've barely stopped thinking about him all day. His generosity with Santa this morning, even his change going in the charity box. People as uptight as Joss Hallissey is supposed to be aren't generally known for doing things like that.

I love walking through town on winter evenings, even though the street decorations are the same tacky neon things that have been up every Christmas since the mid-eighties. Threadbare garlands cross the road above my head, arranged in uneven scallop shapes, a wreath in the centre of each one, invariably with half the bulbs missing. The only thing the council have spent any money on lately is the rope-light word display that reads '*Nadolig Llawen*' and '*croeso i Folkhornton*' – 'Merry Christmas' and 'Welcome to Folkhornton' in Welsh. There's a lopsided tree up beside the fountain in the town square, and at this time of day, everyone I pass has got a spring in their step as they head home. At the upper end of town, I cross the main road and come to the wrought-iron double gate of one of the entrances to Mistletoe Gardens.

The Hallissey Construction van is parked in the gateway, and I go around it and along the red asphalt pathway, past the semi-circular patches of grass and flowerbeds at the foot of tall trees. There are four entrances, and all converge in the centre where the bandstand is.

'Hello.' I approach the stone steps up to the hexagonal bandstand.

A weathervane creaks from on top of the curved roof that's supported by eight ornate posts, while the bandstand itself is surrounded by a low wall with black and gold iron railings on top of it.

'Evening.' Joss doesn't look up from the tape measure he's running along the stone floor.

Maybe Saff's right. Maybe he's going to be an absolute nightmare to work with. I tap the cake box I'm carrying. 'I brought sustenance.'

He holds up a pencil in a 'wait a minute' gesture, leans across to jot something down in an open notebook on the wall, and then unclicks his tape measure and lets it snap back in. He uses the pencil to point to the flat post at the top of the steps where two takeaway cups from the local coffee shop are waiting. 'I brought coffee.'

There's an open tool bag near the top of the steps and Joss chucks his tape measure into it with a clang, then he picks up both the cups and hands one to me. I'm surprised when he sits down on the top step up to the bandstand, and I sit down too, open the cake box, and put it on the step between us.

Instead of complaining like I thought he might, he lifts out a cupcake and peers at it, almost admiringly. 'Thank you.'

'Thank *you*.' I raise my coffee cup and take a sip. 'Ooh, gingerbread latte. An inspired choice, given our project.'

'Figured you were the type of person who'd think it was criminal to drink a non-festive coffee at this time of year.'

'I am.' I use my cup to gesture towards the one in his hand. 'Let me guess – black coffee. The blackest and bitterest of dark coffee, with not a sweetener or sugar or splosh of milk or anything to pep it up in any way?'

'Heck, no. I have enough trouble sleeping without touching caffeine at this time of night.' He raises his cup like he's going to make a toast. 'Decaf tea with vanilla and nutmeg, but it's nice to know you think I like my coffee like my personality.'

I don't say anything, but something niggles at me. No matter how he comes across at first, in our encounters so far, I've learnt two things about Joss – that he's generous and that he's surprising. And that he has trouble sleeping, apparently. And I think there's a lot more to learn.

'Thanks for this.' He pulls back the paper on his Christmas tree cupcake.

'Thought you didn't like cupcakes.'

'I don't.' He bites into it and gets green icing on the tip of his nose, and then wriggles it around like he's trying to cast a spell in *Bewitched*.

I stifle a giggle because it's the most *un*-Joss-Hallissey sight ever, and I'm almost positive he did it on purpose.

He chuckles something that isn't a real laugh and wipes it off, and carries on eating the cupcake by pulling small bits off and popping them into his mouth.

I nearly miss *my* mouth because I'm so focused on watching him. He *is* gorgeous, but there's nothing relaxed or open about the way he's sitting. Hunched over with his head ducked down, the same paint-covered jeans he had on yesterday but with a clean black T-shirt today, and a close-fitting black jacket open over it.

'No wonder they want to get rid of this place. It's dead.'

I'd been so focused on him that I haven't realised he's right. There's no one here apart from us. It's always like this now. Far from the bustling community hub it once was, Mistletoe Gardens is almost an inconvenience, an annoyance to have to cut through instead of the pleasant shortcut it used to be.

Without the council's decorations, the bare trees are dark, the mistletoe in the boughs is nothing more than puffy silhouettes against the night sky, and they've stopped bothering to turn on the streetlamps, so the only lights are from businesses along one side of the far road, and headlights from cars and the lit-up interior of passing buses.

Even the usual December stalls and mistletoe romance didn't do much to pep it up last year. 'This place is... *was*... so special. It's my great-great-grandmother's legacy. She sowed the first mistletoe back in the 1840s.'

'You know mistletoe is a parasite, right? It doesn't have roots of its own, so it feeds from the host tree and gradually sucks all the goodness out of it until it dies. Your however-many-greats nan would probably have been arrested if anyone had caught her – there's a law against deliberately spreading invasive parasitic plants on public land.'

'It's a bit late for that – she's been dead since 1879. It was so romantic. She wanted an excuse to kiss the man she was secretly in love with, but she couldn't find any mistletoe, so she walked for miles to collect some berries and, because she didn't have any trees in her own garden, she sowed them on the branches in the park, expecting them to grow straight away, but no one told her that mistletoe takes years to grow. By the time it had started to sprout, she'd lost touch with the man she'd liked, and then they randomly bumped into each other again while walking here one December evening. She told him that anyone who kissed under the mistletoe was guaranteed another year of blissful happiness together and dared him to disprove it. She got her kiss, and he asked her to marry him a couple of weeks later – on Christmas Day. Apparently it was the proudest day of her life when they renamed the park after the mistletoe she'd sown.'

'*That's* where the legend comes from? Just a tale propagated by a law-breaking, lovesick old biddy from times gone by? No offence to your ancestor.'

I almost burst out laughing at the idea that *that* wouldn't be offensive. 'Don't you think there's something romantic about it, though? Walking through a moonlit wonderland with someone you love. Sipping hot chocolate. Stopping for a kiss under every tree.'

'I don't believe in romance.'

Of course he doesn't. 'What about love?'

'I don't believe in love.'

No wonder he seems so sad. How can anyone go through life not believing in love? 'What do you believe in then?'

He thinks for a moment and looks across at me. 'Misery, solitude, and pizza.'

This time I do burst out laughing, and his lip twitches like he wants to smile, but he frowns and looks away when I catch his eyes.

'You're remarkably tall for a nine-year-old, which I'm assuming is your actual age considering you still believe in fairytales. You can't really think that a kiss under magical mistletoe cements your relationship for another year, can you? It's a fairy-story. *Nothing* can make a relationship work, especially not a parasitic plant in a half-dead tree.'

'All right, when you put it like that, it sounds a bit daft, but it's a lovely tradition to have – a way of making time for your significant other and letting them know they're still important to you. A moonlit mistletoe walk, and a twirl at the Mistletoe Dance – it's a public declaration that this is your person and you'll be in love with them for the rest of your life. This was a central social hub in the olden days – it was an important declaration to make.'

He scoff-laughs *again* and shrugs taut shoulders. 'Things change. The modern world rarely looks up from its phone. No one has time for mistletoe kisses or a place like this nowadays.'

I'm about to protest when there's chirruping nearby, and Joss looks up and says, ''Ello, Rob.'

I look around for someone named Rob, but he inclines his head towards the wall at the side of the steps we're sitting on, where a little robin has landed and is singing to us, his red breast bobbing with a song.

Joss crumbles up the last of his cupcake and goes to tip the crumbs onto the wall, and then screws the empty paper case into a ball and throws it into the nearest bin with perfect aim. 'He's my little buddy. Always comes down when I'm working. So friendly that he nearly gets trodden on because he gets himself right behind my boots and doesn't make a sound.'

He gives the robin a reproachful look, but the bird carries on pecking the crumbs, not bothered by how close Joss is standing.

'And you call him Rob?'

'I call all robins Rob. I think he follows me. I'm convinced he's the same one I see in my garden. He waits outside my door every morning and if I put my hand down with food in it, he steps straight on.'

I barely manage to cover the *awwwwwwwww*. Again with the surprising. Someone who is so abrupt and standoffish is not only kind to Santas, but feeds hungry robins too. 'I didn't know birds were big fans of cake.'

'Birds are fans of anything at this time of year when food is scarce.' He collects the empty bakery box and puts that in the bin too, then sits down to sip his tea again.

'Mervyn's arranged for one of us to meet the caretaker at nine o'clock tomorrow morning and get the spare keys,' I say. 'In the meantime, we've got to be out by six tonight.'

He glances at his watch and groans. He drains the cup, and then leans backwards, his whole body stretching until he can snag the handle of his tool bag and pull it closer. The movement pulls his T-shirt up just enough that I can see a sliver of stomach, and although it shouldn't be even vaguely hot, I can't tear my eyes away for every moment that he's leaning across to root around in the bag.

Eventually he sits back up and pulls his shirt down, his cheeks colouring like he knows where my eyes were. He puts a notebook on his knees and whips a pencil out from behind his ear. 'You need to show me what you want. I can't measure properly until I know exactly what we're building.'

'I don't know. Just a little house that looks like a gingerbread house. I'm not talking about three bedrooms with en suite bathrooms, full plumbing, an attic, and a granny annexe. Something with four walls and two roof sides. And a chimney. I want to use candyfloss to look like smoke coming out of it.'

'How big are we going?'

I glance up behind me. The bandstand is immense. The roof of the huge hexagonal space is way above our heads. 'It's got to be big enough to fit Santa and a couple of children. And I'd love to make it look like a real living room inside, so we'd have a Christmas tree and a fireplace and somewhere for Santa to sit, and a parent would have to stand nearby, and someone to take a pic—'

Joss cuts me off with a kind laugh. 'So as big as possible then?' He jots down measurements and sketches out a traditional house shape, with a front door in the middle, a gable roof, and an off-centre chimney, and I'm hypnotised by his fingers as he draws. They're long and elegant and surprisingly clean for someone who works with his hands.

'That's perfect,' I whisper. 'Exactly the cosy cottage I was picturing.'

He glances up at me, and this time his lips definitely half-tip into half a smile. He scribbles down measurements again and then starts adding details, and I shift closer to see what he's doing.

'Can we put...' I lean over, take the pencil from his hand and draw in two cross-bar windows on either side of the house. 'It's got to have stained glass windows made of melted boiled sweets, and gingerbread houses usually have this circular window above the door.' I draw in one of those too.

'A transom window.'

'Yeah, that.' I glance at him again, impressed. I didn't even know it had a name beyond 'circle window thingy'.

I catch a whiff of his spicy aftershave and realise that if I'm close enough to smell his aftershave then I'm *too* close. How have I not noticed that my elbow is almost on his thigh? I shift away in embarrassment and hand him the pencil back, and he continues sketching on details, tilting the book to show me.

'Thanks, Joss,' I say quietly. I don't know why I'm so touched, but there's something about the amount of effort he's putting in when he was so adamant that he wouldn't get involved.

He meets my eyes briefly, and then goes back to the notebook. 'Let me guess, gumdrops on the roof?'

'Yes! But I'm going to have to find out if they do giant gumdrops, because normal ones will be too small. Everything will have to be supersized. I'm probably going to have to make most of the decorations. I want a really traditional look – bright-white icing, lots of red and green sweets, multicoloured gumdrops to look like Christmas lights, lots of peppermint swirls. Any ideas?'

'You wouldn't like my ideas when it comes to festive things.'

I roll my eyes. 'You've got enough imagination to get involved in building a life-size gingerbread house – you're just going to have to muster up the imagination to *imagine* you're a normal person who likes Christmas and can interact with other humans once in a while.'

He raises an eyebrow. 'Oh, I am, am I?'

'Says the man currently drawing gumdrops onto a gingerbread house.' I point at his notebook. 'Ooh, that's great positioning. One on the tip of every roof tile. I love that. How about icing rosettes around the chimney base with a peppermint swirl at the centre of each one?' I lean over to trace the line with my fingernail, but I've got too close again. My chin is nearly on his shoulder and I pull back so sharply that I crick my neck, and this time he definitely notices the unintended closeness because he springs to his feet so fast that he even frightens the robin. 'It's late, I should measure up.'

He hurries back to his van and returns with an armful of long wooden planks, gets a saw out of the tool bag, and produces a piece of chalk from his pocket.

'Can I help?'

He makes a negative noise, and I feel like a bit of a lemon as I stand at the top of the bandstand steps and watch him as he positions the frame of the house.

'I've got a friend who works with carousels on the Yorkshire coast. He's sending me a pavilion tent by courier tomorrow. It can be rigged up around the edges to keep both the rain and the nosy neighbours out.'

'You've already thought of that?' *Again* with the surprise. I thought he was going to be arrogant and bad-tempered, but he's given a lot of thought to the sensible, logistical side, whereas my mind is caught up on royal icing and gumdrops.

He lays wood down, measures it, cuts it, and marks out chalk lines on the floor, and I stand there watching him. 'Joss, can I ask you something?'

He's got the stick of chalk between his teeth and makes a noise that's neither a yes nor a no. I go for it anyway. 'Why did you really change your mind?'

'It appealed to me.' He stops what he's doing, takes the chalk out of his mouth, and looks me in the eyes as he answers. 'The challenge of doing something so different. The intricacy of it. I'm not much of a commercial builder. I prefer making smaller things.

I like restoring old things and turning them into something new, giving things a new lease of life – upcycling, as they call it nowadays. I like taking time over tiny details. But that doesn't pay the bills, and that's not what Hallissey Construction is about. When I started thinking about this after you left yesterday, I got that same feeling about it. And you, Essie. I wasn't joking this morning. Your enthusiasm and belief in this project is inspiring – it has been since you were on that stage the other day with everyone doubting you. You weren't going to give up on this, and that's inspirational.'

Downing the hot coffee just now didn't make me as flushed as his words do. He surprises me again, though. An honesty I didn't expect. And telling me more about himself than I ever thought he would. Who knew Joss Hallissey had so many layers? 'Can I ask you something else?'

The chalk is between his teeth again and he mutters something that sounds like, 'I really wish you wouldn't.'

But I've never been very good at doing what people want me to. 'I know I've put you on the spot, but do you genuinely have time for this? This is a big ask. It's going to take us most of December. It's a lot to expect, and you obviously have your own job to do as well...'

'And if I say no, you're going to let me walk away without a word, are you? No more chasing, no more bribes, no more begging?'

'I never begged!'

The grin that doesn't reach his eyes crosses his face again, but then he turns serious. 'Yeah. Things are winding down at work. I haven't been actively seeking jobs lately. The company has been in the red for a while and now it's teetering on the edge of being back in the black. We have one job lined up for next year – we're joining forces with a big construction and infrastructure firm. If it goes well, they're going to absorb Hallissey Construction – let my lads keep their jobs and buy me out. There's no point trying to fill our schedules before that. And repairing the roof of the swimming baths isn't a four-man job – the others will be happier if I'm not there.'

'I'm sure that's not true.'

His teeth pull one side of his lower lip into his mouth and the other side tips up into a fraction of a smile. 'Oh, come on. It's like Bob Cratchit when Scrooge leaves the office. While the Bah-Humbug cat is away, the Christmas-loving mice will play. Festive music, mainly, which I ban from jobs I'm working on. One of my lads starts playing it in October, if you can believe that.'

There's something about the way he calls them 'my lads'. The men at the swimming baths the other day must've all been in their twenties. Joss can only be ten to fifteen years older than them at the most, and yet there's a fatherly protectiveness there and a pride that he probably doesn't realise is tingeing his voice. 'I start playing it in September.'

'Of course you do,' he mutters. 'I don't know why I expected anything less from the girl with hair the colour of Rudolph's nose.'

'It's festive. And it's a deep Christmas red, it's nowhere near the colour of Rudolph's nose.'

'I'm glad you've given so much thought to a fictional reindeer's hooter hue.'

His turn of phrase makes me laugh. 'It'll wash out by January. I like to do something festive in December, and this shade of red is the perfect match for my green reindeer antler headband and my Christmas tree earrings.'

For one second, he stops fiddling and tilts his head to the side so his hair catches on the batten of wood he's holding upright. 'It's enough to brighten anyone's day.'

I blush the same shade as my hair because even though I don't think it was meant as a compliment, it sounds a little bit like one, and it makes something inside me perk up. 'Don't you like any Christmas songs?'

'Yeah.' He goes back to fiddling with the wooden batten, trying to get it to line up with the piece on the floor. 'You know the one that goes "Silent Night", but stop at the "Silent" bit. That's the kind of Christmas music I like – the silent kind.'

I once again want to giggle at his way of saying things, but I force it down, because *no one* is allowed to dislike Christmas music on my watch, not even Joss Hallissey. 'You're going to have to get used to it. It's nearly December and we're building a giant gingerbread house. We *have* to have Christmas music playing.'

'I work on building sites – luckily I've got excellent ear defenders.'

I snort. 'You're not seriously going to wear those great big things on your head to block out a bit of Christmas music, are you?'

'No, of course not.' He shoots me that sarcastic grin again. 'It'll also have the additional benefit of blocking out anyone who continually wants to talk to me.'

I glare at him, but it has no effect on the sarcastic grin he's still got on.

He jerks his head to beckon me over. 'Here, hold this.'

I step over the planks of wood and wrap my hands around the piece he's holding, and he crouches down to get the two pieces to fit together. 'What is it you're doing?'

'Marking out the framework. I want you to approve it before I start cutting things. You strike me as the kind of person who would agree to something, then say it wasn't quite right, then want it some other way again, and then finally decide it was right the first time.'

'Oi! There's insulting and there's *insulting*. I work in a bakery. We do custom cakes. Do you have *any* idea how many times I've had to re-do entire cakes because a customer has decided they want pink to green ombre icing instead of pink to red? Or because "Happy B-day" actually *would* be better if it said "Happy Birthday", or "Oops, did I accidentally ask for almond flavouring? I wanted hazelnut", and how many times I've decorated with roses and then they've had a sudden thought that it would look better with pansies, so it gets redone, and then, oh no, wait, it actually would be better with roses after all. I'm not an "endless tweak" kind of person, Joss. I don't know anything about building houses – I trust your judgement.'

He's laughing so hard that he's got a hand braced against the floor to prevent himself falling over. 'Okay, okay, my sincerest apologies. I didn't mean to cause *quite* so much offence.'

He sobers up and continues trying to get the vertical batten to clip onto the horizontal batten, and I can't help watching him work. 'What happened to your company?'

'People hire Hallissey Construction and expect my dad – they're disappointed with the replacement.'

My breath catches because I didn't expect such a direct answer. He's crouching right beside my leg and I have an urge to reach out and give his shoulder a supportive squeeze, a friendly gesture like I would with any other friend, and it takes a *lot* of willpower to remind myself that he *isn't* a friend and he'd probably skitter away at an uninvited touch.

He doesn't take his eyes off what he's doing. 'Are you nosy because you're interested or because there's a prize for providing the best village gossip?'

'It's nothing to do with that, Joss. People genuinely care.'

'Oh, don't make me laugh. People only care if there's something in it for themselves.' He stands up, towering beside me, the gingery scent of his aftershave wrapping around me again as he slots his hand around the wood above my hands. 'Okay, let go.'

I step away, slightly concerned by how much I want to hug this miserable, grumpy man. It's the eyes again. Even in the darkness, that sadness is unhideable. His words are harsh, but his eyes are *broken*.

'We have stuff in common, you know.'

'Two S's in our names,' he suggests, running his snappy tape measure upwards from the base of the batten.

'I get a lot of comparisons to my mum too. She's the confident and dynamic resident committee leader and people expect me to be like that too, but I'm the furthest thing from confident and don't have the courage to stand up for myself, and I *hate* speaking in public.'

He pulls the pencil from behind his ear again to mark the wood. 'Is there anyone who *likes* speaking in public?'

'Well, no, probably not unless they're a politician. I just meant... I know what it's like to be compared to someone that you're just... not.'

'In the nicest way possible, thank God for that. I'm very glad you're not like your mother because there's no way in hell I could spend December building a giant gingerbread house with *her*.'

I'm half-horrified and half-overjoyed. No one insults my mother like that, and yet, he's absolutely right. It's half-compliment and half-insult and I respond with a noise of half-horror and half-laughter, and I'm also really, really touched. I think he was trying to make me feel better about myself, in his own unique way. 'For what it's worth, I always thought your father was a touch loud and overbearing. Things can still be accomplished by people who are quiet and reserved.'

His hands go still on the wood. 'Did you seriously just insult my dead father?'

Oh, God. Oh, *no*. I've overstepped by a country mile. Guilt washes through me. He was joking about my very-much-alive mother, and I've gone and hurled a vicious insult at his beloved dearly departed father. 'I'm so sor—'

'Thank you.' He looks up and meets my eyes. 'No one's ever said that before. I always used to tell him to tone it down to a dull bellow, but he was the kind of man who forced people to like him whether they wanted to or not, whereas I prefer it if people hate me.'

I bite my lip as I look at him. He's the strangest man. Sharp, standoffish, and abrupt, but his voice wavers on those words.

'Please stop looking like you want to hug me. It's mildly terrifying.'

In the seriousness of the moment, I burst into uncontrollable laughter. 'Some ego you've got there,' I repeat my words from the bakery this morning. 'I'd rather hug a piranha.'

'I'm sure they can be quite friendly when you get to know them.' His face is blank, but his voice sounds unsteady.

We look at each other for a few long moments, and then he drops my gaze and shakes his head. 'Right, so the roof...'

'Does it have to be fully wooden? I was hoping for it to be as gingerbread-y as possible.'

'I've never heard gingerbread used as an adjective before.' He raises an eyebrow. 'While I appreciate your commitment to a fully edible house, if multiple tonnes of gingerbread fall on him, Santa will *die*, and so will several small children, and you'll be spending Christmas in prison on negligent manslaughter charges. Assuming murder and chaos *isn't* your aim with this thing, it's my job to make sure it's entirely safe.'

Okay, I hadn't thought of that. 'See? That's why I need you – to prevent criminal convictions and unnecessary bloodshed.'

'Happy to be of help.'

How would I have done this without him? I want to say it aloud, because every moment we're here, I'm even more grateful, but it sounds gushing and false even to me, and he doesn't seem like he's great at accepting praise, and I don't think he'd take me seriously.

He draws chalk lines on the floor where the frame is going to stand and then checks his watch. 'Where did that hour go?'

I look up at the clock on the town hall behind us. It's past six already, but there's no sign of a caretaker coming to lock up. 'Luckily your van is blocking the gate so they can't lock us in for the night.'

'They might have us for anti-social behaviour and disturbing the peace, though. Quick, you grab a six-pack of lager and I'll start spray painting comedy genitalia on the trees.'

It makes me laugh as Joss gathers the marked-up wood and his tool bag and we head back to his van. He switches on a light in the back, illuminating a van full of all sorts of tools and wood and other builder-y stuff I can't identify. He pulls out another piece of wood, measures it against the battens, and then bends to saw it.

I don't realise what he's making until he holds up a brick-sized piece of wood.

'A brick template?'

'For you.'

I go to take it from him, but he pulls it away, digs around for a piece of sandpaper, and then starts rubbing it and turning away to blow the dust off.

'How about you?' he asks while smoothing off a corner. 'Do you have time for this?'

'Yeah.' I look up at him, surprised he's interested enough to ask. 'Even if I don't, I'll make time. My mum's the boss at Dancing Cinnamon – we split the baking between the two of us, Saff looks after the shop floor, and I pick up the slack when Mum has resident committee commitments. This will mean long days and endless nights, but it'll be worth it.'

'The council won't change their minds, you know.'

'You don't know that.'

'Yes, Essie, I do.' He gives me that false smile as he hands me the wooden brick, painstakingly smoothed free of any splinters, and my cold fingertips brush against his warm ones as I take it.

'Why are you helping then?'

He shrugs. 'Dunno. Beats sticking your fingers in a food processor, I suppose.'

I have *no* idea whether he's serious or not, and maybe I don't want to know.

He taps the wooden brick in my hand. 'I don't know the first thing about gingerbread, but get your bricks as close to this as you can, and as uniform as possible, and solid – as hard as they can be. Tomorrow I'll put up the frame. By Friday I'm going to need some gingerbread to start building the walls.'

'Okay.' I've never made gingerbread bricks before, but it can't be that difficult, can it? I'm going to try a few practice runs tonight, and then make a full batch while Mum and Saff are working tomorrow.

He slams the back doors and walks around to the driver's side. 'Do you want a lift home?'

'No. Thanks, though.' I'm again touched by his thoughtfulness. 'I live above the bakery, so just back down the street.' I use the wooden brick to point in the direction I came from.

'Ah, right. I didn't know you lived there.'

'Where are you?'

He points behind him. 'The first tiny village you come to when you go up the valley. One of the little backstreets of detached bungalows. The one with pink roses winding through the privet hedge in summer.'

I've driven past it on bakery deliveries many times. 'It's beautiful up there.'

'It's not mine.' He sighs and rolls his eyes skywards like he's said too much. 'It's where my parents used to live. I'm just staying there until I can sell up in the new year.'

'That's what you meant when you said you wouldn't be a neighbour for much longer?' I ignore the pang in my chest. Three days ago, I'd never even spoken to this man, I have no right to get upset at the thought of him moving away.

'Yeah. Between selling that and the payout for the company, I should be able to afford something decent elsewhere. Very, *very* elsewhere.'

Is Folkhornton really that bad? I want to ask him, but he's clearly got a chip on his shoulder when it comes to this town, and I get the feeling he'll close the conversation down if I mention it. 'Where will you go?'

'I don't know. Somewhere remote. Ideally an island with no other inhabitants. Maybe one off the coast of Scotland. As far away as I can possibly get. It's a shame the commute to the moon is so complicated or I'd go for that.'

I smile even though it doesn't sound like a joke. 'That sounds...'

'Peaceful? Idyllic?' He cuts me off before I can finish the sentence.

I meet his eyes across the van's bonnet. 'Lonely.'

'I've had all I can take of life in the past few years. I need to be alone. No one else to worry about. Not even a pet to get attached to. Just me, off-grid. Living off the land. No need for contact with any other human, ever.'

'You can't grow your own chocolate. And *everyone* needs chocolate.'

'Even the remotest of islands can get chocolate dropped off by seaplane.' The smile he gives me is as sad as his eyes. 'It's all that's keeping me going. The thought of getting away from here for good. Of *not* living in a town like this. Having no expectation on me. Restoring an old house and a whole island by myself, just for me. It's all I want.'

I don't want to say goodnight on such a sad note. 'At least you wouldn't have anyone pestering you to help make giant gingerbread houses.'

'Oh, I'm starting to think *this* could be fun. Futile in terms of saving Mistletoe Gardens, but fun.' He climbs into the van and puts the headlights on, lighting the way for me to cross the road. 'See you tomorrow, Essie.'

When I get to the other side, I turn and wave. 'See you tomorrow, Joss,' I say to myself.

And a passing cyclist who thinks I'm a fruitcake. I stand and watch as he pulls out and drives off, until his van disappears from view, but it takes a *lot* longer to get Joss Hallissey out of my head that night.

4

The Guinness World Record for largest gingerbread house is held by a club in Texas. Built in 2013, the house was 60 foot long, 42 foot wide, and 10 foot tall. It was made with 1,327 kg of sugar, 820 kg of butter, 3,300 kg of flour, 7,200 eggs, and contained 35.8 million calories.

The flat above the bakery is littered with gingerbread bricks. They're slightly smaller than actual builder's bricks, and they're certainly the thickest thing I've ever made with gingerbread – the opposite of the crunchy snap expected from a gingerbread biscuit. I spent the night trying recipes with various quantities of ingredients in them, searching for the one that would hold up to having other bricks piled on top of it, and every surface in my tiny kitchen is covered with remnants of crumbled bricks, overcooked bricks, undercooked bricks, and bricks that look like they should've been on the business end of a fire extinguisher. With every attempt that's gone wrong, I'm doubting myself even more. This seemed like such a good idea at the time, but we're falling at the first hurdle because of me.

I gave up when the clock ticked past 4 a.m. With all the 'it's too soft, it's too hard, it's too burnt, it's too crumbly', I felt like Goldilocks without ever getting to the 'just right' bit, and I knew I had to be up in three and a half hours. So I went to bed, but instead of going to sleep, I thought of Joss Hallissey's face for at least one and a half of those hours.

I yawn as I make a cup of tea and carry it downstairs. I can hear Mum in the bakery kitchen, and I'm hoping that between her and Saff working today, I'll have a chance to perfect my brick-baking skills. It can't be that hard. If I use less bicarb and add more flour, take away some of the syrup...

'Didn't expect you up so early.' Mum looks up from where she's piping out festive-spiced Viennese fingers.

'I'm meeting the Mistletoe Gardens caretaker before nine. You don't know who—'

She interrupts before I can finish asking who the caretaker is. 'That awful Joseph Hallissey isn't going to be there, is he?'

'It only needs to be one of us, and I don't think he's committed enough to be getting here before 9 a.m.'

'No wonder you couldn't sleep. Must be the worry of having to work with *him*.'

'I'm not worried. We measured up last night. He wasn't as bad as I expected him to be.' I feel bad for downplaying it. Joss was actually lovely last night. Kind and thoughtful. The smooth and splinter-free brick template, the headlights so I could see across the road easily, the little robin who clearly thinks he's the best thing since they invented something to slice bread with. Even the coffee he brought. He deserves better than 'not as bad as I expect-ed', but he's the only male this side of the Severn Bridge who Mum *hasn't* tried to get me a date with, and I don't need her getting any ideas. Joss's desire to get away suggests he's been through enough without my mum raking over his love life too.

Mum rolls her eyes. 'What a ringing endorsement. Something's gone horrifically wrong in your life when "not as bad as expected" is the nicest thing anyone can say about you.'

'It's not the *nicest* thing I can say about him, it's just the one I chose to say to you.'

She frowns at my cryptic answer. 'What's wrong with him, anyway? His mum and dad only moved to the area a few years ago, and he wasn't with them. We gathered he'd moved back to run his father's company after he passed away?'

'I'm not working with him to provide you with priority access to village gossip. I don't know the first thing about his life.' I'm certainly not going to share what he's told me about Hallissey Construction and moving away. 'The one thing I do know is that you owe him an apology for the meeting on Monday night. Calling him out like that wasn't right. The only reason he sat for so long was because he's not the kind of person who likes making a scene.'

'He certainly made one.'

'*You* made one. You can't use people's dead relatives to manipulate them. I don't think he's coped very well with losing his father, and that was a horrible thing to do, especially in such a public setting.'

She starts to look guilty. 'I didn't know that, did I? Maybe if he ever spoke or interacted with the group in any way...'

'People have a right to be quiet. They have a right to be different from their parents.'

She ignores me. 'Where's his mother, by the way?'

That casual 'by the way' is a sure-fire sign of gossip-fishing. 'He hasn't said anything about her. He's alone though, so I assume she's passed too.'

'There was obviously something going on. She mysteriously disappeared. Joseph Senior was cagey about it. She stopped coming to events with him and any enquiry as to her whereabouts were met with jolly-but-rehearsed answers. We had a running joke that he'd murdered her and buried her under the patio.' She giggles in a slightly unhinged manner, like she's not entirely sure it *is* a joke.

'Very *Brookside* circa 1993.'

'And then *that* one, Joss, made Joseph's funeral a private affair. Family only. We wanted to go and pay our respects to our friend, but he stopped us. I'd never considered what a difficult time it must've been for him...' She thinks about it for a moment. 'Still, at least we can be sure he's one man I *won't* be trying to set you up with.'

'Small mercies,' I mutter. 'Do you need any help before I go out?'

'No, I've got it under control, but don't be long. I've got a meeting with Mervyn to discuss Mrs Allen and Mr Selman's shared shopfront. He keeps putting his antiques outside and blocking her window display. Honestly, they live next door to each other *and* work next door to each other, you'd think they'd have learnt to communicate by now. Saffie will be on her own if you take too long. I need plenty of time to get ready.'

'No one needs to look as good as you do for a meeting with their worst enemy.' I waggle my eyebrows.

She clicks her tongue. 'I need to intimidate him. Show him that *this* baker is not to be *trifled* with. Trifle, baker, get it?' She giggles at her own joke, and I suspect she's gone a bit giddy at the thought of Mervyn so early in the morning.

I down the rest of my tea and go back upstairs for a quick shower. I pull my hair into Dutch braids and tie them off with holly-leaf bobbles, and pull on a chunky-knit cream sweater and jeans. It's safe to say that no one is going to be intimidated by *my* appearance today.

It's not even daylight as I walk up the road. The streetlamps have gone out and the Christmas lights are off, the council having failed to adjust the automatic timers for the late sunrise times in December. My pace quickens as I get closer to Mistletoe Gardens and thoughts of Joss fill my head. I'm 100 per cent sure he won't be there, but when I reach the road to cross, a beam of headlights illuminates my way.

Joss's van is in the entrance to Mistletoe Gardens, the iron gates still closed behind him. The van engine is running and he lifts a hand in greeting from the front seat, and something in my chest leaps in the air and then flutters back down slowly and I have to double-check I didn't *actually* leap in the air with joy.

I look both ways and run across the road, and Joss leans over and opens the passenger door. 'Jump in. It's freezing and no one's here yet.' He picks up a cardboard tray with two coffee cups in it. 'I brought coffee.'

'I brought breakfast.' I hand him the bag containing two orange and cranberry Chelsea buns that I picked up on my way out of the bakery. I settle myself in the passenger seat and hold my hands over one of the hot-air vents to warm up. 'I didn't expect to see you so early.'

'Couldn't sleep. Intended to get an early start and realised that we'd still be locked out and whoever has currently got the keys wouldn't be here yet. How about you? Actually, don't answer that, I figure you're the type of person who arrives early for everything?'

'That, and for Christmas this year, my mum's bought me a subscription to a dating site. She was about to start going through potential matches so I thought freezing to death out here might be the better option.'

He laughs and hands me a coffee cup. 'And how many are there?'

'Zero. Well, one if you count the bloke whose profile picture is one of those "don't worry, be happy" singing fish and lists "interest in fish" as the number one priority for potential partners. Two if you count the one who I'm 99.5 per cent certain I saw on *Crime-watch* last week.' I take a sip of the gingerbread latte he's got me. 'Thank you.'

He tears open the Dancing Cinnamon paper bag and takes one of the Chelsea buns and holds out the bag for me to take the other. 'Thank *you*,' he says around a mouthful. 'You don't have to keep doing this.'

Not quite the 'I hate gingerbread and flapjacks and brownies' guy I thought he was.

'You don't have to keep doing this.' I indicate to his cup. 'Tea, again?'

'No one drinks tea at this hour. The blackest and bitterest of dark coffee with no sweetener or milk or anything else to pep it up in any way.' He deliberately repeats my words from last night.

'I *knew* it!'

'Yeah, you got me. Coffee is supposed to be punishing at this time of day.'

'No, it's not. Have you even tried the gingerbread latte?'

'Do I look like the kind of person who tries festive-themed drinks?' He raises such a serious eyebrow that it makes me laugh.

'You never know what you might end up liking.'

He lifts his cup and taps it against mine in a toast. 'True. Surprisingly true.' He holds my gaze for a few long moments, and then looks away, his eyes on the opposite side of the road, watching people with their heads down making their way to work.

He breaks a corner off his Chelsea bun, and crumbles it into the opened-out bag on the dashboard, and then carefully folds it up and tucks it into his pocket.

It takes me a truly embarrassing amount of time to work out why. 'That's for your robin friend, isn't it?'

'No, I thought the flowers might be hungry.'

I narrow my eyes until he laughs. 'Of course it's for Rob. I can hear chirping already.'

There's something so calming about sitting with him. The back of his van might be a mess, but the front is meticulous, and smells of *him* – his aftershave and hair product.

The light in the roof is on, and it's so toasty in here that Joss is only wearing a black T-shirt and another pair of ripped and paint-stained jeans, with a huge tear in the thigh of his left leg, showing a patch of skin, and my eyes zero in on it and it takes an inordinate amount of willpower to look away. My fingers are twitching to touch and I have to remind myself that I barely know this man and I cannot go around poking my fingers into every hole in his work jeans.

'Go on, you can if you like.'

'What?' I do a double-take because he must've read my mind, and then my brain quickly scrambles to put two and two together. There's *no* way he's talking about rubbing my fingertips over the skin showing through the rip in his jeans.

He jabs a thumb towards the radio in the dashboard. 'Put music on. And yes, I know it will be Christmas music, and I'll put up with it just for you.'

I look at him for a few moments. His hair is pulled forward and sort of spiked in choppy chunks with some kind of texturising hair clay, and there are dark circles under his eyes that suggest his mention of trouble sleeping was no exaggeration.

I'm so stupidly touched by him offering to have Christmas music on in *his* van that I can't form words. It's the opposite of something I thought Joss Hallissey would do, and he's managed to surprise me yet again.

'You know what, I'm okay just sitting here.' I glance at him. 'It's nice to be quiet sometimes.'

His head is leaning back against the headrest and he looks like he wants to close his eyes and go to sleep, and the desire to touch that patch of skin showing through his jeans is so strong that I have to sit on my hands.

'Did you seriously just invite me to play Christmas music in your own van? That's really lovely of you. Unexpectedly lovely.'

He doesn't look at me, but a small smile spreads across his lips, and it might be the most genuine one I've seen so far.

It isn't long before the glowing clock on the dashboard turns to nine o'clock, but there's no sign of a caretaker, and we sit there for another fifteen minutes before someone finally arrives.

'Oh, you have got to be kidding me.' He catches sight of something in the rear-view mirror. 'Not that charlatan.'

I shift until I can see the pavement behind us in the wing mirror, and sure enough, the Mystical Mistletoe Magi has pushed along her cart of potions and is standing by the gate of Mistletoe Gardens and waving to get our attention. 'Ahh, we know she's the caretaker of the mistletoe in the trees – it makes sense that she'd be a caretaker of the park itself too.'

'Let's see how much she can swindle us out of today,' Joss mutters as he opens the van door and jumps out.

'Aww, don't. She's such a part of Folkhornton.' I clamber out the passenger side too.

'Essie, she's a con-artist. There's no such thing as love potions, just as there's no such thing as magic mistletoe in these gardens. And *what* is with the creepy horse skull?'

'It's in tribute to the *Mari Lwyd*, you know, the old Welsh festive tradition?'

'Oh, yeah,' he mutters. 'Who *wouldn't* want to revive that? Being challenged to a battle of wits on your doorstep by an unseen bloke operating a dead horse's skull covered in bells, and if you lose, it invites itself in and chases you around your own house, snapping its dead jaws at you. There's a reason traditions like this are ancient history.'

'It's just a bit of fun. And it's not a real skull. It's made of wood. She only snaps it if you refuse to buy a potion.'

'Otherwise known as daylight robbery.' He frowns at the Mystical Mistletoe Magi as we walk over to her. 'You're late.'

'I am never late, nor am I ever early. I arrive precisely when I am needed.' She closes her eyes, her eyelids weighed down by a heavy layer of electric-blue eyeshadow and lashings of eyeliner, crosses an arm over her chest, and bows to us. The wooden horse skull on a pole that stands above her, decorated with flowing ribbons and colourful bells, with opening jaws that are operated by a lever in her hand, also bows in our direction.

The Mystical Mistletoe Magi is a local elderly lady who takes responsibility for looking after the mistletoe in the trees of Mistletoe Gardens. She refuses to tell anyone her real name, and her age is disguised by orange-hued foundation and more blusher than a Boots make-up counter. 'Hello, dearies. What a lovely morning!'

Joss glances dubiously upwards. It's overcast and still not-quite-daylight at best, but it's nice to look on the bright side.

'You're our caretaker, are you?' He sounds like he'd have been more thrilled if a murderous ostrich had turned up with the keys. 'And there was me thinking we were coming to meet a groundsman or someone in any kind of official capacity, not some fraud hawking "eye of frog's newt" and "three turns of a sheep's bladder" potions.'

'That's frowned upon these days. Health and safety. I only use top-of-the-line quality ingredients that are all-natural. No bat's breath allowed, at least not without thorough checks and reams of paperwork first. Makes it a nightmare to get imported.'

'Forgive me for finding it difficult to trust someone who won't even tell people their name.'

'I do not need a name. You both know I am the Mystical Mistletoe Magi. You can call me MMM if you prefer.'

'Or "Mmm" for short?' Joss makes a noise like he's tasted something nice, and I nearly choke myself by trying to bite back the laugh that wants to escape.

The MMM looks momentarily offended, but then flashes him a dazzling smile that reveals there's more lipstick on her teeth than there is on her lips. He's undoubtedly not the first sceptic she's dealt with. He's probably not even the first sceptic she's dealt with this morning. She wanders Folkhornton every so often, pushing her cart around Mistletoe Gardens with no real regularity. 'I come when I'm needed,' is what she says if you ask her about it.

She lifts her hand and there's a large jangle of keys dangling from her fingers. I go to take them but she pulls her hand back and the horse's skull jaws snap together. 'I can't hand these keys over to just anyone. I have to be sure you're committed to the magic of the mistletoe. Building a gingerbread house is all well and good, but nothing says "Christmas magic" quite like buying a potion.'

'*No one* saw that coming,' Joss grumbles.

'We'll buy one,' I say as sweetly as possible to make up for his brashness. 'What have you got in stock today?'

She whisks a floaty cover off the cart with a flourish and a puff of smoke. I'll have to ask her how she did that, it would be perfect for the gingerbread house chimney. Tiny glass bottles rattle at the movement, and I pick one up to read the Apothecary-style label on the front.

Repair broken friendships. A potion of bluebell, apple, and acacia to return those we have lost contact with to our lives.

While I'm thinking how nice that sounds, the MMM removes it from my hand and sets it back on the cart. 'You do not choose your own potion, Essie. Your required potion must choose you.'

'Oh, let me guess, it's always the most expensive one that happens to "choose you" at any given time,' Joss says.

'All my potions are equally priced, Mr Hallissey,' she snaps at him, and so does the wooden horse skull for good measure.

It's standing way above our heads and Joss looks like he'd punch it if he could reach it.

'Last I heard, accepting drinks from strangers was a bad idea.'

'I'm not a stranger. I'm your local friendly wisewoman. It's all about wise men at Christmas but it's time that women had a go. None of that frankincense and myrrh rubbish. Girl power all the way.' She holds two fingers up in a V sign, last seen being done by a Spice Girl in the nineties. 'My potions are about believing. By drinking one of these, you are letting the universe know you're ready to welcome this thing into your life. So many people don't get what they deserve because they don't think they deserve it. This is about believing that you *deserve* the thing you want.'

'I'd like to be able to get into a public park without being fleeced for money at quarter past nine in the morning. Do you think one of your potions could help me with that?' Joss puts on a saccharinely sweet voice.

'Oh, I'm not talking about small things like that. My potions are designed to bring your heart's desire – to make *you* believe that it will be yours, whether that's a job, a move, something old or something new, or... love. What you *really* want in the quiet moments that you won't admit to anyone else. The one thing that will make your life better.'

'I could think of a few things,' he mutters, sounding like one of them is a swift blow to his own head.

She waves a hand between the two of us, closes her eyes, and makes a 'woo-ooo' noise. 'For you two, a love potion!'

'Oh, we're not—' we both say hurriedly, our words clashing with each other as we speak at the same time.

'I know that, dearies. Love comes in many formations. May the magic of Mistletoe Gardens guide you to something you love this Christmas, in whatever way that may be.'

She waves a divining finger over the top of her cart and eventually selects two small glass bottles, the same size as food-colouring bottles, and holds them up with long red nails, most of the varnish on the fingers around the edges. 'Five pounds each.'

'You can't sell many of these,' Joss says.

'On the contrary, you'd be surprised by how many people need a little bit of hope in this dark world.'

I watch Joss's Adam's apple bob as he swallows and goes quiet.

'It's romantic,' I say. 'The love potions are always popular with couples under the mistletoe.'

'I bet you think a dozen red roses on Valentine's Day is romantic too. You've missed the line between romance and commercialism. If you need to pay ten quid to a charlatan to prove to your other half that you love them, you're doing something wrong.'

The MMM ignores his comment and moves the hand holding the bottles nearer to us.

I scrabble my purse from my pocket, but Joss has already got his wallet out. 'I've got it.'

I go to protest but he's already handed her a ten-pound note.

'Thank you,' I mouth at him and he flashes both eyebrows at me. That generosity again. No matter how cynical he is, he's paid for mine too. It makes something go warm in my chest. A real gentleman. A *surprising* gentleman.

She hands us a bottle each and I read the label.

A potion of myrtle, coriander, and coltsfoot to bring love into your life this season.

Joss and I unscrew each of our lids and tap the tiny bottles against each other's. 'To love,' I say.

'To getting on with our day without running into any more shysters,' Joss says as we clink bottles. 'Ladies first. If you're going to drop dead, do me a favour and do it *before* I drink mine, okay?'

I tilt the bottle to my lips and down the contents. 'Mmmmmm, full of love and... blackcurrants.'

'Hah.' Joss steels himself with a deep breath and downs the bottle. 'Tastes like Ribena. Oh, what do you know, it *is* Ribena.'

The MMM holds out a recycling box for the empty bottles, and as we chuck them in, Joss suddenly flicks his head and starts blinking rapidly. He pinches the bridge of his nose and looks wobbly on his feet. 'Woah. What *is* that? Something's happening... Ess...'

He sinks down onto one knee, and his eyes open until they meet mine, his hands coming up like he's trying to frame my face. 'Essie Browne, you're the most beautiful girl I've ever seen. Marry me immediately!'

'Oh, get up, you wally.' I reach over and smack his upper arm. 'I thought there was something wrong with you.'

He's laughing as he jumps back to his feet. 'Sorry, it had to be done. Isn't that what's meant to happen after drinking a love potion? You fall for the first person you see? Or could it be this is a great big con?' He strokes his chin like he's deep in thought.

'My potions are not designed to work immediately.' The

MMM sounds like a headteacher scolding her naughtiest pupil. 'You can joke now, but you'll be a believer before the end of the year. You mark my words.' She finally hands us a key to Mistletoe Gardens each.

'Thank you for the *interesting* morning.' He nods to the MMM, who glares at him and makes the horse skull's jaws snap in his direction.

'And people wonder why I hate this town,' he mutters as he goes to open the gate.

'Your derision and bluster may fool some people, but it does not fool me. It isn't love that's hurt you, Mr Hallissey,' the MMM says mystically. 'It's the person you were in love *with*. Love is a gift and we have an unfortunate habit of choosing the wrong people to bestow that gift upon. The magic only happens when you find someone deserving of it.'

'She must've been at the fortune cookies for breakfast,' he says to me once we get through the gate and out of earshot.

'She makes a good point. Life would be so much easier if we always chose the right people.'

'Mr Hallissey!' the MMM bellows after us, and then beckons for him to go back.

She holds out another little bottle and speaks very seriously. 'An extra one for you. On the house. To help you rediscover the joy of the festive season. If anyone needs that, it's you, *Joss*.'

He looks taken aback by her use of his first name, and instead of another barbed comment, he takes it and murmurs a thank you. The MMM beams at me as we walk away again.

'I'm not drinking that,' he says to me.

'Oh, come on. She gave it to you out of the goodness of her heart.'

'It could be poison! Mystical Mistletoe Magi or Mystical

Mistletoe Morgue Supplier. Potions to help you rediscover the joy of the season... with the undertaker.'

I'm laughing so hard that I nearly stumble into a bush. 'She's been making potions for years. No one's died yet.'

'That we know of!' He holds up the little bottle and eyes it.

The printed label reads:

A potion made with calamint, marjoram, and tangerine, to help you rediscover the magic of Christmas and bring back the joy of the festive season.

'You really think I should drink this?'

I look over my shoulder. 'She's watching. It would be polite.'

'On your head be it. If I die, I expect you to stand as a witness at my inquest and tell them exactly what happened. And if I shrink and fall down a rabbit hole, you're solely responsible for rescuing me from Wonderland.'

It's been a long time since anyone made me laugh so much, and I can't help watching his throat working as he downs the bottle. 'Was that so hard?'

'I think it was Vimto. She's single-handedly keeping soft drinks companies in business.' He pinches the bridge of his nose again. 'Wait... Have you got a Santa hat I can borrow?'

'What? Why?'

'I'm feeling all festive. Can we go Christmas carolling tonight? Ooh, can we watch Christmas movies and go festive jumper shopping? Make snow angels? Roast chestnuts on an open fire?'

I smack his arm again. 'I'm glad you amuse yourself because you don't amuse anyone else.'

He laughs, his blue eyes twinkling in a way they haven't before, and for one second, my breath catches. 'You know something, those potions have already had a magical effect.'

'How'd you work that one out?' He quirks an eyebrow, unable to stop himself grinning.

I reach out like I'm going to poke his cheek but stop myself before actually touching him. 'That's the first time I've ever seen you smile. Really, genuinely smile.'

'I smile.'

'Tightly. Sarcastically. Mockingly. Not uninhibitedly like that. That's a thing of beauty.'

He tilts his head like he can't believe I just said that either. If he looks at me, he's going to realise my cheeks have gone the colour of the berries on the holly bushes we're walking past. He blinks for a few moments before he replies. 'I don't find there's much to smile about.'

'That's a terrible thing to say. I know things are awful sometimes, but there's so much that's good about the world too.'

'Not in my part of it.'

I chew my lip again, wishing I hadn't said anything now. I look over my shoulder, expecting to the see the Mystical Mistletoe Magi still watching us, but she's disappeared. Completely disappeared. I push myself onto tiptoes and look all around, but there's no sign of her anywhere, and with that wooden horse head jolting and clattering above her, she's impossible to miss.

Joss follows my gaze. 'That's not creepy *at all*.'

'She's harmless. Pensions aren't generous these days, she's just trying to top up her income. It doesn't do anyone any harm. Her whole "turns up whenever she's needed" thing gives it a magical air.'

'She turns up whenever she sniffs someone's got a spare tenner in their pocket, more like. You can't really believe that rubbish?'

'No, of course not, but it's romantic. Like she said, it's about believing something can come true, like making a wish on a shooting star.'

'Burning balls of gas are no more likely to grant wishes than her repackaged supermarket-bought soft drinks.'

'Oh, give it a rest, Ebenezer.'

He laughs again. 'So you don't think one bottle of that and ol' Grinchy McGrinchFace over here is going to turn into a hip-happy-clap-trappy Christmas lover in the manner of Clark Griswold?'

'I think you're well on your way. You might even try the ginger-bread latte one day.'

'We can count on hell freezing over first.'

'There's one problem with your story.' I grin at him. 'Knowing who Clark Griswold is means you've seen *National Lampoon's Christmas Vacation*. And if you've watched Christmas movies, you're not a completely lost cause.'

'Yeah, because it's funny, not because it's festive.'

I give him a look so disbelieving that he starts laughing again.

We reached the bandstand long ago, and Rob is chirping impatiently from the wall, and Joss greets him as he goes to tip out the Chelsea bun he saved earlier.

'What's the plan for today?' I ask when he's finished cooing at the bird.

'I did some prep work last night, so I've got the frame mostly ready.' He glances at me. 'You don't look like you got much sleep either.'

I groan. 'I couldn't get the bricks right. I was up until four o'clock practising and they all came out wrong. They need to look right, taste good, and be strong enough to support the weight of a house on top of them. It's a lot to ask of a biscuit.'

'In construction, you'd take out water content for a harder cement mix. You'd—'

'Joss, that's *it*! No eggs. I didn't try it without eggs, but if I replace them with a vegan egg substitute powder, it would give the same taste but without the added wetness. They'd come out as a crumblier biscuit without losing their shape.' I squeak in delight. I can't believe I didn't think of this last night.

'You know I'm going to need them by tomorrow, right? The frame will be up today and I'll get the tent rigged around the bandstand when it arrives, I can begin building tomorrow.'

'I'm going back to try it right now. Well, hopefully. Mum's got a meeting with Mervyn and if the shop isn't too busy then I can use the bakery kitchen instead of the cramped one in the flat.'

'Your mum has a lot of *meetings* with Mervyn.' His waggling eyebrows leave no doubt about the implication.

'Yeah, we know. Saff and I are on the case. They went to school together, they were friends once.'

'Were they indeed?' His eyebrows twitch again, making me laugh. 'I happen to know Mervyn's single and looking. Unfortunately, he's infuriated so many people around here that no one will look at him in return.'

'My mum's single too. I don't think she'd be opposed to a relationship – the problem is that most men around here are utterly petrified of her.'

'Maybe we can do something about this. Maybe that love potion wasn't meant for us in the traditional sense, but in as much as we can use the "magic of the mistletoe" for someone else's benefit...'

'I like where you're going with this.' I'm surprised he's even mentioned it. 'I thought you didn't believe in any of that.'

'Ah, I'm only thinking of you. If your mum's happy, she might spend less time trying to match you up with disturbingly fish-obsessed men and terrorising town meetings.'

'I thought you weren't going to be at many more town meetings after December...'

His eyes lock onto mine again. 'Yeah, you're right. I'm not.'

That utter sadness washes over me again. Life has felt brighter in the last couple of days, and I have a niggling feeling that Joss is something to do with that. The thought of him not being here makes me feel sadder than I would've thought possible, considering that on Monday I would've said good riddance. It's amazing what happens when you get to know someone, even a little bit.

'See you later with some brick samples,' I say, and wave goodbye to the robin who's still on the bandstand wall, having finished his crumbs and singing hopefully at Joss for more.

'Good luck.' Joss looks up. 'You'll smash it!'

'Thank you,' I call over my shoulder, not wanting to turn around and see his face again. I walk back towards the bakery with a little extra spring in my step. I've been doubting myself so much, but somehow Joss believing I can do it makes me a little bit more confident too.

The tradition of making gingerbread houses began in Germany in the 1800s, after the publication of Grimm's fairytale, 'Hansel and Gretel'.

'Helloooooo!'

Joss doesn't hide the groan. 'For a moment there, I was thinking how nice Mistletoe Gardens is.' He looks at the resident committee swarming through the gate, carrying boxes and ladders. 'And then *they* turn up.'

'They've volunteered to decorate.' I wave to the gang. 'They're trying to help.'

Joss watches as Douglas from the coffee shop carries a box so big he can barely get his arms around it, and Mr Arkins, in his dino costume, waddles in carrying one end of a huge foldable ladder with Mr Chalke from the shoe shop on the other end. Beryl carries a stack of boxes she can't see over the top of, and Edna has apprehended a supermarket trolley and filled it with tinsel. Mr Selman has got two armfuls of snowflake stake lights that he keeps dropping and every time he bends to pick one up, he drops another one and chases it across the path, the wire trailing behind him and tripping up Mrs Allen, who's carrying another armful of lights. 'I'm not sure Mistletoe Gardens *is* that big. Are they decorating the park or are they going to start here and go in all four directions until they hit a distant seawall?'

The residents continue pouring in, one after another, carrying boxes and bags and flasks of tea and picnic baskets and blankets like they're settling in for the day. Most of them aren't exactly spring chickens and they've still come out in their coats, hats, scarves, and mittens.

'They haven't put half of this stuff up for years. Mervyn must find your mum very... *persuasive*.'

I giggle at his word choice because there are a lot of ways to describe my mum, and *persuasive* is one of the tamer ones. I have no idea how she persuaded Mervyn Prichard to let the residents ransack the council warehouse where decorations are stored, but I suspect the use of thumbscrews was involved.

'Ooo ooo, morning Essie!' Lynette comes towards the bandstand.

'Behave yourself.' I threaten Joss with a warning finger. 'No growling.'

He laughs and then bares his teeth at me, doing a little growl for good measure, and it really shouldn't be as sexy as it is.

'Morning, Joseph,' she says warily.

Joss looks at me like he's surprised word hasn't got around, and I see the moment he realises he's going to have to give up that little bit of himself or put up with being called by his full name.

'Friends call me Joss,' he says eventually, and it makes something *else* go warm inside me. It feels like one more tiny brick out of his wall.

A brief look of joy flits across Lynette's face and she looks around like she's misplaced her megaphone to announce this to the entire park. Instead, she nods approvingly at the house frame Joss has put together in the bandstand.

There are smooth planks of wood forming the bottom, sides, and top of each wall. The two panels for the roof are in the back of Joss's van and one of his lads is coming to help him get them on today.

'Got to admit, I thought it was a bonkers idea when you mentioned it, Essie, but it's all coming together now. Who knew you two would work so well together, eh?'

When I glance at Joss, I'm almost positive there's a hint of redness colouring his cheeks.

'Many happy memories in this old place. My late husband used to make a point of pulling me into the bandstand for a kiss every time we came here, no matter the time of year. He thought the mistletoe magic should be harnessed year-round.' She admires the structure for a few moments and then looks at the crate full of gingerbread bricks at my feet. 'You two look busy, I'll leave you to get on.'

Joss calls after her when she goes to walk away. 'Lynette? I'm sorry for the way I acted that time you approached me at a town meeting. I wasn't dealing with things very well, but you didn't deserve the reaction I gave.'

The chemist owner looks surprised by his apology and it takes her a while to respond. 'Thank you, Joss. Don't worry yourself about it. I'll take down my voodoo dolls of you when I get home.'

She keeps her face remarkably straight for someone who's *obviously* joking, and waves a cheery 'toodle-oo' over her shoulder as she walks away.

I elbow him. 'Look at you being a decent non-werewolf.'

'A decent non-werewolf. That's the kind of compliment I want on my gravestone one day.'

I'd intended to come up and see the frame last night, but it was too late by the time I'd finished making a few batches of ginger-bread bricks. He's also got the tent rigged up around the band-stand, and it's currently pulled back to allow access and let daylight in.

Lynette has gone over to where Beryl is untangling the artifi-cial berry lights that get tucked into the real holly bushes so they give out a red glow. She whispers something to her and they both look in our direction.

'Look at that. Gossip spreading in action.' He crouches down by the bakery crate and picks up a gingerbread brick. 'I'll "test" this wonky one.'

At first I think he means test it for strength, and I almost start laughing when Mr 'I don't like gingerbread' uses the flat of his hand to break a corner off and pops it in his mouth.

The friendly robin is on the bandstand wall next to us, and Joss keeps crumbling pieces off and leaning over to put some down for him, and he eats, singing for more every time it's gone.

'Do you think it'll hold up?'

He grins around a mouthful of gingerbread. 'I knew you could do it, Ess.'

'Really?'

He picks up two gingerbread bricks and bangs them together and then nods, satisfied with the tapping noise they make.

'My mum took one look at them and said they'd fall apart, and she's been a baker for over fifty years, so she'd know.'

'She ever tried to build a life-size gingerbread house?'

I shake my head.

'Then with respect, she wouldn't know.'

That simple. There's something so honest about his uncompli-cated way of putting things. He has no reason for trying to make me feel better about myself, and yet he does, just by being himself.

'There are cracks already.' I pick up one of the bricks and use my little finger to point out a couple of flaws that developed as they cooled.

He cocks his head to the side and I can feel his eyes on me, and I don't dare to move because if I do, he'll see right through me. 'You doubt yourself too much, you know that?'

I do doubt myself, I know that, but my last big idea turned into my biggest failure, and now I'm back where I grew up, working with my mum who's a powerhouse in time management and keeping things together, and somehow manages to keep up with the bakery and her resident committee commitments and still find time for a social life, whereas I'm up until the early hours to get the bakery stocked, and I can't make *anything* without doing a run of practice pieces to iron out any kinks first because something always goes wrong. I can't say any of that to Joss though, so I mouth a 'thank you' at him.

'I guess we could say you're *baking* spirits bright.'

I laugh out loud. Who knew Joss Hallissey had an eye for puns? 'That's genius! That would make an amazing hashtag. Can I use that?'

He shrugs, bemused.

'Saff runs the bakery's social media accounts and is covering the build. A hashtag is a good place to start. I'm supposed to be taking photos today too.'

There's a clatter as Douglas sets his ladder against a tree and starts climbing it, holding a string of lights between his teeth, being fed up to him by Mr Arkins. The dino suit is obviously too bulky for climbing ladders.

Beryl chooses that moment to start playing Christmas music on a battery-operated radio she's brought with her, and not to be outdone, Edna puts on a playlist from her phone, and two competing lots of music clash in the middle of the park.

'Oh, come *on*,' Joss groans. 'When it's just you and me, I can block out the fact I'm doing something Christmassy, but this is too much.'

'Christmas music is the best. It's *supposed* to be out-of-tune and sung with joyful abandonment.'

Yet another station of Christmas carols starts playing through someone else's phone.

'It's like a duet.' I look around. 'Well, a trio. Oh no, Mr Chalke's got an iPod and a Bluetooth speaker out, so it's soon to be a quartet. It's fun to sing them together, like a duet where you perform both parts.'

Joss looks... unconvinced would be a nice way to put it, but undeterred, I sing along to all of them. 'All I want for Christmas is walking in a winter wonder sleigh ride the snowman to the world oh come all ye hark the silver bells.'

It frightens the robin away.

Probably just as well when they start squabbling over the best Christmas song and one turns up their music to drown out the other music.

'Oh no, now there's a fight over whether "Mistletoe and Wine" is better than "Saviour's Day" and they're having a Cliff play-off. A Cliff-off, if you will.'

'I certainly wouldn't mind Cliff-offing myself right now.'

I grin at him. 'Wait until someone throws "21st Century Christmas" into the mix, it'll end in fisticuffs.'

'Can't wait.' He drags the crate of gingerbread bricks across the bandstand and crouches down to line the first brick up with the frame. 'Ess, what am I supposed to use for mortar? You said something about icing?'

'Oh no!' I slap my palm to my forehead and make a noise of frustration. 'I forgot. I've been so caught up in getting the bricks done that I've forgotten to make royal icing. How could I have been so stupid?'

'Essie,' he says calmly, his eyes gleaming with that same bemusement. 'Breathe. There's no rush.'

'You don't understand. This was supposed to go perfectly. I'm supposed to be on top of things like this. I was supposed to help the residents and take photos and—'

'It doesn't have to go perfectly.'

'That's not what—'

'I don't care what your mum would say. It's no big deal. I'll take the photos while you go and make the icing.'

I go to ask if he's sure, but he shoos me away. 'Take your time. And catch your breath because your face is currently the same colour as your hair and an aquatic animal would have taken a breath more recently than you have.'

It makes me smile to myself as I hurry back down the road towards the bakery. I race into the kitchen and start throwing icing sugar and egg whites into the stand mixer, measuring quantities in only the loosest sense. I flap around more than Joss's robin friend would, trying to tell myself I've done this hundreds of times before, even though admittedly, I've never made *quite* this quantity of royal icing in one go, and it isn't long before I'm racing back through town, hauling a food-grade bucket full of icing with me.

Joss isn't in the bandstand when I get back, and I stop at his van and survey the area. The music has quietened down and only two playlists remain, one on either side of the park, each quiet enough for the other side not to hear.

Maybe it really was too much for him and he's gone. Maybe he was so desperate to get out of here that he abandoned the van and left on foot.

'Useful to have one that tall. And that young. And that fit. Not enough young chaps willing to help out the older generation these days.'

'Hmm?' I ask as Mr Arkins glides up in his brown dino suit, his face completely obscured by the window in the dinosaur's neck that he can see out of.

'Got to admit, we thought he might be difficult to work with, but he's been quite pleasant. No growling at all.'

Mr Arkins uses his T-rex arm to indicate the tree where he and Douglas were stringing lights up when I left. Douglas is now at the bottom of the ladder, and Joss is at the top, wrapping fairy lights around a bare branch. 'Douglas had a little slip and he came to help.'

Helping the people he supposedly hates. Surprising.

Mr Arkins goes to help Edna who's spreading a net of lights along the hedges, and when Douglas spots that I've returned, he calls someone else over and insists Joss get back to the gingerbread house.

On the way across the park, Joss is pulled over by Lynette and has a cake forcibly inserted into his mouth, and before he gets back to the bandstand, Beryl has manhandled him into bending low enough that she can reach to tug a red and green hat with elf ears onto his head, except one of the ears has got half a crocheted brain leaking from it.

The robin is hopping back and forth along the bandstand wall, unperturbed by the activity all around us. 'You really like him, don't you?' I say to the bird, unable to take my eyes off Joss as he walks back.

Rob chirps in response.

'Love the hat. If I didn't know better, I'd say you were enjoying yourself.'

'Just trying to be a decent non-werewolf.' He leans over to lift the lid off the bucket I'm carrying and dips a finger in.

'Joss!' I complain as he sucks it clean.

'There is *no* point making a gingerbread house if I can't eat half the equipment. I will never again work on a project where I can eat the mortar *and* the bricks, so let me have my fun. It's the best bit – like scraping the bowl out when your mum made cake mixture when you were litt—' He stops abruptly and his voice wobbles like it's going to break. He holds his hand out for the bucket handle, his tone flat when he continues. 'Time's marching forwards, let's get a move on.'

I hand it over wordlessly, unsure of what caused the change, but unable to shake the feeling that a hug would solve a lot of his problems.

He takes the hat off his head and puts it on the wall, where Rob hops over and tries to peck off the crocheted elf brain. His hair is messed up from it but he doesn't bother to straighten it out. He sets the bucket by the furthest corner of the frame and hauls the crate of gingerbread bricks across with a loud scraping noise, and yanks his tool bag over too.

Pushing him isn't going to help, I know that much, especially with so many people around. 'Royal icing starts drying out on contact with the air. You have to put the lid back on every time you touch it, or it's going to start setting within ten minutes. It needs a few hours to reach full hardness.'

'Thanks.' He nods like he appreciates me not pushing it.

'Ooh, good job, Edna. Very nice, Douglas. Oh yes, just like it used to be.' Mum marches towards the bandstand and I groan.

Joss looks up, looks between me and the approaching figure, and goes back to work on the bricks, sort of shrinking, like if he curls into a small enough ball, she won't see him.

Our red-breasted companion flies off in sheer terror as her heels click along the path.

'Look at this.' Mum whistles as she stands at the bottom of the bandstand steps and looks up at the house frame. 'That's a much better start than I expected.'

'It's all Joss, not me. He's the builder.'

'We're a team.' Joss is kneeling down in front of the frame, laying the first line of gingerbread bricks. 'Essie makes, I build. Neither of us would work without the other.'

I'm surprised because I thought he saw me as more of an annoyance than anything else, but I watch my mum's perfectly made-up face shift. First her mouth opens, then her eyes widen, and then I recognise the excitement that fills her eyes – the kind that's reserved solely for potential matches.

'Isn't Saff on her own in the bakery?' I jump in quickly, hoping to inspire an immediate need to rush back there before this goes the way I think it's going.

'She's got the two Saturday girls.' Mum does a dismissive handwave and stalks up the steps, her grin getting wider. 'Mr Hallisssssssssey.' She draws out his name, probably going for sultry cat but coming across more like a deranged cobra. 'You wouldn't happen to be single, would you?'

'No, I'm a monk.'

'Jolly good.' She licks her lips like the cobra is now preparing to eat a yipping prairie dog it's caught.

'I'm not single, Mrs Browne,' Joss replies without looking up from his work, his tone suggesting he knew this was coming. 'Single implies that one day I might not be single, and that's never going to happen. I don't think of myself in relationship terms – there is no single or taken, I am simply non-existent. A non-entity when it comes to relationships. Think of me as a non-sentient object. A paperclip, if you will, with a similar level of interest in romance, although the paperclip would arguably be *more* interested than myself.'

My mum stops in her tracks and her entire demeanour

changes. Distress fills her eyes and she looks like she's about to well up. Her lip actually starts wobbling, and before I can stop her, she's crossed the bandstand, physically hauled Joss's head up and is cuddling it against her thigh, stroking his hair.

'Oh, you poor darling boy. Who hurt you? Who hurt you so badly that *this* is the result? Do you want me to track her down and poke her with my knitting needles?'

Joss has been yanked backwards on his knees and is hanging in the headlock she's put him in, one hand braced on the floor, looking like he's about to tap out.

She's got confused between wrestling moves and gestures of affection again. 'Mum! Don't suffocate my builder! I need him alive!'

'Was it that prickly poinsettia you were married to?'

'Joss was married?' I say in surprise, and then turn to him. 'You were married?'

'The past tense is the key aspect of that sentence,' he chokes out, barely audible under my mum's vice grip.

'Look at him, Essie,' Mum continues. 'Don't you think he deserves better?'

'I think he's about to lose consciousness.'

'Oops, sorry.' She loosens her grip and he rubs his neck, probably trying to ascertain it isn't broken. 'I see so many people hurt by past relationships who close themselves off to new beginnings and actively shut out the idea of giving love another chance.'

I remember what the MMM said the other morning. *It isn't love that hurt you, Mr Hallissey.* Do they all know something about Joss's marriage that I don't?

'Just because one person hurt you, Mr Hallissey, doesn't mean they all will.' Mum ticks a finger at him.

'Bronwen!' Mrs Allen toddles over. 'Come and settle a dispute for us, will you? Mr Selman is insisting that "You Make It Feel Like

Christmas" is Neil Diamond's best Christmas song when it's plainly "God Rest Ye Merry Gentlemen". Can you help before I strangle him with this tinsel?'

'It's a full-time job being president of the resident committee, you know,' Mum says to us as she hurries after Mrs Allen who's got Christmas decorations in hand and Neil-Diamond-related murder in mind.

'You okay?' I ask Joss. 'You look a little traumatised. My mum tends to have that effect on people.'

He's still on his knees, and he looks up and meets my eyes, holding my gaze for a moment, before he rapidly looks away and goes back to gingerbread brick-laying. 'Fine.'

'I didn't know you were married,' I venture carefully, trying to sound conversational and not interested *at all*, when in reality my brain is racing along at ninety miles per hour. I'm desperate to know more and equally certain that he isn't going to open up to me.

'Past tense,' he repeats.

'When?'

'Essie, in the nicest way possible, I don't want to talk about it.'

'Oh, right. Okay,' I stutter. 'Sorry.'

I sound totally un-sorry, but it's myself I'm annoyed at because I knew that's how it was going to go. I stand there in awkward silence, trying to think of something to say to ease the tension, but Mum comes back before I have a chance.

'The mistletoe is getting to people. What those two need is a damn good snog.'

'With each other?' Joss looks confused and mildly horrified. I can see thoughts of clacking dentures and prune breath running through his mind.

'They've been in love for years and they *still* haven't figured it out for themselves. Maybe the magic of the mistletoe can help them this year.'

Joss meets my eyes and raises an eyebrow, and for some reason, it makes me grin.

'Right, where was I? Oh yes, dates! Have you checked your matches this week, Essie?'

'No, because I'm not inter—'

'Never mind that, it's the weekend so I thought some more men might be ripe for the picking.' She gets her phone out and opens the dating site app. 'Look, this one's a handsome one, don't you think?'

She waves her phone screen in front of my face, briefly showing me a long-haired man in the photo, and then goes over to Joss. 'Look, don't *you* think he's handsome? He and Essie would make a nice couple, wouldn't they?'

'It takes slightly more than *looking* nice.' He doesn't even give her phone a cursory glance.

She scrolls further. 'Ooh, this one's six-foot-four. And this one's got a lovely big bathroom.'

Maybe she's accidentally logged into Rightmove again. 'What type of man posts pictures of his *bathroom* on dating sites? Doesn't that disturb you even slightly?'

'Well, it's an asset, isn't it? Trying to show you that he's got a nice big...' She trails off and stays silent long enough for us to get the innuendo.

'House?' Joss offers, and I burst out laughing.

Mum continues scrolling. 'Ooh, look, this nice chap's just posted that he's in desperate need of a date tonight because he's made reservations but the woman has dropped out. It's only twenty miles away, you could pop there easily on the train.'

'Oh my God, Mum, will you stop? I don't want to be anyone's second choice. I don't want to go on some consolatory date with a guy who considers me only a marginally better option than losing his deposit on the table.'

'He could be your perfect match. It might be fate that his other date dropped out because all along he was destined to meet *you*. I'll send him a quick reply and see if he's filled the position ye—'

'Essie's already got a date tonight, Mrs Browne.' Joss interrupts without looking up from what he's doing.

'She has?' Mum says in surprise.

'She has?' I say warily, wondering what he's up to. 'I mean, I have?'

He lifts his head and grins at me. 'She's going out with my friend Rob.'

Mum looks between us with her mouth hanging open. 'Well, why didn't you say something earlier? How marvellous. What's he like? Is he handsome? Does he have as nice a bathroom as the bloke on here?'

'He's, um, quite short. Red hair, like Essie. He's got a lovely singing voice. They're going to make beautiful music together.'

'Karaoke!' Mum claps her hands together. 'What a brilliant date. I wish you'd said something before I wasted my time looking through these.'

'Didn't want to spoil the fun of looking at all the men with big... bathrooms,' Joss says brightly.

'Ooh, so exciting! I must go and tell the others. Tatty-bye!'

'That was... inventive,' I say when she's out of earshot. 'Thank you. I'm totally ineffectual at standing up to her. I say I'm not interested and she ignores me.'

'How could anyone ignore *you*?'

I'm not sure if he's being sarcastic or if it's a compliment, but for once it doesn't sound like a bad thing. 'Either way, you didn't have to do that. No one is ever usually brave enough to get between me and my mother.'

The robin lands back on the wall again, and Joss fishes some gingerbread crumbs out of the crate and sprinkles them in front of him, and like he can sense me watching, he brushes his hands together and looks over his shoulder at me. 'Relationships only end one way, no one should be forced into that against their wishes. It was the least I could do.'

'Is that what happened to you?'

'I don't want to talk about it, Ess,' he repeats.

I sigh and he glances up at me and then sighs himself. 'At least she confirmed something I've always known.'

'What?'

'My wife cheated. Your mum wouldn't have said that if she hadn't known about it, so she's proved I was right. Everyone in town knew what was going on, and *none* of them had the decency to tell me.'

I suddenly fall in. 'Is that why you hate Folkhornton and everyone in it so much?'

He nods. 'And that was a much-needed and timely reminder. It's easy to get swept along, find myself enjoying this, feeling a sense of community here. It felt nice helping out with those lights this morning. I needed a sharp reminder of the total lack of care or consideration these people showed me.'

'How do you know they knew? Your wife obviously *was* a prickly poinsettia – people like that have a hard time hiding their true person-alities for long, it could've just been something people picked up on.'

He scoffs. 'Is there anything that people *don't* know around here? If gossip was a superpower, they'd all be some plural version of Batman. Any hint of tittle-tattle is like a bat signal lighting up the sky to the residents of Folkhornton. They knew.'

I chew on my lip. 'I didn't know you'd been married.'

'It ended a couple of years ago. We lived in Bristol and only moved back here when my father was ill. Were you even here then?'

I shake my head because I hate even *thinking* about Paris and the time I spent there. 'I lived away for a while. I only came back last year. But for what it's worth, I've not heard anything about it since.'

'It's old news. Someone's life imploding is only interesting when you can gossip about it in real time.'

He sounds so bitter, and I want to stand up for the residents, but he's probably got a point. Not much gets past the town busy-bodies. It's unlikely that an affair would be going on without someone knowing about it.

'I'm sorry.' I kneel down beside him, intending to help with the wall building. 'Even if they did know, that can't be an easy thing to tell someone, Joss.'

'Well, I would rather have heard it from *any* one of them in *any* way than to have found out the way I did. It's proof of what I've always known – people are inherently selfish and do nothing if there isn't something in it for themselves.'

'Maybe they didn't know how to break it to you. You're quite scary.'

'Am I?' He quirks an eyebrow so high that it makes me smile. 'I mean, good. That's exactly what I want. People to stay away from me. Far away.'

'I don't think you mean that.' I knock my shoulder against his where I'm kneeling beside him. 'I think you're quite a nice non-werewolf really.'

This time, he meets my eyes and something flickers in his gaze, and I really, *really* wish I could hug him.

'Stop it.' He holds out a warning finger. 'You've got that huggy look in your eyes again. Don't even think about it.'

I poke my tongue out at him. 'Get over yourself. I'd rather hug a Portuguese Man O' War.'

'Hmm. Squashy.'

'And murderously stingy.'

'Like me.'

I narrow my eyes at him. I think not, somehow.

6

The world's most expensive gingerbread house costs £49,750. It is made with Meridian Black Strap molasses, Ceylon cinnamon, Echire Butter, Suma raw cane sugar, Duchy eggs, rubies, and pearls.

'Your hair smells of gingerbread.'

I'm on my knees in the bandstand, and Joss is showing me how to build a wall with the gingerbread bricks. He's already done a side wall, so we're doing the back one. I look over my shoulder at him where he's kneeling right behind me. 'Saff and I have baked four hundred gingerbread bricks today, there are worse things it could smell of.'

He laughs. 'It wasn't an insult.'

So Joss Hallissey is complimenting me? Blue moons and flying pigs spring to mind. I didn't think Joss Hallissey complimented anyone or anything.

He's set up a string line, taut across the front of the frame, and he digs out trowelfuls of royal icing and splats it in a line, from one edge of the frame to the other, and then uses the tip of his trowel to feather along the centre of it.

'Speaking of not-insults, I have a question.' He slathers icing onto the front end of the brick like he's buttering it, and then places it into the icing along the bottom of the frame. 'Those things you made me in the basket... Why were they so different to everything I've bought from the shop since?'

'I made those ones.' I hadn't realised building a wall would come with such close proximity, and Joss's cinnamon aftershave at such close range is making it difficult to follow the conversation. 'Everything in the bakery is from my great-great-grandmother's recipes, passed down for generations, but the things I made for you were my own recipe.'

He taps the brick down with the handle of his trowel, holds a gauge rod against the side of it, and then balances a spirit level on top. 'They were better.'

'Thanks.' It makes me smile, and his head tilts enough that I know he's watching my smile.

'You should sell those ones in the shop.'

'Tell my mum that,' I mutter, and then backpedal quickly. 'Except for the love of mistletoe, *don't* tell my mum that. She'll kill me if she knows I changed anything.'

He takes another brick and holds it up so I can see what he's doing as he slaps another trowel of icing onto one end of it. 'So you want to make changes and she doesn't?'

He lines that brick up to the last one and presses it down, and then swipes the trowel along the bricks with a well-practised flick, removing the mortar that has splurged out and leaving a neat white line of icing between them. He sits back to do another one, clearly waiting for an answer.

'I think there's room to modernise,' I say as he butters another brick end and adds it to the rapidly growing base of the wall.

'Times have changed. People want different things these days. Things like vegan options, or gluten-free, or nut-free. There are so many different products now, some of which are better than the originals, but my mum won't hear of it, she thinks Folkhornton people are old-fashioned and only want the traditional stuff.'

'Most people in Folkhornton are about eighty, on a good day.'

'People of any age like to try new things. My mum shuts down all my ideas without giving them any thought, and there's nothing I can do about it. She's the boss – I just work there.'

'Line it up, push it down, swipe off the excess.' Joss repeats the process with another couple of bricks, and then pushes the trowel into my hand. 'Your turn.'

Does he seriously think I've been concentrating on bricklaying? I pick up a brick nervously and copy what he's been doing. Icing on the end, spread to the edges, push it into the bed of mortar and cwtch it up to the brick already there, tap it level to the string line. Swipe off the excess that squishes out.

He holds up a hand to give me a high five, and his fingers curl ever so slightly around my hand. 'There you go, you're officially a bricklayer.'

His patience surprises me. I thought he'd have no time for showing me stuff like this – that he'd be irritable and intolerant and say it would be quicker if he did it himself, but he seems surprisingly happy for me to have a go.

I do a couple more before he squeezes a brick he cut earlier into a small space at the end, checks it again with his spirit level and then moves the string line up to the next marker he's put on the frame.

'You ever done anything like this before?' He dumps trowels of royal icing along the top of that row of bricks, feathers a line through it, and then starts off with a small brick, so the mortar lines don't match up and make it look exactly like a brick wall should.

'No. Not to this scale.' I take the trowel when he hands it to me, butter the end of another brick with icing, push it against the first one, and swipe off the excess white goo that splurges out. 'I'd like to do more display pieces, but Mum says it's pointless. In a place like Folkhornton, we're too small to attract new customers. Dancing Cinnamon has stood there for the better part of two centuries – everyone who wants to come there already does. If I spend hours making window display pieces, all it's going to achieve is making our regular customers come in and say "ooh, that's nice" and then buy what they were going to buy anyway. It won't bring in droves of new cake lovers. And she's right. Whenever I put a big fancy cake in the window, people admire it, but don't rush in to order one for themselves.'

I've carried on laying the next row of bricks, getting into the rhythm of it, and Joss leans back to eye it against the string line and make sure it's level. 'What about social media?'

'Saff runs the accounts. We post everything we make, but we're a tiny town and most of our followers don't live nearby.'

He uses the spirit level and then shifts the string line up again for the next row of bricks, and hands me a full-size one to start with this time. 'Online sales?'

'Saff's looked into it, but it's a minefield with couriers and stuff. You're going to get damaged orders and have to refund or scramble to make emergency replacements, and someone's going to have to cover the time for making online orders and we don't have enough staff. I'd like to be able to send things far and wide, but Mum thinks it's more trouble than it's worth, and she's undoubtedly right again.'

'What if she's not?'

'She is, Joss.'

He shrugs as I line the bricks up one by one, scraping and slathering. 'Well, fifteen minutes ago, you didn't think you could build a brick wall, and now look. You *have*.'

I sit back on my knees and my shoulder accidentally bumps into his arm, but he doesn't move away. 'Are you trying to build my confidence?'

'No.' He checks the level and moves the line up for the next row. 'You're very good at what you do, and more people should know that.'

I blush. 'Well, with a bit of luck, pretty soon a *lot* of people will know about our gingerbread house. We need to get people talking online. We need the world to know about Mistletoe Gardens and what Mervyn Prichard and his cronies plan on doing to it.'

'Speaking of the world…' Joss swipes a stray bit of mortar off with his finger and sucks it clean. 'Why would *anyone* move away from Folkhornton and then voluntarily return?'

I give him an analytical look. 'Let me get this straight, you refuse to talk about your life, but you're fine with questioning me about mine?'

'Yeah, because if we're talking about you, we're *not* talking about me, and it's always better that way. I'm intrigued. I only came back because of my father – why does anyone come back if they don't have to?'

'Because it's my home? Because all my friends and family are here?'

He slaps on the base line of icing and waits for me to start laying the bricks again.

I sigh. 'I was dating a French guy who decided to move back to Paris and asked me to go with him. Paris was my dream city – it was the chance of a lifetime. And I thought that what French people really needed was a good, hearty, old-fashioned, traditional English bakery that specialises in the sort of bakes your grandmother would've made.' I glance at him, his head tilted as he listens intently. 'But it turned out that what French people want is the finest French patisserie, and Welsh Cakes are, in fact, *not* the next pastry craze on the continent. So that failed spectacularly and took all of my savings with it, and when the relationship also ended, I was stuck in France, homesick and alone, with no money and nowhere to go. My mum had to pay for the train ticket home. She let me have my job back and move into the flat above the bakery which was being used for storage. I still find flour under the bed to this day.'

He laughs. 'At least you tried?'

'I felt like a huge failure. My mum said it would never work, but I thought I knew better. I believed in myself *too* much. I thought I'd spread my wings and become a chic Parisian, but all I did was amass a collection of striped tops and berets.'

'No string of onions around your neck?'

'I draw the line at strapping root veg to my person.'

We both laugh. Apart from Mum and Saff, I've never told anyone that, and it doesn't feel as exposing as I thought it would. There's something safe about Joss, something trustworthy, something that makes it easy to talk to someone who's such a good listener, even if he doesn't share anything in return.

'Is that why you don't believe in yourself now? And why your mum doesn't take you seriously?'

'I don't know. Both. Either. Neither.'

It's like he can tell how uncomfortable that question has made me, because he uses his trowel to tap the icing and it clicks in response. We've stopped working while I've been talking and it's already starting to set, and we both start buttering bricks and laying them to complete the row.

'The way I see it is that if you can build a giant gingerbread house, you can do anything. Maybe by the time we're done here, you'll believe in yourself again.' He gives me a knowing look, and I'm a certain he can hear the 'I wouldn't bet on it' that plays in my head.

I dye my hair bright red so I look more confident than I am, and Joss Hallissey is the *last* person I expected to understand that.

* * *

'Are you really building a life-size gingerbread house?' A little girl, probably about six years old, with a doll in one hand, drags her grandfather across Mistletoe Gardens at a pace he clearly wasn't expecting. They stand at the foot of the bandstand steps and she looks up in awe, her mouth formed into a 'o' shape, even though there's only a couple of walls up so far.

'We certainly are,' I say. I'm not very good with kids, I never know what to say to them and whatever I choose comes across as patronising even though it's not intended to. 'Do you like ginger-bread houses?'

She nods excitedly.

'Do you know who else likes gingerbread houses?' Joss says, surprising me. I had *not* pegged him for someone who'd voluntarily engage with a child. Or a human in general, really.

The little girl gasps like she knows what he's going to say. The hand her granddad was holding flies to her mouth, and Granddad hooks onto the hood of her coat instead. 'Is it Santa?' she whispers, looking around like the man himself might be listening.

'It is!' Joss matches her excitable tone. 'When this house is done, Santa's going to live here over Christmas. Santa's so excited because, although he's eaten lots of gingerbread houses, he's never lived in one before.'

'Do you know him?'

'Of course we know him. Santa hired us to build this house for him.'

She gasps again like Joss is the most magical person on earth.

'You know what it means when Santa lives in town, right?' Joss is halfway up a ladder, filling the last corner of a wall with gingerbread bricks, but he's got all the time in the world for her.

She does an exaggerated shake of her head, blonde curls whipping back and forth.

'It means everyone in Folkhornton is going to get *much* bigger presents this year because Santa hasn't got so far to carry them. Hauling things about on a sleigh gets *super* tiring, so the elves make the presents as small and lightweight as possible, but when Santa's only got to pop up the road, it doesn't matter how big and heavy things are, so everyone in a town with a life-size gingerbread house gets extra good presents.'

She bounces on the spot, unable to contain her excitement. 'Which is your favourite reindeer?'

'Hmm.' Joss gives it serious consideration. 'Have you seen *The Santa Clause*?'

She nods excitedly.

'I like Comet because he's got a bit of personality, you know? There's too much focus on Rudolph and the glowing nose, no one appreciates the other reindeer, but Santa's sleigh wouldn't get off the ground without them. I think they deserve more gratitude, don't you?'

I glance at the sky for some hint of UFOs or spacecraft because surely an alien abduction and replacement with a pod person is the only explanation for Joss's complete personality change.

'I'm going to make Blitzen my favourite reindeer from now on,' the little girl says. 'I bet no one else says Blitzen is their favourite reindeer.'

'Don't forget Donner,' Joss adds. 'Lots of people forget all about Donner and he deserves some love too.'

'Donner can be my favourite reindeer,' the granddad says to appease her sudden distress that these fictional reindeer will feel left out.

'How about you, Essie?' Joss looks over at me from his ladder. 'Who's your favourite reindeer?'

I nearly crumble like a gingerbread brick under the weight of their expectant gazes. I feel like a lot is riding on my answer.

I run through the poem in my head. On Dasher, on Dancer... nah, everyone knows those names. Donner, Blitzen, and Comet are already taken. Prancer's had films made about him, he doesn't need any extra attention. 'Cupid?' I say, sounding unsure about my answer.

'And Vixen can be Barbie's favourite!' The little girl waves around the doll in her hand.

'There we go, now all the reindeer are equal and won't feel bad about the fact they don't all have red noses.'

Split personality? Spontaneous lobotomy? My grouchy builder has morphed into Santa's Little Helper in the face of a child with a Barbie doll, and there is *no* explanation for it.

'What do you want for Christmas?' Joss asks her.

'I can't tell you! You're not Santa!' She gasps in such horror that it makes him laugh.

'Ahh, I was just testing you and you passed with flying colours. Santa will be very happy.' He jumps off the ladder, picks up the basket of gingerbread stars I brought this morning, and holds it out for her to take one, and then offers it to Granddad too.

'Thank yooooooou,' she calls, the elongated 'o' echoing back to us long after they've gone out the gate.

'Good God, you're lovely.' I stare at him in complete and utter shock. 'Or ill. Are you ill? Have you got a temperature that's frazzled your brain and turned you into a different person?' I barely refrain from putting a hand to his forehead to check. 'A twin brother! That's it, right? You're one of two and you're winding me up by swapping around occasionally and *you're* the nice one?'

He gives me a tight, sarcastic smile as he returns to his ladder.

'Seriously, Joss. Where did that come from? You like children?'

'What kind of monster doesn't like children?'

'You know what I mean. You're kind to children.'

'If I strike you as a person who would be *un*kind to children, something's gone horribly wrong in my life.'

'You know what I mean,' I repeat. He's deliberately avoiding the question. 'You hate everything – I'm glad children have escaped your wrath.'

'I like children because the world hasn't yet turned them into cynical and selfish adults. Like me.' He doesn't look up from the brick he's putting in, but I bite my lip because he sounds so sad.

He speaks after a few moments of silence. 'Am I really so horrible to be around that you think I'd tell a child that Santa doesn't exist? You must think I kick puppies and murder bees in my spare time too.'

'No, of course n—'

'Let children hold onto that childhood innocence for as long as possible. The world will snuff it out soon enough without my input.'

'I know that. You're not usually one for "visions of sugarplums", that's all.'

'I don't even know what a sugarplum is.' The hint of teasing is back in his voice, serious conversation obviously closed.

'I don't know either, actually. That's pretty bad, isn't it? You'd expect a baker to know.'

'I'd expect any self-respecting Christmas lover to know.'

'I'm guessing some kind of Victorian-era festive snack.'

'From the times before they had Lindor and Pringles, obviously. Children were nestled all snug in their beds while visions of... sentient Quality Street danced around their feet...'

I laugh. 'Now *that's* the Joss I know and lo— tolerate,' I amend quickly. He might be okay but I certainly don't love him.

He smiles at me across the gingerbread house, but it's a smile that in no way, shape, or form reaches his eyes, and I can't help wondering how many layers he's hiding under there, and I haven't even peeled back the surface yet.

7

November 21st is National Gingerbread Day in the UK.

In the past few days, we've made over seven hundred bricks, and that's not an exaggeration. It's Wednesday afternoon and the house is coming on fast, thanks to Joss's master brick-laying skills. It's quiet in the bakery, so Saff's on the shop floor and I'm in the kitchen, getting to grips with another batch of bricks. I'm up to my wrists in sticky gingerbread dough when she calls me from out front.

I look down at my brown-covered hands. It isn't a pretty sight, but a customer probably won't appreciate being kept waiting while I scrub it off.

Saff's behind the counter as usual, but the shop is empty, apart from Joss, hovering inside the door.

He grins when I emerge from the kitchen. 'They have plumbers for that, you know.'

I laugh because it does look like I've been unblocking the toilet. 'You know full well it's gingerbread dough, although you're hilarious, as always. It's unusual to see you at this time of day...'

'Yeah, I just came to say I won't be there tonight. I have... um... a thing. That I can't get out of. I wanted to let you know that I can't... work on the gingerbread house tonight.'

'That's okay,' I say, intrigued by his stumbled explanation. Joss doesn't usually stutter or second-guess what he's going to say – he says exactly what he thinks, whether you want him to or not.

He looks different this afternoon. His jeans are smart and non-paint-stained, his black T-shirt is plain and ironed, and he's shaved for the first time in a few days and is wearing a different aftershave, a crisp and cool spearmint one that I've not smelt before. His thick hair has got more product in it than usual and he's made more of an effort with styling it.

'I'm sorry, I can't get out of the... thing...' He looks uneasy. 'I'll shirk off work tomorrow and put in extra time to make up for it.'

'You're not obligated to work on it every day, Joss, you're allowed to have other... things.'

'Okay, so I'll see you tomorrow then?' His hand reaches out, hovering for a moment, and then he cups my elbow and gives it a squeeze, avoiding the dough-covered hands.

I'm sure it's just a friendly gesture, but a tingle goes down my spine, and I'd really like him to never move his hand, ever. Well, not unless he was going to move it to somewhere more interesting than my elbow.

His cheeks take on a red tinge too, and he quickly lets go. He pats his hands on his thighs like he's trying to rally himself. 'See you tomorrow.'

'See you tomorrow,' I repeat, trying to stamp down the disappointment as he opens the door and hesitates like he wants to say something else, his eyes lingering on mine, but eventually all that comes out is yet another 'See you tomorrow,' as he leaves.

We've been doing a few hours' work on the gingerbread house every evening after work, using Joss's industrial floodlights to make up for the lack of daylight. Every night, I take something unsold and Joss brings coffee, and little Rob joins us, chirping and hopping along the bandstand wall like a manager overseeing the project. It's only been a few days, but those evenings in Mistletoe Gardens have become something I look forward to.

'*Duw, duw*, anyone would think he'd see you tomorrow,' Saff says. 'If he'd have said it any more times, he'd have been seeing you a week next Friday.'

His van's outside and I can't take my eyes off him as he gets back in and starts up. I don't realise Saff's speaking until the white van has pulled away and disappeared from view. That was one of the strangest encounters we've had so far. From the elbow touch to Joss seeming so unsure of himself.

'He didn't want me to worry when he didn't turn up. It was nice of him to tell me.'

'Note how he *had* to tell you in person when a text would've sufficed.'

'He's being a gentleman. It's polite.'

'Essie Browne, I've known you since we were six, I know when you're deflecting.' She taps a finger on the counter. 'Come here.'

I go over, holding my dough-covered hands out of the way.

Saff takes my chin between her thumb and forefinger and tilts my head from side to side, examining my face, and I'm blushing from the thought of what she might see there. Other than flour, which I'm liberally coated in, and probably some stray nutmeg too.

'Oh, you have got it *bad*. You really like him, don't you?'

'No, of course not. Not in *that* way. He's a nice enough guy, misunderstood...' I trail off.

'Did you see the way he smiled when you came out? I've never even *seen* him smile before, and that one almost blinded me. It's been a while since you lit up like that too.'

'Don't be daft, it was relief at not having to face a customer in this state.' I wiggle my fingers towards her.

'Do you know what the *thing* is? Why was he so cagey about it?'

'No idea, but he clearly didn't want to talk about it.'

'Maybe he's got a date.'

I look out the window, like the empty space where his van was will somehow give us the answer. 'I don't think he's the dating type, Saff.'

I ignore how uneasy I feel at the prospect of Joss having a date. It would be nothing to do with me if he did. He's obviously been hurt and is protecting himself so hard that it doesn't seem like he'll ever let anyone in again, *plus* he's leaving. There's no point in entertaining anything more than... maybe even friendship is pushing it, but we can certainly tolerate each other until the gingerbread house is done, and then things will go back to normal. I'll be here, and he's selling up and shipping out. 'Did you know he was married?'

'Married? Him?'

'So you didn't know either...' I say, more to myself than to her. Saff's been here all along. Even if I'd missed the gossip while I was living in Paris, she would've heard it.

'Is he behaving himself when you're doing the house together?'

'Yeah, of course. He's surprisingly lovely. Kind, thoughtful, unexpectedly funny. A friend to little birds everywhere. He's working so hard and he's brilliant at his job...' I watch her raised eyebrow getting higher as I speak. 'Why d'you ask?'

She twists her fingers together awkwardly. 'Have you read his reviews on the trade comparison website? They're pretty awful.'

'No,' I say, my voice going up in surprise. I hadn't even thought of doing that. And now I wish I had.

Saff can't get her phone out quick enough as she opens the browser and brings up a page she's previously been looking at. 'They're not good, Ess. Sloppy, slapdash, doesn't care. Lazy. One says he turned up drunk!'

She holds her phone out but I wiggle my fingers again, so she leans over the counter and scrolls through the customer comments so I can see the screen too. I catch words like 'always late' and 'slacking off'.

'That might be his lads, not him personally. They're all quite young and could've still been learning.'

Saff's eyebrow rises again.

'Joss takes pride in what he does. He's careful but efficient. His lads have needed extra help this week, so he's there during the day and in Mistletoe Gardens every evening. He must be knackered, but he never complains.' I keep my eyes on the phone screen as she scrolls slowly. 'These are all from a couple of years ago. And there are a few good ones...'

'Yes. There's one from a little old lady who, although she makes no mention of his workmanship, gave him five stars because, and I quote, he has very nice buttocks!'

'Well, he does!'

We look at each other and burst out laughing.

'Just be careful, okay? I don't think you should get too close to someone who "sat in the van nursing a hangover while young lads did all the work", no matter how nice his buttocks are.'

'Essie, I'm out for the evening.' Mum bustles into the bakery kitchen at six o'clock that night. 'I've got to meet Mervyn about Mrs Allen and Mr Selman's shared driveway. He's parked his car an inch over her boundary line and she's got her dog to pee on it.'

Saff cashed up so I didn't have to stop, and Mum's coming in early tomorrow to do the morning rush, and I'm still up to my elbows in gingerbread dough as I make the eleventh batch of bricks this afternoon, grateful for the multiple bakery ovens and ample fridge space to chill the dough.

'More bricks?' She rolls her eyes, taking in the crates of fresh gingerbread bricks stacked up on the counter. 'I'm going to need you to pick up the slack on an order I haven't had time for.'

'No problem.' My chilled dough is rolled out to three inches thick, and my hand is a blur as I flick the knife along each edge of the brick template, cutting around it, again and again. 'What and when?'

'Three hundred snowflake sugar cookies by tomorrow morning.'

'Three *hundred* biscuits? Tonight?' I say in shock. 'Are you joking?'

'Argoel Accountants are expecting them at nine o'clock tomorrow morning for their staff Christmas party.'

'Mum! You can't dump three hundred snowflake cookies on me at six o'clock in the evening and tell me they've got to be delivered by morning.'

'We're covering for you all the time so you can work on this gingerbread house nonsense. I just need you to do this one little thing for me.'

'What's "little" about three *hundred* biscuits? That's hours of work and I've still got two batches of brick dough chilling in the fridge. When am I supposed to get all this done?'

'Sometimes, Essie, your *real* job has to take priority over playing with edible Lego.'

'I'm trying to save our family legacy. I thought you'd be pleased.'

'It's a lot of work for something that might *not* help.'

'Exactly. We have to do something outstanding. Something that captures people's imagination. We've already increased followers on social media. Our first picture has been "pinned" 275 times. Saff's posting something every day. When we've got more of the house completed, we're going to send photos to the newspapers, and...' I trail off. Her eyes have glazed over and she stopped listening at least three sentences ago. I sigh. 'I'll get them done.'

I look forlornly at the fridge door. The bricks will have to wait. Again.

I feel inexplicably like I'm about to well up. All I wanted was some support. For Mum to hear my plan and say, 'Yes! That'll work! Good job, Essie!' I wanted her to believe in me. Everything I've tried since I got back has been a failure. Every idea I've had has been shut down, and I'm starting to feel that there's no point in continuing to try. I tried to do something big in Paris, and it went horribly wrong, and no one is ever going to let me forget that. The only thing I could do that my mum would approve of is go on dates with random men.

'Good good. Tatty-bye, see you tomorrow.'

'Mum, wait,' I call as she's about to flounce out the door. 'Did you know about Joss's wife?'

She sighs. 'I had a feeling you were going to ask that.'

So he was right. They must've known because I didn't need to specify *what* she knew. 'You did?'

'Of course we did – that spiky bit of holly wasn't subtle about it. She didn't even try to hide what she was up to.'

'Why didn't you tell him?'

'Because he was dealing with so much else. Joseph Senior made no secret that his business was in trouble, and we were all devastated when we heard about his cancer diagnosis. Joss moved here to dig the company out of the doldrums and care for his father. How could we add to that misery, Essie? It's not an easy thing to say, is it? Walk up to a man we didn't know and casually drop it into the conversation? *Sorry your father's dying, your mother's disappeared, your family business is going under, oh, and by the way, your missus is having it off with the personal trainer.*'

'Her personal trainer?' I chew my lip. Joss deserves less of a cliché than that.

'We knew he had a lot on, and she was *flaunting* it, he was going to find out sooner or later, and at that time, we thought it would be better if it was the "later" option.'

'That makes it sound like you had a town meeting about his life.'

'Not at all. It came up at an outdoor yoga class and a few of us expressed that when someone's dealing with all that, you don't want to pile even more on top of them.'

'Oh, great. You chewed over Joss's life between downward facing dogs and lotus positions.'

'He was a stranger, Ess. Joss and his wife only moved here when Joseph Senior was dying. If it had been someone we knew well, maybe it would have been different, but we didn't know him. We didn't know how he'd react. If he'd believe us. If he'd think we were meddling old busybodies. And it wasn't like we had any proof. You can't throw that particular cat amongst those particular pigeons without being *certain*. We did what we thought was best at the time. We were going to tell him once things calmed down, but he found out himself before then. And quite frankly, with his horrible attitude, maybe he deserved it.'

'Mum! You can't say that. He was hurt. His attitude is *because* no one told him. He doesn't trust anyone because none of you told him that... Wait, Hallissey Construction was in trouble *before* Joseph died?'

She nods.

'But Joss said that *he'd* run it into the ground...'

'Joseph Senior didn't say much. He was a paradox of a man – both an oversharer and intensely private. He'd talk at length about some things but not others, like the wife who'd disappeared. He was trying to drum up business, but he told us about the jobs he'd lost because of his illness, how he'd had to miss so many days because of hospital appointments, treatment, operations, and being too weak to do his usual work. He was waiting for Joss to come back and take over – young blood in the company is what he said it needed.'

'So, Joss was supposed to reinvigorate his father's company...'

'Hasn't he?'

I go to answer, but stop myself because anything I say will *not* remain in this room. 'I wouldn't know.'

She looks at me like she knows I clearly know. 'Oh well, mustn't hang around gossiping all night. Three hundred snowflake sugar cookies for Argoel Accountants by 9 a.m. No slacking, okay?'

Slacking? Who does she think she is? If only I was brave enough to say what I was thinking. Instead, I look around at the gingerbread debris covering 90 per cent of the surfaces in the kitchen. Maybe she's right. I *do* have a real job to do, and as much as I'd like to work on the gingerbread house twenty-four hours a day, I have to do the sensible thing that pays the bills.

I cut the final bricks from the dough I was already using, transfer each brick onto oven trays and slide them into the fridge to chill again. The colder gingerbread is when it goes into the oven, the more likely it is to keep its shape, and I sigh while I clean up. I'd been looking forward to a night of gingerbread making, hoping to get enough of a headstart that we could feel like we were actually getting somewhere.

* * *

Eventually I get into the swing of things. Huge batches of dough, rolled out to uniform thickness, a snowflake cookie cutter to stamp out snowflake after snowflake, chill them, bake them, and transfer them onto wire racks to cool before decorating.

I've got the Christmas carol playlist going on my phone and I'm belting them out, safe in the knowledge that no one can hear me. I've got to a particularly Mariah Carey-esque warble on the chorus of 'O Come, All Ye Faithful' when there's a knock on the door.

I stop singing instantly and coldness floods my veins. It's after ten o'clock at night, and I'm alone, not just in the bakery, but in the town itself. No other shops nearby have a flat above them, so there are no neighbours to scream to for help.

'It's me, Ess.' Joss's voice filters through from outside, and I breathe a sigh of relief.

I run through to open the door, and something inside me that's been feeling down since Mum left rapidly brightens up.

'Hello!' I'm so eager that I nearly drop the keys as I fumble with suddenly shaking fingers and yank the door open, letting in a whoosh of cold air. 'I didn't expect to see you tonight!'

I sound so upbeat that I might have swallowed a jingle bell, and my smile is wide enough to power a wind farm off the coast of Scotland. What's wrong with me? I'm *so* glad to see him. *Ridiculously* glad to see him.

Joss has got his hands shoved into his pockets and his shoulders hunched like he's freezing, and although he smiles, his smile is muted and he looks a bit lost.

'Is everything okay?'

'Yeah, of course. I just... needed a walk. Clear my head. I saw your light on and thought I'd say hi.'

'Hi.' The urge to wrap my arms around him and pull him inside is almost impossible to ignore.

'Are you making gingerbread bricks?'

'No.' I glance at the empty shop behind me, like the kitchen will somehow explain itself. 'I've got an order of three hundred snowflake cookies to be delivered by morning. Mum dumped it on me before she left.'

'Oh, right.' He makes a pained face. 'Do you want any help?'

'Can you bake?'

'No.' He looks down at the ground and the word sounds surprisingly disappointed, and then he looks up again. 'But I'm guessing snowflake cookies need icing, and I've got a steady hand.'

He pulls a hand out of his pocket and holds it out to prove it. His hand is shaking, and he frowns like it's a personal betrayal by his own bodyparts and rams it quickly back into his pocket. 'At least, I do when I'm not outside and it's two degrees.'

'Ever used a piping bag before?'

'No, but I can learn.'

I go to answer him, but the timer starts bleeping from the kitchen. 'Sorry, I've got to get those out the oven. The difference between perfectly baked and coal is about ten seconds. Come in, make yourself at home. Lock the door behind you, will you?'

I dash through the shop and yank the oven door open and jump back instinctively to avoid the inevitable blast of steam, and pull the tray out with an oven glove.

'Wow.' Joss appears in the doorway, looking around in awe. 'I feel like Dorothy seeing behind the wizard's curtain but I'm not disappointed.'

'You need tea to warm up.' I flap a teatowel over the top of the oven tray. I can't leave them on it while I make a cuppa or the bottoms will go hard, but he holds a hand up to stop me.

'You're busy. Let me make the tea. A kettle might be the only thing in this room that I don't need to be taught how to use.' He shrugs his coat off his shoulders and lets it slip down, revealing gorgeous arms that I can all too well imagine being tanned in the summer... I mean, no, not *gorgeous* arms. Muscular arms. No, not muscular either. He's a builder, he's got to be able to carry stuff, hasn't he? Practical arms – that's it! Useful arms for his line of work. That is the *only* thing that's interesting about his arms.

'Essie?'

I've got so carried away by thoughts of his arms that I'm staring into space and that's definitely *not* the first time he's tried to get my attention. He's holding his coat up like he's wordlessly asking me what to do with it. I point him towards the hallway between the bakery and the stairs up to my flat and turn my attention back to the snowflakes with such vigour that I accidentally break two while trying to gently persuade them onto the cooling rack.

Joss comes back in, washes his hands, and sets about making two cups of tea like he belongs here. In one corner of the kitchen, there's a kettle and in a tiny cupboard above it, there are tea bags and mugs, ostensibly for emergencies, but mainly so Mum doesn't have the excuse of using my kitchen to go upstairs and have a poke around the flat.

Christmas carols are still playing quietly from my phone on the unit, and although I've devolumed, I'm not turning them off just because Mr Grinch is here. If anyone needs Christmas carols, it's Joss. While that batch of sugar cookies is cooling, I slide another two trays out of the fridge and load them into the oven and set the timer again, trying not to focus on him moving around on the other side of the kitchen.

He puts a steaming mug down in front of me. 'Tell you have some of those going spare.'

I can sense his height behind me, peering over my shoulder,

like I've done to him many times while he's laying gingerbread bricks, looking suspiciously like he might be about to steal one.

I direct him to an oven tray on the other side of the unit, piled high with all the biscuits that have gone wrong so far tonight. 'Unuseables. Broken or slightly burnt – help yourself.'

The way his eyes light up is positively childlike. I've *never* seen anyone look so pleased to see a tray of substandard biscuits before, and it makes something inside me feel a bit giddy.

He takes his mug of tea and crosses the kitchen, picks up a broken snowflake biscuit and pops it into his mouth.

'Oh my God.' He lets out such a moan of pleasure that it makes me blush for very much *non*-food related reasons. 'Do you have any idea how good that is?'

'They're just sugar cookies. Slightly burnt sugar cookies.'

'They're incredible.' He eats another one. 'I regret never coming here before. To think I've been missing out on food like this all along.'

'I thought you "didn't like baked goods"?' I quote him non-verbatim from the first day I met him.

'What I meant was I don't like being bribed.'

'I wasn't trying to bribe you.'

His eyebrow rises so sharply that it practically makes a pinging noise.

'I was trying to apologise via the medium of baked goods. And ask for your advice, and I had *maybe* hoped that your advice might be given more freely if you felt a teeny bit guilty for accepting a large basket of baked goods.'

'I'm glad you did,' he says quietly, all hint of teasing gone from his voice.

Something feels different tonight. He doesn't seem like himself. 'Me too.'

He holds my gaze across the kitchen and his mouth tips into a gentle smile – one that's so genuine, it makes my heart melt.

I sip my tea between rolling out the next batch of chilled dough. Joss's eyes are on me as I stamp out another round of snowflakes and slide them onto a baking tray, and within a few seconds, the timer goes off, and I smoothly remove one batch from the oven and replace it with the next tray from the fridge and reset the timer.

'You're like a machine. A bright carol-singing machine.'

Oops. I hadn't even realised I was still singing along. Usually I'd be self-conscious, but there's something about Joss that makes me feel like I don't have to hide. Maybe it's because he's leaving. It doesn't matter what he thinks of me because once the gingerbread house is done, I'm never going to see him again.

The thought makes me freeze and I drop the cookie I was peeling off the baking paper onto the unit where it breaks in two.

Joss is over in a flash to grab it. He makes that orgasmic noise again. 'Oh my God, that hint of almond, that melt-in-your-mouth texture. They're even better when they're still warm.'

That thought of never seeing him again is hovering at the edge of my mind, and I can't quite reach it to give it a good kick away and tell myself to stop being so silly. I cannot *miss* someone I've only known for a week and a half.

He goes back to the opposite unit and takes another biscuit, and I can feel him watching me again.

'Will you stop a minute?' He finally speaks. 'If you don't eat some of these biscuits, I'm going to devour the entire lot. Stop and drink your tea, please?'

'I can't fail at this, Joss. My mum's already annoyed with me for wasting time on the gingerbread house. I can't show her I'm incapable of fulfilling the most basic orders too.' I take a biscuit and lean against the unit opposite him.

'What's basic about three hundred snowflake cookies? That's a *lot* to put on anyone. It would be a lot to expect from a factory, never mind just one woman.'

'And my mum could manage it in stiletto heels with one hand tied behind her back and a Bluetooth headset in her ear while negotiating resident decoration disputes and inflatable-Santa carnage.'

'It must be nice to be a robot powered by Christmas spirit. Or an elf. You know those elves in *Elf* who can make a thousand Etch-A-Sketches a day?'

I can't help the grin. 'You're giving away your Christmas movie tastes again.'

He beams. 'Just trying to make you smile.'

My heart feels all warm and squishy in my chest. He's the sweetest, most thoughtful guy, and yet I seem to be the only one who sees it.

'It's not that. It's... before. In Paris. She knew I'd fail and I did. She told me I couldn't expect to waltz back in and get my job back when it all went wrong, and then it all went wrong, and I had to beg for my job back, and she's my mum so she couldn't refuse, and I haven't earned her trust back yet. She keeps giving me these little tests, last-minute things dumped on me to prove I'm... I don't know. Dedicated or capable or not going to run away when the going gets tough or something.'

'You're the most dedicated person I've ever met. You came up with an idea to build a life-size gingerbread house, and you refused to give up. The buzz is building in town. People are *talking* about it. And look at these.' He walks over to the stack of crates and lifts a gingerbread brick out. 'By my calculations, there's roughly four hundred bricks here. You've made all these today?'

I do a small nod. 'Saff helped.'

'*You're* incredible, Ess. And you don't give yourself enough credit *or* take enough breaks.'

'Does anyone?' I mutter as he goes back and sits against the unit.

He closes his eyes, bringing the cup of tea to his mouth and letting the steam rising from it warm his nose, which is still red from the cold. He tilts his head like he's listening to the song playing quietly from my phone. 'That's really nice. What is that?'

'"Candlelight Carol" by Aled Jones. He's Welsh. It's a crime for a Welsh person not to listen to Aled Jones at Christmas time.'

He smiles without opening his eyes.

'This is my Christmas carol playlist. I like listening to them. While Taylor Swift singing about Christmas tree farms and an Ed and Elton duet have their place, listening to the older Christmas songs reminds me of Christmas when I was young because we had to sing them in school. It feels like reconnecting with the past, back in the times when Christmas was fun and exciting and not buried under orders of eleventy billion snowflake cookies and thousands of batches of mince pies.'

'I like this. I feel like I know it even though I've never heard it before. It's like being back at the school nativity.'

'Did Joss Hallissey just admit to liking a Christmas song?' I do a pretend gasp of shock, and he smiles but it's a smile that doesn't reach his eyes.

Aled Jones changes to 'We Wish You a Merry Christmas' and he hums along, but there's something wrong. He downs the rest of his tea, but keeps both hands wrapped around the empty mug like it's still capable of warming him.

'How was your thing tonight?'

'It was... a thing. It was fine.' He swallows and doesn't lift his eyes from the floor.

Whatever that thing was, it was *not* fine.

'Icing?' he says quickly, like he's trying to change the subject before I ask about it again.

I go over and make him hold his hand in a loose fist, snip the end off a piping bag and slide a nozzle in. He holds the empty bag, and I roll the top down over his hand, creating a well in the centre for the icing. I hold the outside of his hand while I steady the bag and spoon blue royal icing in.

His eyes are fixated on the spot where our hands are touching, and my fingers are tingling from the touch. I have to wet my lips and swallow to make words work. 'You don't have to squeeze it too hard. Hold the tip above the biscuit so you're directing the line of icing, not dragging it along the surface...'

It's a good job I can ice cookies in my sleep because I have no idea if I'm talking gibberish or not, and Joss's eyes are so focused on our hands that they've gone glassy, and I'm not sure if he's heard a word I've said.

I put the lid back on the icing bowl, shimmy the bag back up, and physically unfurl his fingers from it. I squidge all the icing downwards, twist the top, and hold it out to him.

He swallows and blinks a few times like letting go of his hand has woken him up.

'Hold the twist at the top here so it doesn't all splurge back out, and then use your right hand here to direct it and keep up a gentle pressure, and twist to detach it at the end of each line.' I demonstrate the way to hold it, and then grab a snowflake biscuit and draw a blue snowflake shape. 'They need to be as uniform as possible.'

I pick up an icing pen and add tiny white dots at each tip of the snowflake, and he watches intently, leaning on one elbow on the unit so he can see everything I'm doing. I get another slightly burnt snowflake biscuit and hand him the piping bag. Our fingers brush again as he takes it and I'm sure I imagine the sparkle, but when I look up at him, he blushes and looks away.

The snowflake I iced is on the unit and he copies it perfectly. His hand is still unsteady, and I don't think it has much to do with the temperature outside now. My entire body is zinging every time he gets close, making me feel unsteady too.

'That's really good.' I give the biscuit a nod of approval.

Joss grins and eats it whole. I raise an eyebrow.

'Quality control,' he says with a mouthful. 'Or destroying evidence.'

He takes another snowflake, ices it perfectly, and then eats that one too, and I can't help smiling. It's nice to see him enjoying something because I don't think he enjoys much somehow. While it would be easy to watch him eat biscuits all night, thankfully the timer starts bleeping and I have to rush across the kitchen to rescue another batch from the oven.

The music changes to 'Away in a Manger' and Joss stops to listen to it, his lips mouthing the words to himself as he remembers a song he clearly hasn't heard in a while.

Once I've transferred the snowflakes onto a cooling rack and got the next batch in the oven, I look over at his work.

'I knew you'd be good at that.' I nod to the intricately neat snowflake he's icing. He's done seven practice runs on the imperfect biscuits and only the first two look like practice at all. 'You're ready to move onto the real thing.'

'I'm graduating already?' He cheers. 'And in secondary school, my home economics teacher told me I'd never amount to anything in the kitchen after a particularly bad exploding Pyrex incident in Year Seven.'

He makes me laugh so effortlessly, and yet it constantly

surprises me when he does because he's so serious in so many ways, but I can't help feeling that he's let his guard down lately.

When I'm standing next to him, he nudges his hip into mine so gently that I barely feel it. 'Thanks for letting me help.'

'Letting you...' It's such an odd sentence. *I* should be thanking *him*, and yet he's acting like I've done him a favour by letting him decorate a few snowflakes.

'Yeah,' he says softly. 'I needed... I don't know. Needed to get out of my own head, I guess. I'm glad you were up.'

'Me too.' I echo our words from earlier.

He eats another practice biscuit, and I move them aside and place a cooling rack on the unit instead.

I should walk away, I *know* I should, but his words are so lost and he hasn't even tried to hide the vulnerability in his eyes tonight, and his hand is right there, resting on the unit, and before I can second-guess myself, I slot my fingers around his and give it a soft squeeze. 'You can talk if you want to. Biscuits are really good listeners. They never repeat anything.'

It's pointed, trying to let him know that anything he says to me won't become the next item on the town gossip agenda, but it's easy to see how guarded he is. I doubt he'll ever trust anyone enough to open up, let alone the daughter of the gossip committee's leader.

He doesn't say anything, and I wonder what else I expected. He's never going to trust me. I pull my hand away and go back to rolling out another chilled ball of dough.

The song changes to 'Ding Dong Merrily on High', and I hum along quietly to fill the silence, Joss icing snowflakes while I'm hopping between the cooling racks and the fridge for more dough.

I hear him inhale a couple of times, like he's about to speak, but then he doesn't, and 'Hark, the Herald Angels Sing' cycles round.

'My mum doesn't know who I am.'

My entire body freezes and my breath stops in my throat. Of all the things I was expecting him to blurt out, *that* was not one of them. I turn to face him slowly, terrified that if he realises he's talking, he'll stop immediately.

'I go every Wednesday evening.' His voice is hoarse, tight, and barely above a whisper. 'She doesn't want to be alone with me because she thinks I'm a stranger, so I sit in the communal dining room and read aloud to her. Sometimes the other residents sit and listen too. My mum thinks I'm a member of staff who comes in to read to the nursing home residents every week. She remembers me in that context, but she doesn't know I'm her son.'

My eyes have welled up and there's a lump in my throat.

'It was *A Christmas Carol* tonight. She and the lady in the room next door are excited about Santa coming. Patients with dementia never forget Santa. They forget their own families, they forget how to eat or walk, but Santa *always* inspires a childlike joy in their eyes. They never forget the feeling of Christmas.'

'My God, Joss. I'm so sorry,' I murmur, putting two and two together with what my mum said earlier. 'She's lived in a nursing home since before your father died?'

He nods without looking at me. 'It broke my father's heart to make that decision, but it got to the point where he couldn't cope. At his funeral, she spent half the time wailing uncontrollably, and half the time thinking we were at a big party because she couldn't remember ever being married and thought she'd never seen the man in the photos before.'

He finally looks up and meets my eyes, and *every* bit of sadness in them is explained instantly. 'I'm a wreck tonight because she told me that if she had a son, she'd want him to be just like me. It's the nicest thing she's ever said and I think it broke something inside me.'

His voice cracks and I don't know what to do other than hug him.

'Joss, I know you're not a huggy person, but can I—'

'Yes.' He doesn't even let me finish the sentence, leaving me wondering if he needs a hug as desperately as I need to hug him.

I don't so much hug him as leap on him with such force that he lets out a soft laugh and backs up against the unit to hold us both upright.

'I'm sorry. I'm so sorry.' My heart is breaking for him. *No one* has a clue he's dealing with this, and I feel ridiculously humbled that he's opened up to me. It's something I never thought he'd do.

His arms tighten around me, curling around my back and pulling me tight against him. His chin rests on my shoulder and I can feel every breath shuddering as he tries to keep his emotions under control, and my arms slip around his shoulders, squeezing and rubbing, anything to make him feel less alone.

'I always go, no matter how hard it is. I always think that if I don't go, *that* will be the one day she has a moment of clarity and asks where I am. But it's hopeless. It's been over a year since she even remembered she had a son. She told me about him once. She was so proud of this lovely family he had, a wife who treated him like a king, fantasies of the grandchildren she'd have one day... It was right in the middle of my divorce, and I couldn't tell her who I was, or that the family she was imagining I had was a distant memory. I asked if he ever came to visit and she said he'd taken her on a day out once, and described a date she'd gone on with my dad in their early years together.'

I squeeze him tighter. This man. The tight smiles, the sharp words, the sarcasm, the standoffishness that hides all of this. In the past couple of years, he's lost his dad, his mum, and his wife in three different ways. That's a lot of grief for anyone to handle.

I don't know much about dementia, I have no idea what it's like to lose a parent in this way, and I'm wholly inadequate in trying to find the right words. 'She might not know *you*, but she can sense love. She can sense you're someone who cares about her. She knows, in one way or another, that you're one of "her people", even if she can't place exactly who you are. Don't underestimate that, Joss.'

He mumbles something against my shoulder and curls even tighter around me, holding me closer than I've ever known it was possible to be held.

One of my arms is wrapped around the back of his neck and clinging onto his opposite shoulder, and my other palm is flat on his back, rubbing in circles, trying to speak without words. I lose track of time as we stand there, not speaking, just holding, until we're blasted out of the reverie when the oven timer starts bleeping.

I groan into his shoulder. That timer has got the *worst* timing of any non-sentient device I've ever encountered.

I ignore it.

'Ess,' Joss whispers.

'I can make more biscuits, but I don't think you'll ever let me hug you again. They can wait, you can't.'

'Go on.' He laughs and puts his hands on my hips and pushes me away. 'Yes, I will. I promise.'

I reluctantly disentangle myself from him and race over to yank the tray out of the oven, which lets me know of its disapproval by letting out a blast of steam, and my mind is so caught up that I'm lacking my usual dexterity to avoid it.

They're slightly browner than the rest, but at this point, I don't care. Talking to Joss is more important than a few lightly char-grilled snowflake biscuits.

He probably thinks he's going to get out of saying any more, but as soon as the biscuits are on a cooling rack, I make another cup of tea without a word, because if he uses any words, it'll probably be to object. I walk across the kitchen, slip my hand around his wrist, and pull him to a table in one corner of the large bakery kitchen. He lets me cajole him into a chair and plonk the mug in front of him. I go back to collect mine and sit down opposite him, and put the tray of damaged biscuits between us.

He takes one instead of talking.

'I can't believe this has been going on for so many years and no one knows.'

'Dad never told anyone. You know what he was like – the outgoing life and soul of every party, he didn't want well-meaning neighbours coming round to see if they could do anything. He was the person who did things for everyone else. He didn't want pity or to let anyone see behind his cheerful façade. And when Mum was still lucid enough for self-awareness, she was embarrassed. She didn't want anyone to see her like that. She didn't want visitors who'd realise something wasn't right.'

'When did this start, Joss?' I'm determined not to let him clam up again.

'Honestly, I'm not entirely sure. Mum hid it for a long, long time, and I suspect there was a fair bit of denial on my dad's part too. I think he'd noticed the signs and brushed them off, too afraid to face what they might mean. But then there was an incident and he was forced to face it. One day, he'd been out for the morning, and he came back in, said hello to Mum, and went into the kitchen to make his lunch. While he was eating, the police turned up. Mum had gone upstairs and hidden in the wardrobe to phone them because there was an intruder in the house. She hadn't recognised him.'

I think of Joseph Senior. Very loud, with a booming Welsh accent you could hear from three streets away. The kind of man who called everyone '*butt*' or '*boyo*', despite the fact they weren't his buddy, or his boy, or, indeed, male. Very charming, always the first on hand to help with anything. Joss's parents hadn't lived here long when I left Folkhornton, but long enough for his gregarious father to make an impression. Before I realise I've done it, I've reached out and squeezed Joss's hand. Instead of pulling away like I thought he would, his fingers close over mine.

'By the time the police left, she was lucid again, she kept saying she'd done it as a joke or that one of the neighbours must've called them, but even my dad couldn't deny what had happened. He swore he could cope, and she would have weeks, even months, of normality, of "being a bit forgetful" as my dad put it, but then something like that would happen again.'

He sips his tea and takes another biscuit, and I do the same, not wanting to push him but making it abundantly clear that he isn't allowed to stop talking yet. My arm is still stretched across the table, his fingers clasped between mine, his thumb rubbing mindlessly back and forth over the backs of mine where they're enclosed in his hand.

'My ex and I came down to visit, and although Mum was her normal self, a few things set alarm bells ringing. She asked me if I liked bands that hadn't been heard of since the eighties, and when I spoke, I had the feeling she was looking right through me, and when three o'clock rolled round, she got ready to go out and said she had to pick Joss up from school. It was like she'd gone back in time. She couldn't comprehend that I *was* Joss because she couldn't have a son who was older than she thought she was. We stopped overnight, and the next day, it was like nothing had happened. She had no memory of the day before and told me off for not visiting sooner. My dad was dealing with the cancer diagnosis by this point too, but he hadn't told us. He'd been going through it all on his own. He was planning to beat it and was only going to tell us on the day he was declared cancer-free. But life doesn't work out like you dream it will, does it? He had to tell us when he found out it was spreading and the treatment wasn't helping.'

His voice breaks again and my grip on his hand grows painfully tight. 'No wonder you want to live on a deserted island.'

'I've had enough of life, Ess.' It's not the first time he's used those words, but they make so much more sense now. 'I can't take any more. Even their cat died. They'd had this lovely little rescue cat for twelve years and she died six months after my dad, and Mum remembers her and *still* asks if she can see her, and every time, I have to explain that she's gone, and every time it breaks Mum's heart, and then she forgets and we have to go through it all again. Nothing good ever lasts. I need to be alone, no friends, no family, no pets, nothing to get attached to. It only hurts more in the end.'

'What about seeing your mum? How will you go every week if you don't live here?'

He grunts. 'I haven't quite squared that one up with myself yet. It's soul-destroying every time I see her, it's not doing her any good and it's definitely not doing me any good. It kills another little bit of me every week. At some point, don't I have to give up?' He doesn't sound like he believes the words either. 'I can always come back for visits. Chuck a sleeping bag in the back of the van and stop overnight somewhere. And it won't be for months yet, the business deal will take a while to go through, and...' He trails off, looking exhausted by his own words.

'I'm so sorry,' I say again, wishing I was better with words. I can't think of what to say. I've always been a big believer in actions speaking louder than words, so I get to my feet and go around the table, pulling on his hand until he stands up and I can lean up and slide my arms around his neck again.

He breathes a long sigh as I hold him again. It feels like we've got all the time in the world. It takes a few long minutes for Joss to relax into it. He's tense, upset, probably worried he's said too much, and at first he's stiff and awkward, but I refuse to give up.

I let my hand venture to the back of his neck and pull his head down to my shoulder, and his arms tentatively close around my waist, his hands are open like he's trying to touch as much of me as possible, and eventually his body sags against mine, so much that he stumbles and has to brace a thigh against the table.

I think that sag is the physical weight of one of his walls breaking down, and it makes me squeeze him even tighter, trying to get across how much it means that he told me. That he came here tonight. That he's trusted me with this. That he let me in just a little bit.

'How long has it been since someone hugged you?' I murmur.

'There's this old lady at the nursing home who hugs everyone she sees. Hasn't got a clue who anyone is, mind, but—'

My fingers tighten on his shoulder. 'You know what I meant. Since anyone hugged *you*, Joss?'

He shakes his head, unable to answer.

'Get used to it,' I say into his ear, and he buries his head further into my shoulder, wrapping around me and pulling me tight to him.

Just breathing. Holding. My fingers on his shoulders, his back, his hair. Stroking gently, and he lets me. He holds me, his fingers running softly up and down my back, his breath shuddering when he exhales against my neck. He's going to have five crescent shapes from my nails in that sinewy bit of muscle between neck and shoulder.

'Ess, can you not tel—'

'I promise. Nothing you say to me will *ever* be repeated to anyone.'

He exhales and it sounds like a sigh of relief and his lips press against my hair when he speaks again. 'Thank you.'

It's not just for not telling anyone.

It's because Joss Hallissey needed to talk, and he chose me to listen.

8

In medieval times, ladies would gift their favourite knights a piece of gingerbread for good luck before a tournament.

The next morning, I don't so much wake up as roll over for the millionth time and decide I can't ignore the alarm any longer. I couldn't get Joss out of my head for a *long* time after he left last night. He's my first thought this morning too, although that implies that at some point during the night, I've *stopped* thinking about him, and I most definitely have not.

After that last hug, we stood side by side with our piping bags and iced three hundred blue snowflake outlines with white dots around the edges, glad of the mindless task of decorating. It's a good way to take your mind off things, requiring just enough concentration that you can't think too hard but not so little that your mind wanders to the things you'd rather not think about, and it was nice to see Joss lose himself in it.

Neither Mum nor Saff are due in until nine o'clock, and the ribbon-tied boxes of snowflake cookies are neatly packed into a crate that I've got to deliver to the accountancy firm. I haul myself through a quick shower, counting down the minutes until I can get to Mistletoe Gardens and see Joss.

Especially when I walk out the front door and straight into the side of his van. I blink up at it in the early-morning murk, and I'm not sure if he's so ingrained in my thoughts that I'm hallucinating his van outside.

Joss rolls down the window with a bright grin. 'Good morning.'

Hallucinations don't have smiles like that. 'What are you doing here?'

'Argoel Accountants is right outside town, it's cold and dark, and I didn't like the idea of my favourite baker walking all that way under the weight of three hundred biscuits.' He does a nonchalant shrug down at me from the driver's side window.

'Mary Berry will be so stoked to see you.'

He lets out a loud, unexpected laugh that seems to catch him off-guard, and we smile at each other for too long, until he realises I've got the crate in my arms and jerks his thumb towards the passenger side. Joss leans across to open the door for me and then holds his hands out for the crate. I pass it up to him, appreciating the careful way he slides it onto the seat and fits the middle seat-belt around it.

I'm so surprised to see him this morning. It was *late* when he left last night. Once the snowflake cookies were finished, he insisted on staying to help clean up, package them, and then make another couple of batches of gingerbread bricks with the dough I had waiting in the fridge. He'd quizzed me about when I'd be delivering, but our only delivery vehicle is Mum's car and she took it last night, so walking to the accountancy firm's offices was my only option. I'd thought he was trying to keep the conversation safely off himself, not planning to turn up at exactly the right moment to give me a lift.

And now I'm standing on the road staring lovingly up into his van like a heart-eyes emoji. I shake myself and clamber in, grateful for the warmth coming from the vents and the light in the cab.

As I sit down, Joss indicates a cardboard tray on the dashboard with two coffee cups in. 'Help yourself.'

'Which one?'

'Either. They're both gingerbread lattes.'

I let out a cheer and throw my arms around him.

Of course, it's a *little* bit difficult to hug someone in a van with a bakery crate between you, and what I actually do is bruise my rib on the hard plastic edge and end up with one arm half-around Joss's neck and my face smooshed against his ear. Which has an unfortunate side effect of getting up close and personal with his red-hot fresh ginger aftershave and everything goes a bit hazy.

His warm hand comes up to rub my arm *and* prevent further injury. 'You don't know if I like it yet.' His voice sounds like I'm only partially strangling him.

I disentangle myself and strap in because a seatbelt might go some way towards protecting him against unwanted displays of affection. 'Go on then, *do* you like it?'

'Are you going to murder me with this fluffy gonk if I say no?'

I glance at the little red-and-white gnome hanging from the rear-view mirror. That was *not* there the other day and for some reason it sends a little tingle through me. Joss voluntarily bought something Christmassy. 'I'll let you live for now, at least until we've delivered the cookies.'

His self-satisfied smile grows wider and he leans closer to whisper, 'It's quite possibly the best coffee I've ever had.'

'Hurrah!' I stop myself from hugging him again and victory punch the air instead.

He holds eye contact for a few seconds, and I realise how easy it would be to stare into his eyes all day. Dark blue with flecks of lighter blue, and deep. I've never known anyone who can hide as much behind his eyes as Joss does.

Like he senses it too, he sits back sharply and starts up the van.

I wrap my arm around the crate, holding it in place just to be extra sure of those biscuits arriving in one piece.

'I feel like the Grinch when he goes to return all the presents he's stolen.'

'Wait, you know *How the Grinch Stole Christmas* as well?' I look over at him but his eyes stay firmly fixed on the road as he pulls out. 'We're going to have to start a list of Christmas movies you *haven't* seen.'

'What's your favourite?'

'All of them. The cheesy made-for-TV ones, especially. But I'll always have a soft spot for *It's a Wonderful Life*.'

'Ahh, there we go, Miss Browne, there's one I haven't seen.'

I do a mock gasp of surprise. 'How can you be thirty-eight and have never seen *It's a Wonderful Life*?'

'One of life's great mysteries.' His concentration is on the roundabout as we drive around it and the Argoel Accountants' office block comes into view.

In the car park, I jump out and Joss hands the crate carefully down to me. A security guard has seen us pull in and comes to collect the crate. It's that easy.

It's only twenty to nine by the time we get back – on foot, I wouldn't even have been halfway there by now. Joss pulls up outside Dancing Cinnamon and turns the engine off, and we sit in silence for a few minutes, enjoying the warmth and the light inside the van while the empty street is dark and cold outside.

I don't want to say goodbye to him. I don't want to spend the day at the bakery while he's working on the gingerbread house in Mistletoe Gardens. The thought that he's leaving keeps flitting across my mind, and I've got an urge to spend as much time as possible with him.

'So, load me up with the crates of gingerbread bricks and royal icing and I'll make up for the lost time yesterday.' His voice is hoarse and sounds flatter than usual.

Oh, holly prickles to it. I'm an adult. Time with Joss is more important than a bollocking from my mum. 'I'll come with you.'

'Why?'

'Because I want to.'

He rolls his head along the back of the seat so his eyes are on me. 'Are you channelling Billie Piper in the nineties or something?'

I giggle. 'I'd rather spend the day with you. Every adult has to be adult enough at some point to shirk their responsibilities and build a giant gingerbread house.'

His face breaks into a wide smile that he *cannot* hide, and it makes every atom inside me start fluttering. And probably a few external atoms too. He looks relaxed and happy, and it would be so easy to slide my fingers along his sharp jaw and pull his mouth to mine... Holy mistletoe, what am I saying? Where did *that* come from?

The thought surprises me, as do most things with Joss. Maybe it's the late night, lack of sleep, or overexposure to Joss's aftershave... I don't *actually* want to kiss him, obviously. It was merely an observation. It *would* be easy to kiss him at that angle, if one was so inclined. Which no *one* in this van is, of course.

'We should move, shouldn't we?' he mumbles. He's still got his head tilted towards me, and now I'm thinking of the hug last night and how he let me stroke his hair, and how easy it would be to slip my hand into the textured dark strands now and tuck them back...

I mumble an agreement, but still, neither of us actually move.

'Joss, thank you...' My mouth is dry and the words come out

cracked and unstable.

'For what?'

Being the loveliest person I've known in a really long while. 'For coming. For the coffee. For being a total darling.'

He bursts out laughing, but it's not a happy laugh. 'Okay, now I know you're being sarcastic. Either that or they accidentally spiked that coffee with six daiquiris. You'd have tasted that, right?'

He's got his holey work jeans on again, and I reach over and rest my hand over the biggest tear on the top of his thigh. 'You're a total darling. The only one of us who can't see that is *you*.' I open the door and vault out before I have a chance to be embarrassed.

I go round the front of the van and reach up to open Joss's door. He looks a bit shellshocked and has to blink a few times before his eyes focus on me again. 'Come in and choose what you want for breakfast, and let's get out of here before my mum arrives.'

That thought is enough to make anyone get a wriggle on, and he swings his legs out and jumps down. Once we've loaded crates of gingerbread bricks and two buckets of royal icing into the van, he follows me back inside and looks longingly at the selection of fresh things I've put out for early-morning customers, before he points to an artfully arranged pile in the lower left corner of the display case.

I raise an eyebrow. 'You hate Christmas so much that you want a mince pie for breakfast?'

'I'm only getting it for Rob. He'll enjoy the crust.'

Although he says it as a joke, I have no doubt that he's genuinely chosen something the little robin will enjoy sharing, and I have no complaints about a mince pie for breakfast, so I use the tongs to load two into a bag, and he *still* gets his wallet out to pay.

'Don't you dare.' I'm out from behind the counter and I get my hands on his back and physically turn him around and push him out of the shop before he's had a chance to open it. 'My mum will be here *any* second. We move now or we risk being caught.'

He hums the *Mission Impossible* theme tune as he starts up the van and I lock up the shop and then race around and dive into the passenger side, giggling as he pulls away while I'm still doing up my seatbelt. I feel like a naughty schoolgirl playing truant, racing away from the school just as the headmaster turns up. As we rev away from the shop front, I see Mum's car turning into the car park at the back.

I'm still giggling as I sink back against the seat and breathe a sigh of relief. It's the most joyous I've ever felt before 9 a.m.

* * *

'Oh, come *on*,' Joss groans as he backs up to the gate of Mistletoe Gardens and spots the Mystical Mistletoe Magi in the mirror. 'Dare me to reverse over that creepy horse's skull and crush it into a gazillion pieces.'

His thigh is tantalisingly close without the crate between us and I reach over and give it a gentle smack. 'Folkhornton wouldn't be the same without her.'

'You say that like it's a bad thing,' he mutters as he turns off the engine, leaving the MMM *and* the clacking wooden horse skull unharmed.

'I'm sure she's added more bells and ribbons to it,' I say as we get out of the van.

Joss looks at me across the seats through the open doors. 'Maybe it gets one as a reward for every person it bites.'

I'm *not* going to laugh at him, but we emerge at the back of the van at the same moment, we meet each other's eyes and his mouth twitches, and we both start giggling uncontrollably again.

The MMM watches us with smiling eyes, her eyelids weighed down by a layer of purple eyeliner that's spread so far, it looks like she's got two black eyes.

'Good morning,' I say brightly, my arm pressing into Joss's where he's standing next to me. 'How are you, MMM?'

'Not having as much fun as you two obviously are.' She bows her head to us like she's about to perform a martial arts move.

I look up at Joss again, and he winks at me. She's right, though. Every moment with him is fun. I haven't laughed as much in the last year put together as I have since he came into my life.

'It must be the mistletoe. I met my husband because of this mistletoe, you know.' She taps her nose. 'We were strangers who used to walk our dogs around Mistletoe Gardens and they took a liking to each other, and we found ourselves timing our walks so they could play together, but we accidentally fell in love too. Even canines aren't immune to the magic of the mistletoe!'

Joss snorts. 'Let me guess, it's time for us to buy another potion.'

'Oh, far from it, Mr Hallissey. I'm here on behalf of the mistletoe today. You see, a bunch of it has got itself tangled up there.' She uses the horse's head on the pole to indicate towards a bunch of mistletoe, tied with a red ribbon, that's hanging directly from the ironwork in the centre of the gate. Somehow, I don't think the mistletoe itself had any input in its positioning there.

'I can reach that for you easily.' Joss goes to lift it down, but she makes the horse's head lunge forward so fast that it nearly nips his fingers off.

'Don't touch that! There's a rule that if mistletoe is seen above a locked gate, we cannot let anyone unlock the gate without first acknowledging it with a kiss.'

'Even I'm not tall enough to kiss that.'

I giggle at him being deliberately obtuse, but the MMM clacks the horse's jaws at him again. 'Not the mistletoe, *twmffat*. Each other. If you both wish to pass through the gate, you must first give the mistletoe what it wants.'

'You wouldn't think it would be so difficult to get into a public park that we're carrying the keys to, would you?' he says to me and then turns back to her. 'I didn't realise that cut-off pieces of plant wanted anything. I didn't think they were sentient enough to have needs, wants, and desires. What does it want for Christmas? Has it been to see Santa yet? Oh, maybe it would like a piece of the mince pie I haven't been allowed to eat yet?'

Despite his harsh words, his voice is teasing and good-natured, and the MMM's eyes meet mine as she hears it too.

'All the mistletoe in Mistletoe Gardens wants is to see people happy.' She looks pointedly between us and then says in a slightly threatening manner. 'Especially people who have been sad for too long.'

She waves a cryptic hand while the horse's skull peers down at us menacingly. 'It would be bad luck to let you pass without a kiss.'

'Bad luck...' Joss repeats like he's trying to figure out how it relates to conning us in some way, and his face softens when he fails to find an ulterior motive. His eyes flick to me and then back to the MMM. 'Well, this girl did a beautiful thing for me last night, and I wouldn't want to be responsible for bringing her bad luck.' He tilts his head and points to his cheek, giving me advanced warning before he steps closer.

My hair is half-up in mini space buns tied with silver tinsel today, and his hand comes up, the backs of his fingers inadvertently brushing my jaw as he gathers up the side of my hair and tucks it over my shoulder, and then he bends down and touches his lips to my cheek.

It's the barest touch, a skim of his mouth against my skin, the kind of touch that you wouldn't even feel if your entire body wasn't alight with anticipation of it. His lips are blisteringly hot against my cold skin, and after being clean-shaven last night, there's the smallest hint of a shadow prickling his jaw that makes me feel like steam must be rising from the friction. The tip of his nose is frozen as it presses against my cheekbone, lingering for just a second longer than his lips do, and even though it's mere seconds, it feels like many, many minutes before I sense the chill next to me where he's stepped away and blink open eyes I don't remember closing.

His hand is still in my hair, his fingers closed around the straight strands from where he tucked it aside, like he's forgotten to let go, and I feel weird and wobbly, like I'm still waking up. Maybe I've overslept and Mum's going to bang on the flat door in a minute, demanding to know why I haven't delivered the cookies yet and wake me up from this lovely dream.

The MMM clears her throat, and the sound makes Joss jump and drop my hair.

'The mistletoe will be satisfied *for now*,' the MMM says begrudgingly.

'The *mistletoe* should be satisfied I didn't set it on *fire*,' Joss grumbles.

The horse's skull snaps in his direction.

'Now, if we've paid our dues, maybe we could be permitted entry into this free-to-enter public park.' He gives her a completely false smile. 'If you're *sure* we don't need to buy another potion, that is?'

She matches his sarcastic grin. 'I think the ones you had last time are still working their magic.'

'Look at you being a thoroughly decent charlatan today.' He gets his key out and opens the gate, and I say goodbye to the MMM.

It's not quite daylight as we walk along the red asphalt path of Mistletoe Gardens, meandering towards the bandstand. Each bare tree branch is strung with white LED lights, and if you look at just the right moment, you can almost convince yourself that a fairy has just flitted out of sight. It looks more magical than it's ever looked before. If fairies were going to hang out anywhere, it would be somewhere like this.

I glance up at Joss and his eyes are on all the lights too, and I can still feel the mark on my cheek where he kissed me, and even though I *know* there's no mark there, I wish I had a compact mirror to pull out and check.

We're walking side by side, and our fingers brush with every step. If I moved my hand a smidge to the right, I'd catch his fingers easily. They'd tangle together of their own accord. I'm simultaneously telling myself to be a bit braver and do it and shouting at myself not to be so stupid. We're *just* friends. There can be no finger tangling and cheek kisses that weren't *just* to absolve ourselves of bad luck.

I wet my lips and swallow. 'The only thing I did last night was listen.'

Even though he doesn't look at me, a smile breaks slowly across his face. 'The beautiful thing was that you made me want to tell you. I've never done that before. Never told anyone and definitely never wanted to. Thank you.'

I can feel my lip starting to wobble at how sincere he sounds and there's only one thing for it – I'm going to have to hug him again.

I catch hold of his hand and tug him to a halt and throw my arms around his neck again, a lot easier this time without a plastic crate between us. He stumbles backwards in surprise, and I think he's going to shove me off, but then he laughs and bends down until he can get his arms around my waist and stands back up, lifting me clean off the ground.

He buries his face in my shoulder and his arms cross over my lower back, his fingers curling around my hips on either side, holding me against him. My hands are flat on his back, but how tightly he's holding me gives me the confidence to move them. At first I let my fingertips press a little, and then I let one hand run experimentally up to his shoulder, squeezing when my hand lands there. I don't realise my fingertips have brushed against the back of his neck until a shiver goes through him, and he lets out a little sigh that's completely involuntary and I don't think he's aware of making, but in the worst moments of my life, I'm going to replay that sigh in my head and find comfort in it.

His aftershave is in my nose, mixing with the clean scent of his hair putty, and I'm so overwhelmed with affection for him that I can't help squeezing him impossibly tightly.

'Have you drunk the huggy potion or something this morning?' His words are muffled against my shoulder, but it doesn't sound like he's complaining.

It makes me giggle and... what's the word for feeling light-headed but when your *whole* body goes light-headed?

'Is she watching?' he says into my shoulder.

'No.' I lift my head and look around. 'She's disappeared. Again. So has the mistletoe.'

'Creepy.' He shudders as he puts me down and my hands slide down his arms disappointedly. I could, quite happily, have hugged him all day, and a fair part of the night too, should the need arise.

Instead of stepping back, his hands are still curled around my hips and mine are still on his forearms, and I look up into his eyes.

His eyes are so beautiful. I've never been particularly taken with eyes before, they've always been a superficial thing, something that women are 'supposed' to find attractive, and 'nice eyes' is supposed to be top of the list of desirable qualities in a man, but I've always wondered what difference it makes. Eyes don't make someone attractive, personality does.

From the very first moment I looked into Joss's eyes, I saw something other people don't get to see. Yeah, Joss is gorgeous, but Joss has always been gorgeous. Getting to know him is what makes him attractive.

His blinking slows down and his eyelids look heavy, like he's starting to relax and he doesn't want to open them again, and I'm about to reach up and cup his face, let my thumb rub over his barely stubbled jaw, when there's a whirlwind of chirruping as Rob lands on the path beside our feet and sings his 'give me breakfast' song, sounding like it's not the first time he's tried to get our attention and has decided to take matters into his own hands. Well, wings.

Joss laughs and steps away. 'Morning, Rob. Thanks for reminding us that we left breakfast in the van. I'll run back and get it.'

As he does that, I herd Rob towards the bandstand. 'Probably a good thing you interrupted that before it could go any further,' I say to the red-chested bird. I've fallen for a man who was leaving Folkhornton once before – I'm certainly not going to make that mistake again. I've hugged Joss *way* too many times for one twenty-four-hour period, and Rob can recognise that, even if I can't.

I sit on the steps and Rob hops around next to me, and we both watch Joss jog back with the bakery bag and put some crumbs on the wall for Rob. There's plenty of space on the band-stand steps, but Joss chooses to sit next to me, and I have to hide a reluctant smile behind my mince pie.

There are definitely a few bricks out of Joss's walls this morning.

9

In Germany, Lebkuchen was once used as a currency to pay taxes.

'No, no, I won't hear another word about it, I don't want you both getting cold.' It's the fifth of December and the gingerbread house walls are now so tall that I can't see over them, the wooden roof is on, and Beryl has invited herself inside, arms laden with knitted material that turns out to be a pair of scarves. Mine is knitted in horizontal stripes of white and silver and Joss's is in gold and green, and each end is adorned with half a felt gingerbread man – the head on one end, the body on the other.

Beryl drapes the scarf around my shoulders and demonstrates how it wraps around your neck twice and then the ends fit together with a sewn-in magnet so the gingerbread man's head is reattached to its body.

'You two are doing such a brilliant job here.' Beryl bustles over to Joss, who bends to let her wrap the scarf around his neck. 'I wanted to make you both a little something to say thank you. We all love Mistletoe Gardens and appreciate how hard you're working to save it. Got to admit, a few of us thought you'd lost the plot when you first mentioned it, Essie, but seeing the two of you come together and make something so wonderful is truly inspirational.'

'Never underestimate this girl,' Joss says kindly. 'Imagination and dedication are all it takes to make a real difference.'

'It would be nothing without Joss,' I say to Beryl as she loops the scarf over his head again and clicks his felt gingerbread man together.

'Thank you.' Joss has got a hand on his throat because she's wrapped it so tightly that it might be cutting off his air supply, but he sounds remarkably touched.

'Thank *you* both. I'd be devastated to see this place gone. My husband and I had our second date here – our very first kiss. He'd been too respectful for anything more than a peck on the cheek on the first date, but here, we had a right proper snog under the mistletoe.'

A seventy-something woman using the term 'right proper snog' makes it impossible not to giggle, and when I look over at Joss, he's struggling to hold it together too.

'We came here every December and repeated the kiss under the same tree.' She points out one on the far side of the park. 'We were happy for every year of our marriage. He's been gone for six years now and I still come along every December and bring his urn with me, give it a little kiss for good luck under the same tree. I like to think he's looking down on me from somewhere.'

I've gone from holding back giggles to holding back tears.

'Mind you, he's probably saying to himself, "Look at that silly old barnacle kissing a ceramic jar."'

The withheld tears are replaced by withheld giggles again, and Beryl smiles to herself like that was her intention. 'We met because of this park. He was homeless and sleeping on one of the benches, and we got talking, and I started knitting him socks, and scarves, and jumpers. I didn't realise I'd fallen in love with him until the weather turned and I found myself out here in my dressing gown in the middle of the night during a snowstorm, forcibly persuading him to come home with me because I couldn't bear the thought of him being outside in it. He stayed forever after that night.' She blinks herself back from the memories of her lost love, and I can't help looking over at Joss and the way he's listening so intently.

'I'll leave you two to get on.' Her eyes fall on a basket of roof tile practice pieces. 'Ooh, don't mind if I do. Thanks, Essie.' She helps herself to a thin biscuit in a star shape and bites the corner off as she leaves.

'No, don't! That was my...' I call after her.

'Guess we won't be using the star-shaped tiles then. Too untraditional anyway. Much like these frilly-edged ones.' Joss helps himself to a different tile and scoffs it in a couple of bites. 'Too fussy. We need something simple and easy to cut out, we're going to have to make a *lot* of these.'

'We?'

'I can ice cookies now, I think I can be taught the basics of gingerbread making. Paul Hollywood, watch your back.'

Tiling the roof is our next project after the walls are completed. The gingerbread will have to be thin and strong enough to support the weight of other tiles scalloped above it, and I spent most of last night experimenting with different shapes and fancy edges, but Joss is right, we need a simple rounded edge and enough space for another tile to be layered above so it partially overlaps, and any fanciness can be added with icing and decoration later.

Beryl rearranges a few imperfectly spaced lights in a holly bush, and Joss stands next to me in the gingerbread doorway as we watch her go. 'I didn't think this place meant that much to people. She's gone to all this trouble just because we're *trying* to save it.'

He looks down at his scarf and then over at mine, the felt gingerbread man's head joined to its body in the centre of both our chests. 'This really is remarkably macabre. I'm not sure if it's a gift or a death threat. The line of blood she's used to join it doesn't exactly scream "Christmas", does it? It screams something more along the lines of "help me" or "I'm a psychopath". And it will certainly *cause* some screams if any small children catch sight of it.'

'It's supposed to be frosting.' I can barely speak because he makes me laugh so hard.

'Why is it red? And these bits here are definitely meant to be blood drips.' He points out two drop-shaped bits of red felt at the point where the gingerbread man's neck is cut off.

'It's icing, how you'd repair any broken gingerbread man.'

'Hell of a sense of humour to do it in red.' He holds the end of his out, so the top half of his gingerbread man matches with the bottom half of mine. 'We could clip them together and be chained to each other for the rest of the day, at risk of strangulation if we stray too far.'

While the idea of being knitted to Joss isn't a bad one, we have walls to insert the very last bricks in to, and roof tiles to fathom out.

I glance over at him, his head resting against the wooden door-frame, the scarf hiding half his face. 'You're going to wear it every day, aren't you?'

'I'm never taking it off. I'm going to become like Mr Arkins and be known as "the man in the decapitated gingerbread man scarf". I will fuse with the scarf until I embody the spirit of a decapitated gingerbread man, much like I'm fairly sure Mr Arkins thinks he really is a dino now.'

'No one's ever seen under the costume. Maybe he is.'

Joss laughs as he fiddles with the felt gingerbread man, flicking its head and body together and then apart again, and I'm struck by how happy he looks. Smiling eyes, crinkles at the edges that show he's smiling behind the scarf too, the green and gold stripes are the lightest thing I've ever seen Joss wear, everything else he wears is black. There's simply a lightness about him that wasn't there before.

We're still smiling at each other when Mr Chalke from the shoe shop huffs his way to the bottom of the bandstand steps. 'Goodness me, doesn't it look magical? Hallissey, do you do these for real?'

'For real?' Joss sounds confused.

'Not with gingerbread. I've got a space at the end of my garden and one of these would suit it perfectly. For the grandkids to play in and the wife to potter about in when I want to watch the rugby. Or maybe a bachelor pad where *I* can watch the rugby while the wife potters about in the house.'

'A garden shed?'

'Aye, s'pose so, but one that looks like this. A real little gingerbread house, but one that won't fall apart in the rain. With all the bricks and decorations and stuff.' He waves an all-encompassing hand towards the house.

'I... um...' Joss looks surprised and sounds stuttery. 'I guess I could fit one in before I go.'

Mr Chalke's ears physically prick up. 'Go?'

I realise what's happened at the exact moment Joss does, and I don't know which one of us is more surprised that Joss dropped his guard enough to say something without thinking.

'Off for the Christmas holidays.' He saves the sentence quickly, clearly not willing to share *that* much with the neighbours yet. 'But it would take a bit of working out. Size, logistics, exactly what you want the exterior to look like...'

'A gingerbread house is a bit seasonal,' I say. 'It might look daft in the summer. Maybe you could do more neutral decorations... like green leaves instead of Christmas trees around the edges, and daisy flowers instead of peppermint swirls, and... Oh, maybe we could do interchangeable decorations! Think of how much your grandchildren would love it if they got to take off the decorations in the autumn and turn it into a Christmas house and then in the spring, they could change it back into a summery house, and—'

Behind me, Joss is laughing good-naturedly, but Mr Chalke listens intently. 'The grandkids would be landed with that. Can you do that, Hallissey?'

'Honestly, I've got no idea. I think my baker friend is getting carried away and imagining things you could do with fondant icing, not actual building materials, but...' He meets my eyes and his mouth tips up at one corner. 'But I love a challenge. We'll give it some thought.'

'Consider yourself hired. I'll tell the missus as a Christmas present, she'll be delighted. She's been on at me for a summer-house for ages now.'

He shakes both our hands in turn and shoots one more admiring look towards the gingerbread house.

I make an excited noise through my teeth once he's out of earshot.

Joss smiles at my smile and shakes his head. 'Removable decorations. These things can't be made of gingerbread. They'd need to be stone or concrete.'

'We could do that. You can pour concrete into moulds, right? We could mould our own giant gumdrops.'

'You can't put removable concrete gumdrops on a roof, Ess.

Removable things made of concrete have a tendency to fall off and crush people.' He laughs. 'How is it that I can transfer your vision into gingerbread and now you're transferring it back into concrete?'

'We complement each other?'

'We do something to each other all right,' he mumbles. 'You'll have to help. Think you can pipe concrete out of a piping bag?'

'I'll give it a try.' Anything to extend my time with Joss.

'You really will, won't you? You really believe it's worth it?'

'Yes. Because I can see the way your eyes have lit up.' I don't think he's realised it, but his eyes are lighter than I've ever seen them, and he's beaming with excitement, and trying – and failing – not to show it. 'There's so much we can do with this. Removable decorations. Letting people decorate their own sheds. Can you make coloured concrete?'

'Yep, add powdered pigment to the water.'

'Then that! People could choose their own colour swirls of iced concrete,' I say, wondering if this really *is* a sentence I've just said aloud. 'If removable concrete gumdrops won't work, there are other things we can do. Plywood leaves and a dab of glue. Easter eggs made of exterior wood and cherry blossoms for spring. Those Velcro pads that you stick pictures up with. It would be so much fun to give grandkids a bag full of decorations and tell them to go wild. We coul—'

He envelops me in a bear hug so suddenly that I choke off the sentence. We've both got coats on and the scarf is padding out his chest so it feels like being hugged by a duvet, but Joss voluntarily going in for a hug is certainly a surprise of 'Christmas miracle' proportions.

'You're amazing, do you know that?' His face is pressed against my hair, his mouth right above my ear. 'You're inspirational. You make me think about things I never would've thought possible.

You're unafraid to try anything. You remind me of what it's like to be passionate about something. You make me feel like my whole life is stretching out ahead of me.'

The words take me by such surprise that I struggle to formulate a response. 'Isn't it? You're not dying, are you?'

'I've been metaphorically dying for the past few years. Every inch of joy was gone from my life – until you bounced into it. You make me feel like nothing is impossible.'

A hot flush sizzles through me. 'You're hazardous for anyone's health, Joss Hallissey.'

'Funnily enough, I think the opposite. I think *not* knowing you was hazardous for my health. You're like Penicillin to all the crap.'

'I can honestly say I've never been compared to an antibiotic before. Thanks, I think.'

But really, I'm melting inside. He gives the best compliments. The most unusual, sure, but also the best, because no matter what he says, he's genuine with it, and it makes me feel like I'm about to cry.

Also, like I'm about to suffocate. I pat at his chest to get him to loosen his grip and allow me a few breaths.

Plump white berries grow in amongst masses of glossy green leaves in the high branches of the trees above us, the holly bushes are interspersed with red berry lights, and although the flowerbeds are empty at this time of year, the residents have filled them with artificial red-and-white roses.

With a bit of space between us, I watch him looking across the grounds. 'This is what you enjoy doing? This creative side of building work?'

He makes a noise of agreement. 'Yeah. This is what I wanted to do. Designing buildings as well as building them. I hate the position I've found myself in with Hallissey Construction. My dad was in a financial mess, and since I came back, I've had to take *every* job, no matter what. Jobs where there's no room for creativity or enjoyment. Corporate repair work more than anything else. Soulless office blocks. Fixing roofs. Re-doing staff quarters in buildings that should have been condemned ages ago, stuff that no one but a few miserable employees will ever see. And don't get me wrong, I'm lucky that Mervyn Prichard liked my father enough to keep me on a retainer, so we get first option on all the council's construction work, but I've forgotten that I was young and creative once. I wanted to be an architect. Watching this come to life is a feeling I never thought I'd find again.'

'You said you restore things?' I say, thinking back to one of our earliest conversations. A couple of weeks ago that now feels like months. If anyone had suggested at the time that I'd be standing in a life-size gingerbread house with Joss Hallissey, I'd have laughed in their face.

'I like giving things a second chance at life. I love the creativity, the inventiveness, the challenge of coming up with some way to reuse each thing, to give it a new life, and then seeing people excited about it. It makes me feel the way building this gingerbread house has. I did a lot of it when I was living in Bristol, but I had free time then. I worked as an architect's assistant – my job was nine-to-five so I could spend weekends doing stuff like that. Since I came back here, I've had to spend weekends doing overtime, trying to pull the company back from the brink and earn enough to keep the lads on.'

'And you've done that. Mum told me the company was in trouble long before you took over. You've saved it. You've got a buyer lined up. You've fulfilled your duty, Joss, if that's what it was about. Can't you say no to some of the bigger jobs now and do the smaller things that bring you joy?'

He shakes his head. 'That's a hobby, not a real job.'

His voice is flat and if he sounded any more parrot-like, he'd be squawking and saying, 'Polly want a cracker?'

'Who told you that?'

He sighs. 'My ex, if you must know. Multiple times and loudly. But she was right. One glorified garden shed isn't going to pay the bills. The company has one last job in the new year and then I'm gone. *That's* what I want.'

The chill that goes through me is nothing to do with the December day. 'What will you do for work if you live on an uninhabited island?'

'I don't know. Something office-y. Something I can do remotely and never have to interact with another human. Something that involves a lot of spreadsheets.'

The bone-deep chill comes again. That's the polar opposite of the creative, hands-on, architectural force of nature that Joss is.

'How about you?' he says before I can push him any further. 'This is obviously bringing out your creative side?'

'Doing this with you has been amazing. It's let my imagination run wild. There's no room for creativity at the bakery. Recipes have to be strictly adhered to because that's what our long-time customers expect. Everything has to be uniform, and when I do custom cakes, every little detail is worked out with the customer beforehand. I'm *loving* this. The sky's the limit. I love the way we have to think on our feet, adjust, come up with new ideas, and...' *You, Joss Hallissey. You* are what's made this project so special.

'There has to be other big things you can do. Isn't there such a thing as gingerbread competitions you could enter?'

I shake my head. 'Who am I to compete against seasoned gingerbread masters? I started baking with my nan when I was two. My experience is just that – experience. I have nothing on the professional chefs who enter competitions like that...'

'And you don't believe in yourself.'

'I did once, and I failed spectacularly.'

'Exactly – once. Back then. That has no bearing on now. We haven't failed. Town's busier. You've gained hundreds of followers on social media and the town blog. No one knows how many kids are going to be queuing up to ring one of Santa's sleigh bells or how many couples are going to turn up for a game of tonsil tennis under the mistletoe when we open. It's going to be a chestnut-roasting success.'

His confidence in this never fails to surprise me. 'The council said a deal has been agreed. No amount of followers is going to un-sign a signature on a jargon-filled contract between the council and some house-building contractor.'

'I know Mervyn, all right? I suspect there's still some wiggle room. In fact, I suspect he overstated that about the contract and nothing's been signed at all yet...'

'You don't know that.'

'No.' He sighs. 'Of course I don't. But I've got a sneaking suspicion that Mervyn himself doesn't want Mistletoe Gardens torn down. He's got memories here too. He once told me he'd kissed the woman he loves under the mistletoe years ago, but it didn't work out, and now he returns every year, trying to be brave enough to ask her again.'

'Aww,' I say, although I'm not sure if I'm aww-ing at Mervyn having a human side or Joss being an old romantic at heart. 'This gingerbread house is turning you into a soppy old snowman.'

'You say that like you're not the greatest believer in magical mistletoe.'

I turn to face him. 'It's a nice story, but I've never actually kissed anyone under it. I don't know if it works or not, I'd just like to think there's still a bit of magic in the world because it doesn't feel like there is sometimes.'

'*You've* never kissed anyone under it?' He pretends to do a double-take, but his face is sincere, and his eyes don't leave mine.

'It's never been the right time.' My mouth feels dry and I have to wet my lips. 'I always seem to be single when December comes around and, well, perpetually single for the rest of the year too, and—'

'The men in this town are really, really stupid.'

He says the loveliest things without meaning to. It *should* be a joke and I go to laugh, but something in his eyes makes my breath catch, and suddenly everything goes still and silent, and I'm hyperaware of every breath, and I can feel my pulse beating in my fingertips where they've curled into the sleeve of his coat.

His eyes slide slowly down towards my lips and back up again, his head lowers like he's going to lean his forehead on mine, and I freeze because I'm certain he's going to kiss me. His spiky hair has flopped forward and my hand trails up his arm, caressing his shoulder, tracing up his neck, and his eyes start to drift closed. I tuck his hair back, and he suddenly jolts back to full awareness. His face flares redder than my hair and his eyes widen in confusion, like he's not sure what just happened either.

He goes to shove a hand through his hair and nearly pulls me over too, because our scarves have failed to part. The gingerbread men on either end have magnetised to each other in a rather unfortunate position. Their faces are smushed together so it looks very much like they're kissing, and their legs are, ahem, inappropriately intertwined.

'Oh, I say.' Joss does a perfect impression of Dot Cotton. 'Who knew gingerbread men could be so frisky?'

It breaks the weird tension that's sprung up between us and we both burst out laughing as they re-enact the Kama Sutra of felt gingerbread men.

Joss stands up and comes nearer to me again so we can untangle them.

'Sorry, Ess.' His eyes are downcast. He clearly doesn't mean the tangled gingerbread men. 'I think there's some sort of electrical forcefield in this park from all the Christmas lights and it's making things go a bit funny.'

We both know the Christmas lights aren't even on at this time of day, but there's certainly something making me feel a bit funny whenever I'm with him too.

* * *

By 5 p.m. that evening, the gingerbread house walls are finished, Joss has erected freestanding scaffolding at either side of the house and put up a chimney. His floodlights are lighting up the darkness, and we're both up on the scaffolding, trying to work out the best way to lay the gingerbread roof tiles.

'Good evening, Mr Arkins.' I climb down when I spot an approaching dinosaur.

Mr Arkins stands at the bottom of the bandstand steps and looks up. It's like being a judge on *The Masked Singer* and there should be a crowd chanting, 'Take it off, take it off.' He's carrying two dinosaurs in his... paw? Hoof? What would be the technical term for a dinosaur's foot? Joss and I both go to the bottom of the steps and he hands us one each. It's a keyring with a small plastic T-rex wearing a Santa hat hanging from it. Who doesn't love a festive dino, right?

'What have we done to deserve these?' Joss looks touched.

'I wanted to say how much I appreciate what you're doing. I don't know how the Folkhornton council can consider destroying Mistletoe Gardens. They know how much it means to us.' His voice is as muffled as usual through the dino suit, but there's passion in his words. 'I've written a strongly worded letter, but the words of an old man are worthless compared to the money they'll rake in by selling this land to some moral-free housing conglomerate. It's just a little something to remember me by when this is all over.'

'Are you going somewhere?' My voice catches in my throat. We might take the mickey out of Mr Arkins and his never-removed dino suit, but he's a *huge* part of Folkhornton. He's raised many a smile when I glance out the bakery window and see a dinosaur toddling down the street, or when I hear children excitedly chattering about the dinosaur they just saw.

'I don't know. My wife and I have been talking since we heard the news, and we're both wondering if it's time to move on.'

Mr Arkins has a wife? Now *that* is something I did not know.

'The shop isn't doing as well as it once was,' he continues. 'And her business is struggling too. We're both long past retirement age, and without Mistletoe Gardens... and the memories we have here... It's been thirty-five years...' He chokes up and stops talking.

'What has?' Joss's face is full of concern and his question is gentle, leaving no doubt that it doesn't have to be answered if Mr Arkins doesn't want to.

'You see that stone over there?' Mr Arkins points out an area on the western side of the gardens where there's a large, flat stone against a tree trunk. The grass in front of it is always neatly trimmed, and there's a potted rose standing next to it that blooms into yellow flowers every summer. 'That's a memorial to our son.'

I can't help the intake of breath. I had no idea that was a memorial or that Mr Arkins had ever had a child.

'M. A.,' Joss says slowly. 'The initials chiselled into one corner.'

'Mason Arkins. I did that myself. We wanted something natural, something that would stand there for generations to come but not look out of place. I wanted to make a mark in some way to show it wasn't a random stone – that it meant something.'

I'd never even noticed there was anything carved into it.

'He was six years old. Killed by a drunk driver. It happened on the road out there.' He points to the opposite side of Mistletoe Gardens. 'We were waiting to cross at the lights and the car careened straight into us. Mason was killed outright. My injuries were minor in comparison to our grief, but they couldn't be hidden. My silly costume hides a multitude of scars.'

'It's not silly.' I hadn't realised tears were building in my eyes until the movement lets them spill over.

'I do it as a way of remembering him. That's where the idea for the shop came from. Mason was dinosaur obsessed. He wanted dinosaur *everything*. He was upset when we went shopping and there wasn't much dinosaur stuff around in those hazy pre-internet days. I lost my job because of my injuries and my grief. My wife too. I probably could've overcome the injuries, but the grief was insurmountable. We got to the point where our savings were running out and we *had* to work again, but I wanted to do something worthwhile. Something to bring smiles to children's faces. Dinosaurs made Mason happy and a whole shop of them would make other kids happy too. But I had facial scarring, injuries that had required skin grafts and couldn't be hidden. I thought coming face to face with children would scare them half to death. One of my wife's cousins had a fancy dress shop and made me a dinosaur costume. Mason would've been overjoyed to see a dinosaur running a dinosaur shop, and it just stuck.'

'It became easier to face the world from behind a mask.' There's a shiver in Joss's voice that makes me look over at him.

The oversized dino head nods. 'And now they're going to tear down Mistletoe Gardens and take our last connection to him with it.'

'No, they're not.' I can see the set of Joss's jaw, the gritted teeth, his eyes glistening with unshed tears. 'It's not too late. I *know* that nothing's been signed yet – we can turn it around.'

'I hope you're right, young man.' The dino bows to us. 'You're doing a wonderful job. Even I'll be stopping by to see Santa when it's done.'

'If you've got a Santa hat that will fit, maybe kids would like their photo taken with you too,' I say as a joke.

'Oh my God.' Joss gasps and gestures towards a gap between benches in the path around the bandstand. 'We could set up an area over here. Somewhere for you to sit, a bit of set building and some gingerbread dinosaurs to tie in with the theme... Kids can come and meet the prehistoric version of Santa! I would've *loved* that as a child. To be fair, I'm thirty-eight and I will still be *first* in the queue to sit on your knee. I think this place is causing me to regress or something.'

'The magic of Christmas,' Mr Arkins says. 'Never is there any other time of year when it's so easy to slip back into your childhood ideals and believe you're young again. If Santa doesn't mind sharing the spotlight, I'd be delighted to be part of it.'

'Yes!' Joss barely refrains from jumping for joy.

'Thank you for giving an old man a listening ear.' Mr Arkins starts to walk away.

'Are you okay to get home?' Joss calls after him. 'I could give you a lift or walk with you?'

'No, no, I'm fine, dear fellow. I'm only a couple of streets outside of town. Lovely of you to offer, though. Got yourself a real gentleman there, Essie.'

I glance at Joss too. I'm constantly surprised by this man. For all his bluster and as many times as he says he doesn't care about this town or anyone in it, he *really* cares about Mr Arkins tonight. And the idea of kids who love dinos getting to share their

Christmas with Mr Arkins too... Joss turned Mr Arkins's sadness into something positive.

I don't realise I've migrated across the steps until I touch his arm. 'You okay?'

'Yeah.' He looks as surprised by the touch as I am, then he blinks his eyes closed and pinches the bridge of his nose. 'Just wasn't expecting that. I never realised a place like this could mean *that* much. I had no idea about his son – I thought he was just a bit barmy.'

I let my hand trail up his arm until my fingers close around the curve of muscle between his neck and shoulder and pull him down to my level so he's seeing the same thing. 'As you stand here, wearing a decapitated gingerbread man scarf and watching a seventy-eight-year-old man dressed as a dinosaur waddling away from a park full of magical mistletoe, how can you even consider leaving this place?'

His arm slides around my waist, the weight of it resting on my lower back, and he leans his head to the side so it rests against mine for a brief moment. 'One of life's great mysteries.'

He doesn't sound as convinced as the last time he said it.

10

The world's biggest gingerbread man was made by IKEA in Oslo
and weighed 650 kg.

'Are you... singing?' I ask as I walk up to the bandstand. It's 11 a.m.
and we had a morning rush at Dancing Cinnamon, so I'm later
than I should be.

'Nope. Just happy to be here. Helping to *bake* Christmas merry
and bright.'

He's certainly making *something* merry and bright, all right.
'How can you be so chirpy when you must've got even less sleep
than I did last night?'

Joss and I spent most of yesterday evening making gingerbread roof tiles, and now he's up on the scaffolding, setting out the
first line along the bottom edge of the roof.

'Just glad to be *baking* spirits bright again.' He laughs. 'Sorry,
the tiredness is making me punchy. *Pun*-chy, get it?'

I think of the miserable guy I met three weeks ago. You
wouldn't think they were the same person.

He bites the corner off another tile and grins down at me

before he starts singing to the tune of 'O Christmas Tree'. 'Oh gingerbread, oh gingerbread, how lovely are thy spices. We ice your head, we bite your limbs, we make scarves out of your body parts... Oh gingerbread, oh gingerbread, oh bara sinsir, most lovely.'

He even manages to substitute the 'o tannenbaum' line with the Welsh word for gingerbread.

I have to bite into my fist to stop laughing, and when that fails, I laugh so hard that I give myself hiccups. '*What* did they put in your coffee this morning? Because I'm fairly sure they need a licence to serve it at this time of day.'

He leans over the scaffolding and grins down at me. 'I realised how happy I am to be here. A father and his kids walked past on their way to school this morning and they stood staring at it in awe. It put a massive smile on their faces, and it felt *really* good. Every day when I get in the van, I hesitate at the door and feel weighed down by the day ahead, but as I was getting in the van this morning, I realised I haven't had a single moment of dread since I met you. I'd forgotten what it's like to enjoy a job. It's been a long while since I cared about my work, but this is something totally different. It feels important. Like I'm part of something that really matters.'

He's lying across the scaffold board to position the tiles, covering the back of them in a thick zigzag of royal icing, and leaning down to hold each one in place for a few seconds before the icing takes its grip. 'And I got another job offer this morning. A summer house. A lady showed me a photo of her cottage garden full of gnomes and mushrooms and lights, and she wants something magical looking to fit in with the fairytale theme.'

'Are you going to do it?'

'I said I'd let her know. I don't know. It's the sort of thing I'd like to do, but one or two small jobs won't cover expenses. Maybe it's something I could do on my own, after the company's sold, before I...'

Leave. I mentally finish the sentence he can't seem to complete. I can't quite comprehend how much I'm going to miss him. It's a truly unreal amount for someone who wasn't even on my radar last month.

Mr Arkins is around the other side of the bandstand, setting up an area for children to have their pictures taken with the festive dino, and he's not only managed to get a Santa hat on top of the dino head, but he's also been able to get a festive jumper on, so now his dino costume is wearing a knitted jumper depicting a Christmassy tyrannosaurus sitting in front of a Christmas tree, with the words 'Tree-rex' underneath, and the star on top of the Christmas tree actually flashes.

Mr Arkins truly is a joy to the world.

'Mr Hallissey!' Edna comes across the gardens waving something in her hand.

'You all right, Edna?' Joss climbs off the scaffolding and heads towards his workbench, which is outside on the path today. With the walls built and the scaffolding up, there's no room for it in the bandstand.

'I could do with some advice and I thought you'd be the ideal person to ask.' She fans herself with the paint brochures she's holding. 'I want to give my shed a lick of paint, but there's all this jargon about textured or smooth or breathable, and acrylic or latex or oil-based. I've got overwhelmed by it all.'

Edna spreads her collection of paint samples across the workbench, and Joss leans on his elbows and looks them over. He listens to her garbled worries and explains in simple detail what each word means and why she would or wouldn't want each one. He talks through options with endless patience, and she's looking a lot less flustered after a few minutes, especially when he offers to use his trade discount and get it cheaper for her.

'You don't want to do the job, do you?' she asks as he pushes himself up to stand at full height again.

'Well, I...' Joss is suddenly tongue-tied.

'Oh, would you, Mr Hallissey?' Edna jumps in on his silence. 'I was going to ask my son but he's always too busy. I'll pay, of course, and provide copious amounts of tea and biscuits. You'd be the answer to my prayers.'

He looks blindsided for a moment, and then a smile he's trying to hide creeps onto his face. 'Only on the condition that you stop calling me Mr Hallissey and start calling me Joss.'

Edna squeaks in delight. 'I *knew* you were the right person to ask. Thank you so much, Mr Hal— Joss.'

He grabs a pen and marks up her best options in the brochures, pops his phone number on the bottom in case she has any more questions, and tells her he'll be in touch to measure up.

Joy is pouring from her as she toddles back towards town, clutching her brochures tightly.

I knock my arm against his as we watch her go. 'Look at you getting *all* the work today. All of it.'

He beams at me. 'I like doing stuff like that. Stuff where you make someone's life easier. Builders have a reputation for being rip-off merchants who are all too happy to take advantage of little old ladies who don't understand jargon and inflate prices for people who won't know any better, and I've always wanted to be the antithesis of that. To do small jobs, individual rather than corporate, to charge reasonable prices and take payment in instalments for anyone who can't afford to pay it all at once. That's what my father wanted when he started out, but things got off-track as his company grew. He ended up doing big jobs for big money that he couldn't keep up with. I prefer the one-on-one stuff where you're taking a weight off someone's shoulders and—'

He's cut off by my phone ringing and although I'm intending to ignore it, 'Mum' flashes up on the screen, and you can't *not* answer a phone call from your mum.

'Essie!' she barks into the phone before I've even said hello. 'I need you back here *right now*! I've just taken an order for two hundred mince pies by six o'clock tonight! Saffie and I can't manage on our own. I know you've got better things to do, but I don't employ you to play with gingerbread in Mistletoe Gardens all day!'

'I'm not play—' My protest is cut off before it's begun.

'Your real job has to take priority. We've been more than accommodating so far, but we need all hands on deck for this one. Get back to the bakery *now*!'

She hangs up before I can protest again. I feel horrible. I've been doing as much as I can in both the bakery *and* the ginger-bread house, and she makes me feel like I've abandoned them in favour of something new and shiny, when the reality is that I spend every night working until the early hours of the morning to make sure I don't let any of my responsibilities slide, and I don't think Mum even realises.

Joss is back on the scaffolding, sticking gingerbread roof tiles on with royal icing, and I walk up the bandstand steps and look up at him. 'Mum's got a huge mince pie order,' I start, turning my phone over in my hands. 'They need—'

'It's fine, Ess. That's your job. That *should* be your priority. Go. I'll carry on here.'

'But...' I didn't get here early enough this morning, and now it's not even lunchtime and I've got to go again. I was looking forward to getting up on the scaffolding at the other side and doing the roof between us. I feel like I'm achieving something here, and I *like* working with someone who makes me feel like I *can* achieve something. At Dancing Cinnamon, I'm doing the same thing over and over again, and suggesting anything new is swiftly met with comments about getting ideas above my station, and there are reminders at every turn of what happened last time I got any big ideas.

My phone rings again before I have a chance to think up a counter-argument, and it's Mum's name on the screen. Clearly I haven't moved fast enough.

'I'll come back to do some decorating later,' I stutter to Joss eventually. 'Make up for lost time once the mince pie crisis has been averted.'

'A mince pie emergency waits for no man.' He glances down at me and I smile at him, but a sadness has settled over both of us. He was so happy just now and I was skipping up the road and humming Christmas carols on my way here because I was looking forward to seeing him, but that phone call is a sharp reminder that this is only temporary, and when December ends, so does this... whatever this is between us. We've been spending too much time together, getting too close, and although he's been having fun, he hasn't said a single word about *not* leaving Folkhornton in the new year, and what I'm feeling for Joss isn't something that can be switched off like Christmas lights in January.

I shove my hands into my pockets and force one foot in front of the other as I walk away, my decapitated gingerbread man scarf flapping over my shoulder as if the felt gingerbread man is reaching out for its other half.

11

Before engaging in orgies, Romans ate anatomically correct versions of an early form of gingerbread to fuel their libidos!

Dancing Cinnamon is in chaos. We're used to dealing with big orders, but two hundred mince pies in five hours' time is a big ask, even for us. An impromptu Christmas party for a youth training charity that makes you wonder why they couldn't have made it slightly less impromptu.

Mum's making batch after batch of pastry, I'm rolling it out and cutting pie bases and fitting them into the baking tins, Saff's on filling duty, then it's back to me for a pie lid, a pastry decoration, and an eggwash. We've got an oven each, and timers are going off left, right, and centre, and no one knows which one is bleeping until we've all checked to make sure our own pies aren't about to set off the smoke alarm.

You'd think we'd all be concentrating on the task at hand, but Mum's waxing lyrical about the latest batch of single men on the dating site she bought me a subscription to.

'This one's got a horse.' She points a gloved finger to a photo on her phone. 'You always wanted a pony for Christmas when you were little.'

'I like horses as much as the next person, but I've never considered them a personality trait before.'

'You're being difficult. You've had loads of messages from potential matches and you haven't even looked at them.'

'I'm not inter—'

'Look at this one.'

—*ested*, I finish in my head.

Mum scrolls the page and shoves the phone towards me on the unit. I don't bother to look.

'He's got lovely big teeth.' She carries on like subtitles you can't turn off. 'You know what they say about men with big teeth.'

'They're good at eating salad?' Saff offers.

'That's *feet*, Mum. And not a conversation that any living human should be forced into with their mother.'

She ignores me. 'You've got a message here from one saying he'd love to date a baker and he wants to know what cake you'd make him on your first date. You can be *really* flirty when you answer.'

'I'm not going to ans—'

'Something sexy, like a raspberry ripple. That brings to mind all sorts of swirls and curves and things. Nothing square and boring like a Battenberg. Give it some thought before you reply, it's a marvellous conversation opener.'

'I quite like a Battenberg,' Saff says, taking pity on me between scoops of fruity mincemeat filling. 'Different colours, marzipan, can't go wrong.'

'Mum, I don't want a guy who thinks that's a sexy approach. He's probably hoping to get a free cake out of it along with a one-night fumble. I want a guy who's kind and lovely, who says he doesn't like cake just to be difficult but then ends up eating more of it than I do...'

'That's quite a specific request. A bit odd. Shall I add it to your profile?' She sounds confused as the reference goes straight over her head.

'No!' Saff and I shout in unison.

Mum pouts as she goes back to kneading pastry.

We carry on like a little production line. Kneading, rolling, cutting shapes, filling, and baking. After a couple of hours, Mum's phone rings and she snatches it up, but not before Saff and I have seen Mervyn's name splashed across the screen. She cradles the phone protectively and runs upstairs with it.

'You could just tell her there's something between you and Joss,' Saff says when we're alone. 'She'd be *begging* you to spend time with him then.'

'There isn't, Saff.' I sigh. 'There can't be. And it doesn't matter because he's leaving in the new year.'

'What's wrong today? You looked so gloomy when you came in. I told Bron we could manage between us but she was having none of it. You clearly didn't want to come back.'

'I didn't,' I admit in a whisper because the last thing I want is for Mum to overhear. 'This has awakened a creativity in me and Joss fuels that. The more time I spend doing the gingerbread house, the less time I want to spend making batches of mince pies I've made seventy thousand times before. And then there's Joss...' I drop my circular cookie cutter onto the work surface, and bang my head down onto my arms.

'The others have been talking about him, you know. The other shopkeepers have mentioned their surprise at how helpful he is. People like him.'

That makes butterflies dance inside me. His kindness has won the villagers over too. It proves he can't hide that heart of gold, no matter how hard he tries. 'He's like a hazelnut. Hard and unappealing on the outside, it's incredibly hard work to crack that solid shell, but when you do, he... becomes a Ferrero Rocher.'

Saff's mouth drops open. 'Okay, you've *never* compared a guy to your favourite chocolate before. Is there something *really* going on between you? Ess, do you *seriously* like Joss Hal—'

'What's all this about Joss Hallissey?' Having crept down the stairs, Mum appears in the kitchen doorway and I have no idea how long she's been listening.

She puts her phone back on the unit and I look between it and her pink-tinged cheeks. 'Important resident committee business, was it?'

'Vitally important. Mr Selman's Christmas tree is growing over Mrs Allen's fence, so she took his decorations off that half and put her own up, and he's threatening retaliatory forces of sticking a pin in her inflatable Christmas flamingos. Mervyn's trying to find a diplomatic solution that doesn't involve the murder of any Christmas decorations.'

'If nothing else comes out of today, at least we've learned there is such a thing as inflatable Christmas flamingos.'

'Don't try to change the subject, missy. I want to know what's going on with you and Joss.'

'Nothing.' It's not exactly untrue.

'Don't think I don't know about that little trick you two pulled the other day. Beryl told me that Rob is what he calls that little bird. There was no date, was there? He's trying to keep you for himself, you mark my words.'

I laugh, even though the thought of Joss wanting me for himself sends a not-unpleasant tingle racing through my body.

'I hear he's leaving.' Mum's purposely trying to sound casual.

'He *is* leaving.'

'I don't think you should fall in love with another man who's leaving town, Essie.'

'The difference is the last one actually wanted me to go with him. Joss is leaving so no one ever finds him again.' I try to ignore the stone that settles in my stomach. Folkhornton will feel a lot smaller without him.

'It's probably for the best. I don't trust that one.'

'Why?' I'm surprised because she seemed to like him at first. That day she nearly strangled him, for example. She often shows affection via the medium of grievous bodily harm. 'Because he's quiet and doesn't like getting involved in other people's business?'

'No, there's something about him. He's hiding something.'

I think of his mum and how he doesn't want anyone to know, how Joseph Senior must've hidden so much too. 'There's a lot going on that you don't know about. Besides, you're all missing the point – he's leaving.'

'Exactly. What you need is a nice, stable man.'

'That makes me sound like I need a garden fence.'

'He's bad news, Essie. I've got a feeling about him. He's going to break your heart.'

I do a false laugh. 'Of course he's not. There are no hearts involved, it's just gingerbread.'

Mum and Saff both fix me with a look that says they believe me about as much as I believe myself.

12

In ancient times, a woman in love could ask a folk medicine prac-
titioner to bake a gingerbread man in the likeness of the object of
her affections. If she could get him to eat it, he was guaranteed to
fall madly in love with her! Women are also known to have eaten
'gingerbread husbands' to increase their chances of finding the
real thing!

After the mince pies are collected and Mum and Saff have left, I've
tidied up, made a cuppa and wolfed down something to eat, it's
9 p.m., and I'm standing at the bottom of the stairs, trying to
persuade myself to go up to bed, but I can't get the gingerbread
house out of my head.

I'd intended to go back up to the gardens as soon as we were
finished with the mince pie order, but I hadn't expected it to be so
late. I've got to get up at 5 a.m. to start baking for the day ahead,
but I *know* I'll lie awake tossing and turning. While my body is
tired after the busy day, my mind is far from it. I go back into the
kitchen and make a batch of royal icing. I can do something useful
for a couple of hours. I can make a start on the decorating, and it'll

be a surprise to Joss when he arrives in the morning, and it might allay some of the guilt at having to abandon him today.

It's a cloudy December night as I walk up the road, the footsteps of my winter boots echoing across the brick paving stones. The Christmas lights are still on, but they've had a makeover. There's a tasteful 'Nadolig Llawen' emblazoned across the street, and sprays of LED snowflakes hanging from each lamppost. Blue icicles with white snowflakes criss-cross the road ahead like ribbons, and there are reindeer that flash alternately and appear to chase each other around town.

At the beginning of December, they were the same old decrepit decs that had been languishing in the council's storage room since the mid-eighties, but these look new and modern. Shops are busier lately, and people have been posting photos from their visits to Folkhornton – not just of the gingerbread house, but the other parts of town too, the quaint shops, the fountain, the town tree and the Christmas decorations. Either Mum's had the thumbscrews on Mervyn again or there have been enough extra visitors to make the council consider it worthwhile to upgrade.

I feel a pang when the empty gateway comes into view. I *miss* seeing his van there, as it has been every time I approach Mistletoe Gardens lately. My keys rattle loudly as I undo the gate and lock it behind me.

'Ess, is that you?'

A voice in the darkness *should* make me jump, but I know Joss's gentle Welsh accent so well that it sends butterflies scattering through me instead, and the bucket of icing bangs my legs as I hurry towards the shadow sitting on the bandstand steps.

This is Mistletoe Gardens at its most magical. A warm orange glow coming from the old-fashioned streetlamps, and every bare tree branch is wrapped in twinkling micro lights. The hedge atop a wall that forms the perimeter of the gardens is covered with a glowing net of fairy lights, and the holly bushes are interspersed with red ball lights that give the impression that the berries themselves are glowing.

But nothing makes me happier than seeing Joss sitting there. I don't realise how much I've missed him until it takes all my willpower not to throw my arms around him. 'Hi! What are you doing here?'

'Honestly? I don't know. Went for a walk, ended up here.' He looks up and even in the darkness, I can see he's smiling. 'Thinking, I guess.'

'About...?'

'I'm not sure I've worked that bit out yet either.'

I go up the steps to stow the bucket of icing inside the gingerbread house, surprised to see Joss has finished laying the entirety of the roof tiles today, and then I sit down on the step beside him. 'You okay?'

'Yeah.' He glances over at me. 'Better than I've been for ages, actually. I just wanted to spend some time here, to appreciate what we're trying to save. Mistletoe Gardens didn't matter to me until recently. No one in Folkhornton did.'

I like how he uses the past tense without even realising it.

'After you left this morning, Douglas came over to ask if he could help seeing as I was flying solo, then Beryl brought me a cup of tea and a biscuit, then Mr Arkins started painting the backdrop for his festive dino area and chattered the whole time, and I felt like I was an important part of something really special...' He looks over at me again. 'Why are you smiling like that?'

I laugh and then put a hand to my face to check, but he's right, I'm grinning because *he* sounds so happy. Folkhornton is funny like that – it creeps up on you and before you know it, you've fallen in love with the place. And Joss is obviously feeling it too, but he's holding himself back, probably because of his history with this place and the people in it. It seems like a good moment to broach a difficult subject. 'The only reason they didn't tell you about your wife and the personal trainer was because they didn't want to pile more misery on top of what you were already dealing with.'

His head snaps up and he looks at me for a long moment. 'So you *do* know.'

'I asked my mum after she mentioned it here. I wasn't being nosy – I wanted to know if you were right about everyone knowing.'

'And?'

'They were trying to find a way to tell you, but you found out before they could.'

'Yes.' A shiver goes through him. 'On the day of my father's funeral, my ex booked a session at the gym. I thought it was a bit odd, because you'd expect your wife to go to your father's funeral with you, right? But I didn't want to argue about it, and I thought maybe she was too upset, maybe she didn't want to cry in public, maybe she knew I'd have my hands full with my mum and didn't want me to worry about supporting her too, so I let it go. Afterwards, I was driving home and I passed the gym – it was after closing time but her car was still in the car park, so I thought I'd go in and see if she wanted to go out for dinner and toast my father in our own private way, and I walked in on... well, let's just say, there was a *workout* of a different kind going on. One that involved a lot less clothes than a traditional workout, and a *truly* inventive use of a fitness ball that had probably never been violated like that before.'

'Wow. That's awful, Joss.' I reach over and give his forearm a squeeze through the sleeve of his coat. 'I'm sorry.'

'Don't be. It wasn't a good relationship. I'd been so caught up in what was happening with my parents that I hadn't noticed how bad things had got between us. When my mum started going downhill, and then my dad's diagnosis, I went completely numb. I got through each day on autopilot. When I look back, I remember almost nothing from that last year living in Bristol because I wasn't "there". I could have a conversation with someone, blink, and not have a clue what they'd said. I was blank, staring at things but not seeing them. I drove down here every weekend, and my ex thought that should "get it out of my system" and then I could focus on the week ahead, but I was preoccupied all the time. I pulled away from our friends. I didn't want to do anything or go anywhere. She thought I should be able to switch it off when it was inconvenient.'

'If only grief worked like that,' I murmur.

'They were both still alive. It wasn't—'

'Of course it was. Grief doesn't start exclusively at the point someone dies. Grief for the person your mum used to be. Grief for your father's diagnosis. Grief over what was inevitably coming.'

He goes quiet, thinking it over. 'I've never thought of it like that before.'

My hand is still on his forearm and I squeeze it again, and he shifts just a little bit closer to me on the step. 'I'm guessing there was a decision you had to make about coming back here too?'

'Yeah, but it was a decision with only one option. I'd always known that I'd take over my father's company one day, didn't expect it to be that soon or in those circumstances, but that's the way it had to be. My wife isn't from here, and she didn't want to move back here with me. She thought I was throwing away a good job with prospects for a failing building company that was in a hole of debt deeper than any of its broken-down JCBs could dig, but I'd made a promise to my father and I couldn't let him down. The lads who worked for him are all young fathers with families to support

– I couldn't let them down either. I didn't cope well after he died. I didn't care about the business. I resented it. I hated everything. I drank too much and didn't turn up when I was supposed to. Those lads kept the business going when I couldn't. That's why I have to do this one last job in January – to make sure they're taken care of.'

'So that's where all the bad reviews come from...'

His face screws up in confusion and he tilts his head until he can catch my eyes. 'You've read my reviews?'

Maybe I shouldn't have said that. 'Saff has. She was being the overprotective best friend.'

'So Saff thinks she's got something to protect you from in me...' His hand twists around until he can get his fingers under mine and lift my hand from his arm. He pulls my hand to his mouth and presses his lips to the back of it, burning on this chilly night, and my breath shudders as I let it out slowly.

'Where on earth would she get that idea from?' I murmur, barely audible. It's a good thing I'm already sitting down because I'd have had to sit down pretty swiftly after that, and I'm equally glad he's not looking at my face because it's probably glowing brighter than the holly berry lights in the nearby bushes right now.

'A total mystery,' he concurs, my hand still held to his mouth, the movement of his lips making his stubble graze against my skin in the tingliest way possible, causing a shiver that's not the traditional kind of shiver.

And I *have* to ignore it. I'm feeling something for Joss, but it's something that can never be anything more. This could go further, I know it could. The things I felt when he kissed my cheek the other day, the tingles I'm feeling now... *if* he was staying... but he's not.

'Seeing as we're oversharing tonight, how about you?' Joss has let my hand drop from his jaw, but our still-joined hands are resting on his thigh. 'What really happened in Paris?'

'I'd been dating this guy for a couple of years. He was French. Younger than me, but it hadn't seemed to matter at first. No one had ever treated me as nicely he did. It was a whirlwind of romance. I'd always waxed lyrical about how much I'd love to live in Paris, but it was just daydreaming about something I'd never do. And then he got a job offer in Paris. He asked me to move there with him, and I... I think I'd talked myself into it rather than it being something I wanted to do, you know? There was this guy who I thought I was in love with, offering me a chance to do something wild and daring and so far removed from this little Welsh town, and I thought I'd be stupid to say no. I had this idea of taking a piece of Wales to Paris and starting my own bakery there. I even called it *Cannelle Dansante*, and thought it would be just like here, except I'd be my own boss, and it would be something new that Parisians and tourists alike would flock to.

'He found a tiny little flat for us to live in, and I found a tiny little shop to rent. The flat was awful and the shop was awful. I sunk everything I had into doing it up and buying equipment, convinced it would be worth it in the end. He was only a couple of years younger than me, but it felt like he'd dragged his granny along to the City of Light with him. He had new work friends and he wanted to go out partying and enjoying the city atmosphere, and I was baking all the time, from the early hours until midday, and then spending the rest of the day on my feet, trying to encourage people into my empty shop. I was too tired to do the fun things he wanted to do. We argued all the time. He went and did the fun things with his friends from work and came back tipsy and smelling of other people's perfume.

'The relationship was over and we were barely tolerated housemates in an apartment that wasn't big enough to avoid each other. I couldn't tell Mum how wrong it had all gone because she'd told me I was making a big mistake and I'd ignored her. Saff was so excited and supportive and wanted to live vicariously through me, and I couldn't tell her how much I'd let her down. The bakery was an abysmal failure. I worked so hard and was lucky if I sold one or two cakes a day. I had to pull out – I had no money left to keep funnelling in and getting nothing back. My ex found someone else and wanted to move her into his flat, and I had nowhere to go. I had to swallow my pride and beg Mum to help me get home.'

'Oh, Ess, I'm sorry.' He covers my hand with his other one and squeezes it between them both. 'I know your confidence was knocked, but I didn't realise how big the knock was.'

'More like a crater,' I mutter, wondering why I'm saying this to Joss Hallissey, of all people. Even Mum and Saff don't know the true extent of how miserable I was in Paris, but Joss makes it impossible not to talk to him. 'I stopped trusting myself and believing I know what's best for me. I should have listened to my mum. She could foresee how it was going to go. I stopped trusting my own judgement, and anything I do now, I think it's going to end in failure, and everyone else does too.'

'No, they *don't*.' His words are pointed and he tugs my hand until I look over and meet his eyes, and it makes me realise that I've welled up. I look away quickly, trying to swipe tears away before he notices.

From the way he squeezes my hand, he's noticed, but he doesn't push it. Instead, he puts his elbows on his knees and leans on them without letting go. My arm is between his arms and my hand is still clasped in his, and his chin is resting on it. 'Sometimes you have to make mistakes before you know they're mistakes. That's just how life is. And it's not a bad thing to have jumped headfirst into something and given it your all. Whether it worked out or not, it takes courage to do that. *That* is something to be proud of, no matter the end result. And it takes guts to admit you failed too. To come back with your head held high and try to move on, and to still have this creativity and this drive to do something special and to single-handedly make it happen, even when you aren't sure you can do it.'

'It helps if other people are sure.' I give his hand a purposeful squeeze so he knows exactly who I mean.

His mouth tips into an involuntary smile and he looks across at me again. 'Since the moment you plonked a basket of baked goods in front of me in the swimming baths lobby, the one thing it's been *impossible* to do is doubt you, Ess.'

My breath catches and I have to hold it to stop it escaping as a sob. He has no idea how much that means to me... and how much of an impact it's had to work with someone so encouraging and confidence-building, and I'm overwhelmed by a sudden urge to kiss him.

And I *cannot* kiss someone who won't be here this time next month.

Instead, without giving him a chance to protest, I jump to my feet and go up onto the step behind him. I put a hand on his back for balance as I fit one leg on either side of his body and sit down. I lean forwards and slip both my arms around him, pulling him back against me. 'Sorry, but you can't say things like that and not expect to have a cwtch, whether you like it or not.'

He laughs, sounding like he doesn't mind anywhere near as much as he would have a few weeks ago. His hands cover mine and he lets out a happy-sounding sigh and relaxes in my arms, and I squeeze him tighter.

It's quite possibly the strangest cwtch I've ever had, but that's the thing about a Welsh cwtch – it's so much more than a hug. You can hug anyone, but only someone you *really* care about gets a cwtch.

He leans backwards until his lips brush all-too-briefly against my cheek. 'Thank you for making life make sense again.'

I close my eyes and rest my head against his. There's none of his usual styling product tonight, his hair is soft and barely dry after a shower, and he smells of shampoo, and I have to force myself not to nuzzle it with my nose.

Sitting here holding him soothes something inside of me. Everything feels better when I'm with Joss.

Until the thought of Joss not being here rears its ugly head again.

'Do you think it's still going to make sense on an isolated island? You can't live alone forever and shut out the whole world because *one* ex was a complete jingle bell-end.'

'It's not just because of that. It's everything. It's all been too much. The only thing that's kept me going for the past two years is holding onto the fact I'm leaving soon and never coming back, and you're making me want to stay, and I can't—' His voice breaks and he runs out of breath.

In my mind, I cling onto that 'making me want to stay' line because it sends a flutter of hope through me. Instead of pushing him any further, I squeeze him with my knees on either side of his body, holding him tightly, and I lose track of time as long minutes tick by. Not another word needs to be said tonight, but in the back of my mind is the one thing I don't know how I'm ever going to say – goodbye to him in January.

13

In 1444, Swedish nuns made gingerbread as a cure for indigestion.

It's a gorgeous night. The clouds are keeping the temperature up, and our combined body heat is doing a good job at keeping the December chill out. The roof of the bandstand is surrounded by blue cluster lights that hang down like icicles, and each one of the tall trees around the gardens is covered with a sheen of white lights, illuminating the bundles of mistletoe leaves in every canopy. The whole place is alight with fairy lights, like a perfect North Pole-esque garden where you'd expect to see Santa's elves jingling their way between workshops.

'This is so beautiful,' Joss whispers.

It really does feel like the magic of Mistletoe Gardens is sparkling around us. 'The magic of the mistletoe.'

He laughs. 'Any tingle in the air around here is the poor National Grid frazzling as it tries to provide electricity to all those Christmas lights.'

It makes me laugh out loud because it's such a *Joss* comment to make.

'We should do something, shouldn't we?' He stretches like he's waking up.

'We're not going to get this finished on time if we don't.' Even as I say it, my arms automatically tighten around him because I don't want to let him go. But the whole project has taken longer than I thought. It's the thirteenth of December today, and there's only a few more days until we're meant to be open for the public to look around.

He sounds as reluctant as I am, but the clock on the town hall behind us shows we've been sitting here for over an hour. It feels much colder than it was before and I miss the body contact instantly when we start to move, but he's right, no matter how much I'd like to sit here all night, I came with the intention of icing some swirls, and decorating has to be the priority now.

He holds a piping bag while I poke in a nozzle and then squirt red gel food colouring in lines up the side of the bag, spoon in white royal icing, twist it all down, and then do another one so we've got a bag each. 'The colouring will mix with the icing and give a red-and-white swirl effect. We should do rosettes up every side, underneath the overhang of the roof, around the window frames, and around the base of the chimney. Pop a real peppermint swirl sweet in the middle of each one when you're done for a finishing touch.'

I open the bag of red-and-white swirled sweets I brought with me and stand it on the scaffolding where we can both reach it, and I start at the corner where the front and side wall meet and pipe wide rosettes of icing up the edge, and Joss goes to the opposite end and starts there. We're both quiet, although Joss puts his phone next to the peppermint swirls and finds a station that plays old-fashioned Christmas carols, and the quiet sound of 'Joy to the World' fills the night.

He takes his time to avoid mistakes, and I can't help peeking at the intense concentration on his face, the way he screws up his nose as he focuses, his jaw working as he sucks peppermint sweets. Every so often, he looks over and meets my eyes with a smile that lights up his face and sets off butterflies inside me, and our hands brush every time we reach for peppermint swirls at the same moment.

It isn't long before the gentle soundtrack of Christmas carols is joined by yawning. It's late, the clock has somehow crept round to 1 a.m. already, and Joss is clearly tired. His soft humming of Christmas carols is interrupted by loud yawns.

'Do you want to go home?' I ask from the opposite side of the gingerbread house.

'That would involve saying goodnight to you, so no. Not yet.'

I blush at his honesty *and* because I'm feeling the same way.

His words make me feel warmer than the physical work does, and it's easy to lose track of time as I refill piping bags, open the second bag of peppermint sweets, and we keep going for at least another hour before the bucket of icing is empty and the gingerbread house has its first official decorations.

We finish with me on a stepladder, piping red-streaked white rosettes along the underside of the roof, and Joss up on the scaffolding, piping them around the base of the chimney.

He's tidying up by the time I clamber down, yawning myself now. We close the gingerbread-tiled door and stand at the bottom of the bandstand steps, looking up at our handiwork.

The rosettes have hidden the edges of the wooden frame, so it's starting to look like a real gingerbread house, and I get the sense of childlike wonder I'd hoped for when I look up at it. What child *hasn't* dreamed of living inside a gingerbread house? If I'd seen this as a little girl, I would've been awestruck. I'd have begged my parents to bring me here every day.

'It's enough to make anyone believe in magic,' he murmurs and then holds his hand out. 'It's late, I'll walk you home.'

I go to protest that I'm an adult and can manage five minutes down the road without assistance, but there's never a bad excuse to spend extra time with Joss. I slip my hand into his, and neither of us let go until we get back to the bakery.

We stop outside and as soon as I've pushed the key into the lock, he holds his free hand out for my other hand. 'Thanks for tonight, Ess. I've never told anyone what happened with my ex-wife and I didn't realise how much I needed to. How can I ever thank you?'

'Be my date for the Mistletoe Dance.' The words come out of my mouth so fast that I'm unsure if I actually said them. 'Just as friends. I don't want to go with a seventy-eight-year-old man dressed as a dinosaur and my mum is not going to stop until she's set me up with some random psychopath from the world of online dating. If this is the last year of Mistletoe Gardens, she isn't going to rest until I've got a date because it's a Browne family legacy to kiss under the mistletoe and I'm the only one who hasn't done it yet, and if I'm going with you, she'll at least think there's a chance and leave me alone...'

'Urgh, Ess, I *never* go to those things. Everyone is going to be there. I don't like parties and mixing and dancing and Christmas music and...' He's trying to be annoyed, but his eyes are twinkling and a smile sneaks onto his face. 'Okay.'

I throw my arms around him, and like he did the other day, he lifts me up and spins us both around, and then sets me down again, his fingers caressing my back as mine slip from his shoulder and trail down his arm. Everything around us goes very still. We're so close. A slight tilt of my head, a tiny push up onto my tiptoes... the way his head has automatically dipped towards me. It's the most perfect angle for a kiss, and my fingers curl into his coat, and I can feel his breath catch. His tongue touches his bottom lip and his eyes close, but neither of us makes the first move, and we stand there, frozen in time until he laughs an awkward laugh and pulls away.

'Are you okay to get home? That's quite a walk without the van.'

'Only half an hour, and I could do with the fresh air. Clear my head.'

'You say that a lot.'

'Got a lot of things taking over my thought processes lately.'

Haven't we *all*? 'Gingerbread, right?'

His eyes lock onto mine and his tongue peeks out to wet his lips. 'Yeah. Right.' The comment sounds sarcastic, but his eyes are dark and serious, and I know he definitely *isn't* talking about gingerbread. I get a little flutter. Is Joss feeling the things I'm feeling too? I'm not entirely sure that it isn't my brain having a conniption due to overexposure to his gorgeous aftershave that overpowers the ever-present scent of gingerbread, but if he's feeling something too then it *must* be real, right?

'Text me when you get home safe, all right?' I force myself to say eventually, because we're just standing here, staring at each other, willing the night not to end yet.

'I'm a thirty-eight-year-old man. I don't nee—'

'You're never too old or too male for someone to care you're okay. I'll worry about you all night if you don't let me know you've got back safely.'

'Okay. Goodnight.' He's gone all blushy as he takes a step backwards without dropping eye contact.

I've never had a 'romantic comedy moment' in real life before, but his eyes stay on mine as he walks backwards... Until he walks into a lamppost, jumps in surprise, and gives it a glare that suggests it moved itself into his path just to be awkward. It makes me giggle and he starts laughing too, and with one last smile, he turns and walks away properly.

I stay paused at the door, certain he's going to turn back before he gets out of sight, and he does. Another moment straight out of a film. The butterflies have barely had time to settle before they take off again.

I go up to my flat, make a cuppa and have a shower, and by the time I get into bed, my phone buzzes with a message from Joss.

Home safe.

Seeing his name makes me smile, and I'm about to reply when another message flashes through.

Thanks, Ess. Been a long time since anyone cared.

I type back:

Goodnight. Sleep well.

I stare at the kiss emoji, debating whether to add it or not... Oh, what the heck. So far tonight, I've held his hand, forcibly hugged him, accidentally asked him to be my date, and nearly snogged him. At this point, a kiss emoji makes no difference. I add it and send the message.

The reply comes back:

Sweet dreams.

With a kiss emoji. I snuggle down in bed with my phone on the pillow and let the butterflies do their somersaults and swan dives.

14

In Norway, the city of Bergen makes an entire town built from gingerbread every year.

'Good morning,' I say cheerily as I walk into Mistletoe Gardens on Thursday. Joss is sitting on his workbench outside the bandstand with his legs dangling over the side, sipping a coffee.

He looks up and gives me a smile that brightens his face, but does nothing to hide the dark circles under his eyes.

'You're here early.'

'Couldn't sleep.' He holds out the cardboard takeaway coffee tray with one cup left in it, and I put the box I brought containing two stollen muffins down on the workbench beside him.

The hunch that seems to be settled over his shoulders lifts for a moment as he tears into it and takes a bite of the muffin. His eyes drift shut with pleasure and he makes a noise that probably means 'thank you' in dolphin.

I take my coffee and stollen muffin and turn around to sit against the workbench next to him, and he shuffles nearer until his thigh is pressed against mine, and I'm sitting close enough to feel his shoulders sag again.

'How was your mum last night?' It's been two days since the night of icing swirls in the dark, opening up to each other, and kiss emojis, and I only saw Joss for a little while yesterday morning before he had to leave.

'She was okay.' It takes him a while to answer. 'I told her about you.'

'Me?' My throat has to work hard to stop myself choking on the piece of muffin I've just swallowed.

'She's always happy to sit and have a chat with me, and last night she decided I was positively glowing.'

'Probably literally, after all those luminous marshmallow Krispie Cakes you ate yesterday.'

Joss and I spent the morning making giant gumdrops by mixing melted marshmallow and Rice Krispies and moulding them into silicone muffin moulds to get their size and shape. To get their colour, we used enough food colouring to make them bioluminescent, and as usual, Joss ate most of the mixture.

He laughs, but it's a sad, tired laugh. 'It was nice. It felt normal for a minute. Like when I used to come home and we'd have a catch-up in the kitchen. I'd sit at the island in the middle with a cuppa while she insisted on cooking because she was convinced I wasn't eating properly in Bristol. I told her about the gingerbread house and she let me show her a photo. It was a nice moment. There have been more of those lately.'

'Do those moments make it harder in the long run?'

'Yes.' He lets out a sigh. 'It's a reminder of who she used to be. The mother I miss so much. A flash of hope in an illness where there is no hope. A harsh punch of how much I *wish* I could sit there and really talk to my mum. I can't even call her Mum any more. It's disturbing for someone who can't remember ever having children to be called Mum.'

'I'm sorry, Joss.' My hands are full, and so are his, so I press my thigh harder against his and lean forwards until I can see him over my shoulder.

He looks exhausted. The dark circles make the lines around his eyes stand out more than usual, and there's a slump to his shoulders that he seems unable to lift. 'Did you sleep last night?'

He thinks about it for a moment. 'Define sleep.'

I laugh. 'If you need me to define it, you clearly didn't.'

His pale face breaks into a smile. 'Honestly, no, not much. But on the plus side, I *am* now probably owed the Guinness World Record for staring at the ceiling. Will you be my plus one to the awards ceremony?'

I laugh, but it isn't funny, not really. I want to slip my arm around him and hold him close, but before I can figure out the logistics from this angle, he flops against me. His body leans heavily on mine and his head drops to the side to rest on my shoulder, and he lets out another long sigh.

I turn my head until I can rub my chin against his forehead, just to let him know I don't mind him there.

'You okay?' I whisper into his hair.

'Yeah. I got them to put more shots of espresso in my coffee than is probably legal. I just need a minute for it to kick in and I'll be up and at 'em.'

'We've got all the time in the world.'

His face shifts into a smile against my shoulder, and he's quiet for a while. So quiet that I'm not entirely sure he hasn't fallen asleep. Even his grip on the coffee cup in his lap goes lax, and it feels like the most open and unguarded Joss has ever been. And I realise how oddly content I am. The smell of gingerbread in my nose, a hot gingerbread latte warming me up, and this beautiful soul trusting me enough to let his walls down in my presence...

And then the familiar sound of clacking startles us out of the morning reverie.

'Haven't we suffered enough?' Joss groans and rolls his forehead against my shoulder like he's trying to hide, but the kind-hearted tone in his voice doesn't match the words.

I wave as the Mystical Mistletoe Magi pushes her cart of potions towards us, the wooden horse's head click-clacking above her, and her shawl billowing in the breeze as she totters to a halt.

'Hello, MMM.' I'm always pleased to see her. It's like Mr Arkins in his dino suit – Folkhornton wouldn't be Folkhornton without her.

I'm surprised when Joss doesn't move but stays leaning against me. Either he doesn't mind her seeing him this relaxed, or he's too tired to sit upright.

'Don't you two look cosy on such a chilly day?'

'My cockles are warmed by your presence, MMM.' His voice is dripping with sarcasm, and I have to bite down a laugh.

'While I'm proud to have that effect on the ventricles of your heart, Mr Hallissey, I'm prouder to see my potion working.' She stands back and looks us over, and the horse's head peers down too. 'I've seen plenty of people fall in love, but I've never seen anyone literally melt into love before.'

I can *feel* the scathing look he gives her. 'No one's in love, charlatan.'

I smack at his knee for being so rude, and he instantly tightens his legs and holds my hand in place by squeezing it between his knees. It's definitely not *love*, but Joss is so open and intimate lately, and I once again wonder what this *could* be if he wasn't leaving.

'Cold fingers,' he mumbles under his breath, like he needs to warm them up for me.

'You've made an interesting assumption, Mr Hallissey. Nowhere, anywhere, did anyone suggest that potion was to make you fall in love with each other. It was to bring love back into your life in whatever form that may take. How you chose to interpret that is your own doing.'

'I don't believe in love.'

'Of course you don't,' she says sagely. 'All of your feelings about love are associated with something negative. All you need is to meet someone who makes you see the positive side again. Love is magical. Falling in love is the universe's way of letting us have a fairytale of our own. Your problem is that you gave your heart to someone who ripped it to shreds rather than cherishing it, and you let that injury fester and scar, rather than realising some people just aren't meant for each other, and others *are*. When a heart has been broken – whether by romantic love or by grief for people who are no longer with us – it can come back stronger and warmer rather than harder and colder, and it's okay to let yourself fall again. It takes more courage to trust again than it does to shut down.'

'I'm too tired to make sense of that,' he mutters. 'Needless psychoanalysis aside, what can we do for you this morning, MMM? Come to shake us down for more cash?'

'Actually, I came to show you this.' She produces a dinosaur magazine from amongst the folds of her oversized shawl. 'Page fourteen.'

'There are actual magazines dedicated to this sort of thing?' Joss lifts his head and pushes himself upright, and I miss the feeling of him leaning against me. I take the mag and hold it so we can both see it.

'What do a giant gingerbread house and a festive dinosaur

have in common? This small Welsh town is all too happy to tell you.' I read the headline aloud.

There's a two-page spread with a photo of the gingerbread house and one of Mr Arkins painting dinosaurs onto his snowy background scenery, and on the opposite page, a picture of one of the biggest trees filled with balls of mistletoe.

It's a festive story of a tiny town versus a heartless council. As the council move to bulldoze Mistletoe Gardens, the only green space in Folkhornton in the South Wales valleys, the residents are fighting back. Local baker Essie Browne and local builder Joss Hallissey have teamed up to build a life-size gingerbread house, from which Santa will meet and greet children, but why stop at Santa? Folkhornton is going one step further, by also offering a meet-and-greet with their very own Christmas dinosaur, also known as Mr Arkins of The Dinosaur Shop.

The article goes on to explain the legend of the mistletoe, and give dates and times for when Mistletoe Gardens will be open, and lists the stalls that will be run by the locals.

'Mr Arkins must've done this,' I say. 'I didn't know anything about it.'

Joss makes a noise of agreement. 'This is the first physical thing I've seen, everything else has been online. That's fantastic.'

'They've got a large readership. The Dinosaur Shop stocks copies and sells out every month,' MMM says. 'Mr Arkins believes in what you're doing here. We all do. You've created the impossible.'

I glance up at the gingerbread house. I've been so caught up in getting everything done on time that it's easy to forget how far we've come. Between us, we've *actually* built a life-size gingerbread house. Something that I suggested three weeks ago and never believed we could actually do. And we've done it, just the two of us.

Joss catches my eyes and his mouth tips up into a smile that makes his eyes look brighter, despite the tiredness still clouding them.

'You can keep that, dearies. You keep it, Mr Hallissey.' The MMM takes it from my hand and thrusts it towards Joss. 'Proof of what you've achieved here, *together*. It's you who needs the strongest reminder of how magic can happen when you're willing to let it.'

I expect Joss to say something sarcastic, but he takes the magazine and thanks her for it, his fingers tracing over the cover with reverence. 'Go on then, what potions have you got on offer today?'

I'm not sure which one of us is most surprised – me, the MMM, or possibly Joss himself for actually asking. Without a word, he shifts on the workbench until he can pull his wallet out of his back pocket. I go to get my purse out, but his hand touches my wrist, stopping me.

The MMM is so taken aback by his request that she forgets all the smoke and fanfare to whip the cloth off her cart as she peruses the bottles that clink together every time she moves.

She eventually picks up two of them. 'These are just the ticket.'

Joss holds out a crisp ten-pound note to her, and she takes it, and then encloses a bottle in each of our hands, the labels concealed. 'Don't look at them until after I've gone.'

'So we can't ask for a refund when the labels say "Robinson's Orange Squash"?'

'So you can work out the importance for yourself, Mr Hallissey.' She gives him a sarcastic smile and says goodbye, and we both watch as she click-clacks her way to the gate, the horse's head jingling with bells, its ribbons trailing in the breeze behind it.

'I do not like that woman,' he mutters.

'Well, you must be doing something right because the horse's head didn't snap at you once today. And you *asked* for her potions.'

'I felt sorry for her. She can't get much custom, and she's an old lady peddling her wares on a cold mid-December morning. She needs that tenner more than I do.'

'I think you like her more than you're letting on.'

'She's just weird. Quirky.' He rolls his eyes like he's about to say something he'll regret. 'I'd miss her if she wasn't about, all right? There's something comforting about her presence, like a kindly grandma who you might not see very often but you know will always be there with dry homemade cakes and ugly sweaters knitted for you.'

My hand is still closed around the bottle, and I hold it up and tap it against his. 'Thank you. Again. Ready to see what's in store for us today?'

He holds his hand up so the side is resting against mine, counts down from three, and we both open our fingers.

'Believe in yourself,' I read aloud. 'Burdock, chicory, neroli. When you're convinced you can't do something, it becomes a self-fulfilling prophecy.'

'Believe in others,' Joss says. 'When you're convinced other people will let you down, it becomes a self-fulfilling prophecy.'

He twists the lid off and holds up the little bottle to toast against mine. 'Cheers to whatever's in these bottles not being poisonous.'

We clink the little bottles and down them in one.

'Dr Pepper, no doubt about it.'

'Canada Dry, I think. A staple of any nineties childhood.'

He laughs, and it makes something tingle inside me, so much so that I take leave of my senses and drop my head to the side so it rests against his shoulder.

I feel him move to look down at me and his lips inadvertently brush my forehead as he speaks. 'You believe in yourself yet?'

'I'm starting to. When I look at what we've done here, yes... But it doesn't make any difference in the long run. It's not going to make my mum take me seriously. It's not going to make her let me go in a different direction with the bakery. And I still don't have the courage to push myself forwards and be shut down again.' I shift my head but I'm at the wrong angle to catch his eyes. 'What about you? Are you starting to believe in other people?'

'Some of them, I suppose.'

'Any specific ones?' I ask, cringing at how needy I sound.

He laughs and rubs his cheek against my hair. 'One very specific one indeed.'

'Mr Arkins, right?'

He laughs out loud. 'It's definitely *not* Mr Arkins, Ess.'

I can't think of anything else to say that won't lead to having to confront the butterflies in my belly, and we sit there for a while longer, my head on his shoulder and his head on mine as the sky turns to full daylight, revealing cloudy grey skies so typical of this time of year in Wales.

'It looks good, right?' I whisper, my eyes on the bandstand.

As well as the rooftop gumdrops I installed last night, this morning the house has windows in the once-empty window frames, which I made by melting Glacier Mints while Joss was visiting his mum yesterday.

'It looks nearly finished.' His tone doesn't sound as excited as it should be, and I lift my head to meet his eyes, and the same feeling is reflected back at me. While it will be amazing to see the house finished, it will also mean my time with Joss is over and it isn't right to feel this amount of pure dread at the thought of saying goodbye to him.

* * *

All I can hear is yawning. For the past few hours, all I've heard is yawning. I'm up on the scaffolding, piping lines of white icing in neat semi-circles around the edges of every gingerbread roof tile, and finishing off each one with a blob in the centre that holds on a real gumdrop in alternating red and green colours.

I can hear Joss's jaw crick because his mouth isn't wide enough to accommodate the size of yawn that's trying to escape.

Darkness set in hours ago, and we're working by the light of Joss's floodlights, and even though I'm rushing to finish the roof, it's still six o'clock before I climb down and make my announcement. 'Right, that's it. Tools down. Early night.'

Joss does a sarcastic laugh from inside the house, where he's gluing flames made out of melted orange sweets into the gingerbread brick fireplace he built today. 'We open tomorrow night. We haven't got a tree in yet, nor have we actually *got* a tree, we haven't done the window boxes, I haven't finished icing this mantelpiece, and there are *no* decorations inside. No one's having an early night.'

'Look at me,' I say from the doorway.

He does.

'Joss, your eyes are bloodshot and can barely focus and, interspersed with the yawning, all I can hear is you swearing at yourself for making mistakes. You need to go home and sleep, and come back refreshed tomorrow. We're arguably wasting more time by pushing onwards when we both really need a break.'

'We don't have time for a break.'

I sigh. I know he's right – tomorrow night is when Mistletoe Gardens opens to the public. The gingerbread house is supposed to be finished by then, and Santa arrives on Saturday morning and will hopefully have children queuing in their droves to visit him, but Joss currently looks like he could sleep through a squashing by Santa's sleigh, and I've been too knackered to focus and keep having to wipe icing off and re-do it.

It's been a quiet day in the park. Early drizzle turned to heavy rain, coupled with a bitingly cold wind that's put most people off their Christmas shopping and kept residents indoors. We've had the tent drawn around the bandstand all day, and our only visitor has been a very wet Rob, chirping from the wall outside to demand extra food, and making the most of the damp ground to peck for worms in the grass.

'Do you want to watch a movie?' I blurt out.

'Would it be a Christmas movie?' he asks without looking up.

'It's December fifteenth, of *course* it will be a Christmas movie.'

'Why? Where?' He looks around and then over at me. '*Here*?'

'You're exhausted, Joss. I'm trying to send you home for an early night and you refuse, so the next best thing is finishing work early and relaxing.' I point down into town towards the bakery. 'I can be back in ten minutes with my laptop, my Netflix subscription, blankets, and cinnamon popcorn.'

He makes a wanton noise. 'I am weak in the face of cinnamon popcorn.'

I laugh and shrug my coat on. 'Be back before you know it.'

He looks like he's about to protest, so I walk out through the gap in the tent before he has a chance. The rain from earlier hasn't eased, and I splosh through the damp streets and get to the bakery in record time. I stuff a rucksack with as many cosy blankets as I can find, slide in my laptop, make a flask of hot chocolate and a huge bucket of microwave popcorn which I coat with a mixture of butter, brown sugar, and cinnamon, and then fill up two hot water bottles to keep us warm.

The streets are as empty as they've been all day, and the Christmas lights are dulled by the rain dripping from them, and by the time I get back to Mistletoe Gardens, Joss has turned off the floodlights and turned on all the Christmas lights inside the gingerbread house, and set up a little area where we can recline against a plank of wood leaning on a tool box, and there's a nest on the floor made from a bouncy-looking pile of clean dustsheets from his van.

'Oh, wow.' It's the first time I've seen the gingerbread house in the dark with the fairy lights on, each set a multicoloured rainbow of lights sparkling from inside the gumdrops I pushed each LED bulb into, hung around each of the four window frames, a set around the doorframe, and Joss is arranging a pre-lit garland of holly leaves and cinnamon sticks across the gingerbread mantelpiece.

He looks up. 'Never mind watching a Christmas movie – I feel like I've stepped *into* one. Even Hollywood set designers wouldn't build a set this good. I can feel the festiveness seeping into my veins.'

'Look at this place, Joss.' I don't want to raise my voice too loudly in case it breaks the spell. 'It feels like magic. Like our own little Christmassy den. We built a gingerbread house. I know it still needs decorations to turn it into a cosy living room inside, but this is exactly the sort of place where elves would hang out in the North Pole.' I thrust the hot bucket of popcorn at him. 'What Christmas film have you never seen?'

'I... um...'

I remember an earlier conversation as I point at the nest he's set up. *'It's a Wonderful Life* it is then. Get comfy.'

He laughs a tired laugh at being bossed around, but willingly obeys, settling down in the bubble of dustsheets as I hand him a hot water bottle, throw two red blankets with gingerbread men on them at him, and pour two cups of hot chocolate out of the flask. He's set up another tool box at a perfect height to put the laptop on, so I position it where we can both see it, and the dongs of the bell in the opening credits reverberate through the gingerbread house.

I sit down beside Joss in the nest. He's got one hand wrapped around his hot chocolate, the other is stuffing popcorn into his mouth, and the hot water bottle is held against his chest. I settle back against the angled wooden board so I'm half-reclining, put the hot water bottle on my stomach, pull my fleece blanket over me, and sip my hot chocolate. It's damp and cold outside, but in here, it's a cosy little burrow. It feels like we're in a magical Christmas cottage, away from the rest of the world, where no one will ever find us.

Joss moves the bucket of popcorn nearer, closing the space between us until he's sitting next to me, and then he reclines too, wriggling around until he's comfy, and I look over at him and grin. 'Most Christmassy thing you've ever done?'

He's got a soppy smile on his face that looks like he couldn't get rid of it if he wanted to, and it answers the question for me.

When the hot chocolate is gone, the popcorn bucket is mostly empty, and George Bailey is telling Mary he'll lasso the moon for her onscreen, Joss spreads an arm out towards me, silently asking if I want to snuggle up against him, and it's a good thing the hot chocolate *has* gone because I would definitely have spilled it in my rush to shift closer, until his arm wraps around my shoulders and pulls me into his side.

He lets out a long breath and sinks further down, leaning his head back on the wood behind us, and I do the same, listening to the sound of the rain pattering on the roof of the bandstand high above our little house.

It's the most perfect, warm, cosy, and festive romantic moment I've ever experienced.

Joss has to swallow before he speaks. 'If anyone had told me a month ago that I'd be lying inside a gingerbread house, watching *It's a Wonderful Life*, and cuddling the most beautiful person I've ever met, I'd never have believed them.'

I've got one of the blankets pulled up to my nose, and my face flares so hot that I'm surprised my cheeks don't singe a hole straight through it. 'You're too tired to know what you're saying.'

'Nah, I'm not.' His voice is starting to slur and his eyes are barely open. 'I never knew it was possible to enjoy Christmas this much.'

It sends a zingy thrill through me because he sounds *so* happy.

He lifts his head to watch the film, but I suspect the chances of him making it to the end are slim to zero. To be honest, I don't think the chances of him staying awake for the next five minutes are all that good either.

He's blinking slow, and every time his eyes close, it takes longer for him to open them again. His head starts to nod forwards, and each time, he jerks awake with a start, blinking wide eyes open.

By the fifth time, I've had enough. When his head drops forward this time, I slide my arm around the back of his neck, tangle my hand in his hair, and tug his head down onto my shoulder. 'Close your eyes, lovely boy. Let yourself be as tired as you are.'

'How'd I get this lucky, Ess...' His words slur so much that he can't finish the sentence, and I squeeze him tightly.

He's asleep before his head touches my shoulder. His whole body melts against mine, and he lets out a sigh and snuggles in. I kiss his forehead. 'Night, Joss.'

I keep my arm around him, stroking his hair from the other side, holding him tight as his breathing evens out. His hot water bottle has fallen onto me and I gently ease them both between our bodies, keeping us warm, and I pull another blanket over so it covers us both, not wanting to jostle him too much in case he wakes up.

It might not get *It's a Wonderful Life* ticked off his bucket list of Christmas movies, but at least it gets him to relax and catch up on some much-needed rest.

The combination of the warm drink, warm body beside me, and festive cosiness of the gingerbread house makes my eyes drift closed, and I rest my head against Joss's soft hair and let myself doze too.

George Bailey is realising what Bedford Falls would be like if he'd never existed when I blink back to awareness of my surroundings. Joss hasn't moved an inch, but the film is almost over, a couple of hours that I don't remember passing. I'm hyper-aware of how content I feel. Still warm, still snug, my hand still in Joss's hair, my mouth smushed against his forehead.

He starts to stir too, and my fingers tighten in his hair. 'Don't wake up yet,' I whisper.

'I assure you, I have woken up. This conversation would be a little difficult if I hadn't.' His voice is a low croak, sexily rough with sleep.

I hold him tighter. I feel so safe and free in this moment, like I could say anything and he wouldn't judge me. 'I meant, don't *jump* up yet, let me cwtch you for a moment longer.'

Surprisingly, his head stays on my shoulder and he snuggles in closer. His arm snakes around me and he holds me tight. He exhales and his body relaxes against mine again.

The ending of the film plays on the laptop, and although my eyes are on it, all I can concentrate on is Joss. I wonder if he's enjoying this closeness as much as I am. My fingers graze his dark hair where they're still holding his head, and he turns into it, his fingers trailing up and down my opposite arm under the blanket, his arm a heavy weight across my body, and I let my lips brush across his forehead again, and his little sigh of happiness is one of the best things I've ever heard in my life.

It's only when 'the end' appears that he starts to move. He stretches luxuriously and turns his head to nuzzle into my hair, and then his lips press against my jaw, just a gentle kiss laid there, making me glad I'm not currently standing upright because I soon wouldn't be. It takes *all* my willpower not to curl my hand in his hair and drag his lips to mine.

'Joss,' I mumble for no real reason – a warning to stop or a plea for him to go further. I *want* him to go further, but the sensible side of me *knows* that he has to stop. After the disaster of the last time I fell in love, if I ever let a man get close again, it will be someone who there's a future with. It can't be someone who's about to up and leave.

He gets the message and changes tack. His nose is freezing and he rubs the tip of it against my cheek, making me jump at the sudden coldness and smack at his leg. We're both laughing as we roll away from each other. He pushes himself up to sit on his knees, and I get to my feet, groaning as my back protests that thirty-six is too old to be napping on a stone floor.

As I start tidying, he reaches out and catches my wrist. 'I know I was already asleep when I said it, but I meant what I said – I don't know how I got lucky enough to have you in my life. My marriage break-up knocked me sideways. It made me feel like I was worth nothing. For you to just sit there and hold me while I slept for no reason other than caring about me...' He shakes his head like he can't find the right words.

It takes every ounce of willpower to *not* tackle him to the floor in the biggest bear hug in the history of the world. I hold his beautiful blue eyes and he blinks back at me, not hiding anything tonight. His eyes show every bit of hurt and sadness that's taken over his life in recent years, but tonight they reflect the twinkling of multicoloured Christmas lights too, and despite the dull night and the lingering tiredness, they look brighter than I've ever seen them.

His eyes close and he lifts my hand to his mouth until his lips graze across the sensitive skin of my inner wrist, and I make an unrecognisable sound that could most probably be likened to a whimper. It should be illegal for a man to do that unless they're immediately going to follow it up with *much* more explicit things.

He suddenly comes to his senses, drops my wrist, and starts gathering dustsheets. 'I'll drive you back, I'm not having you walking through the rain again.'

When everything's cleared away, he turns out the last of the fairy lights and I stand inside the door and look around. The outside is complete now, apart from a puff of candyfloss in the chimney to look like smoke coming out, but the inside is going to be a lot of work tomorrow.

Joss comes to stand next to me in the darkness and drops an arm around my shoulder. 'Ess, you know where I live, right?' I nod and he continues. 'Will you come up to the house tomorrow morning? I've got something to show you before we start decorating the inside.'

I glance up at him but it's too dark to see his face. 'Of course.'

I want to prod and wheedle for more information, but he sounds so nervous that it definitely isn't the time for teasing curiosity.

His arm tightens briefly around my shoulders, and then he nods to the dark house in front of us. 'Nearly done.'

'Nearly done,' I repeat, trying to convince myself that his voice sounds as sad as I feel. Although I'm proud of having got this far, it also means that once the inside is decorated, that's *it*. It's done. This time with Joss is over, and I'm really, *really* not ready for it to end yet.

15

Queen Victoria gave her beloved dog, Dash, two pieces of gingerbread as Christmas presents.

It's hammering down the following morning as I walk through
quiet streets towards the edge of the tiny village where Joss lives.
My raincoat is drenched, and there's an umbrella dangling from
my hand that wouldn't stand up to the relentless wind and had
blown inside out so many times that I'd given up on it before I got
out of Folkhornton town centre.

No one else is daft enough to be out in this weather, but I woke
up early and couldn't stop thinking about Joss, and how much it
felt like a huge deal for him to invite me to his house. I'd plaited
my hair last night and taken it out this morning for a bouncy set
of red waves, which turned into a frizzy drowned gerbil approxi-
mately four seconds after I set foot outside. My hood is pulled
tight under my chin, and the only other sign of life on the roads is
a bus that splashes me as it zooms through an ever-increasing
puddle.

Twenty minutes later, I can't get any wetter as I turn into the tiny back lane of modern bungalows covered in tasteful white Christmas lights and surrounded by neat evergreen hedgerows. Joss's bungalow is on the corner, detached from its neighbours, with a wide stone path up to an off-pink door.

I stop in my tracks when I see the most prominent thing in his garden. There's a 'for sale' sign standing proudly on the lawn.

It hits me like, well, a 'for sale' sign to the face. I imagine the feeling would be similar had it leapt from its post and attacked me.

A 'for sale' sign is so final.

I know he's leaving, I know he's selling his parents' bungalow, but I never realised it was on the market. I thought it was some unascertained time in the future, not that he was literally selling it *as we speak*. He could be holding open house days or showing potential buyers around. A 'for sale' sign doesn't just mean he's leaving, it means he's leaving *imminently*.

I stare at it for an abnormal amount of time. It prickles my skin like it's broken into splinters that are needling at me. I thought there was hope. That spending time in Folkhornton again, enjoying doing the gingerbread house and getting to know the residents... I've thought that if he would admit to himself that it's not as bad as he thought, then maybe he'd stay. But you can't argue with a 'for sale' sign, can you?

There are rivulets of rainwater running down my face and my rainproof coat is fast becoming *non*-rainproof, so I force myself to walk up to the door *without* kicking the sign over, even though I want to.

I knock but instead of an answer, I follow my ears to the sound of a power tool coming from around the side of the bungalow. There's a garage attached at the back, the door raised and light spilling out into the dull morning. Inside there are piles of wood and furniture and tools, clamps, and workbenches, and Joss is leaning over one of them, smoothing out wood with an electric planer. I wait for him to finish before I knock.

'Ess!' Joss jumps at my interruption, and then his entire face lights up with an unrelenting grin. 'You're early. I was about to jump in the van and pick you up so you didn't have to walk in this weather.'

I don't mention that I'm early because I couldn't wait to see him. Instead of pacing the bakery, watching the clock until it was a reasonable time to set off, I convinced myself I'd need time to find the place and left early, and now it's barely half past eight when we'd said nine o'clock.

He bites his lip as he looks me over. 'Let me get you a towel, you're soaked.'

I dump my bag on an empty workbench, and he holds his hands out for the dripping wet bit of fabric that was once my coat, and then disappears into the house, leaving me shivering as I take in the chaos of the obviously well-used workshop, sawdust covering the floor, his van parked on the driveway outside rather than in here where it should be. There are stacks of furniture, old and falling apart, and other pieces that are only half made.

Joss returns with a huge towel that he holds open for me, and I take it gratefully and wrap myself in the soft fluffiness of it.

I peer at him, hopefully looking less like a drowned rat and more like a... well, a drowned rat wrapped in a towel, but still. 'How'd you sleep?'

'Like a proverbial log. I don't know what you did to me last night, but that was the first time I haven't stared at the ceiling in... a couple of years. I feel almost human again this morning.'

I can't help smiling to myself. Sometimes a night off really is the best medicine.

'This place is amazing. What are you up to in here?' I look around the garage, my fingers trailing over a chipped carousel horse with a missing ear. In the clutter, I can make out an intricate metalwork bench with four legs rusting away, old fencing, a mangled but ornate ironwork gate, and piles of indistinguishable wood. But there's not just old stuff. There's old stuff made into new stuff too.

'This is what you do,' I say to myself, looking at an outdoor table and chairs with pastel flowers ingrained into the wood.

'That's a garden set for my neighbour.' He points to the right, presumably meaning the next bungalow along. 'She was really kind to me when I first moved in. That was the first thing her late husband bought for their house fifty-something years ago. It was falling apart and she asked if I'd get rid of it for her, but she was really upset at having to throw it out. She doesn't know, but I've given it a new lease of life, repainted the flowers and preserved them with resin, replaced the rotting wood with something more solid, and waterproofed it. She likes sitting out in her garden in the nice weather. I'm going to give it to her as a thank you before I leave.'

I force words out past the lump in my throat. 'It's perfect. That's the loveliest thing to do, Joss.'

'She brought me food every night at first. She's a little old thing, I doubt she could manage to cook for herself most of the time, but she cooked for me too because I was existing on an, ahem, *liquid* diet. Even if I was too drunk to slur a thank you in her direction, she still came with a steaming bowl of food every night. This was the least I could do. When I got my head back on straight, I started going round there to do any little jobs she couldn't manage herself.'

Do not go and hug him. Do *not* go and hug him. My eyes fall on the hacked-up remains of a bench. A bench that was made in memoriam to a much-loved local lollipop man who had guided children safely to and from school for decades. A bench that was put up in his honour after he died last year. A bench that was stolen from Folkhornton town centre mere months after being put up. I gasp in horror. 'Why do you have that?'

My head is filled with thoughts about what a stolen bench is doing in Joss's garage. Has everything I've thought about him been wrong? Is he really a thief, a vandal, destroying things for his own pleasure? There's no mistaking which bench it is. A plaque with Mr Leonard's name is on the wood. Kids took to carving thank-you messages into it once it was installed next to the fountain, all of which are still there.

'That's actually what I wanted to show you...' Joss glances at it and then at me, and a look of horror crosses his face and he holds his hands up. 'Okay, okay, I know it looks bad, but it's not what you think.'

'It was stolen from the town a few months ago! What's it doing in your garage?'

'It wasn't stolen. Okay, it was kind of stolen but not in the way you think.' He rolls his eyes with a huff. 'The council employs Hallissey Construction to do a lot of jobs for them, and they wanted rid of it but they didn't want the wrath of the townspeople that getting rid of it would incur. I was legitimately employed to remove it in the middle of the night without anyone knowing. It's stolen in as much as I was told to throw it on the tip, but I couldn't toss it aside like it didn't mean anything, so I kept it.'

'And now you're cutting it up.'

'I'm making it into a throne for Santa to sit on in the gingerbread house. That's what I wanted to show you.'

'Why?'

'Because it'd be a bit uncomfortable sitting on the floor? And Santa's old, probably hasn't got the knees for it...'

'No, I meant...'

'I thought it deserved a second chance at life.' He switches the electric planer on again. 'Did you know Mr Leonard used to visit nursing homes dressed as Santa and give out gifts? Some of the residents in Mum's nursing home have no family or visitors bringing them gifts to open, but he had something for everyone, and more importantly than that, he had *time* for everyone. I spoke to him often. He'd lost his wife to dementia and he wanted to give something back. I thought Mr Leonard would approve of using it for this. Sort of a full circle thing.'

'You are a *gorgeous* human being, Joss Hallissey.'

His face turns the colour of Santa's sleigh, and he mumbles something unintelligible and continues planing.

And I'm not having that.

I march across, get my hand around his and make him stop. I tangle my fingers around both of his hands, while my other one slides up to his jaw to cup his face and hold him in place until he looks at me.

'You put on this front so no one sees what a lovely person you are because you don't think you deserve anyone to like you. You're beautiful, Joss. Inside and out. And I think it's been a long time since anyone told you that, a longer time since you let anyone get close enough to see it, and an even longer time since *you* believed it. And that is not okay. You have a heart of gold and I am never going to stop telling you that. And one day, you're going to believe me.'

His eyes close and his head grows heavy in my hand. 'I'm leaving, Ess. I can't...'

'So, what, we won't still be friends? There's no such thing as phones, emails, text messages?'

'I don't think that'll be enough.'

I *know* it won't be enough, but I don't say it out loud.

His eyes open and he ducks down to press his lips against my cheek, and then he stands upright and pulls away, showing me the incredible throne he's made – solid, chunky wood with ornate mistletoe leaves carved along the back and legs, and some of the thank-you messages from children retained in the woodwork.

'Everyone's going to know.'

'That's okay. Maybe they *should* know. Do you like it?'

I squeeze his hand. 'I *love* it.'

'I'm just finishing off the feet. I'll give it a coat of red-tinted varnish tonight and it'll be ready for Santa by tomorrow morning.'

There are so many things I want to say, and most of them involve throwing my arms around him and begging him to stay, but I force myself to do nothing more than mumble another compliment about the festive throne that I know he won't believe.

'I brought breakfast,' I say eventually.

He looks uncertain, and I get the feeling he wasn't intending to invite me inside. His eyes flick between my bag and the door through to the house like he's trying to calculate how to make breakfast in the garage work.

'It's marzipan loaf cake,' I say, knowing that Joss can be brought around to most things by the promise of baked goods.

He hesitates for a moment longer, and then seems to take in the towel still wrapped around me and my still-dripping hair. 'You'll have to put up with my attempt at coffee.'

I pick up my bag and follow him through into a narrow tiled kitchen, with wooden cupboard doors and pink floral prints on the lemon walls, and although it's very pretty, it's very *not* Joss. I put the bakery bag down on the unit and he sets a coffeemaker going, and because the kitchen is so tiny, points me through to a larger living room. 'There's a radiator in there you can stand by to dry out. Coffee won't be a minute.'

He's already laid my coat across a radiator in the narrow hallway, and I go into the living room, glad there's a mirror on the wall. I attempt to towel-dry my hair, but it's going to do nothing but turn into a mass of frizz, so I pull a band out and put it into a messy bun on top.

'No Christmas decorations?' I call out.

'I don't like Christmas, remember?'

Yeah, I remember, but it still surprises me. He's embracing everything in Mistletoe Gardens, but the most Christmassy thing here is his decapitated gingerbread man scarf hanging on a hook in the hallway. And the felt blood dripping from the neckline detracts from its festiveness a bit.

'I think you like Christmas a little bit,' I say when he carries in two mugs of coffee and puts them carefully down on two coasters on the mahogany coffee table, and then goes back for two plates with the slices of marzipan loaf cake on them.

'I like how much *you* like Christmas.' He sits down and invites me to do the same, and I *should*, but I can't help wandering around the room. Mismatched armchairs and an Easy Riser recliner that doesn't look like it's been sat in for a couple of years. His mum's chair tidy hooked over the arm. A cross-stitch magazine rolled up and poking out. I know the date on it will be a few years ago.

It's so... not him. There is nothing of Joss in this place whatsoever. From the paisley rug on the living room floor, the flowery curtains, the dried-out potpourri on a side table, to the framed photographs on the mantelpiece showing photos of his mum and dad on their wedding day, Joss and his ex on their wedding day, and one of their late cat, presumably not on its wedding day.

It's a house where an elderly man and woman live, not a thirty-eight-year-old bachelor.

'Do you actually live here?' I was trying to be sensitive about it, but his eyes are on me as I look around, and it doesn't make sense.

'Yes, of course. For the past two years. Since the day of my father's funeral...'

I go over and perch next to him on the sofa. Because he does seem perched. Like he's sitting in someone else's house, being careful not to mess anything up. The garage was the only part that had any hint of Joss to it.

Despite telling myself not to touch him, my fingers rub gently across his shoulder.

'I sleep on the sofa,' he blurts out. 'We were going to sell it straight away, but when my marriage ended, I needed somewhere to go, so I stopped here temporarily. It isn't where I grew up or anything like that. My mum was struggling with stairs a few years ago so they sold our house and downsized to a bungalow, so this is not like a sentimental childhood home or anything. This is my parents' home. I feel like I'm house-sitting. Like they're going to come back at any moment. For as long as I stay here, there will always be that possibility. I'll always be able to believe that I'm looking out the window waiting for their car to pull in.'

I bite my lip because it makes me want to cry *again*. No wonder he doesn't feel at home here. 'What if you were going to stay? Would you make it yours or find somewhere else?'

'I like it here. It's quiet. My neighbours are lovely. And recently, I've been thinking... I saw some gorgeous laminate flooring, it would look so good in here, and I nearly bought it, but... And seeing your big kitchen made me think I'd knock through the wall of the hallway and expand my tiny kitchen, but...'

Every sentence ends with a but.

'We could easily Joss-ify this place.' I nudge my shoulder against his. 'I'd help if you wanted a hand changing things up. I know you're a builder and I'm never *quite* clear on which end to hold a paintbrush, but you've helped me out with baking, there's no reason we can't share each other's skills. If it seems overwhelming or like something you can't face tackling by yourself, or if it would feel like you were saying goodbye and you didn't want to do that alone, or...' I trail off because he's staring at me like I've sprouted a red nose and started singing 'Here Comes Santa Claus'.

'I hear it's best if you go for the end *without* wet paint on it.'

He's deflecting and we both know it.

'I know this isn't healthy, but meeting you... This is the first time I've *cared*. The first time I've *wanted* to...' He searches for the words. 'To actually live here.'

'You're allowed to be happy again. I know life has slammed you into a few rocks, maybe you've got a few holes in your hull, but you haven't sunk yet. It's okay to patch them up and keep going until one day you're ready to float again.'

He stutters something that isn't an actual word. 'It's too early for that sort of metaphor, Ess.'

Maybe it has got a little deeper than I intended, so I sip my coffee and when I put the mug back, I deliberately put it next to the coaster rather than on it.

He raises an eyebrow, but a grin spreads across his face, and then he reaches across, picks up the mug and places it deliberately onto the coaster.

Oh, well, it was worth a try. 'Baby steps are fine too.'

'It was me who varnished this coffee table, more like.'

A laugh escapes that's *so* unexpected that the sheer suddenness of it makes me laugh even harder. Joss quirks an eyebrow, but his lips are twitching, and it isn't long before we're both laughing much harder than anything was actually funny, and the tension in Joss's shoulders dissipates. 'Thank you. It's been a long time since there was laughter inside these walls.'

'Thank you for showing me.'

This is a huge part of his armour that *no one* has seen behind and I know it means something special that he let me in.

Gingerbread figures were quite unusual in times gone by – one museum displays a nineteenth-century gingerbread mould in the shape of a chicken wearing trousers!

Despite having the whole interior of the gingerbread house to decorate today, it's half past nine before we pull up at the gates of Mistletoe Gardens and find them... open.

'That's not good,' Joss says.

I angle my head so I can see the reflection in the passenger side mirror and catch sight of a group of locals, all gathered around the bandstand. 'Neither is that.'

A sinking feeling grows in the pit of my stomach. Why are the gates open? Why are so many villagers inside?

'Oh, thank goodness you're here!' Beryl shouts so loudly that we can hear her before we've opened the van doors. She's hurrying towards us, a knitted hat on her head that's doing nothing to keep her dry.

'Oh, Essie, Joss, it's terrible. After all your hard work...' She continues when we jump out of the van. 'We don't know what can have happened. Vandals. Yobs. Mr Chalke was walking his dog this morning when he noticed the gates open. The tent was open, and...' She trails off, like it's too bad to verbalise. 'He tried phoning the bakery, but there was no answer.'

'I was at...' I glance at Joss and he looks worriedly back at me.

We can see the bandstand from here, but half the tent is pulled, hiding the gingerbread house from view, and my mind is filled with visions of what can have befallen it. Has it been vandalised? Broken up? Spray painted by drunken youths who have broken into the park?

'What exactly has happened?' Joss asks her as we hurry along the path to the colourfully anoraked gathering of locals, staring miserably at the bandstand from under an array of umbrellas.

'It was like this when I got here,' Mr Chalke says. 'The gate had been left unlocked and someone's obviously been in and opened the tent. I'm so sorry, you two – the rain's got in.'

I didn't realise Joss was holding my hand until his grip tightens as we walk up the bandstand steps. I'm expecting the worst. What if the whole gingerbread house is crumbled to pieces on the floor? What if someone's done something awful to it?

It's still up, that's something. The front looks okay. Undamaged.

'It'll be okay,' Joss murmurs, squeezing my hand again as we walk around the house.

It will not be okay. As soon as we're there, I know what's happened before I've seen it. The strength of the wind this morning and the force of the rain. The tent was around the bandstand to keep the weather out, and with the tent left open, it wouldn't stand a chance. Without that tent, the gingerbread house had *no* protection from the weather.

Joss swears.

I want to cry from the second I pluck up the courage to peer around his shoulder.

The back end and the left side of the house are drenched. At least a quarter of the roof tiles have slid off and are a pile of gumdrop-dotted mush on the floor, and the walls, the bricks... They're still *there*, but the gingerbread has absorbed the water and expanded like a sponge, and when I press my finger to one of the soggy bricks, it makes a big, mushy hole.

The royal icing surrounding them is as solid as stone, but the bricks are unsaveable. A huge chunk of both the side and the back of the house is ruined, along with about a quarter of the roof.

Mistletoe Gardens is supposed to be opening *tonight*. People are expecting to look around the gingerbread house *tonight*. We've got Santa arriving at nine o'clock tomorrow morning to meet and greet the first children, and so far there's *nothing* inside. It was already an overwhelming task to get it decorated today, but now it feels insurmountable. What can we do with this? Drying it out is impossible and there certainly isn't time to re-do it.

Panic is building inside me. This has all been for nothing. We've failed at the very last moment. All of this work, all of this time, all of this effort, and it falls apart on the very last day – literally.

Joss swears again as he reaches up and fixes the tent. It looks like someone's got the pulleys tangled and been unable to get it back the way it should be. But who? And how? How did someone get in with the gates locked? And why would they interfere with the tent at all?

Beryl comes up to the bandstand railings. 'Are you okay, Essie?'

'Who would do this?' I say in despair at her kindly words. The gathered residents are all standing around, looking wet and upset and at a loss for what to do, much like me.

'Maybe one of you left it open last night,' Lynette ventures. 'Maybe it wasn't malicious, but just a careless accident. Nothing else has been damaged.'

'The tent was closed last night. We...' I trail off before admitting Joss and I spent the evening curled up together inside the gingerbread house.

'Then *one* of you must've left the gates unlocked and someone's got in and done it.' She gestures towards Joss, whose back is turned as he examines the roof.

I can hear whispers of 'Hallissey' going through the group.

'You know what he's like,' someone mutters. 'Untrustworthy, unreliable, drunk half the time according to his reviews.'

'Wouldn't be surprised,' the other one says in response. 'Leopards don't change their spots.'

'Total opposite of his father.'

There are other mutterings about how wonderful Joseph Hallissey Senior was, and while I'm sure he was, so is *my* Joss, and that feeling of protectiveness washes over me again. Joss has worked ridiculously hard lately, on the gingerbread house *and* to change his attitude towards the Folkhornton residents. He doesn't deserve the things still being uttered about him behind his back. He's gone round the other side of the house to check for damage now, but if he overhears that our neighbours still think this way about him, it's exactly what will make him want to leave instantly. I'm devastated about the damage to the gingerbread house, but the readiness to blame Joss is even more upsetting, and it makes fire crackle through my veins.

'Actually, I watched Joss lock up last night,' I say loudly. 'We left together. We arrived together just now. The tent was closed and the gates were locked. Whoever did this, it wasn't either of us.'

I don't know if it's because they've known me since I was little or because of who my mum is, but they obviously believe me because it puts an end to the grumblings. In fact, what it actually does is give them something else to gabble about. Leaving together, arriving together, and not being at the bakery this morning add up to give the impression I spent the night with Joss, and finding out how or why the gates were open is suddenly less important in the grand scheme of gossip-related things.

'We can fix this.' Joss's arm wraps around me and he pulls me tight against him, his voice soft but determined.

'We're opening *today*, Joss. We didn't have time to decorate the inside as it was, we certainly don't have time to remake God-only-knows how much gingerbread and repair the roo—'

'We can help,' Beryl says.

'Oh, yes!' Mr Chalke exclaims. The rest of the residents call their agreement too. 'Anything you need. We'll all help, won't we?'

Another chant of agreement that makes me feel so emotional that my eyes start welling up again. The residents of Folkhornton all coming together to help us with this daft project that no one believed in at first.

'You two have been single-handedly trying to save Mistletoe Gardens for weeks – it's about time we all chipped in,' Lynette calls.

'Hear, hear,' Mr Arkins says from inside his dino suit.

'Right.' Joss claps his hands together. 'For every minute these wet bricks are here, the moisture is seeping into the undamaged bricks surrounding them. Ess and I are going to stay here and start stripping them *now*.'

I appreciate his practical side, the way he gets on with things and takes charge like he's running a building site. He quickly counts the damaged bricks and tiles.

'We need at least two hundred bricks and seventy-four roof tiles. Who can make gingerbread?'

'I love making gingerbread! I do it with my grandchildren every year!' Edna calls.

'And me! I've even made a few gingerbread houses in my time!'

'Same here! My husband wouldn't believe it was Christmas without a batch of gingerbread on the go!'

'Well, Essie's mum doesn't know it yet, but you're going to use the bakery kitchen to combine your gingerbread expertise and make what we need. Are you up for the challenge?'

Six ladies cheer and link arms as they take off towards Dancing Cinnamon like they're following a yellow brick road. Mum and Saff aren't going to know what's hit them.

'The recipe's in my head!' I yell after the gang of ladies. 'Oh, and Saff's! Ask Saff, she knows where everything is.'

I have no idea if they hear me. 'No one's even set up their stalls yet. That's what they were supposed to be doing today, not helping us.'

'That doesn't matter,' Lynette says. 'Have you seen the Facebook page? People are coming from all over tonight. I could display my wares in a bin bag and it would still be the best night ever.'

'No one's going to come out in this weather.' I glance up at the heavy grey clouds that have turned from pouring rain to drizzle now.

'Forecast says it's going to brighten up later.' Mr Arkins holds up his phone in his dino paw. He waddles over to the railings, his outfit keeping him dry, although the ginormous T-rex head looks a bit worse for wear. 'What else do you need?'

'Everything.' I sigh. This is hopeless.

'A tre—'

'I know exactly where we can get a tree!' Mr Arkins says before Joss has finished the word. 'Come on, Douglas, we'll be responsible for the tree. A six-footer should do nicely.' He hooks a dino claw around an unsuspecting Douglas's wrist and drags him out of the gate.

'And decorations?' I say to the remaining residents who are still waiting for instructions. 'We were going to go for an edible theme...'

'I'll string some popcorn!' Mrs Allen exclaims.

'And I've got a batch of salt dough waiting for my grandchildren, we can use that,' Mr Selman says.

'How about marshmallows around the door?'

'And M&Ms around the windows, like the gingerbread houses I always buy from Dancing Cinnamon, Essie?'

The tears turn into laughter as the offers of help flood in. I meet Joss's shining eyes as everyone dashes away in every direction, and he holds a hand out, and squeezes mine when I slip it into his. 'We've got this.'

Three simple words that mean such a lot. His calm voice and reassuring Welsh accent make it easy to believe him, to trust him and his bright smile, and for a moment, it really does feel like we've got this, all of us.

Joss goes over to get tools out of his van and returns with a bucket and gives me a pair of his paint-stained builder's gloves that feel nice when I slip them onto my hands.

'Why'd you say that just now?' He starts shovelling up the pile of wet gingerbread mush that was once the beautifully tiled roof. 'You'd already got in the van when I locked up last night. You *didn't* see me do it.'

'Doesn't matter. I trust you, Joss. If you say you locked up, you locked up.'

'Yeah, but... I don't need you to lie for me. I didn't hear what was said but I can guess what it was – people are blaming me, and that's fine. I don't care what they think of me.'

'Yes, you do.'

He raises an eyebrow.

I sigh. 'When I first suggested this, a majority of those people didn't think it was possible. Apart from *you*. You believed in me when no one else did. Your reviews from two years ago don't reflect who you are now. Everyone knows that really – they were just upset and lashing out.'

I get the feeling he wants to say something more, but there isn't time. He nudges his arm gently against mine instead.

I start dismantling the gingerbread wall, pulling the soaking wet biscuit out in sloppy clumps and dumping them into the bucket. The sadness at how much effort has been wasted is replaced by an urge to get it fixed. Joss is above me on the scaffolding, stripping the remaining damaged tiles from the roof and cleaning off the wooden base, ready for new tiles.

The wet gingerbread comes out easily, but the royal icing is as solid as concrete, unaffected by the deluge of rainwater, and Joss produces a coping saw to cut it out piece by piece. He's sandpapering royal icing from the roof and I'm sawing chunks of it from the wall when my phone beeps with a text from Saff.

Six locals have just invaded the kitchen and ransacked the place before remembering to ask me for gingerbread brick instructions. Your mum's as hopping mad as a box of really angry, health-and-safety-conscious frogs. It's great fun!

I show Joss when he climbs down from the roof, and he laughs. 'We're doing okay here. Gingerbread is a lot quicker to get out than it is to put in. You should go and superv—'

He's cut off by another van pulling up alongside his in the gateway, and the three boys from Hallissey Construction jump out.

'You called your lads?'

'Of course I did. Forget the swimming baths roof, *this* is the most important job I've ever done.'

'Joss...' Keeping my gingerbread-covered gloves away from his clothes, I do the nearest impression of throwing my arms around him, and he does the same, keeping his hands off my body but still managing to squeeze me with his arms.

'It'll be okay. We'll make this right, I promise.'

His gentle voice against my hair is so reassuring. The kind of man you can rely on. Pragmatic, sensible, and trustworthy. I wish there were more people like him in my life.

The lads are making their way over so he releases me. 'Go and supervise the gingerbread baking before your mum has a meltdown.'

As I leave, Mr Arkins and Douglas come back, carrying a tree between them, and two of the lads rush over to take it from them, and the fact the older generation have got three other young 'uns to help now leaves me walking down the street towards the bakery feeling much lighter than I have until now. Even the drizzle has stopped, although heavy steel-blue clouds still hang in the sky.

'Essie!' Mum demands from behind the counter before I've got the door fully open. 'Why have six of our neighbours invaded my kitchen, taken Saff hostage, and started making gingerbread? What on earth is going on up there in the gardens?'

While I'm sure the group of women told her, I reiterate what's happened with the gingerbread house.

'Let me guess, Hallissey made a mistake. Or a *deliberate* mistake.'

'What? No! Neither!'

'I told you this project was silly from the get-go. It's always been an unfeasible, fairytale-esque whim. And if you'd had *anyone* other than him doing it with you, then—'

'Then it wouldn't be the house it is now,' I finish for her, grateful when a customer comes in and I grab the chance to escape.

The kitchen is lost under a cloud of flour and spices so large that meteorologists will be along to study it at any moment, and I'm greeted by the embodiment of the term 'organised chaos'.

The ladies have taken over like this is a factory production line and Saff's walking around like some sort of foreman. They've divided into three pairs, and one team are mixing dry ingredients, one team are on wet ingredients, and one team are on rolling and cutting around the template. There's already a load of gingerbread bricks cooling down on a wire rack, and according to the beeping timer that Edna hasn't heard with her hearing aids, there's another one due out a few minutes ago.

Saff steps in and rescues it from the oven before it gets too singed, and Edna turns up the volume of the timer, swiftly deafening about 75 per cent of the Folkhornton population and continuing to bang it like *it* is the thing that's not working.

It's the most lively our little kitchen has been for years as I start on the first batch of royal icing. The ladies keep up a constant chatter about what they're doing for Christmas, what presents they've bought their grandchildren, and what they're cooking on the big day, and it's easy to get lost in, to carry on with a task that I've done so many times lately that I no longer need to concentrate.

'I'll help,' Mum says when I reappear on the shop floor, trying to balance a bucket of royal icing, a crate of warm gingerbread bricks, and the M&Ms that were requested earlier.

With the ladies in the swing of things, Saff covers the shop again, while Mum wrestles the crate from me and barges out the door before I have a chance to protest.

'I can manage.' I hurry after her. 'I know you don't approve of this project.'

'I want to see what's going on,' she says. 'If criminal damage has taken place in my constituency, I need to know.'

'And there was me thinking you wanted to help.'

'I don't like seeing you waste your time on this, Essie. It's a daft project that's never going to go anywhere, and it's got you tangled up with a man who's leaving anyway.'

'*You* called Joss out at that meeting!' I say incredulously. 'I'd forgotten he existed, and he was so unfriendly that I would never have asked him. *You're* the one who dragged him into it.'

'I didn't know he was leaving then. I didn't know there'd be anything between you.'

'There isn't anything between us.' I sound sulky, because there *is* something, but it isn't something I can deal with right now.

'I called on him in that meeting because I expected him to do exactly what he did – to bark something disparaging and storm out. I *didn't* know you'd go and beg him for help...' She stops in surprise when we arrive at Mistletoe Gardens.

It's the busiest we've ever seen it. Someone's turned all the Christmas lights on early and they brighten up the dullness of the day. The whole place is buzzing louder than the buzziest beehive.

Mum spots Douglas and swaps the crate for the bag of M&Ms I'm holding, leaving me to stare at the gingerbread house in surprise.

Inside, the tree is set up in one corner, strung with shimmering multicoloured lights, and a group of villagers are threading strands of popcorn and cranberries onto strings. Mr Selman has got a plate full of gingerbread men, iced with thin white outlines, and is currently tying on red ribbons to hang them on the tree. Mrs Allen is making a door wreath out of Haribo and having a little bit *too* much fun impaling the gummy bears. One of Joss's lads is up on a stepladder, piping rosettes of icing across the inside of the roof, hiding all hint of the wooden frame, and outside the bandstand, the other two construction workers are setting up stalls for the shopkeepers ready for tonight, and in the middle of it all, Joss is up on the scaffolding, arranging clouds of white candyfloss in the chimney to look like smoke.

Like he can sense me watching him, he turns and beams at me, and starts climbing down as I walk across the gardens.

Inside the gingerbread house, someone's phone is playing 'Candlelight Carol', and the residents are having a sing-along. Like an out-of-tune choir. Who don't know the words. Or agree on the language because some are singing in Welsh and some are singing in English. But in a weird way, it works.

'Now *that* is a Christmas miracle,' I say to Joss as he takes the crate of bricks from my arms. 'They're not even bickering over whether "Mull of Kintyre" is really a Christmas song or not. *How* did you do that?'

'They asked me what my favourite Christmas song is and I said that one I heard at your place the other day, and off they went.' He gives me a wink. 'And "Mull of Kintyre" definitely *is* a Christmas song.'

'Essie!' They make my name blend seamlessly into the tune of 'Candlelight Carol' without breaking stride on their singing. Beryl has brought in a garden chair and is merrily crocheting snowflakes with sparkly white wool for the tree. She adds a face depicting a look of agony to the centre of each one.

Joss has cleared every inch of the water-damaged gingerbread, and he hands me a brick-laying trowel and plunges his own into the bucket of royal icing, starting to slather the mortar on top of the remaining wall, while I start at the side, still unable to believe so many of our neighbours have come to help us.

'Didn't think we'd be doing this again anytime soon.' Joss grins at me from around the corner of the house, close enough that we can share the bucket of icing.

'Didn't think we'd be doing this again ev— uh oh.'

Mervyn Prichard is strolling along the path, chatting to a man who's holding his phone out like he's recording the conversation.

'These are the trees that hold our magical mistletoe,' Mervyn is saying. 'Legend has it that anyone who shares a kiss under our mistletoe on a cold December night is guaranteed another year of happiness in their relationship.'

'Do you have any personal experience of the power of the mistletoe?'

Mervyn goes red and stutters into the reporter's phone for a minute. 'Well, I did, um, er... once... back when we were younger, kids, really.' He isn't aware of Joss and me watching. 'I once kissed the most beautiful, poised, graceful woman I've ever met, but, well, things went a bit wrong. She married my friend but then he died and it all got a bit awkward, and we ended up on opposing sides of the wrong argument, and... Oh dear, don't print that.' He clears his throat, looking embarrassed by his oversharing. 'Well, it didn't work out for us, but maybe the mistletoe will give us another chance one day. Christmas magic and all that!' He chortles but there's a telltale wobble in his usually booming Welsh voice.

'Poised and graceful,' I say to Joss. 'That sounds like my mum. And she says Mervyn's always hanging around the mistletoe when she's here in December. And my dad *was* his friend before he married my mum. And Mum always talks about a mistletoe kiss that got away. Could that have been him?'

'Whenever Mervyn's talked about the woman he kissed under the mistletoe, he says it's too late and too much has happened between them...'

'They *have* to be talking about each other.'

'Hmm.' I can hear the cogs turning in Joss's mind. 'We're going to have to give this one some thought, Miss Browne...'

'And this is where they're putting the finishing touches to the gingerbread house.' Mervyn gestures towards it proudly and then does a double-take and realises that half the wall and roof are missing. 'Oh, blimey, what's happened here?' He looks at us then back at the journalist. 'Don't record that bit. Hang on a minute, will you?'

He looks up at Joss and me from the path outside the bandstand. 'Oh, dear me, that doesn't look good. It's opening tonight, is it not?'

'It is.' I sound more confident than I feel. Even with so many hands on deck, it still feels like an impossible task.

'You were saying, Mr Prichard?' the journalist prompts.

'Well, we appear to have had a bit of an... accident?' He looks at us questioningly.

'It'll be fini—' Joss doesn't get to finish his reassurance.

I hear the screech before I see the whirlwind of brown curls come tornado-ing across the grass like Taz from the *Looney Tunes*. 'You!'

'Me?' Mervyn looks taken aback as my mum points an accusatory finger at him.

'*Someone's* sabotaged the gingerbread house and it'll take less than three guesses to work out *who*! Come to enjoy the spoils of your victory, have you?'

'I don't know what you're talking about, Bronwen.' To be fair to Mervyn, he does look genuinely clueless.

'You'd have a key to the gates,' Mum snarls at him. 'Apart from these two, you're the *only* other person with a key. What a coincidence!'

'Well, yes, er, I do have a key. For security reasons, obviously, but it's in my office. Untouched. Locked in a secure cabinet. I'm sorry, I really don't know what's going on here. Has someone done this deliberately?'

Joss gives him a rundown of what's happened.

'And you think *I'd* do that?' He looks helplessly between us, Mum, and the journalist. 'No, no, no. This gingerbread house is the best thing that's happened to Folkhornton in ages. We were trending on Twitter this morning. Mostly people asking where Folkhornton is, but still. Last year's *Bake Off* winner tweeted about the gingerbread house! We've got celebrities "liking" our posts! A *Sewing Bee* contestant tweeted about Beryl's decapitated gingerbread man scarves! I've got a cake influencer annoyed that she didn't have a chance to do a daily vlog of the build. I don't even know what a vlog is. Or a cake influencer, for that matter. People are talking about the gingerbread house all over the internet. I'm concerned that we won't have enough parking spaces to accommodate all the people who are planning to come and see it. The *last* thing I'd want to do is damage it.'

'Does that mean you aren't going to bulldoze Mistletoe Gardens in January then?' Mum punctuates the question with a well-timed stamp of her foot.

'Oh, well, I can't really comment on matters like that, you see...'

'Who's that you're talking to?' Mum's eyes zero in on the journalist.

'This chap is from *Bulletin: Wales*, he's come to do a story on the opening night of Mistletoe Gardens, and—'

'And I bet you're taking full credit for it, aren't you?' She whips round to the journalist and wags a finger at him. 'He's taking advantage of what they've done. They're doing this to save the park *from* him, and here he is, using you to pretend he's all Santa Claus when really he's the Grinch! No! Worse than the Grinch! Scroooooooge! Oh, wait, no, Scrooge learned his lesson in the end too. Someone who's worse than the Grinch and Scrooge combined but with *no* redeeming features by the end!' Being concise never was my mum's strong point.

The journalist, unused to a full onslaught by my mum, looks a bit unsteady on his feet. 'Rumours of sabotage, council and residents at war, a giant gingerbread house, and...' The poor man looks alarmed as Mr Arkins appears in the gateway carrying a Christmas stocking. '...someone dressed as a dinosaur. It really is all happening in Folkhornton this Christmas, folks.' The journalist speaks into his phone. Probably not *quite* the headline we were hoping for.

He goes to wander around Mistletoe Gardens and take photographs for his piece, and Mervyn turns back to my mum. 'Bronwen, please. You can't honestly think...'

'I *think* the facts speak for themselves.'

'But what would I have to gain? The gingerbread house is bringing in tourism and getting people talking. Our footfall has been higher this December than it has for decades. This is the *last* thing I'd want to compromise. Surely you can see that?'

'No, I can't.' Mum's voice is wavering like she doesn't want to admit that Mervyn's speaking sense. She gets frustrated at being unable to hide the shake in it. 'I'm going back to oversee the chaos in the bakery. I'll bring the next lot of bricks up and *he* had better be gone by then or I... I won't be responsible for my actions.'

Mervyn looks at us helplessly while she stalks away. He actually looks like he's about to cry. 'I'm sorry. I had nothing to do with this. I don't know who's responsible.'

He chases after the journalist, trying to persuade him to take pictures of the decorations rather than Beryl's macabre crochet creations, including a snowman whose crocheted carrot nose can be pushed so far into his stuffed head that it comes out the other side.

'That went well,' Joss says, and his deadpan tone makes me

laugh. 'Absolutely ideal timing. When we were thinking about ways of getting them together, a blazing row *really* helps.' He glances up at the biggest tree. 'Maybe a little Christmas magic is overdue.'

'They've had worse rows than that. I'm sure they could get over it with a little... nudge or two.'

'Talking of getting over things, we need to get *on* with this or we're never going to be ready.' Joss nods to the clock on the town hall building. 'It's already nearly lunchtime.'

'Do you honestly think—'

'Yes,' he says simply. 'Yes, we can do it. With this many people onboard, we'll be done before nightfall.'

'That sounds suspiciously like you have faith in your neighbours, Joss Hallissey.'

His cheeks redden but he doesn't contradict me as he goes back to laying gingerbread bricks, filling the empty parts of the wall, refusing to meet my eyes, and hope breathes inside me.

Maybe it's not too late for Christmas magic in *all* senses of the word.

17

Three million ounces of ground ginger are sold every festive
season – enough to make 450 million gingerbread men!

Mistletoe Gardens is the busiest I've ever seen it. In all the years
I've stood here on December nights, wrapped up in gloves, and a
scarf and hat, selling cakes to happy couples, I can never
remember a year when it's been this crowded on opening night.
I'm at the Dancing Cinnamon stall on the path around the bandstand. Beryl is selling her festive creations to my right, and
Douglas from the coffee shop has got a hot chocolate stall to my
left. All the others are here too, manning their own stalls offering
handmade gifts and crafts.

Mum and Saff closed the bakery early to get everything made,
and a couple of the ladies hadn't had enough of the gingerbread
making and stayed to help, so I could stay in the park and make
sure everything was done.

It's incredible to see the gingerbread house finished. Multicoloured fairy lights are wrapped around the Rice Krispie cake
gumdrops on the roof, making it look like they're actually lit up,

and strings of actual gumdrop lights give off a soft jelly-like glow around every window, and the doorframe is lit up by white snowflake lights. Even the Haribo wreath has got micro lights entwined around it. My last finishing touch today was the icicles hanging from the roof – made of royal icing and finished with a sprinkle of edible glitter. The bandstand itself has tinsel and lights wrapped around every post and red ribbon bows on each railing. The whole park smells of gingerbread and icing sugar, with a hint of peppermint. Lights are glimmering all around me, and the trees are never more beautiful than when their bare boughs are glowing with the ice-white lights that cover each branch like a net and illuminate the bundles of mistletoe growing high above us.

I can't imagine there being a more romantic place in the world.

Right on cue, something tingles at the back of my neck and I look over my shoulder to see Joss coming towards me. He's been missing for the past couple of hours, and I'd started to wonder if he wasn't coming back.

I serve a customer wanting a mini-Yule log, and the instant she's left, he sidles up and stands next to me.

He smells of solvent-based paint and I realise where he's been. 'You went to varnish Santa's throne, didn't you?'

'It would never have been ready for tomorrow morning if I hadn't.'

'Didn't think you'd come back.'

'Wouldn't have skipped it for the world.' I think he intended to sound sarcastic, but it accidentally comes out sounding genuine, and it makes me realise how much I missed him tonight.

He's been here all day, a constant reassurance, a sparkle in his eyes every time I've caught them across the busy park, a warm smile that makes me forget everything else outside of it, but since we finished repairing the walls and gluing new roof tiles in place,

Joss and I have been pulled in opposite directions. While I stayed on the scaffolding, icing the new tiles so they blended in with the old ones, Joss went to help with everything from tangled tree lights to wonky-legged stalls to a crying child who was inconsolable that Santa doesn't arrive until tomorrow.

This might be the first time I've breathed all day. My hair is still up in the messy bun I put it in in Joss's living room this morning, and that feels like a lifetime ago, not less than twelve hours. I'm not sure my feet have ever ached this much in my life and my lower back is protesting every movement, but I also feel magical and sparkly. This is all because of something *I* said – and something *we* did. The park is teeming with people, and I'm serving so many customers that we're going to sell out earlier than ever before at this rate.

'Aww,' Joss says at the sight of an elderly couple clinging onto each other as they totter from one tree to the next and stop for a kiss underneath each one. 'So sweet.'

'They've just told me this is the twenty-first year they've kissed under our mistletoe, and they credit it with keeping their marriage going.'

He's quiet as he watches them, his expression something close to wistful.

'How do you ever let someone in again? How do you ever be that open with someone who can hurt you?' he murmurs, sounding more like he's talking to himself than to me. 'Look at them, they're *so* in love. You can tell they're each other's whole world. How do you ever trust someone that much? How do you *ever* know they won't chuck in the towel when things get difficult?'

'I think you know when you've found someone who lights up your world, someone who will *always* be worth fighting for because your life would be infinitely darker without them in it.' I shouldn't have said it out loud. It's too close to the bone of what

I'm feeling for Joss, and I can sense his eyes on me. I look stead-fastly ahead, refusing to look over at him, and after a few moments, he moves away and busies himself with straightening up the baskets of gingerbread men displayed on the table.

Customers fill the awkward silence.

This is *it* now for the gingerbread house. Once Santa is installed in the morning, we're done. There will undoubtedly be patch-ups to do – because I can't imagine many children or adults walking around a life-size gingerbread house without having a nibble – but I can cover those. Joss has taken on jobs from the locals and has to go and measure up and give quotes for them before Christmas.

That's the pervading sense of sadness tonight. It should be a happy night. I don't know if we've done enough to save Mistletoe Gardens, but I can't imagine Mervyn seeing this amount of people and still thinking it's a good idea to tear it down, but the ginger-bread house is complete, and therefore so is my time with Joss.

For tonight, though, he stays by my side, helping me serve customers until the stall is empty. He makes himself invaluable to others too, and by the end of the evening, every shopkeeper in Folkhornton is wishing he was a regular fixture every year.

By ten o'clock, the visitors have trailed off, the stalls are completely empty, and most of the villagers have taken their frozen toes and frostbitten fingers home for a warming cuppa.

The gingerbread house has elicited gasps of delight, promises to bring their children to see it at the weekend, and I can almost hear the internet groaning under the weight of the photos being posted. It *has* to be a good thing. It has to have made our voice loud enough to be heard over the clanging of money from apart-ment blocks or whatever the council are planning on doing with this beautiful space.

Joss is sitting on the front of the Dancing Cinnamon table and

I'm leaning over it from behind, trying to stretch out my lower back which is making it abundantly clear that I haven't been off my feet for the past fourteen hours, and if I stay still for much longer, I could easily fall asleep.

'What would you say if I had a plan?' Maybe I was half-asleep already because Joss's voice makes me jump in the quiet night. 'A not-totally-above-board plan? That might involve a bit of, ahem, covert persuasion of your mum and Mervyn?'

'I'd say your plans have been excellent until now, and I trust you in all your underhanded glory. I'm listening...'

He goes to speak, but Lynette bustles up before he has a chance. 'Oh, look at you two. You haven't stopped all day. Why don't you go for a wander, maybe steal a little of that mistletoe magic for yourselves?' Her pointed look leaves no doubt about exactly what she's implying, but I'm too tired to correct her, and Joss pushes himself off the table and holds out a hand to pull me upright.

'How d'you feel about breakfast?' he asks once we're out of earshot and wandering around the gardens. The weather has cleared and left a sky sparkling with stars and a crescent moon hiding behind the tops of distant trees.

'Well, it's not my favourite meal but still highly recommended. You need something to soak up the caffeine.'

He laughs. 'No, I meant making it. I'm thinking a romantic meal for two in the gingerbread house, with just the teeny tiny issue of not being allowed out until they've thought about their actions and made up. They're never going to get anywhere if they keep avoiding each other. Mervyn saw your mum earlier but was too nervous to speak to her. And when she saw him, she scarpered. They just need a little... nudge, and the only time it'll be unoccupied is before Santa arrives in the morning, so a romantic candlelit breakfast. We've just got to lure them both here at the same time. What do you think?'

'I think you're a genius, Joss Hallissey. Cupid should have you on his payroll,' I say smoothly to cover my surprise at *Joss* coming up with something so romantic. Joss who is the sworn enemy of all things love. A little bit of annoyance prickles at me too. He *is* a romantic at heart – he's just *too* determined not to let himself feel anything again. It connects to something I've thought a few times lately – Joss could be so happy here, if he'd just *let* himself.

The conversation slips into easy silence. The gentle sound of 'O Holy Night' fills the gardens from a speaker in the bandstand, and we're walking so close that if I tilted my head slightly, it would rest on his shoulder. For some inexplicable reason, he hasn't let go of my hand and I haven't let go of his. It has to mean something, doesn't it? Joss and I are *way* closer than just friends, I know that even if I don't want to admit it... does he know it too?

Something feels different tonight. I can feel something thrumming between us. Every inch of my body is alive and goosebumps are racing up my arm from the way his fingers are softly rubbing my hand. If Christmas magic was real, it feels like this would be the night it would make itself known.

'As sickeningly romantic as you imagined it?' It's an attempt to ease the tension and confront the awkwardness of wandering around the most romantic place in Wales with someone you're not actually romantic with.

'Worse, but somehow, I don't mind. I can see how people fall in love here – why so many make a point of coming every year. A way of reaffirming your love for each other and letting the other person know they're important enough *to* make that effort every year.'

'This is *exactly* why Mistletoe Gardens is so important to so many people. That's what I've been wanting you to see all along.' I knock my shoulder against his arm. 'You'll be telling me you like Christmas next.'

He fixes me with a piercing stare. '*Everything* about Christmas has been appealing lately.'

The happy dance inside me is cut off by a wolf-whistle from behind us and Lynette pointing frantically upwards. We're standing directly under the biggest cluster of mistletoe in the branches above our heads.

'We appear to have wandered into the path of some magic mistletoe.'

I expect him to yank me away faster than one of Santa's reindeer on a Christmas Eve flight, but he stops. 'Isn't it bad luck not to?'

'Yeah, but you don't—'

'What if I want to?' His tongue wets his lips and somehow I've turned around to face him, and my hand has fallen out of his. I reach up and brush my fingers through his hair, and his eyes drift closed.

Desire for him is pulling in me, warring with the practical side of things, like the 'for sale' sign outside his house. He hasn't said anything to suggest he *isn't* leaving, and I'm so attached to him in such a short space of time. I can't imagine never looking into his eyes again. Never running my fingers through his hair again. Never cwtching him again. Never getting to kiss him at all.

It's like I'm outside of us, looking on from afar, watching myself let something wonderful slip away because I'm not brave enough to admit how much I like him.

And I know I'll regret this moment for the rest of my life if I don't do *something*.

Somehow his arm has slid around my back and pulled me closer so our bodies are pressed against each other, and for the first time, I *really* believe in the magic of Mistletoe Gardens because I can feel the air zinging around me as our bodies move against each other's, burning heat in the chilly night, and everything about this moment feels right.

This is it. Every flirtatious smile has been leading up to this. Every lingering touch, every longing look. I didn't realise they'd been longing looks until this moment, but pure longing is what zips through every part of my body, and my fingertips curl into Joss's shoulder while my other hand brushes his hair back.

I don't remember closing my eyes, but my other senses take over. The gingery smell of his aftershave. The softness of his jumper where my hand has slid under his coat. The grabbable texture of his hair now most of the product has been washed out by the earlier rain. His forehead touches mine as his hand cups my face, his thumb stroking my jaw, the tip of his nose brushing against mine, his lips millimetres away. I can feel his every breath, and how each one matches the way I'm barely breathing. It's the kind of kiss I've always dreamed of happening to me under the mistletoe one day. And then...

He's gone.

He jumps back so quickly that he hits the tree trunk with such force, I'm surprised he doesn't leave a dent in it. He swears. 'I'm sorry. I'm so sorry.'

We blink at each other for a few moments, my brain still trying to catch up with the sudden shift in atmosphere.

'I'm sorry, I shouldn't have... I don't know what I was thinking. I *wasn't* thinking, not at all.' He flicks his head like he's trying to clear it.

I was leaning heavily on Joss and his sudden departure leaves me flailing on the damp grass, struggling for both balance *and* to get my head around what just happened.

'That was too close.' He's pacing back and forth across the tree roots now, annoyed with someone, although I'm not sure if it's me or himself.

'It's fine. I wanted to.'

'I *wanted* to, but I can't. I can't kiss you, Ess.'

'Why not?' The sudden switch has left me reeling. I'm still feeling unbalanced, and... annoyed. Annoyed that he would let things get that far and *then* pull back.

'Honestly? Really, truly, honestly?'

I nod.

'Because the moment I kiss you, I'm going to fall in love with you, and I can't do that. I can't do it again, Ess. I want to be alone. I *need* to be alone in this life.' He looks up and meets my eyes, and his are hard, cold, closed-off, and... scared.

'What if you don't?' I stutter, struggling to make sense of it.

He tries to respond, but scrubs a hand over his face when no words come out.

Anger takes over. 'Do you even realise what you just said? Don't tell me you're *going* to fall in love with me, so the solution is just *not* to kiss me. You can't say something like that, Joss!'

'You knew what you were getting in to,' he mutters. 'You *know* I'm messed up when it comes to relationships. Everyone told you to stay away from me, and *this* is why.'

I really don't think this is the *exact* reason they had in mind.

'I'm sorry. This has all got too much. We're too close. I never meant...'

'You never meant to let someone in again? You never meant to let your guard down? Or you never meant to let yourself live again?'

He stares at me for a few moments. 'All of the above. I'm sorry. Goodnight.'

I'm open-mouthed and staring after him as he stalks away.

How *dare* he? We've got so close and he's been so open with me. He *wanted* that tonight. And I wanted him to know how much I like him. I go to shout after him, but he's moved so fast that I'd need to scream, and making a public scene won't help matters. I direct a noise of frustration upwards towards the mistletoe and kick at an innocent tree root and then feel guilty and apologise to it. It's not the tree's fault, nor the mistletoe's. It's *our* fault. I knew better than to let myself fall for someone who wasn't open to a relationship, and Joss should've known better than to let himself get close to me when he knew there was no chance of anything *really* happening between us.

Anger gives way to sadness and acceptance.

Maybe he's right. We've been caught up in a bubble here. Spending every day and most evenings together. I can't get enough of Joss. And he *is* leaving. He's never pretended otherwise. It's *my* desire for him to stay that's convinced me there's a chance for us, but maybe I'm wrong.

Maybe he was right to stop it before it went any further.

I've always thought love was the most powerful emotion of all and that Christmas magic would overcome all obstacles, but maybe there's not enough magic in this mistletoe to heal all scars.

18

At the Ritz-Carlton in Arizona, there's a life-size gingerbread house that doubles as a restaurant and seats six people!

Joss thinks sunglasses will hide how sad his eyes are as we haul a table and two chairs from the back of his van the following morning. Neither of us have mentioned last night, but the air is tight between us and communication is limited to singular words.

I was half-expecting him not to turn up after what happened, but I should've known Joss isn't the kind of person to back out of a commitment because of something as trivial as a kiss, or more specifically, a *not*-kiss, and his van was waiting outside the bakery this morning, the usual tray of two coffees on the dashboard, like nothing's different.

In the gingerbread house, we put the table and chairs beside the tree, where there's plenty of room while Santa's throne is still waiting in the van, and he runs down to collect two festive breakfasts from the coffee shop, while I turn all the fairy lights on, and lay the table in the most romantic way possible, complete with fancy plates, festive table decorations, candles, nutcracker candlestick holders, and a framed school photograph to remind Mum and Mervyn of the good old days when they still tolerated each other.

'One last thing,' Joss says when he comes back with the food. He's taken the sunglasses off but he still won't look at me as he rests a ladder against a tree trunk, and goes up it until he can snip a chunk of mistletoe from the lowest bundle.

'You're not supposed to do that.' I watch him climb down, tie a loop of red ribbon around the stems and reach up to hang it from an icing rosette on the ceiling.

'Extenuating circumstances,' he says with a smile that doesn't reach his eyes.

It's by far the most words we've said to each other all morning.

The next phase of the plan is the hard part. I get out my phone and dial Mum's number. It's quarter past eight, she'll be getting ready for work by now anyway. I try to make my voice sound panicked when she answers.

'Mum! There's an emergency at the gingerbread house. I need your help. Can you come to Mistletoe Gardens *immediately*?' I hang up, purposely not staying on the line long enough for her to ask questions, and Joss makes the same phone call to Mervyn.

'Now we wait,' he mutters as he hangs up and pockets his phone. He goes down a couple of steps and sits, and the robin lands on the wall and starts chirping, but Joss ignores him.

'You aren't even going to talk to Rob?' I'm still standing in the bandstand, leaning on the railings, and trying not to look at the way he's sitting, his back hunched, his shoulders drooping.

'He's getting too attached to me. I'm leaving – he needs to stop relying on me.'

It's a thinly veiled insinuation. It's not *just* Rob he's talking about. 'What if he thinks you're worth relying on?'

'He'd be mistaken.' He fixes me with a hard look over his

shoulder, but when I meet his eyes, he blinks and softness crosses his face, and he looks away.

'Joss...' I start, but the gate rattles as Mervyn arrives and Joss darts over to open it.

'Oh, dear, dear,' Mervyn's muttering as he comes in. 'Whatever's happened now? It's been one thing after ano— oh, hello, Essie, I didn't realise you were here as well. What's going on?'

'Another little emergency.' Joss takes over smoothly. We hadn't planned any further than getting them both here, but luckily neither live far away, and the telltale clicking of heels on pavement saves us from having to stall for long.

'You know what, it'd be easier to show you.' Joss bundles Mervyn inside the house to hide him from Mum's sight as I go over to open the opposite gate and let her in.

'Haven't you had enough emergencies for one week?' Mum looks disappointed in me. 'Honestly, this thing is more trouble than it's worth if it's going to keep falling apart like this.'

Joss is pretending to show Mervyn something, hiding him behind the Christmas tree as Mum approaches the bandstand.

'Why've you got a candle burning in there? For goodness' sake, what are your nan's best Christmas plates doin—' Mum's marching up the bandstand steps, and the game's up as soon as Mervyn hears her voice.

As he starts questioning what's going on, I give Mum a gentle shove to get her inside the door at the exact same moment as Joss slips out, and between us we slam it shut, and pull a stack of bakery crates across the front to prevent them from opening it.

'The emergency was your breakfasts going cold!' I call in.

'It's the time of year for making up,' Joss adds. 'You two have known each other for years, you clearly care about each other, and there's a bunch of mistletoe in there that would like to know just how *much*. Neither of you are coming out until you've apologised and admitted that you're each other's long-lost mistletoe kiss!'

'You've got two options – you can either admit how you feel about each other, or you'll have to break the walls down, and I know neither of you are going to do that.' I seriously, seriously hope not, at least.

'He tried to destroy your gingerbread house!' Mum yells in indignation.

'Mervyn didn't do that,' Joss says. 'I don't know who did, but it's not his style.'

'I didn't, Bron.' Mervyn's agreement is muffled from behind the thick walls.

'He wants to bulldoze Mistletoe Gardens!' Mum shouts. I'm pretty sure I hear a foot stamp to go with it.

'I'm sure you could *persuade* him otherwise.' I waggle my eyebrows at Joss and then remember we're on not-really-speaking terms and I shouldn't be waggling *anything* in his direction.

'This looks like a jolly nice breakfast,' Mervyn says. 'It'd be a shame to waste it.'

There's a scrape of a chair being pulled out and I look at Joss again in glee. His eyes have lit up for the first time this morning. Until now, he's looked like he's lost the will to live. It doesn't take away the metaphorical elephant between us, but every time we glance at each other, for just a second, it's like last night didn't happen.

'We should give them some privacy,' I say, even though I want to eavesdrop more than anything.

He half-heartedly agrees and goes to stand on the grass underneath a tree – thankfully one without mistletoe in it. I have no intention of following him, but his eyes stay on me as I walk down the bandstand steps, and he inclines his head, inviting me over.

I'm still in two minds about last night. Half of me wants to yell at him for the mixed signals. He's let me think there was something between us, even though no matter what *is* between us, he wasn't ever going to let himself feel it, but the other half of me is excruciatingly embarrassed. Did I *really* misinterpret his signals so badly? Did I throw myself at him? He's been so open. So touchy-feely. He's let me into his house, his head, and I thought his heart too. But how did I think this was going to end? Joss is surrounded by walls that are too high for anyone to get over. I've always known that, I just wanted to believe otherwise. Just like with Paris. If I'm honest, I knew that would be a mistake before I went, but I wanted to believe otherwise. This whole thing is just another failure that *I* could've prevented by listening to reason.

I reluctantly go and stand next to him. Any other day, I'd have been itching to get a bit closer, for him to slip his arm around me, but today, I wish I could walk away and pretend last night was nothing but a bad dream.

'Hi,' he says carefully, like it's the first time we've spoken all morning.

'Hello.' I give him a polite nod. It feels weird and wrong and so very awkward. I should *never* have ventured anywhere near that mistletoe last night.

His hand creeps over until his little finger brushes against the back of mine. 'Ess, I'm sor—'

'Excuse me?' A well-dressed man carrying a briefcase is striding towards us. Mistletoe Gardens isn't supposed to be open to the public yet, but I never went back and locked the gate after Mum came in. 'Are you the creators of this masterpiece?'

He looks towards the gingerbread house, and I wonder what he'd think if he knew we've currently got two people trapped inside it.

'We are,' Joss confirms.

'Delightful work. Can't stop thinking about it, and more

importantly, my customers can't stop talking about it. Wife's gonna bring the kiddos at the weekend. Proposition for you – I run the Presto Hotel Group, and I want one of these in my lobby next Christmas. Actually, in *all* of my lobbies. We have fourteen hotels across the South Wales area, employ our own Santa every year and run our own winter wonderland in every hotel, and this is exactly the sort of thing that would give our guests that money-can't-buy magical experience. Except money *can* buy, obviously, ho ho.' He whisks two business cards out of his suit pocket and hands us one each. 'I'd like to employ you to build one of these in each of my hotel branches next Christmas – team of chefs at your disposal and plenty of staff to help. And in our flagship Cardiff branch... Do you think you could do one for Easter? All the pastel colours and fluffy chicks and patterned eggs, home for the Easter Bunny – also on the payroll, spends every Easter weekend with us, keeps the children amused with egg hunts and crafting while parents relax and enjoy our facilities. An Easter-themed ginger-bread house would be a massive draw.'

My mind is flooded with images of an Easter gingerbread house. Egg-shaped biscuits decorated in lemon, baby blue, and lilac patterns, delicate chicks, supersized chocolate-cornflake nests with Cadbury's Mini Eggs in them instead of gumdrops on the roof, gingerbread bunnies dotted around, swirls of pastel icing finished with speckled chocolate eggs instead of peppermint sweets. Excitement dances inside me like my veins are running with fizzy pop bubbles. 'Oh, my gosh, yes! We'd love t—' I stop myself. I'm forgetting that Joss and I aren't a 'we'. I can't speak for both of us.

I look at him and his face is alight with joy. I *know* he's picturing Easter substitutions in place of festive ones, like I am. And the possibilities. Building this has tapped into my creative side and shown me what's been missing from my life. This is the sort of thing I wish I could do more of, but can't because of the limitations of Dancing Cinnamon. Being employed to make something like this on a regular basis makes life seem limitless.

'I honestly believe there's no end to the magic we can create,' the hotelier continues. 'After Easter, maybe something for the summer too – a tropical, biscuity, summer house? I don't know, you're the experts, but I'd be overjoyed to discuss all possibilities with you both in the new year. I'm really excited about this and what it could bring to our hotels.'

Joss is grinning down at the business card in his hand, smiling so widely that his jaw must be aching. He looks up and meets my eyes, and... his face falls. His smile is replaced by a hard line and his forehead creases with a frown.

'I can't. I won't be available next year.' He hands the business card back to the businessman. 'I'm sure Essie would be willing to do it again with a different builder, but I won't be involved. I'm sorry.'

'Oh.' The hotelier looks as surprised as I am. 'Well, that is a shame. Never mind, though, I'm sure we can work something out.' He pulls a pen from his suit pocket and writes something on the business card, and then hands the second one to me as well. 'This is my direct line. I'll look forward to a discussion with you in January. Please do ring as soon as you can, I'd like to get contracts in place early so we all know where we stand and have ample time to plan. Thank you for your time, I must dash.' He stops to look up at the gingerbread house as he walks away, shaking his head in wonder. 'Marvellous. Simply marvellous.'

I stare after him, but I'm numb with shock. All the fizzing joy has gone flat. Getting to build life-size gingerbread houses for the next year is more than I'd ever dreamed of, but the thought of doing it without Joss takes away every ounce of excitement and makes it seem daunting rather than fun. The words on the card blur in front of my eyes. I'm holding an open invitation from one of the best-known hotel firms in Wales. This is spectacular, and suddenly, it feels grim and disappointing.

Joss is silent. He looks downtrodden and defeated.

'You can't honestly think I could do this without you?' I stutter out eventually, my voice sounding hoarse and unsteady.

'Builders are a dime a dozen. And now people have seen this, you won't have so much ridicule in trying to find anoth—'

'Joss, this house is special because of *you*. You're not replaceable. You believed in me when I really needed it.'

'When any builder sees this, they'll believe in you too.'

'You believed without seeing. That's the point. That's what Christmas is all about. Believing in magic without seeing it. Like Santa. Christmas wouldn't be Christmas if children didn't believe in the impossible – in something they've never seen.'

'You're not Santa and I'm not a child.'

'You know what I mean. You're the only person who believed we could do this, no matter how impossible it seemed. I don't want to do it again with someone else – I want to do it with *you*.'

'I won't be here, Ess. You know that.'

The hand holding the business card feels disconnected, like it doesn't really belong to me, and Joss is pacing, his hands shoved into his pockets, and it's all just too much, and I finally snap. 'Joss, stop. For one freaking second, will you take off your mask?'

'I'm not—'

'Yes, you are, and we both know it. I know what you've been through, but you can't stop life hurting you by never connecting with another human being ever again. You push people away rather than let them in. You're the loveliest guy in the world, but you pretend to be horrible in case anyone dares to like you. You have an opportunity here – we both do. A chance to do something that matters. A chance to take your father's company in the direction *you* want it to go in.'

'I never wanted to turn it into a bakery.'

I frown at him for being deliberately obtuse. 'Pretending not to understand what I mean doesn't stop you hearing it. *We* have loved doing this. This has been the best December ever for me, and no matter how much you growl and grunt, I *know* you've loved it too. From the very beginning, you've told me that this creative, small-scale work is what appeals to you, and I've watched it make you come alive. You don't want to go and live on an isolated island somewhere – you just think it's the best way to protect yourself. And don't get me started on doing a remote-based paperworky job. That's the furthest thing from you, Joss.'

'Exactly tha—'

'No! Not "exactly that". All that stuff didn't happen because you're *you*, it happened because life is cruel and it's rubbish sometimes, but there are bright moments too, and those are the ones you cling onto with both hands – not run away from in case they end up going wrong.'

'Essie...'

'No, you need to hear this. You're happy and you're turning your back on that "just in case" it doesn't last. Yes, things suck. Yes, people die, or get horrible illnesses. Yes, people cheat, but sometimes they don't. Sometimes you meet the *right* people and they fall in bloody love with you, and—'

He cuts me off with such a surprise kiss that I stumble backwards and his arms encircle my body, holding me upright.

'What are you...' The sentence is garbled against his mouth, and somewhere in the depths of my spinning mind, I think I should be pushing him off and giving him a smack for good measure, but I also know how hurt he's been. I know what he said last night, and I know how much he's been holding back and how much it means for him to let himself kiss me, and I'm incapable of doing anything other than melting against him, because Joss has just given himself permission to fall in love.

It's too late for me. I've been slowly falling in love with him since the moment I looked into his eyes in the debris-ridden swimming baths lobby all those weeks ago, but I've been holding back, knowing he's leaving, knowing he's too guarded to let himself go, but this kiss is the one that lets everything go.

My hand is in his hair, gripping it tightly in my fingers as our mouths explore each other's, desperately grasping and clinging on, and I feel myself going light-headed, overwhelmed by the kiss that's been desperate to break loose for weeks.

His hand is on my lower back, the other somehow managing to support my neck and stroke my hair at the same time, and mine is under his jacket, running up and down his chest, and happiness takes over, and everything feels right with the world again.

He pulls back slightly, just enough to let me know it's about an immediate need to breathe and not because he wants to end the kiss, and I gulp in air too, my forehead pressed against his, my fingers shaking from how tightly they're curled into Joss's hair and T-shirt, and I'm not sure if I'm laughing or crying, and it's all too much after the warring emotions since last night, too many ups and downs and near misses and almost kisses. In a park full of mistletoe, we've somehow managed to kiss under the *one* tree without mistletoe in it, and I can feel Joss being engulfed by the same emotions, can feel him trying to get shaky breaths under control, and I force myself to loosen my grip, smooth down his T-shirt and stroke his hair gently rather than trying to tear it out. I've always thought that if I ever kissed him, it would be a one-time thing and I'd have to get *all* the kiss out in one desperate, clawing, clutching go, and I have to give myself a shaky pep talk. This isn't a one-off. This is the first of many kisses. It *has* to be.

When Joss's lips touch mine again, it's soft, gentle, and cautious. Careful and teasing in the fun way, a chance to recover my breath, to appreciate the delicious burn of his stubble, and he lets out that happy sigh that I last heard when he fell asleep in my arms, and I make a noise of contentment at how *right* it feels.

His arms grow tighter and mine run over more of his body, exploring, making him shiver as I caress the back of his neck, and somehow our lips leave each other's long enough for my arms to sneak around his neck and pull him into a hug as he trails kisses across my jaw, and then lets himself be held. His hands slide across my back, lifting me up, squeezing me to him, and my lips find his cheek and press a kiss to his cheekbone, and that's it.

I can *feel* the moment his walls crumble because it's like a physical weight leaves him. His legs give out and suddenly I'm straddling him on the grass, my hand is in his hair, protecting his head from banging against tree roots as we dive back into the kiss from our now horizontal position.

When we pull back, gasping for air, I shakily sit back on my knees, my legs on either side of his body where he's lying on the ground and he blinks up at me with a dazed look in his eyes and a dopey grin that gets wider with every second.

'Holy mistletoe,' I murmur, feeling fizzy and fluttery and like I've downed a couple of bottles of the world's most expensive champagne. 'What are you playing at? After last night...'

'You deserve better than me. And I want to *be* better than me, so I'm trying to do the opposite of what I would've done before I met you, in the hopes I can somehow be the person you deserve. Does that make sense?'

'No! Not even slightly!'

He laughs and lifts a hand to rub his eyes, stopping to tuck my hair back as he drops it again. 'After *that*, my brain is too scrambled for coherent sentences.'

I know how he feels.

'I've been alone for a long time, even while I was married – *you've* made me see that. You've made me realise I don't have to face everything alone. You've shown me what it's like when someone really, truly cares about someone else, and I'm not ready to give that up. That night I told you about my mum... I always thought it was a weakness, but telling you made me feel stronger. I don't want to go back to the withdrawn and growly person I was before you burst into my world.'

He drops his head back into my hand that's still between his skull and the tree root. 'I'm sorry about last night. I didn't mean to lead you on. I wanted to kiss you so badly, but when it came to it, there were too many feelings and I ran away rather than facing them head-on, and...'

'Okay, enough talking.' I slide the other hand into his hair and push his head back until I can kiss him again.

Both our chests are heaving when we pull back this time, the sky has brightened into daylight, and if anyone walked past and caught sight of us in this position, they would *not* assume that kissing was *all* we've been up to.

I stroke his face, and let my fingers trace his jaw, still trying to get my head around this turn of events and the rollercoaster of emotions since last night.

'So this means you're going to—' I don't get a chance to ask him if he's planning to stay in Folkhornton because the sound of banging filters through the haze of oxygen deprivation. 'We forgot Mum and Mervyn.'

'I don't think they'll mind having a little bit longer.' He surges up to fit his mouth against mine again and it's so easy to lose myself in him, his aftershave, his touch...

'Essie!' There's a shriek from the gingerbread house. A seriously loud shriek.

Joss groans. 'How long do you think we've got before they start trying to eat their way out?'

'Essie!' Mum's shriek is louder this time, and it sounds distressed rather than angry.

'Something's wrong.' I scramble off Joss and hold a hand out to pull him up. 'That's not angry shouting, that's panicked shouting.'

My phone rings and Mum's name is on the screen.

'All right, all right, we're coming,' I say as I answer it one-handed.

'Stop doing that! I can see you through the windows!' she yells into the handset. 'Don't kiss him! I will break this boiled-sweet glass if I have to – don't think I won't!'

We race up the bandstand steps, trying to work out what's gone wrong. Have they had another row? Has there been a medical emergency? Has Mervyn tried something untoward and had his fingers, or *worse*, bitten off?

At the sound of the bakery crate blockade being moved, Mum starts screeching from inside again. 'Get us out of here right now!' She sounds like the most spoilt of celebrities in a jungle with Ant and Dec on standby.

She storms out like a dragon on fire, nearly tearing the door off its hinges in her wake. I peer inside warily, but Mervyn is sitting at the table with his head in his hands. He looks unscathed and there's no sign of blood anywhere. 'What happened?'

'Nothing happened in there, but quite a flaming lot happened out here! Someone's got some explaining to do!'

'It was just a joke. We didn't think you'd mind, Mrs Browne,' Joss says.

She whirls around and brandishes her fist at him. '*You*! You despicable swine! Taking advantage of my daughter like that!'

'It's all right, Mum, I wanted to kiss him. He wasn't doing anything wrong.'

'*He* has been doing something wrong since the moment you met him!' She turns back to me and the fury on her face melts into something like pity. 'You're a silly girl, Essie. A silly, silly girl. You get so caught up in romance and Christmas magic that you fail to see what's right in front of you.'

'What are you talking about?' I go to take a step nearer to Joss, ready to defend him if she's going to say he isn't good enough for me or mention him leaving, but her hand closes around my wrist.

'Come away from him.' She pulls me down the steps like I'm a toddler having a tantrum in the crisp aisle. 'He isn't what you think he is.'

'What?' I say.

'What?' Joss says.

From inside the gingerbread house, Mervyn groans.

'I've told you he was untrustworthy from day one,' Mum barks as I try to wriggle my wrist out of her grasp. She's going to put me in one of those anti-pull harnesses that you buy for naughty puppies in a minute.

'No, you haven't, you tried to set me up with him at one point.'

'That was before! Before I got a sense of his true colours. He's certainly got you fooled. Everyone in this town has fallen head-over-heels for his act, but he hasn't pulled the wool over my eyes, no siree!'

Joss pinches the bridge of his nose and makes a noise of... distress? Or... understanding?

Please don't be understanding.

I swallow hard, despite the fact my mouth has gone bone dry. I look between the two of them helplessly. 'What the hell is going on here?'

Mum finally takes pity on my cluelessness. 'Mervyn's just told me some very interesting information,' she says to me and then fixes her eyes on Joss. 'Maybe you could do us the honour of being honest too, Mr Hallissey.'

Joss's face has flared red and his eyes don't lift from the ground. 'I don't know what you're talking about.'

A sinking feeling washes over me from head to toe. Someone who doesn't know what she's talking about wouldn't look *that* guilty.

Mum's lip curls and she practically hisses at him. 'Are you going to tell her or am I?'

That has got to be one of the worst sentences in the English language. It implies that not only is there something awful to be told, but that you're one of the last people to know what it is.

Joss goes to speak, but nothing comes out.

'I'll help you out, Mr Hallissey, seeing as honesty isn't your strong point. Why don't you start by telling Essie *exactly* which contractor has been hired to tear down Mistletoe Gardens?'

19

Gingerbread was once a status symbol. When spices were prohibitively expensive, serving up lavishly spiced gingerbread was seen as a way of demonstrating wealth and affluence.

The whole world falls in on itself.

There are tears in my eyes before I've had a chance to process the sentence. 'You?' I splutter out. It would have been indecipherable had it been more than one word.

'No,' Joss says. 'No, no, no, no, no. Not in that way.'

This time, I *know* he's lying. 'You?' I demand again.

He lets out a long sigh. 'Yes. Me. But things have changed. It isn't as bad as it sounds. I'm not still going to do it, obviously.'

I take a step backwards like hearing that simple 'yes' was a physical blow. It's too much to process. 'The people who are tearing down Mistletoe Gardens are Hallissey Construction?'

His silence is an answer in itself.

'But you've helped,' I say more to myself than to him, feeling lost in a swirling sea of thoughts that don't make sense. 'You even got your lads to help. Why would you do that? Why would you do all this? Why would you help us save Mistletoe Gardens when you knew we were trying to save it *from* you?'

'I don't know.' He shoves his hands into his pockets without looking at me. 'I wasn't going to get involved.'

'Involved?' I've clearly inherited my mother's screechiness without realising it.

'I didn't think it would do any harm. I was just going to give you a bit of advice, but then I got here and measured up and I wanted to carry on. And you, Essie. God, *you*. With every gingerbread brick we've put up, you've pulled bricks out of *my* walls. I've fallen for you more every day. Do you honestly think I meant for this to happen?'

'I don't know what you did or didn't mean. How can anything you've said be true? You *don't* want to save the thing we're trying to save – you *are* the thing that's going to destroy it.'

'I wanted to tell you – I just didn't know how. I've been wanting to get out of doing the job, but I needed to make sure my lads would be okay when the company was sold.'

'The "one last job".' I suddenly realise what he means and it makes it even worse somehow. 'The "one last job" you've talked about having in January. *This* is what that is?'

He doesn't give so much as a nod, but he doesn't need to.

I scoff at myself, annoyed at my own stupidity. 'You've told me about it without actually telling me. How can you have sat there and talked about this important job you had coming up *without* mentioning it was to tear down Mistletoe Gardens?' I shake my head at myself, at him, at anyone. It seems like a moment for head shaking. '*What* were you thinking? What *are* you thinking? How did you think I wouldn't find out? How could you say everything you've just said while knowing that *you* are the one who's destroying what we're trying to save?'

'I hated this town, Essie. I didn't care. I didn't understand that

Mistletoe Gardens was important to people. Since I took over Hallissey Construction, I've done every job that was asked of me without stopping to think about anything other than the paycheque at the end. *You've* changed that. You've made me care again. You've made me want to do work that matters to people.'

'This gingerbread house matters to me. I thought it mattered to you as well.'

'It does.'

'Right, so will you personally be driving the JCB that pulls it down in January, some sort of sadistic satisfaction like a gingerbread-scented game of Jenga when it topples, or will you keep an emotional distance by delegating that job to one of your lads?'

'I told you Hallissey Construction is being absorbed by a larger company. The housing firm who are putting in the apartment blocks. To sell my company and ensure my lads have jobs to go back to, I have to do this.'

'Oh, it just gets better. Not only are you tearing down Mistletoe Gardens, you're cosying up with the people who are putting up soulless tower blocks on top of it.'

'I'll be gone by then.'

'Oh, that's okay then. Wash your hands of all responsibility? This has been nothing but a game to you? Playing with gingerbread to amuse yourself while business was slow in December?'

'No, of course not.'

I don't know when Mum let go of my wrist, but I have full control of both arms again, and while I'd quite like to use them to punch Joss, I force myself to turn away and take deep breaths. My voice hasn't lowered since the revelation, and outside the hedge surrounding Mistletoe Gardens, the first shoppers are starting to venture into town. There's no way *everyone* isn't going to know about this before the clock on the town hall strikes ten anyway – I don't need anyone getting a head start on the gossip.

Joss is still in the bandstand and I'm at the bottom of the steps, looking up at him. 'You knew from the very beginning? From that day in the swimming baths? Why the hell didn't you say, "You know what, I can't help you because actually there's a conflict of interests here. Goodbye, good luck"?'

'Because I liked you. You're... magnetic. I couldn't stop thinking about you. I came into the bakery the next day and I was going to tell you that bricks were what you needed, but then I'd agreed to help before I realised what was happening. I thought we'd meet in the park, I'd give you some measurements and that would be that, no further involvement, and then... there was that magnetism again. I couldn't tear myself away. And I meant what I said.' He gestures to the gingerbread house. 'This small-scale creative work is my favourite thing in the world. I loved every minute – because of it *and* because of you.'

'This is the most ridiculous thing I've ever heard. Two minutes ago, I was kissing you. We were ecstatically happy.' My voice is rising again and I force myself to suck in a breath. 'Talk about keeping your enemies close. I suppose Mistletoe Gardens is just another thing the council wants removed without anyone knowing about it? Just another "legitimate employment" for Mervyn's favourite lapdog?'

Mervyn's appeared in the doorway of the gingerbread house, and he holds his hands up like he doesn't want to be dragged into it.

'I'm sorry.' Joss's jaw clenches. 'This was never meant to go as far as it did. Essie, I'm not going to take this job. I'm on your side now.'

I laugh so sharply that I set my own teeth on edge. 'This isn't about the job *now*. It's about the fact you haven't been honest since the moment we met. The only true thing you've said to me is on that first day when you said you didn't care if they buried Mistletoe Gardens. Or, more specifically, if *you* buried it.'

'Ess, that's not...' He trails off, probably unable to finish any sentence that isn't a total falsehood.

I expect there to be a satisfied look on Mum's face, but she looks pained, and a queue is forming outside the gate, children waiting to see Santa, who will undoubtedly be along any minute, and you can't argue in front of Santa, can you?

'When she said you were going to break my heart, I didn't think it would be because of something so two-faced or deceitful. It's everything I thought you *weren't*, Joseph Hallissey.'

I know the name will sting him, and that's exactly what I want.

'Maybe we should go,' Mum says gently.

'Yeah, I think that's a really good idea.'

Mum's got her arm around my shoulders as we dodge past the queue of excited children, and run headfirst into Santa, who's got his hands on his belly and is doing a 'ho ho ho' and waving to everyone he passes as he strides jollily towards the gardens.

'Good morning, ladies. Ho, ho, ho!'

'Oh, piss off!' I snap at him, and then feel ridiculously guilty at the gobsmacked look on his face.

I told Santa to piss off. Has there ever been a worse Christmas than that?

20

In the fourteenth century, people believed that eating ginger-bread in the shape of letters would improve their intelligence.

Nutcrackers make everything better, which is why I'm in the bakery kitchen the next day, making two of them out of Rice Krispies and marshmallow. Generally, you don't need to over-mix puffed rice cereal and marshmallow for it to hold its shape, but this particular mixture is the bakery equivalent of a punching bag.

Saff has given me a hug and left me to it, but Mum stands in the doorway, looking on. 'I don't even want to know what you're doing.'

'I'm making two giant nutcrackers – one for either side of the gingerbread house door to give it that extra "wow factor". I've got a ton of leftover Rice Krispies and marshmallows from making the gumdrops, I may as well use them, and then fondant icing can give them their colours and features.'

I'm huffing and puffing over the worktop, growling occasion-ally when thoughts of Joss enter my head every zero-point-two of a second. There's a huge bowl rolling around in front of me, and

I'm up to my elbows in a mixture of cereal and marshmallow. I must look *more* than marginally deranged, and before long the cereal is going to be less 'puffed rice' and more 'powdered rice' as I knead it like I'm wringing someone's neck.

'It's a good job no one's going to be eating that, it'll be as tough as old boots.'

'That's not the point. The point is...' All right, I don't actually know what the point is, but two life-size edible nutcrackers will make a good photo opportunity and I have to do *something*. I'm not giving up on Mistletoe Gardens because of Joss. In fact, I'm even more determined to make the council see things from the residents' point of view now. 'The point is for there to be something at the gingerbread house that Joss isn't involved in. Something that isn't touched by his lies. He touched my heart and a part of my soul that I haven't let go for a very long time and now that feels tainted too.'

I've got a couple of wooden blocks as a base with dowels in them to hold each of the nutcracker's legs straight, and I take a handful of mixture and start moulding it around both dowels.

It's five days before Christmas, it's not like we have any orders until the inevitable rush of catering for New Year's parties next week. Most people have finished their Christmas shopping so town is quiet, and Mistletoe Gardens is bustling with people looking around the gingerbread house, visiting Santa, buying goods, and stopping to kiss their loved ones under definitely-*not*-magical mistletoe. So I'm told, anyway. I haven't been brave enough to venture up there in case Joss is around. Not that I think he will be. Now the truth is out, he has no reason to carry on this ridiculous ruse.

'You were right.' I slap another handful of sticky marshmallow mixture on and use my hands to mould it into a vague figure-eight shape that will be built up until it becomes his legs.

'I'm sorry, Essie, I know it wasn't what you wanted to hear.'

'Just another failure, isn't it? Another place in my life where I should have listened to you. Another thing you told me would go wrong, and lo and behold, it did.'

'You did something amazing with that gingerbread house. *Both* of you. It was an ambitious project and I've got to admit I didn't think you could do it, but you've proved me totally wrong. I should have believed in you from the start.'

I'm trying to find a way of saying that this is about Joss, not the gingerbread house, when Mum pushes herself off the doorframe and walks across the kitchen to stand on the opposite side of the unit. 'But I know this is about much more than that.'

My eyes are welling up *again* and I have to bite the inside of my lip to stop it wobbling.

'You really liked him.' She doesn't phrase it as a question.

I nod because I'm going to cry if I speak.

She seems softer today. With bare feet instead of her trademark heels and her face free of pristine make-up, she's almost like the mum I remember from when I was little, before my dad died and she filled her life with fighting the fights of Folkhornton residents.

'Why?' I say, feeling the familiar despondency set in. 'Why did you see it when I didn't?'

'I didn't, Ess. I wanted to see you two together at first – it was only when I heard about his plans to move away that I tried to dissuade you from getting any closer. I didn't want you to fall for *another* man who's not staying in Folkhornton. I couldn't bear a repeat of last time.'

'Last time? With France?' I tilt my head as I think about it. 'You thought I was going to leave *with* Joss?'

'After last time… I don't want to lose you again, and if you got close to someone who was leaving, I thought you might too.' She focuses on a mark on the unit instead of looking at me.

'Mum.' Now I'm nearly crying for a different reason. 'Paris was the worst time of my life. I was so homesick that it was like a physical pain. No one should be *that* unhappy in such a beautiful city, but I was, because there's nowhere I love more in the world than this daft little Welsh town with its gossiping residents and cranky crochet creations and dinosaur suits, and you and Saff. I feel like I've only just got back – the *last* thing I want to do is go anywhere else. Joss was... *is*... leaving to get away from everyone and everything about this place. I love everyone and everything about this place. There was never any question of me going with him. I don't even want to leave Folkhornton long enough for a holiday at this point.'

'Really?'

'Really. Is that *really* what your dislike of Joss has been about?'

She nods. It's such a rare thing for my mum to be on mute.

'I knew it didn't make sense. I knew you'd usually have been all over him as a potential match. It only changed when you found out he was leaving.'

'I wanted you to meet someone local. I thought if you met someone here and settled down with a nice homely chap, you wouldn't have any reason to go anywhere.'

'That's what the dating desperation has been about?' I make a noise of frustration. 'Mum, why didn't you just say? I don't want to date anyone – from here, there, or anywhere. I wanted to be on my own for a while and get back on my feet. I didn't mean to feel anything for Joss, it just happened.'

'He gave you what we all should have given you from the start – support.'

'You've never believed in me,' I say quietly, trying to focus on squeezing and smooshing the nutcracker's legs into shape rather than overthink what I've needed to say for a while. 'You don't want me to leave, but you give me no responsibility with the bakery. You don't listen to my ideas. You think I'm going to fail at everything.'

'I think your ideas are often too big for a small town like this.' She sounds like she's been expecting this conversation for a long while too. 'Or needless, like introducing vegan or gluten-free options when most of our customers are perfectly happy with things as they are.'

'Like a life-size gingerbread house? Like two five-foot-tall nutcrackers? And maybe some customers are happy, but maybe some people never come in here because Dancing Cinnamon is so set in its ways that we don't cater for their dietary needs.' I round the top of the nutcracker's legs and start piling on Rice Krispie mixture for the wider torso. Things can't get much worse than what happened with Joss – I may as well confront the other problems in my life too. In for a penny and all that. 'And it's not just that. I want to be able to do more things like this. Things that are big. Things that matter. Things that make people gasp in awe. Things that get people talking. Things for a good cause. I feel like sometimes you don't want to be here, you'd rather be doing resident committee work, and that's fine because I'm here to pick up the slack, but it doesn't work both ways. You do nothing but complain if I ask you to cover for me so I can go and do other things. I've worked here since I was ten years old. I love it, but I don't want this to be the only thing I do for the rest of my life. I want to do something outside of Folkhornton without leaving Folkhornton.'

'The internet again?'

'I don't know. But there's a market for big pieces like this to be commissioned. It wouldn't be a full-time job, but I don't want to keep working until three o'clock in the morning, doing batch after batch of the same thing, over and over again until I die.'

'Okay.'

'Okay?' I blink in surprise, my hands stuck in a very unbecoming position in what will be the nutcracker's crotch area. 'Okay to what?'

'You're right. You've more than proved you're capable of everything I throw at you *and* anything you dream up yourself. Maybe it *is* time I stepped back a little and gave more responsibility to you and Saff. Do you think we need extra staff?'

'The only time we haven't been chasing our tails lately is when our neighbours helped us out on Friday. Yes, we need more staff!'

'I'm not eavesdropping, but I agree!' Saff calls from the shop floor.

I look at Mum and we both burst out laughing.

'There's something else.' For the first time since Saturday morning, I think of the two business cards that are on the table inside the door in the flat, silently preparing me to pluck up the courage to pick up the phone in January. 'Joss and I were offered a contract to build gingerbread houses in all Presto Hotel Group lobbies.' I tell her about the idea of Easter and summer gingerbread houses too. 'At first I couldn't contemplate it without Joss, but doing this...' I use my fingers to carve out a groove in the nutcracker's torso where his candyfloss beard will go. 'I love it. It brings me to life. I want to do it. Even if it's just me.'

She's quiet for so long that she might be getting ready to explode, and I duck behind the Rice Krispie nutcracker, using it as a shield.

'The Easter one should be shortbread. Much more fitting for springtime.'

Just when I think I can't cry any more, my eyes fill up again. 'You'd be okay with that?'

'Make sure they put up a sign advertising Dancing Cinnamon so we can benefit from the exposure as well, but yes. Of course. If it's what you want to do, I'm behind you all the way. I've tried to pile responsibility on you here so you'd see how much I need you, but seeing you in Mistletoe Gardens with Joss… I'm pushing you away by not supporting your vision for the bakery and expecting you to blindly carry on as I did when I took over from your nan.'

'I just want some recognition that I'm a valid part of the team here, not just a dogsbody when you don't fancy doing three hundred millionaire's shortbreads in an hour.'

'I actually like the mindless batches of biscuit after biscuit. It's a bit of quiet time. I like to get away from being the resident leader once in a while. It's too much sometimes.'

My mum is human under her perfectly poised demeanour. I go around the worktop and give her a hug while keeping my sticky, marshmallowy hands out of the way.

'Come on then.' I've never seen my mum cry before, but she's patting her eyes as she pulls away. 'Let's get these nutcrackers made. If you want my help, that is.'

'I'd love it.'

Maybe some good can come out of this. Maybe a new understanding between me and my mum. Even if she drives me barmy sometimes, Joss's situation with his mum has made me realise that one day, it might be too late to tell her how much I love her.

She's not usually a very hands-on baker, but she washes her hands and then plunges them straight into the sticky mixture. She starts on the legs of the second nutcracker while I round off the torso of the first one and start forming the head.

I nudge my arm into hers as I knead another batch of the mixture. 'How did your date with Mervyn go?'

'It was… nice. I wanted to be angry at you two for tricking us, but once he got me to sit down and start eating, I forgot all about it and enjoyed the time with nothing else on the agenda. Usually Mervyn and I have business meetings, there's always something to discuss, usually something we disagree on, but this time, it was nice just to catch up and talk about each other's lives.'

'Are you going to do it again sometime?' I waggle my eyebrows.

'I don't know. It's a bit awkward, isn't it?'

'At least he was honest. If he hadn't told you, when would I have found out about Joss? When the first JCB pitched up in January?'

'He could've told us weeks ago and none of this would have happened.'

'He probably didn't think it was his place.' Look at me, defending Mervyn Prichard. Never a stranger thing has happened. 'I think he was good friends with Joss's father and he looks out for Joss now. He was probably walking a thin line between that and letting the secret slip.'

'Hmm.' She thinks it over. 'I've promised to save a waltz for him at the Mistletoe Dance, but I'm not sure if I should now. And what about Mistletoe Gardens? I don't want to tango with someone who's going to destroy a place that means so much to our family and this town.'

'Mervyn's not solely responsible. It's the whole council who make the decisions, he's just the frontman for this area. He might not always behave the way you want him to, but I think he's a decent man at heart. He deserves a chance. And he likes you. You kissed him once.'

'Many moons ago.' Mum's cheeks have gone a shade of red that I've never seen before given that her skin is usually hidden underneath porcelain-like foundation. 'I know what will cheer you up!' she exclaims, trying to change the subject. 'How about a date for the Mistletoe Dance?'

'Oh my God, will you stop? It's not funny now. No more. Cancel that subscription to the dating site because I never was interested and now I'm even less interested.'

'It might make you feel better to walk in with a gorgeous man on your arm.'

'Okay, firstly, I'm not going. Secondly, I'm not going. And thirdly, there are escort services for that, which is irrelevant because, oh yes, I'm not going.'

'Essie! You can't miss the Mistletoe Dance!'

'I agree!' Saff shouts. 'Still not eavesdropping, mind.'

'I'm not in a very Mistletoe Dance-y mood.'

'I need you there. You're my wingwoman with Mervyn. I haven't dated in decades. I don't know what to do.'

'Just be yourself. You haven't scared him off yet and he's been on the spiky end of your dragon tongue many times. Besides, I'm not the right person to ask. We've proved once and for all that I know *nothing* about relationships.'

'You bought your dress months ago!' Saff calls through. 'You can't let it sit in its garment bag unworn.'

'It'll still be there next year. Maybe I'll have got over Joss by then and feel like celebrating Christmas. For this year, I'm going to hibernate until January, maybe catch up on my to-read list and my Netflix watch list.'

Both of them fall silent. At the moment, it feels like I won't ever get over Joss, and no amount of reading, watching, and hiding in the flat will change that.

'Santa will be there, you owe him an apology,' Mum says.

'Oh, God, did you have to remind me? I can't believe I told Santa to piss off. Talk about putting myself on the naughty list.'

'At least you didn't tell him to insert his "ho ho ho" into any unpleasant orifices!' Saff calls. Hopefully not in front of any customers.

'I'll do a reconnaissance mission beforehand to make sure *he* isn't there.'

Oh, great, I hadn't even thought of that. The possibility of Joss being there makes it an even less appealing prospect.

Mum watches my face fall. 'He's never come to one before, it's not like he's going to start now after all that's happened between you.'

'It's not just that. Everyone knows.'

'Not everyone.' She clearly means *everyone* including their dog, their cat, their uncle, and the Koi carp in their great-aunt's garden pond.

'You didn't do anything wrong, Essie, he did. This was on him, not you.'

'I trusted him. I let myself fall head-over-heels for him.' My emotions are hanging on by a thread today and as I punch, push, and pull Rice Krispie cake mixture into a vague top-hat shape for the nutcracker's headdress, I feel the familiar sting of tears yet again. 'I want to wallow. I don't want to pretend to be happy and festive. I've done enough Christmassing this year.'

Saff appears in the doorway. 'There's a rumour going around that Mr Arkins is going to take his dino costume off.'

'No way. It'd be a cold day in hell before that happens.'

'Isn't that worth it? Don't you want to go just a teeny little bit for the prospect of our favourite dinosaur being unmasked?'

'Never going to happen.' I roll out red fondant icing for the nutcracker's jacket. 'Not the dino unmasking, and definitely not me going to the Mistletoe Dance. End of story.'

21

In the times before paper was widely available, important news
was shared on slabs of gingerbread.

I'm *not* going to the Mistletoe Dance, but somehow Saff's done my
make-up, Mum's done my hair, and I've ended up in my 1950s
Audrey Hepburn-style deep green dress.

Once the five-foot-tall nutcrackers were finished on Monday,
with fondant eyes, teeth, and moustaches, a Toblerone lever on
the back, liquorice whirls for buttons on their jackets, and edible
gold decorations on their fondant-black boots, I didn't want to
run into Joss at Mistletoe Gardens, so Mum and Saff took them
up to the gingerbread house in exchange for me agreeing to
deliver the buffet food to the town hall before the Mistletoe
Dance.

And apparently I'm not allowed to attend without blending in
with the party atmosphere, so now I'm in the town hall right
before the Mistletoe Dance starts, and I look for all the world like
I'm going. But I'm not.

'You will save a dance for me, won't you, Essie dear?' Mr

Arkins is on a stepladder, using his dino claws to put a pin in a string of festive bunting that keeps making a break for freedom.

'Oh, I'm not—'

'I'm old, you know. We never know when our *last* Mistletoe Dance might be. You wouldn't leave an old man standing forlornly in the middle of the dance floor, would you?'

Guilt prickles at me and I mumble something that's neither an agreement nor disagreement.

The town hall is decked out in all its festive glory. There are streamers and foil garlands, and the main lights have been switched for low-light red and green bulbs that cast a festive glow across the room.

'Oh, Essie, I'm so glad you're here,' Lynette says.

'I was worried you wouldn't come.' Beryl embraces me like I've been away for three years, not hiding out in the bakery for a couple of days.

I expected my first post-Joss encounter to be full of questions, but none of them mention him, and I carry on setting out mini-sausage rolls, mince pies, and shortbread stars, and when my crates are unloaded, I stack them and go to move, but I'm surrounded.

'Look at this photo on Instagram.' Douglas pushes his phone under my nose, and I pull back and blink to focus on a photo of the gingerbread house that some influencer has posted. 'She's got 27,000 followers, you know. We might get that many by next year.'

'Look at this headline, Essie.' Another phone is pushed towards me, and Mr Chalke reads aloud. 'Must have this Christmas – giant nutcrackers made of breakfast cereal. Have you ever seen anything like this? A life-size nutcracker you can *eat*!' It's written by an excitable young reporter and he repeats it in the same tone.

'People have been phoning up to ask if they can book tickets for the Mistletoe Dance! Tickets! Like a real event! Usually it's just a few of us lot, but *looook*, cars are already parking on the pavement!'

'Oh no, that means I'm going to get blocked in. I need to get going...' I look towards the door. There's a sea of villagers between me and it, and they're all thrusting phones and tablets in my direction. I honestly don't think I'm going to be able to swim through them to escape.

They're proudly showing social media posts about our gingerbread house, articles about money-hungry councils, and stories of children visiting Santa in the 'most magical grotto in the UK'.

'Mervyn's going to make an announcement tonight,' Lynette says excitedly.

I *want* to be here for that. And Mum's right, it's *not* like Joss is going to come. I wouldn't imagine Joss is going to show his face again until he rocks up in Mistletoe Gardens in January with a fleet of excavators. Unless Mervyn's announcement tonight says otherwise, and *that* I want to hear.

There's something about Christmas that makes it a time for traditions, and coming to the Mistletoe Dance is one of ours. Mum, Saff, and I always come together. So does everyone else from Folkhornton. It's fun, festive, free, and a nice way of wishing your neighbours a Happy Christmas and saying goodbye to another year in Folkhornton. Dance partners are swapped and you find yourself dancing with anyone and everyone, from elderly gents in dino costumes to tipsy old ladies who have had one too many mulled wines or gone a bit giddy on overexposure to Johnny Mathis's Christmas classics.

Each dance ends with a peck on the cheek under a bunch of mistletoe, which is hung from the ceiling in a criss-cross pattern, so every available space is covered by a bunch of glossy green leaves and pearly white berries.

And what am I going to do instead – put a Christmas film on TV and eat seventeen times my bodyweight in After Eights and Cadbury's Roses? Sit there alone, thinking about (a) Joss, or (b) how much fun everyone's having in the town hall without me? Neither of those options sounds appealing.

'Oh, good, you're here,' Mum says, looking like a Christmas angel in her mid-blue chiffon dress.

'Why do I think you engineered that, hmm?'

'Me? Nonsense? The locals haven't seen you for a couple of days, they had a lot to show you.'

'And you happen to know *that's* how I didn't manage to zip in and out like I'd planned...'

'Have you seen Mervyn yet?' She looks around the room, deliberately ignoring my accusation. 'Word is there's an announcement being made tonight about the future of Mistletoe Gardens. You must stay and listen. It's *bound* to be good news with the gingerbread house getting so much attention.'

'So everyone's saying. And Mervyn did say how much footfall is up, and Folkhornton has been swarming this week. He'd be stupid to push ahead, right?'

'Well, he certainly won't be getting a dance under the mistletoe with me if he does, or anything else, for that matter. Rather than post a quiet update on the website, he's waited until everyone's gathered together to share the good news. I'm sure of it.'

'Right. Good.' Although I've barely stopped thinking of Joss since Saturday morning, they've been thoughts of anger and feeling sorry for myself, but for the first time, I think about what it will mean for his company if he loses this job. The lads he employs mean the world to him. Will there be another job they can get involved in, or will he be back to square one? If the larger housing firm find out about Joss's involvement in saving Mistletoe Gardens, will they penalise him for it?

I hadn't thought of that before. With everything that's been going on, it's been easy to get caught up in the lies he told rather than the good he did. That gingerbread house wouldn't exist without him, but Joss has compromised the guaranteed buy-out of his father's company to help me with it.

Maybe it doesn't matter either way. If Mervyn's announcement is a positive one, then Joss will be leaving in January, and if it isn't a positive one, then Joss will be demolishing Mistletoe Gardens and *then* leaving. The last thing I need to do is get any more entangled with the man.

The town hall is filling up rapidly. It's the kind of Christmas party where there's something for everyone, for young 'uns who want to dance the night away with a special someone, for the older residents who aren't mobile enough for dancing any more and want to sit at the tables around the edge of the hall, have some drinks and nibbles, and catch up with their friends, and for people like me, who just want to concentrate on something that *isn't* Joss Hallissey and appreciate so many others feeling the joy of Christmas, even when 'festive' is the last thing I'm feeling.

Just when I need something to take my mind off Joss, Mr Arkins, who had disappeared for a while, waddles up to me in his dinosaur costume. He's managed to get a bowtie and a sparkly jacket on, and holds his T-rex arm out. The song is about to change, and I *did* promise him a dance.

'This is the busiest Mistletoe Dance I can remember,' I say as he leads me onto the dance floor. So many people have come that the town hall is at close-to-bursting capacity, and it's not just locals – people have read about Folkhornton's Christmas celebrations and turned out in full. There's even a couple of reporters lurking on the sidelines. Our little local celebration of the mistletoe my great-great-grandmother planted so many years ago is now a newsworthy event.

Mr Arkins nods his dinosaur head but doesn't otherwise respond.

The song that starts up is 'Candlelight Carol', Joss's favourite Christmas song, and it makes my heart feel like a fist is being squeezed around it. At least Christmas is only once a year because this song is forever going to remind me of him. It's a slow, touching ballad, and the dance floor around us is filled with happy couples, arms around each other, heads nestled on shoulders, loving looks into each other's eyes... And here's me – dancing with an elderly man dressed as a T-rex. Nothing has ever encapsulated my life in a more accurate way.

Usually Mr Arkins is chatty but he's silent tonight. I know he's got a wife, but I've never seen him with anyone, and if she's here, she certainly doesn't seem to mind him dancing with women half his age. Maybe she thinks the costume is enough to put anyone off.

One hand holds mine stretched out in front of us, his dino mitt curled around my fingers, and his other hand respectfully on my elbow, as we twirl around the dance floor, the dino suit so padded that it keeps a respectable distance between us as we dodge other couples who are waltzing to this melodic hymn.

How different tonight would've been if Joss was my date. How much I'd been looking forward to dancing with him all night, until our feet burned and our bodies ached and we *definitely* finished each dance with a kiss beneath the mistletoe.

I miss him. I *wish* we could go back to how things were a few days ago.

If only we could erase the last few days... No, the last few weeks, so Joss and I could meet again without this thing between us.

That deep, pulling sadness drags at me again, and Mr Arkins's dino mitt squeezes my fingers like he can sense it.

'Candlelight Carol' ends and 'Where Are You Christmas' by Faith Hill begins, and Mr Arkins makes no move to dance with anyone else, and I appreciate his kind silence and the time without any expectation on me.

Saff looks like a princess in her deep-pink dress, and has been the recipient of *many* dance invitations tonight, so when I spot her alone when our fourth song ends, I excuse myself from Mr Arkins, who still hasn't uttered a single word.

Mr Arkins's shoulders slump, and somehow, despite being completely hidden inside the costume, he still manages to look disappointed. He lifts a claw like he wants to say something, but no words come out. Something weird is going on here tonight. Everyone in Folkhornton is fairly barmy anyway, but the excitement of Christmas and Mervyn's upcoming announcement must have sent them all over the edge.

I make my way over to where Saff's standing by one of the buffet tables. It's the first time I've seen her since this afternoon. 'You look beauti—'

'Oh, never mind that!' She gives me a hug, bouncing us both up and down like she's going to explode. 'I've got gossip I'm bursting to share and no one else is even vaguely interested! Did you know Mr Arkins and the MMM are married?'

'Noooooo! No! Seriously?' My eyes follow Saff's gaze to where the MMM is on the other side of the room. '*She's* the wife he's mentioned? Oh my God, wait until I tell—' I cut myself off. I *can't* tell Joss. I shake my head at myself, annoyed at how desperately I *want* to tell him. He'll never believe it.

'How on earth did you find that out? And why isn't *everyone* talking about it?'

'It's old news, apparently. Everyone's known for years.'

'I haven't!'

'I haven't either!'

'Are we unwittingly turning into my mother by standing here gossiping like a pair of old biddies?'

'We might be, but I don't care.' She giggles and demolishes another cheese straw. 'So?'

'So... what?' I ask in confusion at the charged tone in her voice, like she's clearly expecting an answer.

She pushes both eyebrows forward and looks pointedly across the room to where the MMM is talking to an elderly man I've never seen before.

The MMM looks so different without her clacking horse head and cart full of clinking bottles. Even from across the room, I can tell her make-up is done perfectly, and she looks pretty in a sparkly silver dress, a world away from the hippy character she embodies most of the time.

'I told you it was going to happen,' Saff says.

'What?'

'Loooook!'

I look across the room, but I can't see what she's on about. 'Saffie, either you've been at the mulled wine or you're going to need to explain yourself.'

'The man with MMM! It's *him*.'

'Him who?' I squint at the man, but I don't recognise him.

'It's Mr Arkins.'

I laugh. 'Don't be ridiculous. That's not Mr Arkins. Mr Arkins is over there.' I jerk my head over my shoulder. The dinosaur is still hovering at the edge of the dance floor where I left him.

'He introduced himself just now. MMM had to give me a reviving potion, them being married *and* him taking his costume off was too much drama all at once.'

'It can't be. You've definitely been at the mulled wine.' I laugh again, even though something niggles about the whole thing.

'No, it really is, Ess.'

'But if that's Mr Arkins...' My finger points at him and then turns slowly towards the dinosaur. 'Who the hell is that?'

Things start to make sense. The lack of speaking. The movement of a much younger man. I've never understood the idea of a red mist before, but I'm suddenly so angry that everything takes on a red sheen and I let out a growl of my own. 'Three guesses – it starts with "J" and ends with "I'm a tit".'

I'm already stalking across the dance floor and the man in the dinosaur costume takes a step back warily.

'Do you think this is funny?' I demand when I'm standing in front of him, looking up at roughly where his face should be.

The dinosaur shakes its head.

'I know it's you, Joss.'

'I'm sorry,' he says, muffled inside the dinosaur suit. 'I didn't want you to go with a seventy-eight-year-old man dressed as a dinosaur.'

'So you came *as* a seventy-eight-year-old man dressed as a dinosaur?' I fold my arms.

'I promised to be your date and I didn't want to break a promise. I just wanted to talk to you, Ess. This wasn't supposed to go the way it has.'

'It wouldn't have gone any way at all if you'd told me the truth from day one. Do you know, I actually felt sorry for you just now? I actually started worrying about what you were going to do. I missed you. I wished I was dancing with you. And I actually was, but it's another one of your lies. A woman should have a choice about who she dances with, and you knew that if you'd asked, the answer would have been no, so you took that choice away by pretending to be someone else in disguise.'

'I'm sorry.' He swallows hard, and I realise I can hear it because the room has gone deathly silent and *every* eye is on us. 'I hadn't thought of it like that. I didn't mean it in that way.'

'Take the head off, will you? I'm having an argument with a man dressed as a dinosaur.'

He reaches up until he can lift the dinosaur head from his shoulders. His dark hair is sticking up in all directions, but he doesn't fix it. He tries to give me a smile but it's halted by the glare I give him, and he tucks the dinosaur head under his arm.

'Great, now I'm having an argument with a man holding a giant dinosaur head under his arm,' I mutter.

'I was going to speak as soon as we were alone, but I clammed up. I knew you'd walk away if you heard my voice. I'm sorry, it was meant to be a joke – padding in case you hit me. I honestly hadn't thought about it in that way.'

I make a noise of frustration and Joss shoves a hand through his hair. 'Please let me explain. This whole thing has gone so wrong, and it was never meant to be this way. *Please* talk to me, Essie.'

'Why should I?'

'I don't know,' he says eventually, looking downtrodden and defeated after the amount of time it's taken him to come up with an answer. 'Because something happened between us in Mistletoe Gardens? Because I don't want our December to end like this? Please give me a minute. I made you something.' He lifts a hand and beckons Mr Arkins over, although he hardly needs to because everyone is hanging on our every word, and Mr Arkins is already returning after collecting something from a side room.

'Hello, Essie, it's me,' he says as he approaches, holding out a... something on a large plate.

'What *is* that?'

'It's a gingerbread house,' Joss says and then glances at it again. 'Well, it was meant to be a gingerbread house. I think we can all agree baking isn't my strong suit. It's meant to be a replica of *our* gingerbread house. I was hoping I'd picked up enough knowledge from you to be able to recreate it. I wanted it to be a reminder, I guess. A way of saying "look what we did together" even though I've wrecked everything.'

'It's sort of collapsing.' I go to poke it and then think better of it in case the whole thing crumbles at the slightest touch.

Mr Arkins, who has a shock of Albert Einstein-esque white hair that I've never seen before, holds the plate up and to be fair, it's the saddest looking gingerbread house I've ever seen. Although it really is a perfect replica of our gingerbread house, complete with piped roof tiles, peppermint swirls, melted Glacier Mint windows, and a rainbow of gumdrops along the roof. He's even piped green lines around the door to represent the marshmallow Christmas trees, and made a tiny wreath of gummy bears.

The only problem is that he clearly has no experience of making gingerbread, and the biscuits look much darker than they should be, but they're also far too soft, so the walls are bowing inwards under the weight of the roof, and the edges are wonky so nothing joins up quite where it should. I didn't expect it to make me emotional, but I can feel myself melting at the sweetness of this gesture.

'I didn't realise it was *that* bad,' Joss says gently, and I pat my face to realise tears have leaked from my eyes. I thought I was holding it together better than that.

'Borrowing the dino suit was my idea,' Mr Arkins says. 'Don't blame Joss. I've been thinking about taking it off for a while now, since I spoke to you two in Mistletoe Gardens, and this seemed like the perfect time. I thought it might give you a chance to talk things over. It's often easier to say things to someone you can't see.'

I take the gingerbread house from Mr Arkins and he backs

away to give us some privacy. 'What am I supposed to do with this, Joss?'

'I don't know. I'd say eat it, but I'm not sure how edible it will be.'

I look down at the forlorn plate in my hands. Eating it definitely doesn't sound like the best plan.

Joss sighs, and for the first time, I look up into his eyes and they look sadder than ever before, and that desire to hug him is still burning in me. I know this is all his fault, but I still care about him, and I still want to take that sadness away.

'I'm sorry, Ess.' He says it so quietly that no one can overhear it. 'I know I've messed up, but I'm begging you to give me another chance. I've been feeling... God, I don't know... *something* for you. Something's happened between us... please don't throw that away because I screwed up. I know I should have told you and I'd do anything to take it back.'

He sounds so sincere, and I'm wavering. The gingerbread house is such a nice gesture. I didn't realise something so simple would touch me so much, but that's what Joss is like – little things add up to mean a lot, like a coffee each day. Something that on the surface means very little, but something so kind and caring that shows Joss to be the opposite of his reputation.

I can feel the eyes of everyone in the town hall on me now, waiting with bated breath for me to turn around, pull him into my arms and cry 'all is forgiven'. I can hear people whispering as the silence goes on. Locals muttering explanations to strangers, residents mumbling between themselves, everyone watching me, expecting a happy ending to this Christmas love story, but it's all too much.

'How can I trust you? How can I ever know what was or wasn't real? How can anyone ever know whose side you were on? Trying to save the gardens while also being the person employed to destroy it. How do I know you weren't already working for them? How do I know that damage from the rain wasn't caused by you? How do I know the gingerbread house isn't yet another thing the council employed you to spirit away in the middle of the night? Because you were right, I didn't see you lock up that night, but I *trusted* you'd done it... and you've proved that you cannot be trusted.'

He steps backwards like I've thumped him. 'You think that was me?'

'I didn't. Everyone else thought it might've been, and I defended you. The point isn't whether you did or didn't lock up that night – the point is that I will never be able to trust anything you say because I don't know if you had an ulterior motive.'

'Essie, I didn't...' He stumbles for words, and I can tell I've hurt him. He looks crestfallen, and I instantly regret suggesting it. Joss might have lied about some things, but I *know* he didn't do that.

'Excuse me for interrupting?' Mr Arkins comes over again. 'I'm the one who left the tent open. I should have owned up days ago. I'm so sorry.'

'You?' Joss and I say in unison.

It's so odd to see Mr Arkins's face and how red it's gone. 'I'm sorry, you two. My wife and I are still the caretakers, we kept our own keys for security reasons, and I couldn't sleep that morning and thought I'd come down and do some work on the dinosaur background, only I couldn't figure out how those floodlights of yours work, so I opened the tent for some light from the street-lamps. It was only a bit of drizzle, I didn't think anything of it, but then I couldn't get the tent closed again. All the ropes had got tangled, and I couldn't reach to undo them, and I felt like such a silly old fool. I didn't feel steady enough on my feet to go up on a ladder, especially dressed like such a wally. I was so embarrassed by my old age limitations that I forgot to lock the gate behind me.

I didn't mean to do any harm. I had no idea the drizzle would turn into belting rain. I did try to phone the bakery when I realised how heavy it had got, but you weren't there, Essie. I'm so sorry – both for doing it and for not owning up. I didn't want people to think I was a daft old man dressed like a numpty, even though I *am* a daft old man dressed like a numpty.'

It makes me smile. Bless him. 'It's okay, we got there in the end.'

'With a little help from our friends,' Joss adds, inclining his head towards the room.

Mr Arkins gives us both a hug, and I catch Joss's eyes and mouth 'sorry' at him. He gives me a half-smile that shows exactly how awkward things are between us.

Mr Arkins holds both our hands and gives each a good shake. 'I'm sorry. I should have admitted it straight away.'

'Don't worry about it. You helped put it right – we couldn't have done it without you.' Joss gives him a reassuring pat on the shoulder. 'Looking back, I can tell how awful you felt that day.'

'Are we "all good" as the kids say?'

'We're all good.' We both speak at the same time again.

'Sorry, I shouldn't have said that,' I say to Joss when Mr Arkins goes back to the MMM.

'It's all right, I deserve it. I know I should've told you about the job, but once I didn't on that first day, I didn't know how to broach the subject, and the longer it went on, the worse it—'

'Can I have everyone's attention, please?' Mervyn's voice booms so loudly from the stage that he probably doesn't need the squealing microphone he's got.

This is it. The moment we find out that the gingerbread house was all worthwhile. The moment that Mervyn announces the housing development is off and Mistletoe Gardens gets to stay.

Except... Mervyn looks nervous – more nervous than he'd

look if he was about to deliver good news. There's a sudden sinking feeling in the pit of my stomach and my hands are shaking where they're holding onto the plate.

I tell myself not to be so silly. Folkhornton has been crammed lately. The Mistletoe Gardens opening night was the busiest anyone had ever seen it. Parents have been bringing children from miles away to visit Santa in the gingerbread house and stopping for a wander around a town they've never been to before. Footfall is up. Takings are up. Every number that the council will have been crunching is going in the right direction. There can only be one outcome – surely, surely, they won't still destroy the place after all this?

'I'd like to say a few words about the ongoing efforts to save Mistletoe Gardens...' Mervyn gulps and has a sip of water. 'I know some of you will be hoping for a different outcome, and while the campaign has been amusing to watch and done a great deal of good for our beloved town, I'm sorry to inform you that the council's position has not changed. Mistletoe Gardens *will* be pulled down in January to make way for an exciting new housing development, which will see us welcome many new friends and neighbours. Although the gardens are a much-loved part of town, and we appreciate—'

'You patronising bas—' Mr Chalke goes to shout and Beryl wallops him round the head.

'Demand for property is at an all-time high,' Mervyn continues unperturbed. 'It would be unforgivable for us, as a council trying to do what's best for Folkhornton—'

'What's best for your own pockets, more like!' someone else heckles from the crowd.

'Right, well, this will bring more money into Folkhornton in the long run, and I'm sure you'll join me in welcoming many new residents, which will have a knock-on effect on the local economy and grow your businesses overall, and I'm sure we all want that, don't we?'

'I'll give him something to knock his effect on!' Mum yells, unseen, from the other side of the room.

Like that old saying that you could hear a pin drop, well, in this room, you could hear a snowflake land. The absolute silence looks like it unnerves Mervyn more than abuse would have, and he quickly signs off and scuttles away from the microphone, presumably to go into hiding for the next few years... A couple of centuries should do it.

There's so much devastation throughout the room. I knew everyone loved Mistletoe Gardens, but I hadn't realised how much until this moment. No one expected things to go this way. The gingerbread house has captured imaginations far and wide, more so than I ever thought it would, and *everyone* expected the council to react accordingly.

And now people are blinking at each other in shock.

The stone that started in the pit of my stomach feels like it grows into a boulder and sinks right through me, making me feel desolate and defeated. We tried so hard and I loved every minute of it because I was so sure it would be worth it in the end.

And it isn't. It wasn't enough.

'Despicable!' Someone finally breaks the silence.

'It's our fault. We should have used it more. We're all guilty of rushing through Mistletoe Gardens but never stopping to appreciate it.'

'Money-grabbing beagles!' Someone else shakes a fist towards the stage, even though Mervyn is nowhere to be seen.

Lynette has got a nail file out of her handbag and looks like she's using her nails to sharpen *it*. Douglas is turning over a beer coaster, looking like he's contemplating how much bodily harm he could do with it.

And Joss has... got his phone out.

Why has he got his phone out? It's not exactly a moment to capture for posterity, is it? 'Did you always know this would be the response? At the beginning of this, you were adamant they wouldn't change their minds. You had insider info even back then?'

'I knew they expected protests and wouldn't be swayed by them, but things changed. The gingerbread house has brought so many tourists in and got so many people talking online – the sensible thing would be to embrace that, not demolish it, not now. I thought we had a chance.'

'So did I,' I mutter, meaning it in all senses of the word. A chance of saving Mistletoe Gardens and a chance of something special happening between us. 'But I've been wrong about a lot of things lately.'

I hold up the plate in my hands. 'Thank you for the gingerbread house. It will probably last longer than Mistletoe Gardens.'

With that, I turn and stomp out, leaving the wide double doors swinging behind me. I know the loss of the park is not *his* fault, but so much of this could've gone differently if he'd just been honest from the start.

As predicted, Mum's car is landlocked on the pavement outside, seeing as I'd only popped by to drop off the food, a few long hours ago now. This evening feels like it's simultaneously been going on for days and has lasted about ten minutes. The anticipation of the last couple of hours, knowing that this was the night we'd find out it had all been worth it, and then the crushing disappointment of *that*. Mervyn's cold and heartless speech, and Joss. Joss in the dino suit. Joss being involved in this. Joss knowing from the very beginning that this was the likely outcome. He even told me. He *told* me, and I didn't believe *him*.

The passenger side door opens and I have a brief moment of

panic that thinking about Joss has somehow summoned him, but a pink satin-covered leg slides in, and Saff plonks herself into the seat next to me.

'Well, that was a Mistletoe Dance I won't forget for all the wrong reasons.' She reaches over and gives my knee a squeeze. 'I'm sorry about the gardens. I didn't think it would go that way.'

I nod mutely, because I'm biting my lip to stop myself crying, and the tears are going to break loose if I unclamp my teeth.

After all our years of being best friends, she can tell. 'Did you see your mum and Mervyn dancing?'

I nod again, appreciating the question to take my mind off the things that will make me cry. 'They've barely taken their eyes off each other all night. I have a strong suspicion that *might* have changed since his announcement though. Wouldn't be surprised if he's missing a few limbs and at least one appendage by now.'

'The point is, you and I have been trying for years to get them to admit their feelings for each other. Joss managed it in a few short weeks. He can't be *all* bad.'

'You knew he was going to do that tonight? That's why you were so desperate for me to go?'

'I didn't know he was going to dress up as a dinosaur. To be fair, no one would've seen *that* coming, but your mum told me earlier that he'd be there.'

'*Mum* knew?' I say in surprise. 'All of that pushing to get me there and she *knew* Joss was going to turn up?'

Saff nods to the plate on my lap. 'He made you gingerbread. That's sweet.'

I break off the chimney and pop it into my mouth, and Saff reaches over to break a corner off the roof, and her face slowly shifts into revulsion and she opens the car door to spit it out. 'Oh my God, that's disgusting. *What* has he done to that?'

'At a guess, he burnt the butter, sugar, and syrup mixture, then put the oven on too high a temperature, so he's somehow managed to charcoal the biscuits on the outside while leaving them soggy on the inside. It really is impressively bad.'

'It's a lot of effort to go to. The gesture is sweet, even if the execution... suggests he shouldn't give up the day job, ever.' She shudders again and then her eyes soften when she looks at me. 'I've watched something really special blossom between you two in the past few weeks. Are you sure that's worth walking away from over a little white lie?'

'It's not just one, though, is it? Everything he said was under false pretences. He knew it would never work and he went along with it anyway. I feel like a child being indulged, like he's let me have my fun while knowing full well it would come to nothing. And tonight in the stupid costume. He could've just walked up to me and asked me to dance, but no, he even had to steal a dance.'

'For what it's worth, I don't think he meant it to come across that way. It's quite funny, really.' She glances at my face. 'I mean, maybe not right now, but in time, you might be able to laugh at it.'

She reaches over to pluck a gumdrop off the roof. And then a Smartie that acts as a miniature version of the peppermint swirls. Generally, anything Joss *hasn't* baked is safe to eat. 'Are you blocked in?'

I nod, my mouth full of really, truly *awful* gingerbread.

'That's Mr Selman's car, I'll go and get him to move it.'

'Never mind. I'll walk. I want to go through the gardens for one last time.'

Saff chews her lip. 'It doesn't have to be the end. We must be able to appeal. A petition, maybe? The bandstand is quite old, maybe we could apply for a listed status or something?'

'It's the end, Saff. If building a giant gingerbread house didn't do it, nothing will. That's it. The council have made up their minds. There's nothing left to try.' I leave the plate on the seat, get out of the car and cross the road. I lean on the railings that separate Mistletoe Gardens from the main road and look in. The trees are lit up and the cluster lights are glowing blue around the bandstand roof.

'I'm sorry I couldn't save you,' I whisper to it as I let the tears fall, finally letting loose all the emotions I've been pushing down since I found out about Joss the other day. This December felt important, not just for saving Mistletoe Gardens, but for me and Joss as well. It feels like we came *so* close to something magical happening, but in the end, love, Christmas magic, and giant gingerbread houses belong in a storybook, and it's time for me to stop believing they can ever be part of real life.

22

In fifteenth-century Germany, they took gingerbread baking so seriously that you had to belong to a gingerbread guild to make it. By the seventeenth century, gingerbread making was a profession in itself and only gingerbread bakers were allowed to bake it.

'Essie!'

It's Christmas Eve morning and I'm wiping down the counters in Dancing Cinnamon when the hammering on the door starts.

'All right, it's not even nine yet,' I say loudly as I walk across the shop and open up to let Saff in. 'Why didn't you go round the back like usual?'

'Never mind that, you need to come up to Mistletoe Gardens *now.*'

'Good morning to you too. And no, thank you. I've had just about all the mistletoe I can take.'

Unsurprisingly, after the Mistletoe Dance last night, I couldn't quiet my mind enough to sleep, and this morning, the tiredness is pressing down on me, along with the complete desolation at how hard we've worked and the fact that we've still failed.

'Seriously, Ess. There's something you need to see.'

'There's no one to cover the shop.'

'Close the shop. Town's dead – *everyone* is in Mistletoe Gardens.'

'Is *he* there?'

She knows who I mean without me having to say it. 'Kind of.'

'Then thank you, but no. I saw more than enough of Joss last night.' It burns to pretend I don't have feelings for him, and admittedly my interest is mildly piqued, but whatever he's up to, it's nothing to do with me any more.

'Then at least look at this.' She gets her phone out, taps the screen a few times, and hands it over.

The video is titled *Heartless council grab money over giant gingerbread house festivity*, and it takes me a few moments of watching to realise what I'm seeing. 'What is Mervyn's speech from last night doing on YouTube?'

'Never mind that.' She reaches over and points to the screen. 'Look at how many views it's got.'

My eyes flick down, pass uninterestedly over the number, and then I realise what I've read and stare at it in shock – 122,752. 'That's *impossible*. It can't have got that many views since last night. What's going on here? Why would someone film that? And who?'

'Considering that's your shoulder...' She leans across and points out a shoulder at the bottom right corner of the video. 'There's only one person who was standing behind you who could've filmed from that angle.'

Joss with his phone out. That bit suddenly makes sense, although the *why* is unclear. 'Joss has done this?'

'Why don't you come and see what's happening in Mistletoe Gardens?'

And she's clearly not going to elaborate any further. I grab my coat and follow her out the door. She's certainly right about one thing – the streets are deserted. All right, it's 9 a.m. on Christmas Eve, it's always quiet, but never *this* quiet. The lack of activity is downright eerie, in fact.

And as we approach Mistletoe Gardens, I can see why. Although the gates are closed, there are a *lot* of people gathered around the railings and hedges outside, chanting and holding up placards reading 'Mistletoe murderers!' and 'Money over magic!'

'What the...' I mutter as Saff produces a key from her pocket and lets us in, shutting the gate quickly before any of the protesters get in. 'How did you get that?'

'Joss gave it to me so I could come and get you. He's a little...'

'...tied up?' I finish for her as my eyes fall on the bandstand. 'What the *hell*?'

I have no intention of laughing, but an unexpected giggle bursts out because it's such an absurd sight that this must be some kind of heartbreak-induced fever dream. Joss is sitting on the steps of the bandstand, chained to the railings. Also chained to the railings in a circle around the bandstand are ten dinosaurs.

'Essie!' Beryl calls from inside one of the dino suits.

Like one mass of giant dinosaurs, they all turn and wave to me at the same time. Even Rob, who's bobbing along the bandstand wall, turns to look at me.

'What the hell?' I repeat, because there really is *no* other response. What else are you supposed to say when confronted by ten dinosaurs chained to a bandstand?

'Hello, Essie!' That's Douglas, muffled from inside a suit.

'Happy Christmas Eve!' That one's Lynette.

It's everyone. They all call out greetings to me like this is a completely normal scene to come across.

I try to avoid looking at Joss, the only one not wearing a dino suit, but his eyes are shining and his smile is beaming, and my resolve is softening as I approach the bandstand.

'What are you playing at?' I ask, although it doesn't seem like a bad thing this time. One of his wrists is chained to the bandstand railing, and the other is chained to the sawn-off 'for sale' sign from outside his house, which is lying on the steps next to him.

'We're doing what we should have done from the beginning.' His grin gets even wider. 'We're saving Mistletoe Gardens.'

'By chaining yourself to the bandstand? When you already know the council "won't be swayed by protests"?' I quote his own words from last night.

'They might not be swayed by protests, but they *will* be swayed by viral bad press, and look at this lot. We've got ten dinosaurs chained to a bandstand with a giant gingerbread house inside. Do you honestly think this *isn't* going to go viral?'

I hadn't seen Mervyn until now, but Joss inclines his head towards the opposite gate, where Mervyn is pacing up and down on the pavement outside, a phone pressed to his ear, looking positively grey with worry.

'Remember the journalist from *Bulletin: Wales* who Mervyn was talking to the other day?' Joss lifts a chained hand to gesture towards a man standing to one side. 'He's been kind enough to come out on Christmas Eve to cover the story. He's broken it on Twitter this morning, and we're currently trending not just in the UK, but in several European countries as well.'

The journalist barely lifts his head to give me a nod, his fingers flying over the screen of his tablet like he can't keep up with comments.

'Turns out that if you're lucky enough to live in a barmy little town where the residents are willing to dress up as festive dinos and chain themselves to a bandstand, people are *very* interested. Headline news on *Bulletin: Wales*, and it's only a matter of time until national newspapers pick up the story.' His voice rises on the last part of the sentence, loud enough for Mervyn to hear, who looks over and gives us all a glare. 'Costumes provided by Mr Arkins, of course.'

One of the dinosaurs lifts a claw and salutes me.

'I've given everyone warming potions,' MMM says from inside another one. She's the only identifiable dino because she's got the wooden horse's head with her, clacking randomly in Mervyn's direction.

'The man talks sense, Essie.'

'Mum?' I say in surprise. My *mum* got into a dinosaur suit? My pristinely styled, never without perfectly coiffed hair and flawless make-up mother is voluntarily dressed as a dino with a Christmas hat on? How on earth has Joss pulled this one off? Bribery? Blackmail?

My eyes fall on him again and his mouth twitches. 'We've gone about this all wrong. We've got nothing but good press for Folkhornton. The gingerbread house has only served to strengthen the council's position. It's made people *want* to move into their housing complex. What we haven't done is show them up for the money-grabbing, mistletoe murdering, greedy cupcakes they are. They don't need good press – they need bad press. We don't need people to know what we're trying to save – we need people to know what they're willing to destroy for profit. It's all about the slant of the story. Did you see the video?'

'Why did you film that?'

'Because I had a feeling it was going to go that way, and the gingerbread house has given us a platform. The council aren't going to listen to the residents, but they might listen to the thousands of unsavoury comments and promises to boycott Folkhornton, their housing development, and any future projects by the housing development firm. They've already pulled out, Ess.

Mervyn has no one to tear down Mistletoe Gardens and no one to build his apartment blocks. Anyone unscrupulous enough to take on that contract has got a lot of backlash to contend with. I'd hazard a guess that it'll be more trouble than it's worth.'

'What about you?'

'I quit. My firm officially pulled out last night, although I think we both know that I unofficially pulled out weeks ago.'

'What about your lads? Their future jobs?'

'Their future jobs are with me.'

My heart flutters despite myself. I don't want to care. I don't *want* to feel that flicker of excitement that he might mean what I think he means, but hope blossoms like a cherry tree in spring and my insides feel like they're vibrating with anticipation. Maybe it says something that I'm still *this* eager for him to stay. 'Why are you holding a "for sale" sign?'

'Because I'm not selling my house *or* my company. I'm not leaving Folkhornton.'

I don't realise I'm going to cry until tears run down my cheeks. 'Why not?'

'Because the person I love more than anyone else in the world is here. Even if you never talk to me again. Even if it takes years to earn your trust back. I'm not giving up on us. And I'm not going anywhere. Metaphorically or literally.' He rattles the chains. 'This lot can come and go as they please. They're elderly – the end of December isn't exactly the ideal time to keep them chained up outside, no matter how much insulation the dino suits provide, but I'm here for the duration. As long as someone will feed me?'

Ten dinosaurs promise they will.

'In my entire life, I've never been happier than I have been in these gardens with you. I'm not giving up on this, Ess. It means so much to so many people, but especially to me. And you.' Joss hasn't got a lot of slack on the chains holding him, but he sits forward and jerks his head to beckon me closer. 'I'm sorry about last night. I have no excuse other than being an idiot. I didn't mean to trick you into dancing with me – I just wasn't brave enough to speak when I should have spoken. I actually thought it might make you laugh and ease the tension between us, but I let it go on too long and messed up again. I'm sorry.'

He sounds so genuine, and him being here, going to all this effort, not giving up when I had, and... staying. I didn't realise how badly I wanted him to stay until now, and the relief of hearing it is making it hard to remember why I was angry with him. I'd given up on Mistletoe Gardens last night, I thought there was nowhere to go from there, but he hasn't. And that says a lot.

'I said a really stupid thing last Friday night that's been haunting me ever since, and I want to apologise for that.' His smile turns from confident to nervous, and he wets his lips and swallows a few times before speaking. 'I said that if I kissed you, I was going to fall in love with you, but that was a lie. I was already in love with you and I was trying to convince myself I wasn't. I'm head-over-dinosaur-tails in love with you. I have been for weeks. I fell in love in the swimming baths lobby – the moment you put the basket down in the exact spot I was about to mark up. You took one look and saw *me*. You saw straight past all the walls I put up. You're the first person in forever who looked into my eyes rather than listening to my words. I didn't know how much I needed someone to remind me of who I used to be until you did. I feel like I've been hit round the face with a railway sleeper every time I'm with you. I haven't felt important to anyone in a really long time, and you don't just make me feel important – you make me feel like the only other person on the planet. I know I've broken your trust, but I also know something magical happened here in the past few weeks, and I'm not walking away. You've made me want to sail again.'

I melt at the reference to my metaphor from days ago. 'You're going to catch your death if you stay out here in the cold for too long.'

'Just need something to warm me up.' He waggles his eyebrows, and that's it. I burst into a mix of laughing and crying, and Rob squawks and flies off in fright as I dive on Joss.

I'm kneeling on the steps in front of him, and I hold his face in my hands and tilt his head until I can press my lips carefully against his. Both his hands are tied up so he can't do anything but sit there and *be* kissed, but he arches his chest to get closer and makes a noise in the back of his throat. He leans into the kiss, pushing himself up to chase after my lips when I go to pull away, and I shift until I can look down at him, one hand holding his head as the other strokes his hair. 'I fell in love with you too. From that first moment, you let me see a part of you that no one else got to see. Everything felt special from that moment on.'

He somehow manages to push himself up until he can kiss me again. It's restrained and not as fevered as it would be if he could use his hands, and if we didn't have an audience watching on, and if I hadn't just heard the click of the journalist's camera and a collective 'awwwww' from the dinosaurs.

'Hallissey, this has got to stop.' Mervyn marches in and then looks between us awkwardly as I scramble out of Joss's lap and back onto my feet. 'Oh, well, not *that*, you two continue with that as and when you wish.' He looks around like he might be trying to determine which costume my mum's in, then he clears his throat and pulls his shoulders back like he's trying to rally himself. 'I'm sure you think you're very clever, but this ends *now* or Folkhornton council will be forced to remove your company from the pool of contractors we employ.'

I have a moment of panic that if Joss is staying and keeping his business, this could sway him.

'That's okay, go ahead.' He gives Mervyn a lackadaisical grin. 'It's not the sort of work I want to do any more anyway.'

'What's got into you today?' I ask, intrigued by his sudden self-assuredness.

'One of the many things that's been missing from my life in recent years is my ability to judge whether I'm doing the right thing or not, but for once, I know I am.'

It makes me want to kiss him again, but I force myself not to with so many people looking on. Out of the corner of my eye, I see Saff go across to open the gate again, and I can see Joss's eyes change as he watches whoever's come in.

The kiss has left him lying backwards across the steps and he pulls himself upright again. 'Use the space.'

'What?' Mervyn looks as confused as I am.

'You said yourself, Mistletoe Gardens is dead space. One hundred and twenty thou—'

'A hundred and sixty thousand now,' the journalist interrupts.

Joss grins. 'A hundred and *sixty* thousand people have seen you say it now. Mistletoe Gardens is unused land, nothing more than a shortcut from one side of town to the other, but we've proved that you can utilise the space and make something great out of it. This place has stood here since 1848 – you want to move forward, but I propose we move backwards. Back to the glory days Essie's told me about. Back to concerts in the park and picnics on the grass. You earn money from selling cheap tickets to live music events or open-air theatre plays. Turn summer evenings into something special here. Let the shopkeepers set up their stalls in the warm weather too. Throw the gates open to local crafters or local classes that can be taken outdoors. Food festivals. Spring-time flower shows when the flowerbeds burst into life. Hire the bandstand out to local firms for advertising or art installations, and keep in mind that Hallissey Construction will be hiring it every December to build a life-size gingerbread house. There is so much we can do with this space that will cost a *lot* less than destroying it and building an ugly eyesore that no one wants in its place. All we need to do is think outside the box.'

He's animated and inspiring, and bright and confident, and engaging. Even the protesters outside have quietened down to listen to him.

'I think it's a jolly good idea.'

'Me too.'

I jump at two voices behind me, and spin around to see two men standing there. One is tall and dressed in a suit, and one is short and looks like he fell out of bed less than five minutes ago. There are other men and women following too. Saff has stayed by the gate to let them in as they arrive.

Mervyn looks up in surprise. 'Do you?'

The men give first me and then Joss a smile and shake our hands in turn, and Joss's chains do some very undignified rattling as they introduce themselves. 'Board members of the Folkhornton council. Couldn't ignore the buzz we're hearing from down here this morning. We had no idea there was so much opposition to our proposal for Mistletoe Gardens, or that there were any other proposals in place – ones that make far more sense, at that. Mervyn, why haven't you told us this?'

'It's only just... I mean, I've only just heard...' A tongue-tied Mervyn looks greyer than he did earlier.

'And look at this masterpiece.' The tall one climbs over the chains and goes to look around the gingerbread house, while the shorter one yawns and goes to do damage control with the journalist, and the others reach the bandstand and look quite alarmed at the sight of ten dinosaurs waving excitedly.

'Did you call them?' I whisper to Joss.

'I might've done.'

'Well, I certainly won't be voting to pull this down.' The tall man climbs over Joss on the steps and returns to the path. 'When's the next board meeting?'

'I think we're having an impromptu one now,' one of the women says.

Joss grins like this was exactly his intention.

'Oh, well, that makes life easier.' The other man returns and claps his hands together. 'Anyone in favour of getting rid of Mistletoe Gardens?'

Silence. Absolute silence.

Apart from Edna who mishears the question and shouts, 'Aye!' despite not being on the council *and* not being in favour of it.

'I think that's a pretty clear response.' Another man gestures towards the journalist. 'Can you make sure you print that bit *really* clearly? Folkhornton's had more than enough bad press for one day.'

'No one wants to see the end of Mistletoe Gardens,' a councilwoman says. 'I met my husband here, you know. He was coming out of the gate as I was walking in and we collided. Love at first sight.'

'Thank you for your contribution.' The tall first man shakes both mine and Joss's hands. 'I hope you'll be around for a long time to come, Folkhornton council needs some young blood and fresh thinking. Give some thought to your vision for Mistletoe Gardens and we'll invite you both in to discuss it with all board members after Christmas.'

'Mervyn, a word?' Three of them beckon Mervyn to one side, while another one asks if we mind him taking a photo to show his children.

'Santa will be here later if you want to bring them down,' Lynette informs him.

'Santa too?' He looks positively childlike. 'We had no idea all this was going on in Folkhornton. We tend to each cover an area of our own and leave decisions to each local councillor, but clearly there's room for a more community-minded approach. I apologise for being so out of touch.'

Mervyn sees the board members out of the gate and safely past the protesters, who are starting to dwindle away, and returns looking suitably scolded. 'Someone's not happy with me.'

'More than one person!' Mum hollers, but her bark is somewhat diminished by layers of dino padding.

'I'm sorry if I've misjudged this.' Mervyn wrings his hands together. 'I got caught up in the numbers and figures in the proposals. I didn't look at the local feeling and love for Mistletoe Gardens. I didn't think any of you would care.'

'So that's that then,' Mr Arkins announces, and the dinosaurs start undoing themselves from their handcuffs.

'Joss, I didn't mean what I said just now.' Mervyn clears his throat. 'Hallissey Construction is an important part of Folkhornton. I would never dishonour your father by ending our contract with you. I hope you'll accept my apology and continue to work with us.'

'That's great, my lads will be thrilled, but I'm going to take more of a backseat from now on.'

'Could anyone help me out of this?' Mum asks, her head sticking out of the dinosaur costume's neck. Mervyn can't volunteer fast enough, and Mum doesn't wallop him, which has got to be a good sign.

'You're going to take a backseat?' I turn to Joss.

'Yep. Firstly, we've got gingerbread houses to build if you're still up for that hotel job. And secondly, my lads love the corporate repair jobs, and I hate them, so I'm going to let them take the reins, while I do... whatever anyone wants me to.'

'Like a handyman?'

'Exactly that. I love doing little things that make a difference, and over the past few weeks, I've realised there are a lot of people in Folkhornton with no one else to turn to. If they've got a leaking tap or a light bulb they can't reach to change, people let these things go because they don't have the money to call someone out, or they think it's too trivial, or they don't know who to trust. It might not seem like much, but finally putting up a panel in a fence that's been down for months is something small to me but makes a difference to whoever needs it done. That's what I want to do.'

'I've got a list as long as my scarf for him in January,' Beryl calls over. 'I'm going to knit him a jumper in thanks, but he won't tell me if he'd prefer a zombie or a vampire on it.'

'Surprise me, Beryl,' Joss replies. We both know it will end up being some disturbing cross between a zombie *and* a vampire.

'Talking of surprising things...' I sit on the step between him and the 'for sale' sign.

He leans his chin on his shoulder to look across at me. 'I know I've screwed everything up, Ess, but I've never felt this way before. I never intended to fall for anyone ever again, and then you burst into my life in bright red festive colour. I want to kiss under the mistletoe every December and build gingerbread houses with you for the rest of my life.'

'That's good because you're certainly dreadful at building them on your own. I still can't work out what you did to that poor thing.'

He laughs and hangs his head in shame, and I reach over and run my fingers through his hair, until he looks up with a smile, and I shift over until I can kiss him again.

No one's found the key to let Joss out of his chains yet, so his hands are still unusable, and we're surrounded by several dinosaurs in various states of undress, so it's nothing more than a soft kiss, my hands on his neck, his hair, stroking his face as I fit my lips against his gently, just once, but once is never enough, and it turns into kissing him over and over again, a press of lips that means so much more because I know Joss isn't holding anything back now. He chases my mouth whenever I pull away, and makes a noise of disappointment when I pull back and realise the world's gone silent.

I blink upwards in surprise to see Saff has crept over from the gingerbread house and is holding a bunch of mistletoe above our heads, while trying to stop giggling and shush the others.

Joss blinks open eyes that look blissfully dazed and it takes him a while to make the connection between the bunch of mistletoe we cut down for Mum and Mervyn the other day, and the fact it's now being dangled above our heads, and then his eyes sparkle and his face breaks into an impossibly wide grin.

He pushes himself up to press his lips to my cheek. 'We got our kiss under the mistletoe after all.'

I rub my nose against his. 'The first of many.'

23

Even Shakespeare loved gingerbread! To quote *Love's Labour's Lost* – 'An I had but one penny in the world, thou shouldst have it to buy ginger-bread.'

I've never seen Mistletoe Gardens on Christmas Eve night. Like most people, I'm usually curled up under blankets on the sofa, watching festive films and eating a rhino's bodyweight in chocolate, but tonight, the residents of Folkhornton are having a private celebration.

There's hot chocolate, mulled wine, and after everything this morning, Mum went back to the bakery and made several batches of candy cane cupcakes while she ruminated on whether Mervyn could be forgiven or not, and now everyone's come out to toast to Mistletoe Gardens, even Santa, which somewhat undermines the illusion that he might be the real thing, or he'd be otherwise occupied on Christmas Eve.

Joss and I are huddled on the bandstand wall. My head is on his shoulder, and our hands are tangled together, and I don't think I've ever felt this contented and peaceful.

Mr Arkins and the MMM, who turns out to be called Martha, are wandering the mistletoe path and stopping for a peck under every tree. She looks like she's making the most of not having to kiss a dinosaur.

Everyone's feeling the love tonight; even Mrs Allen and Mr Selman, the warring neighbours Mum and Mervyn have been trying to get together for months, are wandering arm-in-arm.

'Nothing's unforgivable at Christmas.' Joss moves his head to indicate where Mum and Mervyn are slow-dancing under a tree full of mistletoe as 'Candlelight Carol' plays softly from someone's phone.

'He did the right thing in the end. That counts for a lot.' I lift an arm over Joss's shoulder to pull him into a hug, and we sit there for a while, enjoying each other's warmth on a chilly Christmas evening, and when we eventually disentangle ourselves, Mum's walking towards us.

'Ess, can I talk to you for a minute?' She jerks her head to indicate I should follow her under a tree, and looks around until she can beckon Saff over too.

'Is everything okay?' I sip my cup of hot chocolate from Douglas's coffee shop stall.

'How would you girls feel about more responsibility at the bakery? Or maybe... less interference would be a better way to put it.'

I look at Saff. 'We're listening...'

'When I was baking earlier, I wasn't just thinking about Mervyn. Those nice chaps this morning offered me a job on the council. They think Mervyn needs a mitigating influence, and they want someone to speak for the residents to prevent something like this happening again. I know we need more staff, but you've both proved yourself capable of handling things without my input, and if I'm honest, I'm ready to step back from Dancing

Cinnamon, even if it's taken me a while to admit it to myself. My heart is with my resident work now. What do you think?'

Saff is clearly trying to hide her thoughts behind a paper cup of mulled wine. 'The council aren't going to know what's hit them.'

'Poor Mervyn!' I add.

Mum laughs and smacks my shoulder. 'I know you want to do bigger things, fancier display pieces, and you've got help with the construction angle now.' She glances over her shoulder towards Joss. 'And if you think new options and online sales are the way to go, then I'll fully support you in that, and I'll keep my beak out.' She looks between us. 'Unless you want my beak in?'

'No!' Saff and I say in unison.

'Just don't take your beak too far. We wouldn't mind a little bit of your beak every now and then. You're still the matriarch of Dancing Cinnamon, like Nan was when you took over, and her mum must've been when she took over.'

'Don't you dare call me a matriarch – it makes me sound like I'm ninety years old!'

We have a group hug and then she flaps a hand in front of her face excitedly. 'Ooh, I can't wait to tell Mervyn. Who'd have thought it, eh? Little old me – resident representative for Folkhornton council. I've made enough of a nuisance of myself over the years, I suppose they think I'll be less trouble if they pay me.'

'Oh, have they got another thing coming.'

Mum looks like she wants to argue and then shrugs instead. 'Yep, they really have.'

Joss is watching the couples in love and friends enjoying a perfect festive night when I walk back over to the bandstand. Instead of sitting back down, I stand in front of him for a hug as I tell him what's just happened.

'Do you know, I've never felt sorry for our council before, but your mum is going to tear the place to shreds.' He grins up at me. 'And it's exactly what they need.'

'Speaking of things we need,' I say as Martha the MMM walks over, no sign of the horse's head tonight.

'Congratulations on a good job done well, dearies.'

'It was everyone, not just us. Can't take credit for it,' Joss says.

'You two have inspired everyone, Mr Hallissey. We're all making plans for how we can utilise Mistletoe Gardens in the warmer weather. We won't be taking it for granted any longer. You've made us appreciate what's been right in front of us all along.'

'No potions tonight?' Joss asks her.

'Exactly what I wanted to talk to you about. Can I use you two in my marketing materials? You're proof that a love potion worked.'

'I thought it "wasn't to make us fall in love with each other"?' Joss quotes what she said to us last week.

'Oh, nonsense, it was to make you fall in love with whatever brings joy back into your lives. And you clearly bring joy into each other's lives, therefore, it worked.'

With an arm over his shoulder, I look down into his deep, unhidden eyes. 'Yes, we do,' I murmur, loving the way his lips curve into a smile.

'Just one problem though, MMM.' Joss's fingers squeeze my sides. 'I was in love with Essie long before one of your potions touched my lips.'

'Ah, but were you? Were you really?'

'Yes!'

'Well, my customers aren't going to know that, are they? Details schmeetails!' She walks off with a wave.

'You say that, but you *did* rediscover the joy of Christmas, just like that potion she gave you,' I say to him when she's gone back to join Mr Arkins under another bunch of mistletoe.

'I don't think it was much to do with the potion.' His arms tighten around me and his chin presses into my shoulder.

'You don't know that. Maybe there's something in it.'

'Capri Sun, most likely.'

I slip my hand into his and pull him up, and we walk over to the biggest tree, the one my Victorian great-great-grandmother pushed the first mistletoe berries into all those years ago.

'I know what you've got in mind...' Joss says with a teasing tone.

'Something I've wanted to do for a very, very long time – kiss someone I love under the mistletoe in Mistletoe Gardens.'

'Do you want me to go and get Beryl for you?'

Instead of walloping him, I pull his head down, leaving no doubt about *who* I want to kiss.

The kiss is everything I hoped it would be. Christmas magic tingles all around us, and my hand feels like it's sparkling as I trail my fingers up Joss's arm to grip at his shoulder, and he surprises me by dipping me in a proper Hollywood kiss – a real movie-moment that I've always wished would happen in real life, but never has until now.

I squeal in delight and he nearly drops me. But you can't have it all.

'Do you believe in the magic of Mistletoe Gardens yet?' I whisper, my forehead resting against his when we pull back.

'Something magical has happened in the past few weeks. I don't know if it was Christmas magic, mistletoe, or just being in the right place at the right time, but I've never been happier than I am right now.'

He always knows exactly what to say.

'Me neither.' I push myself up on tiptoes to brush my lips against his cheek.

'I still think the electric forcefield of all these Christmas lights has frazzled our brains, though.'

It makes me giggle and he pulls me into the tightest hug. My arms slide around his neck and he bends to hold me tightly, and if we stayed here like this for the rest of the night, it would be the most perfect way to spend Christmas Eve.

Whether there's any such thing as magical mistletoe or not, maybe the only thing any of us need is to find someone who makes the world seem a little bit more magical than it did before.

ACKNOWLEDGMENTS

Thank you, Mum. Always my first and most important reader! I'm eternally grateful for your constant patience, support, encouragement, and belief in me. Thank you for always being there for me – I don't know what I'd do without you. Love you lots!

Thank you Bill, Toby, Cathie, and Bev for your continued love, enthusiasm, and support. Thank you to Jayne Lloyd and Charlotte McFall for being such wonderful friends.

Thank you to my best friend and beloved fellow house goblin, Marie Landry, for making every day better just by existing. I love you to bits. Thank you for being the *best* best friend in the history of the world!

A big shoutout to some Facebook groups who support me tirelessly and are an absolute pleasure to be part of. If you're looking for book-loving groups filled with lovely readers who will be good for your soul (but terrible for your to-read list!) then I highly recommend joining The Friendly Book Community, Heidi Swain and Friends, Chick Lit and Prosecco, The Socially Distanced Book Club, and Bookswap Central. Thank you so much to all members and admins of these wonderful groups who put in so much effort to make little communities that are a joy to belong to!

Thank you to my fantastic agent, Amanda Preston, and my brilliant editor Emily Ruston, along with the rest of the wonderful and hardworking Boldwood team and the lovely Boldwood authors! It's a joy to belong to Team Boldwood!

And finally, thank *you* for reading! I hope you enjoyed getting lost in the mistletoe magic of Essie and Joss's story and will join me again for the next book – there are many more happily ever afters to come!

ABOUT THE AUTHOR

Jaimie Admans is the bestselling author of several romantic comedies. She lives in South Wales.

Sign up to Jaimie Adman's mailing list for news, competitions and updates on future books.

Visit Jaimie's website: https://jaimieadmans.com/

Follow Jaimie on social media:

twitter.com/be_the_spark
facebook.com/jaimieadmansbooks
instagram.com/jaimieadmans1

ALSO BY JAIMIE ADMANS

Boldwood

Boldwood Books is an award-winning fiction publishing company seeking out the best stories from around the world.

Find out more at
www.boldwoodbooks.com

Join our reader community for brilliant books, competitions and offers!

Follow us
#BoldBookClub

Sign up to our weekly deals newsletter

https://bit.ly/BoldwoodBNewsletter